LIFE DURING WARTIME

Focusing on novels with contemporary concerns, Bantam New Fiction introduces some of the most exciting voices at work today. Look for these titles wherever Bantam New Fiction is sold:

BANTAM NEW FICTION
LIFE DURING WARTIME
LUCIUS SHEPARD

BANTAM BOOKS
TORONTO • NEW YORK • LONDON • SYDNEY • AUCKLAND

LIFE DURING WARTIME
A Bantam Book / October 1987

Library of Congress Cataloging-in-Publication Data

Shepard, Lucius.
  Life during wartime.

  (Bantam new fiction)
  I. Title.
PS3569.H3939L5 1987   813'.54   87-47562
ISBN 0-553-34381-5

Published simultaneously in the United States and Canada

PRINTED IN THE UNITED STATES OF AMERICA

FG   0 9 8 7 6 5 4 3 2 1

For Terry Carr

I'd like to acknowledge the support and friendship of the following during the writing of this book: Gardner Dozois, Susan Caspar, Lori Houck, Craig Spector, Jack and Jeanne Dann, Jim Kelly, John Kessel, Kim Stanley Robinson, Greg and Jane Smith, Beth Meacham, Tappan King, and "Shorty."

R AND R

Always the same story
Four Romans dead, and five Carthaginians . . .

—Federico García Lorca

CHAPTER ONE

O ne of the new Sikorsky gunships, an element of the First Air Cavalry with the words *Whispering Death* painted on its side, gave Mingolla and Gilbey and Baylor a lift from the Ant Farm to San Francisco de Juticlan, a small town located inside the green zone, which on the latest maps was designated Free Occupied Guatemala. To the east of this green zone lay an undesignated band of yellow that crossed the country from the Mexican border to the Caribbean. The Ant Farm was a firebase on the eastern edge of the yellow band, and it was from there that Mingolla—an artillery specialist not yet twenty-one years old—lobbed shells into an area that the maps depicted in black-and-white terrain markings. And thus it was that he often thought of himself as engaged in a struggle to keep the world safe for primary colors.

Mingolla and his buddies could have taken their R and R in Rio or Caracas, but they had noticed that the men who visited these cities had a tendency to grow careless upon their return; they understood from this that the more exuberant your R and R, the more likely you were to end up a casualty, and so they always opted for the lesser distractions of the Guatemalan towns. They were not really friends; they had little in common, and under different circumstances they might well have been enemies. But taking their R and R together had come to be a ritual of survival, and once they had reached the town of their choice, they would go their separate ways and perform further rituals. Because the three had survived so much already, they believed that if they continued to perform these same rituals they would complete their tours unscathed. They had never acknowledged their belief to one another, speaking of it only obliquely—that, too, was part of the ritual—and had this belief been challenged they would have admitted its irrationality; yet they would also have pointed out that the strange character of the war acted to enforce it.

The gunship set down at an airbase a mile west of town, a concrete strip penned in on three sides by barracks and offices, with the jungle rising behind them. At the center of the strip another Sikorsky was practicing takeoffs and landings—a drunken, camouflage-colored dragonfly—and two others were hovering overhead like anxious parents. As Mingolla jumped out, a hot breeze fluttered his shirt. He was wearing civvies for the first time in weeks, and they felt flimsy compared to his combat gear; he glanced around nervously, half-expecting an unseen enemy to take advantage of his exposure. Some mechanics were lounging in the shade of a chopper whose cockpit had been destroyed, leaving fanglike shards of plastic curving from the charred metal. Dusty jeeps trundled back and forth between the buildings; a brace of crisply starched lieutenants was making a brisk beeline toward a forklift stacked high with aluminum coffins. Afternoon sunlight fired dazzles on the seams and handles of the coffins, and through the heat haze the distant line of barracks shifted like waves in a troubled olive-drab sea. The incongruity of the scene—its what's-wrong-with-this-picture mix of the horrid and the commonplace—wrenched at Mingolla. His left hand trembled, and the light seemed to grow brighter, making him weak and vague. He leaned against the Sikorsky's rocket pod to steady himself. Far above, contrails were fraying in the deep blue range of the sky: XL-16s off to blow holes in Nicaragua. He stared after them with something akin to longing, listening for their engines, but heard only the spacy whisper of the Sikorsky's.

Gilbey hopped down from the hatch that led to the computer deck behind the cockpit; he brushed imaginary dirt from his jeans, sauntered over to Mingolla, and stood with hands on hips: a short muscular kid whose blond crewcut and petulant mouth gave him the look of a grumpy child. Baylor stuck his head out of the hatch and worriedly scanned the horizon. Then he, too, hopped down. He was tall and rawboned, a couple of years older than Mingolla, with lank black hair and pimply olive skin and features so sharp that they appeared to have been hatcheted into shape. He rested a hand on the side of the Sikorsky, but almost instantly, noticing that he was touching the flaming letter *W* in *Whispering Death,* he jerked the hand away as if he'd been scorched. Three days before there had been an all-out assault on the Ant Farm, and Baylor had not recovered from it. Neither had Mingolla. It was hard to tell whether Gilbey had been affected.

One of the Sikorsky's pilots cracked the cockpit door. "Y'all can catch a ride into Frisco at the PX," he said, his voice muffled by the black bubble of his visor. The sun shone a white blaze on the visor, making it seem that the helmet contained night and a single star.

"Where's the PX?" asked Gilbey.

The pilot said something too muffled to be understood.

"What?" said Gilbey.

Again the pilot's response was muffled, and Gilbey became angry. "Take that damn thing off!" he said.

"This?" The pilot pointed to his visor. "What for?"

"So I can hear what the hell you saying."

"You can hear now, can'tcha?"

"Okay," said Gilbey, his voice tight. "Where's the goddamn PX?"

The pilot's reply was unintelligible; his faceless mask regarded Gilbey with inscrutable intent.

Gilbey balled up his fists. "Take that son of a bitch off!"

"Can't do it, soldier," said the second pilot, leaning over so that the two black bubbles were nearly side by side. "These here doobies"—he tapped his visor—"they got microcircuits that beams shit into our eyes. 'Fects the optic nerve. Makes it so we can see the beaners even when they undercover. Longer we wear 'em, the better we see."

Baylor laughed edgily, and Gilbey said, "Bullshit!" Mingolla naturally assumed that the pilots were putting Gilbey on, or else their reluctance to remove the helmets stemmed from a superstition, perhaps from a deluded belief that the visors actually did bestow special powers. But given a war in which combat drugs were issued and psychics predicted enemy movements, anything was possible, even microcircuits that enhanced vision.

"You don't wanna see us, nohow," said the first pilot. "The beams fuck up our faces. We're deformed-lookin' mothers."

"Course you might not notice the changes," said the second pilot. "Lotsa people don't. But if you did, it'd mess you up."

Imagining the pilots' deformities sent a sick chill mounting from Mingolla's stomach. Gilbey, however, wasn't buying it. "You think I'm stupid?" he shouted, his neck reddening.

"Naw," said the first pilot. "We can *see* you ain't stupid. We can see lotsa shit other people can't, 'cause of the beams."

"All kindsa weird stuff," chipped in the second pilot. "Like souls."

"Ghosts."

"Even the future."

"The future's our best thing," said the first pilot. "You guys wanna know what's ahead, we'll tell you."

They nodded in unison, the blaze of sunlight sliding across both visors: two evil robots responding to the same program.

Gilbey lunged for the cockpit door. The first pilot slammed it shut, and Gilbey pounded on the plastic, screaming curses. The second pilot flipped a switch on the control console, and a moment later his amplified voice boomed out, "Make straight past that forklift till you hit the barracks. You'll run right into the PX."

It took both Mingolla and Baylor to drag Gilbey away from the Sikorsky, and he didn't stop shouting until they drew near the forklift with its load of coffins: a giant's treasure of enormous silver ingots. Then he grew silent and lowered his eyes. They wangled a ride with an MP corporal outside the PX, and as the jeep hummed across the concrete, Mingolla glanced over

6

at the Sikorsky that had transported them. The two pilots had spread a canvas on the ground, had stripped to shorts, and were sunning themselves. But they had not removed their helmets. The weird juxtaposition of tanned bodies and black heads disturbed Mingolla, reminding him of an old movie in which a guy had gone through a matter transmitter along with a fly and had ended up with the fly's head on his shoulders. Maybe, he thought, the pilots' story about the helmets was true: they were impossible to remove. Maybe the war had gotten that strange.

The MP corporal noticed him watching the pilots and let out a barking laugh. "Those guys," he said, with the flat emphatic tone of a man who knew whereof he spoke, "are fuckin' nuts!"

Six years before, San Francisco de Juticlan had been a scatter of thatched huts and concrete-block structures deployed among palms and banana leaves on the east bank of the Rio Dulce, at the junction of the river and a gravel road that connected with the Pan American Highway; but it had since grown to occupy substantial sections of both banks, increased by dozens of bars and brothels: stucco cubes painted all the colors of the rainbow, with a fantastic bestiary of neon signs mounted atop their tin roofs. Dragons; unicorns; fiery birds; centaurs. The MP corporal told Mingolla that the signs were not advertisements but coded symbols of pride; for example, from the representation of a winged red tiger crouched among green lilies and blue crosses, you could deduce that the owner was wealthy, a member of a Catholic secret society, and ambivalent toward government policies. Old signs were constantly being dismantled, and larger, more ornate ones erected in their stead as testament to improved profits, and this warfare of light and image was appropriate to the time and place because San Francisco de Juticlan was less a town than a symptom of war. Though by night the sky above it was radiant, at ground level it was mean and squalid. Pariah dogs foraged in piles of garbage, hard-bitten whores spat from the windows, and, according to the corporal, it was not unusual to stumble across a corpse, likely a victim of the gangs of abandoned children who lived in the fringes of the jungle. Narrow streets of tawny dirt cut between the bars, carpeted with a litter of flattened cans and feces and broken glass; refugees begged at every corner, displaying burns and bullet wounds. Many of the buildings had been thrown up with such haste that their walls were tilted, their roofs canted, and this made the shadows they cast appear exaggerated in their jaggedness, like shadows in the work of a psychotic artist, giving visual expression to a pervasive undercurrent of tension. Yet as Mingolla moved along, he felt at ease, almost happy. His mood was due in part to his hunch that it was going to be one hell of an R and R (he had learned to trust his hunches); but it spoke mainly to the fact that towns like this had become for him a kind of afterlife, a reward for having endured a harsh term of existence.

The corporal dropped them off at a drugstore, where Mingolla bought a box of stationery, and then they stopped for a drink at the Club Demonio: a tiny place whose whitewashed walls were shined to faint phosphorescence by the glare of purple light bulbs dangling from the ceiling like radioactive fruit. The club was packed with soldiers and whores, most sitting at tables around a dance floor not much bigger than a king-size mattress. Two couples were swaying to a ballad that welled from a jukebox encaged in chicken wire and two-by-fours; veils of cigarette smoke drifted with underwater slowness above their heads. Some of the soldiers were mauling their whores, and one whore was trying to steal the wallet of a soldier who was on the verge of passing out; her hand worked between his legs, encouraging him to thrust his hips forward, and when he did this, she pried with her other hand at the wallet stuck in the back pocket of his tight-fitting jeans. But all the action seemed listless, halfhearted, as if the dimness and syrupy music had thickened the air and were hampering movement. Mingolla took a seat at the bar. The bartender glanced at him inquiringly, his pupils becoming cored with purple reflections, and Mingolla said, "Beer."

"Hey, check that out!" Gilbey slid onto an adjoining stool and jerked his thumb toward a whore at the end of the bar. Her skirt was hiked to mid-thigh, and her breasts, judging by their

8

fullness and lack of sag, were likely the product of elective surgery.

"Nice," said Mingolla, disinterested. The bartender set a bottle of beer in front of him, and he had a swig; it tasted sour, watery, like a distillation of the stale air.

Baylor slumped onto the stool next to Gilbey and buried his face in his hands. Gilbey said something to him that Mingolla didn't catch, and Baylor lifted his head. "I ain't goin' back," he said.

"Aw, Jesus!" said Gilbey. "Don't start that crap."

In the half-dark Baylor's eye sockets were clotted with shadows. His stare locked onto Mingolla. "They'll get us next time," he said. "We should head downriver. They got boats in Livingston that'll take you to Panama."

"Panama!" sneered Gilbey. "Nothin' there 'cept more beaners."

"We'll be okay at the Farm," offered Mingolla. "Things get too heavy, they'll pull us back."

" 'Too heavy'?" A vein throbbed in Baylor's temple. "What the fuck you call 'too heavy'?"

"Screw this!" Gilbey heaved up from his stool. "You deal with him, man," he said to Mingolla. He gestured at the big-breasted whore. "I'm gonna climb Mount Silicon."

"Nine o'clock," said Mingolla. "The PX. Okay?"

Gilbey said, "Yeah," and moved off. Baylor took over his stool and leaned close to Mingolla. "You know I'm right," he said in an urgent whisper. "They almost got us this time."

"Air Cav'll handle 'em," said Mingolla, affecting nonchalance. He opened the box of stationery and unclipped a pen from his shirt pocket.

"You *know* I'm right," Baylor repeated.

Mingolla tapped the pen against his lips, pretending to be distracted.

"Air Cav!" said Baylor with a despairing laugh. "Air Cav ain't gonna do squat!"

"Why don't you put on some decent tunes?" Mingolla suggested. "See if they got any Prowler on the box."

"Dammit!" Baylor grabbed his wrist. "Don't you understand, man? This shit ain't workin' no more!"

9

Mingolla shook him off. "Maybe you need some change," he said coldly; he dug out a handful of coins and tossed them on the counter. "There! There's some change."

"I'm tellin' you . . ."

"I don't wanna hear it!" snapped Mingolla.

"You don't wanna hear it?" said Baylor, incredulous. He was on the verge of losing control, his dark face slick with sweat, one eyelid fluttering. He pounded the countertop for emphasis. "Man, you better hear it! 'Cause we don't pull somethin' together soon, *real* soon, we're gonna fuckin' die! You hear that, don'tcha?"

Mingolla caught him by the shirtfront. "Shut up!"

"I ain't shuttin' up!" Baylor shrilled. "You and Gilbey, man, you think you can save your ass by stickin' your head in the sand. But I'm gonna make you listen." He threw back his head, and his voice rose to a shout. "We're gonna die!"

The way he shouted it—almost gleefully, like a kid yelling a dirty word to spite his parents—pissed Mingolla off. He was sick of Baylor's scenes. Without planning it, he hit him, pulling the punch at the last instant. Kept a hold of his shirt and clipped him on the jaw, just enough to rock back his head. Baylor blinked at him, stunned, his mouth open. Blood seeped from his gums. At the opposite end of the counter, the bartender was leaning beside a choirlike arrangement of liquor bottles, watching Mingolla and Baylor, and some of the soldiers were watching, too: they looked pleased, as if they had been hoping for a spot of violence to liven things up. Mingolla felt debased by their attentiveness, ashamed of his bullying. "Hey, I'm sorry, man," he said. "I . . ."

"I don't give a shit 'bout you're sorry," said Baylor, rubbing his mouth. "Don't give a shit 'bout nothin' 'cept gettin' the hell outta here."

"Leave it alone, all right?"

But Baylor wouldn't leave it alone. He continued to argue, adopting the long-suffering tone of someone carrying on bravely in the face of great injustice. Mingolla tried to ignore him by studying the label on his beer bottle: a red and black graphic portraying a Guatemalan soldier, his rifle upheld in victory. It

10

was an attractive design, putting him in mind of the poster work he had done before being drafted; but considering the unreliability of Guatemalan troops, he perceived the heroic pose as a bad joke. Mingolla gouged a trench through the center of the label with his thumbnail.

At last Baylor gave it up and sat staring down at the warped veneer of the counter. Mingolla let him sit a minute; then, without shifting his gaze from the bottle, he said, "Why don't you put on some decent tunes?"

Baylor tucked his chin onto his chest, maintaining a stubborn silence.

"It's your only option, man," Mingolla went on. "What else you gonna do?"

"You're crazy," said Baylor; he flicked his eyes toward Mingolla and hissed it like a curse. "Crazy!"

"You gonna take off for Panama by yourself? Un-unh. You know the three of us got something going. We come this far together, and if you just hang tough, we'll go home together."

"I don't know," said Baylor. "I don't know anymore."

"Look at it this way," said Mingolla. "Maybe we're all three of us right. Maybe Panama *is* the answer, but the time just isn't ripe. If that's true, me and Gilbey will see it sooner or later."

With a heavy sigh, Baylor got to his feet. "You ain't never gonna see it, man," he said dejectedly.

Mingolla had a swallow of beer. "Check if they got any Prowler on the box. I could relate to some Prowler."

Baylor stood for a moment, indecisive. He started for the jukebox, then veered toward the door. Mingolla tensed, preparing to run after him. But Baylor stopped and walked back over to the bar. Lines of strain were etched deep in his forehead. "Okay," he said, a catch in his voice. "Okay. What time tomorrow? Nine o'clock?"

"Right," said Mingolla, turning away: "The PX."

Out of the corner of his eye he saw Baylor cross the room and bend over the jukebox to inspect the selections. He felt relieved. This was the way all their R and Rs had begun, with Gilbey chasing a whore and Baylor feeding the jukebox while he wrote a letter home. On their first R and R he had written his parents about the war and its bizarre forms of attrition; then, realizing that the letter would alarm his mother, he had torn it up and written another, saying merely that he was fine. He would tear this letter up as well, but he wondered how his father would react if he were to read it. Most likely with anger. His father was a firm believer in God and country, and though Mingolla understood the futility of adhering to any moral code in light of the insanity around him, he had found that something of his father's tenets had been ingrained in him: he would never be able to desert as Baylor kept insisting. He knew it wasn't that simple, that other factors, too, were responsible for his devotion to duty; but since his father would have been happy to accept the responsibility, Mingolla tended to blame it on him. He tried to picture what his parents were doing at that moment—father watching the Mets on TV, mother puttering in the garden—and then, holding those images in mind, he began to write.

Dear Mom and Dad,
    In your last letter you asked if I thought we were winning the war. Down here you'd get a lot of blank stares in response to that question, because most people have a perspective on the war to which the overall result isn't relevant. Like there's a guy I know who has this rap about how the war is a magical operation of immense proportions, how the movements of the planes and troops are inscribing a mystical sign on the surface of reality, and to survive you have to figure out your location within the design and move accordingly. I'm sure that sounds crazy, but down here everybody's crazy the same way (some shrink's actually done a study on the incidence of superstition among the occupation forces). They're all looking for a magic that will ensure their survival. You may find it hard to believe that I subscribe to this sort of thing, but I do. I carve my initials on the shell casings, wear parrot feathers inside my helmet . . . and a lot more.
    To get back to your question, I'll try to do better than a blank stare, but I can't give you a simple yes or no. The matter can't be summed up that neatly. But I can illustrate the situation by telling you a story and let you draw your own conclusions. There are hundreds of stories that would do, but the one that comes to mind now concerns the Lost Patrol. . . .

A Prowler tune blasted from the jukebox, and Mingolla broke off writing to listen: it was a furious, jittery music, fueled—it seemed—by the same aggressive paranoia that had generated the war. People shoved back chairs, overturned tables, and began dancing in the vacated spaces; they were crammed together, able to do no more than shuffle in rhythm, but their tread set the light bulbs jiggling at the ends of their cords, the purple glare slopping over the walls. A slim, acne-scarred whore came to dance in front of Mingolla, shaking her breasts, holding out her arms to him. Her face was corpse-pale in the unsteady light, her smile a dead leer. Trickling from one eye, like some exquisite secretion of death, was a black tear of sweat and mascara. Mingolla couldn't be sure he was seeing her right. His left hand started trembling, and for a couple of seconds the entire scene lost its cohesiveness. Everything looked scattered, unrecognizable, embedded in a separate context from everything else: a welter of meaningless objects bobbing up and down on a tide of deranged music. Then somebody opened the door, admitting a wedge of sunlight, and the room settled back to normal. Scowling, the whore danced away. Mingolla breathed easier. The tremors in his hand subsided. He spotted Baylor near the door talking to a scruffy Guatemalan guy . . . probably a coke connection. Coke was Baylor's panacea, his remedy for fear and desperation. He always returned from R and R bleary-eyed and prone to nosebleeds, boasting about the great dope he'd scored. Pleased that he was following routine, Mingolla went back to his letter.

Remember me telling you that the Green Berets took drugs to make them better fighters? Most everyone calls the drugs "Sammy," which is short for "samurai." They come in ampule form, and when you pop them under your nose for the next thirty minutes or so you feel like a cross between a Medal of Honor winner and Superman. The trouble is that a lot of Berets overdo them and flip out. They sell them on the black market, too, and some guys use them for sport. They take the ampules and fight each other in pits . . . like human cockfights.

Anyway, about two years ago a patrol of Berets went on patrol

13

up in Fire Zone Emerald, not far from my base, and they didn't come back. They were listed MIA. A month or so after they'd disappeared, somebody started ripping off ampules from various dispensaries. At first the crimes were chalked up to guerrillas, but then a doctor caught sight of the robbers and said they were Americans. They were wearing rotted fatigues, acting nuts. An artist did a sketch of their leader according to the doctor's description, and it turned out to be a dead ringer for the sergeant of that missing patrol. After that they were sighted all over the place. Some of the sightings were obviously false, but others sounded like the real thing. They were said to have shot down a couple of our choppers and to have knocked over a supply column near Zacapa.

I'd never put much stock in the story, to tell you the truth, but about four months ago this infantryman came walking out of the jungle and reported to the firebase. He claimed he'd been captured by the Lost Patrol, and when I heard his story, I believed him. He said they had told him that they weren't Americans anymore but citizens of the jungle. They lived like animals, sleeping under palm fronds, popping the ampules night and day. They were crazy, but they'd become geniuses at survival. They knew everything about the jungle. When the weather was going to change, what animals were near. And they had this weird religion based on the beams of light that would shine down through the canopy. They'd sit under those beams, like saints being blessed by God, and rave about the purity of the light, the joys of killing, and the new world they were going to build.

So that's what occurs to me when you ask your question, Mom and Dad. The Lost Patrol. I'm not attempting to be circumspect in order to make a point about the horrors of war. Not at all. When I think about the Lost Patrol I'm not thinking about how sad and crazy they are. I'm wondering what it is they see in that light, wondering if it might be of help to me. And maybe therein lies your answer. . . .

It was nearly sunset by the time Mingolla left the bar to begin the second part of his ritual, to wander innocent as a tourist through the native quarter, partaking of whatever fell to hand, maybe having dinner with a Guatemalan family, or buddying up with a soldier from another outfit and going to church, or hanging out with some young guys who'd ask him about America. He had done each of these on previous R and Rs, and his pretense of innocence always amused him. If he were to follow his inner directives, he would burn out the horrors of the firebase with whores and drugs; but on that first R and R—stunned by the experience of combat and needing solitude—a protracted walk had been his course of action, and he was committed not only to repeating it but to recapturing his dazed mental set: it would not do to half-ass the ritual. In this instance, given recent events at the Ant Farm, he did not have to work very hard to achieve confusion.

The Río Dulce was a wide blue river, heaving with a light chop. Thick jungle hedged its banks, and yellowish reed beds grew out from both shores. At the spot where the gravel road ended was a concrete pier, and moored to it a barge that served as a ferry; it was already loaded with its full complement of vehicles—two trucks—and carried about thirty pedestrians. Mingolla boarded and stood in the stern beside three infantrymen who were still wearing their combat suits and helmets, holding double-barreled rifles that were connected by flexible tubing to backpack computers; through their smoked faceplates he could see green reflections from the readouts on their visor displays. They made him uneasy, reminding him of the two pilots, and he felt better after they had removed their helmets and proved to have normal human faces. Spanning a third of the way across the river was a sweeping curve of white concrete supported by slender columns, like a piece fallen out of a Dali landscape: a bridge upon which construction had been halted. Mingolla had noticed it from the air just before landing and hadn't thought much about it; but now the sight took him by storm. It seemed less an unfinished bridge than a monument to some exalted ideal, more beautiful than any finished bridge could be. And as he stood rapt, with the ferry's oily smoke farting out around him, he sensed that there was an analogue of that beautiful curving shape inside him, that he, too, was a road ending in midair. It gave him confidence to associate himself with such loftiness and purity, and for a moment he let himself

15

believe that he also might have—as the upward-angled terminus of the bridge implied—a point of completion lying far
beyond the one anticipated by the architects of this fate.

On the west bank past the town the gravel road was lined
with stalls: skeletal frameworks of brushwood poles roofed with
palm thatch. Children chased in and out among them, pretending to aim and fire at one another with stalks of sugarcane. But
hardly any soldiers were in evidence. The crowds that moved
along the road were composed mostly of Indians: young couples too shy to hold hands; old men who looked lost and poked
litter with their canes; dumpy matrons who made outraged
faces at the high prices; shoeless farmers who kept their backs
ramrod-straight and wore grave expressions and carried their
money knotted in handkerchiefs. At one of the stalls Mingolla
bought a fish sandwich and a Coca-Cola. He sat on a stool and
ate contentedly, relishing the hot bread and the spicy meat
cooked inside it, watching the passing parade. Gray clouds
were bulking up and moving in from the south, from the Caribbean; now and then a flight of XL-16s would arrow northward
toward the oil fields beyond Lake Izabal, where the fighting was
very bad. Twilight fell. The lights of town began to be picked
out sharply against the empurpling air. Guitars were plucked,
hoarse voices sang, the crowds thinned. Mingolla ordered another sandwich and Coke. He leaned back, sipped and chewed,
steeping himself in the good magic of the land, the sweetness of
the moment. Beside the sandwich stall, four old women were
squatting by a cooking fire, preparing chicken stew and corn
fritters; scraps of black ash drifted up from the flames, and as
twilight deepened, it seemed these scraps were pieces of a
jigsaw puzzle that were fitting together overhead into the image
of a starless night.

Darkness closed in, the crowds thickened again, and
Mingolla continued his walk, strolling past stalls with necklaces
of light bulbs strung along their frames, wires leading off them
to generators whose rattle drowned out the chirring of frogs and
crickets. Stalls selling plastic rosaries, Chinese switchblades, tin
lanterns; others selling embroidered Indian shirts, flour-sack
trousers, wooden masks; others yet where old men in shabby

suit coats sat cross-legged behind pyramids of tomatoes and melons and green peppers, each with a candle cemented in melted wax atop them, like primitive altars. Laughter, shrieks, vendors shouting. Mingolla breathed in perfume, charcoal smoke, the scents of rotting fruit. He began to idle from stall to stall, buying a few souvenirs for friends back in New York, feeling part of the hustle, the noise, the shining black air, and eventually he came to a stall around which forty or fifty people had gathered, blocking all but its thatched roof from view. A woman's amplified voice cried out, *"La mariposa!"* Excited squeals from the crowd. Again the woman cried out, *"El cuchillo!"* The two words she had called—the butterfly and the knife—intrigued Mingolla, and he peered over heads.

Framed by the thatch and rickety poles, a dusky-skinned young woman was turning a handle that spun a wire cage: it was filled with white plastic cubes, bolted to a plank counter. Her black hair was pulled back from her face, tied behind her neck, and she wore a red sundress that left her shoulders bare. She stopped cranking, reached into the cage, and without looking plucked one of the cubes; she examined it, picked up a microphone, and cried, *"La luna!"* A bearded man pushed forward and handed her a card. She checked the card, comparing it against some cubes that were lined up on the counter; then she gave the man a few bills of Guatemalan currency.

The composition of the game appealed to Mingolla. The dark woman; her red dress and cryptic words; the runelike shadow of the wire cage—all this seemed magical, an image out of an occult dream. Part of the crowd moved off, accompanying the winner, and Mingolla let himself be forced closer by new arrivals pressing in from behind. He secured a position at the corner of the stall, fought to maintain it against the eddying of the crowd, and, on glancing up, he saw the woman smiling at him from a couple of feet away, holding out a card and a pencil stub. "Only ten cents Guatemalan," she said in American-sounding English.

The people flanking Mingolla urged him to play, grinning and clapping him on the back. But he didn't need urging. He knew he was going to win: it was the clearest premonition he had ever had, and it was signaled mostly by the woman herself. He felt a powerful attraction to her. It was as if she were a source of heat . . . not of heat alone but also of vitality, sensuality, and now that he was within range, that heat was washing over him, making him aware of a sexual tension developing between them, bringing with it the knowledge that he would win. The strength of the attraction surprised him, because his first impression had been that she was exotic-looking but not beautiful. Though slim, she was a little wide-hipped, and her breasts, mounded high and served up in separate scoops by her tight bodice, were quite small. Her face, like her coloring, had an East Indian cast, its features too large and voluptuous to suit the delicate bone structure; yet they were so expressive, so finely cut, that their disproportion came to seem a virtue. Except that it was thinner, the cheeks hollowed, the face might have belonged to one of those handmaidens found on Hindu religious posters, kneeling beneath Krishna's throne. Very sexy, very serene. That serenity, Mingolla decided, wasn't just a veneer. It ran deep. But at the moment he was more interested in her breasts. They looked nice pushed up like that, gleaming with a sheen of sweat. Two helpings of shaky pudding.

The woman waggled the card, and he took it: a simplified bingo card with symbols instead of letters and numbers. "Good luck," she said, and laughed, as if in reaction to some private irony. Then she began to spin the cage.

Mingolla didn't recognize many of the words she called, but an old man cozied up to him and pointed to the appropriate square whenever he got a match. Soon several rows were almost complete. "*La manzana!*" cried the woman, and the old man tugged at Mingolla's sleeve, shouting, "*Se ganó!*"

As the woman checked his card, Mingolla thought about the mystery she presented. Her calmness, her unaccented English, and the upper-class background it implied made her seem out of place here. Could be she was a student, her education interrupted by the war . . . though she might be a bit too old for that. He figured her to be twenty-two or twenty-three. Graduate school, maybe. But there was an air of worldliness about her that didn't support that theory. He watched her eyes dart back and forth between the card and the plastic cubes. Large heavy-lidded eyes. The whites stood in such sharp contrast to her dusky skin that they looked fake: milky stones with black centers.

"You see?" she said, handing him his winnings—about three dollars—and another card.

"See what?" Mingolla asked, perplexed.

But she had already begun to spin the cage again.

He won three of the next seven cards. People congratulated him, shaking their heads in amazement; the old man cozied up further, suggesting in sign language that he was the agency responsible for Mingolla's good fortune. Mingolla, however, was nervous. His ritual was founded on a principle of small miracles, and though he was certain the woman was cheating on his behalf (that, he assumed, had been the meaning of her laughter, her "You see?"), though his luck was not really luck, its excessiveness menaced that principle. He lost three cards in a row, but thereafter won two of four and grew even more nervous. He considered leaving. But what if it *was* luck? Leaving might run him afoul of a higher principle, interfere with some cosmic process and draw down misfortune. It was a ridiculous idea, but he couldn't bring himself to risk the faint chance that it might be true.

He continued to win. The people who had congratulated him became disgruntled and drifted off, and when there was only a handful of players left, the woman closed down the game. A grimy street kid materialized from the shadows and began dismantling the equipment. Unbolting the wire cage, unplugging the microphone, boxing up the plastic cubes, stuffing it all into a burlap sack. The woman moved out from behind the stall and leaned against one of the roof poles. Half-smiling, she cocked her head, appraising Mingolla, and then—just as the silence between them began to get prickly—she said, "My name's Debora."

"David." Mingolla felt as awkward as a fourteen-year-old; he had to resist the urge to jam his hands into his pockets and look away. "Why'd you cheat?" he asked; in trying to cover his nervousness, he said it too loudly and it sounded like an accusation.

"I wanted to get your attention," she said. "I'm . . . interested in you. Didn't you notice?"

"I didn't want to take it for granted."

She laughed. "I approve! It's always best to be cautious."

He liked her laughter; it had an easiness that made him think she would celebrate the least good thing.

Three men passed by arm in arm, singing drunkenly. One yelled at Debora, and she responded with an angry burst of Spanish. Mingolla could guess what had been said, that she had been insulted for associating with an American. "Maybe we should go somewhere," he said. "Get off the streets."

"After he's finished." She gestured at the boy, who was now taking down the string of light bulbs. "It's funny," she said. "I have the gift myself, and I'm usually uncomfortable around anyone else who has it. But not with you."

"The gift?" Mingolla thought he knew what she was referring to, but was leery about admitting to it.

"What do you call it? ESP?"

He gave up the idea of denying it. "I never put a name on it," he said.

"It's strong in you. I'm surprised you're not with Psicorps."

He wanted to impress her, to cloak himself in a mystery equal to hers. "How do you know I'm not?"

"I could tell." She pulled a black purse from behind the counter. "After drug therapy there's a change in the gift, in the way it comes across. It doesn't feel as hot, for one thing." She glanced up from the purse. "Or don't you perceive it that way? As heat."

"I've been around people who felt hot to me," he said. "But I didn't know what it meant."

"That's what it means . . . sometimes." She stuffed some bills into her purse. "So, why aren't you with Psicorps?"

Mingolla thought back to his first interview with a Psicorps agent: a pale, balding man with the innocent look around the eyes that some blind people have. While Mingolla had talked, the agent had fondled the ring Mingolla had given him to hold, paying no mind to what was being said, and had gazed off distractedly, as if listening for echoes. "They tried hard to

20

recruit me," Mingolla said. "But I didn't see much point. Those guys think they're mental wizards or something, but all they do is predict stuff, and they're wrong half the time. And I was scared of the drugs, too. I heard they had bad side-effects."

"Like what?"

"I don't know . . . I heard they did bad stuff to your head, changed your personality."

"You're lucky it was voluntary," she said. "Here they just snap you up."

The boy said something to her; he swung the burlap sack over his shoulder, and after a rapidfire exchange of Spanish he ran off toward the river. The crowds were still thick, but more than half the stalls had shut down; those that remained open looked—with their thatched roofs and strung lights and beshawled women—like crude nativity scenes ranging the darkness. Beyond the stalls, neon signs winked on and off: a chaotic menagerie of silver eagles and crimson spiders and indigo dragons. Watching them burn and vanish, Mingolla experienced a wave of dizziness. Things were starting to appear disconnected as they had at the Club Demonio.

"Don't you feel well?" she asked.

"I'm just tired."

She turned him to face her, put her hands on his shoulders. "No," she said. "It's something else."

The weight of her hands and the smell of her perfume helped to steady him. "There was an assault on the firebase a few days ago," he said. "It's still with me a little, y'know."

She gave his shoulders a squeeze and stepped back. "Maybe I can do something." She said this with such gravity, he thought she must have something specific in mind. "How's that?" he asked.

"I'll tell you at dinner . . . that is, if you're buying." She took his arm, jollying him. "You owe me that much, don't you think, after all your good luck?"

"Why aren't *you* with Psicorps?" he asked as they walked.

She didn't answer immediately, keeping her head down, nudging a scrap of cellophane with her toe. They were moving

21

along an uncrowded street, bordered on the left by the river—a channel of sluggish black lacquer—and on the right by the windowless rear walls of some bars. Overhead, behind a latticework of supports, a neon lion shed a baleful green nimbus. "I was in school in Miami when they started testing here," she said at last. "And after I came home, my family got on the wrong side of Department Six. You know Department Six?"

"I've heard some stuff."

"Sadists don't make efficient bureaucrats," she said. "There were a lot of people taken into the prison the same day we were. We were all supposed to be tested, but the guards started beating people, and everything got confused. No one was sure who'd been tested and who hadn't. It ended up that some of us were passed through without the tests."

Their footsteps crunched in the dirt; husky jukebox voices cried out for love from the next street over. "What happened?" Mingolla asked.

"To my family?" She shrugged. "Dead. No one ever bothered to confirm it, but it wasn't necessary. Confirmation, I mean." She went a few steps in silence. "As for me . . ." A muscle bunched at the corner of her mouth. "I did what I had to."

He was tempted to ask for specifics, but thought better of it. "I'm sorry," he said, and then kicked himself for having made such a banal comment.

They passed a bar lorded over by a grinning red-and-purple neon ape. Mingolla wondered it these glowing figures had meaning for guerrillas with binoculars in the hills: burned-out tubes signaling times of attack or troop movements. He cocked an eye toward Debora. She didn't look despondent as she had a second before, and that accorded with his impression that her calmness was a product of self-control, that her emotions were strong but held in tight check and let out only for exercise. From the river came a solitary splash, some cold fleck of life surfacing briefly, then returning to its long, ignorant glide through the darkness . . . and his life no different really, though maybe less graceful. How strange it was to be walking beside this woman who gave off heat like a candle flame, with earth

22

and sky blended into a black gas, and neon totems standing guard overhead.

"Shit," said Debora under her breath.

It surprised him to hear her curse. "What is it?"

"Nothing," she said wearily. "Just 'shit.' " She pointed ahead and quickened her pace. "Here we are."

The restaurant was a working-class place that occupied the ground floor of a hotel: a two-story building of yellow concrete block with a buzzing Fanta sign hung above the entrance. Hundreds of moths swarmed about the sign, flickering white against the darkness, and in front of the steps stood a group of teenage boys who were throwing knives at an iguana. The iguana was tied by its hind legs to the step railing. It had amber eyes, a hide the color of boiled cabbage, and was digging its claws into the dirt and arching its neck like a pint-size dragon about to take flight. As Mingolla and Debora walked up, one of the boys scored a hit in the iguana's tail and it flipped high into the air, shaking loose the knife. The boys passed around a bottle of rum to celebrate.

Except for the waiter—a pudgy young man leaning beside a door that opened into a smoke-filled kitchen—the place was empty. Glaring overhead lights shined up the grease spots on the plastic tablecloths and made the uneven thicknesses of the yellow paint appear to be dripping. The concrete floor was freckled with dark stains that Mingolla discovered to be the remains of insects. The food turned out to be decent, however, and Mingolla shoveled down a plateful of chicken and rice before Debora had half-finished hers. She ate delicately, chewing each bite a long time, and he had to carry the conversation. He told her about New York, his painting, how a couple of galleries had shown interest even though he was just a student. He compared his work to Rauschenberg, to Silvestre. Not as good, of course. Not yet. He had the notion that everything he told her—no matter its irrelevance to the moment—was securing the relationship, establishing subtle ties: he pictured the two of them enwebbed in a network of luminous threads that acted as conduits for their attraction. He could feel her heat more strongly than ever, and he wondered what it would be like to make love to her, to be swallowed by that perception of heat.

23

The instant he wondered this, she glanced up and smiled, as if sharing the thought. He wanted to ratify his sense of intimacy, to tell her something he had told no one else, and so—having only one important secret—he told her about the ritual.

She laid down her fork and gave him a penetrating look. "You can't really believe that," she said.

"I know it sounds—"

"Ridiculous," she broke in. "That's how it sounds."

"It's the truth," he said defiantly.

She picked up her fork again, pushed around some grains of rice. "How is it for you," she said, "when you have a premonition? I mean, what happens? Do you have dreams, hear voices?"

"Sometimes I just know things," he said, taken aback by her abrupt change of subject. "And sometimes I see pictures. It's like with a TV that's not working right. Fuzziness at first, then a sharp image."

"With me, it's dreams. And hallucinations. I don't know what else to call them." Her lips thinned; she sighed, appearing to have reached some decision. "When I first saw you, just for a second, you were wearing battle gear. There were inputs on the gauntlets, cables attached to the helmet. The faceplate was shattered, and your face . . . it was pale, bloody." She put her hand out to cover his. "What I saw was very clear, David. You can't go back."

He hadn't described artilleryman's gear to her, and no way could she have seen it. Shaken, he said, "Where am I gonna go?"

"Panama," she said. "I can help you get there."

She suddenly snapped into focus. You could find her, dozens like her, in any of the R and R towns. Preaching pacifism, encouraging desertion. Do-gooders, most with guerrilla connections. And that, he realized, must be how she had known about his gear. She had probably gathered information on the different types of units in order to lend authenticity to her dire pronouncements. His opinion of her wasn't diminished; on the contrary, it went up a notch. She was risking her life by talking to him. But her mystery had been dimmed.

"I can't do that," he said.

"Why not? Don't you believe me?"

"It wouldn't make any difference if I did."

"I . . ."

"Look," he said. "This friend of mine, he's always trying to convince me to desert, and there've been times I wanted to. But it's just not in me. My feet won't move that way. Maybe you don't understand, but that's how it is."

"This childish thing that you do with your two friends," she said after a pause. "That's what's holding you here, isn't it?"

"It isn't childish."

"That's exactly what it is. Like a child walking home in the dark and thinking that if he doesn't look at the shadows, nothing will jump out at him."

"You don't understand," he said.

"No, I suppose I don't." Angry, she threw her napkin down on the table and stared intently at her plate as if reading some oracle from the chicken bones.

"Let's talk about something else," said Mingolla.

"I have to go," she said coldly.

"Because I won't desert?"

"Because of what'll happen if you don't." She leaned toward him, her voice burred with emotion. "Because knowing what I do about your future, I don't want to wind up in bed with you."

Her intensity frightened him. Maybe she *had* been telling the truth. But he dismissed the possibility. "Stay," he said. "We'll talk some more about it."

"You wouldn't listen." She picked up her purse and got to her feet.

The waiter ambled over and laid the check beside Mingolla's plate; he pulled a plastic bag filled with marijuana from his apron pocket and dangled it in front of Mingolla. "Gotta get her in the mood, man," he said. Debora railed at him in Spanish. He shrugged and moved off, his slow-footed walk an advertisement for his goods.

"Meet me tomorrow then," said Mingolla. "We can talk more about it tomorrow."

25

"No."

"Why don't you gimme a break?" he said. "This is all coming down pretty fast, y'know. I get here this afternoon, meet you, and an hour later you're saying, 'Death is in the cards, and Panama's your only hope.' I need some time to think. Maybe by tomorrow I'll have a different attitude."

Her expression softened, but she shook her head, no.

"Don't you think it's worth it?"

She lowered her eyes, fussed with the zipper of her purse a second, and let out a rueful hiss. "Where do you want to meet?"

"How 'bout the pier on this side? 'Round noon."

She hesitated. "All right." She came around to his side of the table, bent down, and brushed her lips across his cheek. He tried to pull her close and deepen the kiss, but she slipped away. He felt giddy, overheated. "You really gonna be there?" he asked.

She nodded but seemed troubled, and she didn't look back before vanishing down the steps.

Mingolla sat awhile, thinking about the kiss, its promise. He might have stayed even longer, but three drunken soldiers staggered in and began knocking over chairs, giving the waiter a hard time. Annoyed, Mingolla went to the door and stood taking in hits of humid air. Moths were loosely constellated on the curved plastic of the Fanta sign, trying to get next to the bright heat inside it, and he had a sense of relation, of sharing their yearning for the impossible. He started down the steps but was brought up short. The teenage boys had gone; however, their captive iguana lay on the bottom step, bloody and unmoving. Bluish gray strings spilled from a gash in its throat. It was such a clear sign of bad luck, Mingolla went back inside and checked into the hotel upstairs.

The hotel corridors stank of urine and disinfectant. A drunken Indian with his fly unzipped and a bloody mouth was pounding on one of the doors. As Mingolla passed him, he bowed and made a sweeping gesture, a parody of welcome. Then he went back to his pounding. Mingolla's room was a windowless cell five feet wide and coffin-length, furnished with a sink and a cot and a chair. Cobwebs and dust clotted the glass of the transom, reducing the hallway light to a cold bluish white glow. The walls were filmy with more cobwebs, and the sheets were so dirty that they appeared to have a pattern. He lay down and closed his eyes, thinking of Debora. About ripping off that red dress and giving her a vicious screwing. How she'd cry out. That both made him ashamed and gave him a hard-on. He tried to think about making love to her tenderly. But tenderness, it seemed, was beyond him. He went flaccid. Jerking off wasn't worth the effort, he decided. He started to unbutton his shirt, remembered the sheets, and figured he'd be better off with his clothes on.

In the blackness behind his lids he began to see explosive flashes, and within those flashes were images of the assault on the Ant Farm. The mist, the tunnels. He blotted them out with the image of Debora's face, but they kept coming back. Finally he opened his eyes. Two . . . no, three fuzzy-looking black stars were silhouetted against the transom. It was only when they began to crawl that he recognized them as spiders. Big ones. He wasn't usually afraid of spiders, but these particular spiders terrified him. If he hit them with his shoe, he'd break the glass and they'd eject him from the hotel. He didn't want to kill them with his hands. After a while he sat up, switched on the overhead, and searched under the cot. There weren't any more spiders. He lay back down, feeling shaky and short of breath. Wishing he could talk to someone, hear a familiar voice. "It's okay," he said to the dark air. But that didn't help. And for a long time, until he felt secure enough to sleep, he watched the three black stars crawling across the transom, moving toward the center, touching one another, moving apart, never making any real progress, never straying from their area of bright confinement, their universe of curdled, frozen light.

CHAPTER TWO

In the morning Mingolla crossed to the west bank and walked toward the airbase. It was already hot, but the air still held a trace of freshness and the sweat that beaded on his forehead felt clean and healthy. White dust was settling along the gravel road, testifying to the recent passage of traffic; past the town and the cutoff that led to the uncompleted bridge, high walls of vegetation crowded close to the road, and from within them he heard monkeys and insects and birds: sharp sounds that enlivened him, making him conscious of the play of his muscles. About halfway to the base he spotted six Guatemalan soldiers coming out of the jungle, dragging a couple of bodies; they tossed them onto the hood of their jeep, where two other bodies were lying. Drawing near, Mingolla saw that the dead were naked children, each with a neat hole in his back. He had intended to walk on past, but one of the soldiers—a gnomish copper-skinned man in dark blue fatigues—blocked his path and demanded to check his papers. All the soldiers gathered around to study the papers, whispering, turning them sideways, scratching their heads. Used to such hassles, Mingolla paid them no attention and looked at the dead children.

They were scrawny, sun-darkened, lying face-down with their ragged hair hanging a fringe off the hood; their skins were pocked by infected mosquito bites, and the flesh around the bullet holes was ridged up and bruised. Judging by their size,

Mingolla guessed them to be about ten years old; but then he noticed that one was a girl with a teenage fullness to her buttocks, her breasts squashed against the metal. That made him indignant. They were only wild children who survived by robbing and killing, and the Guatemalan soldiers were only doing their duty: they performed a function comparable to that of the birds that hunted ticks on the hide of a rhinoceros, keeping their American beast pest-free and happy. But it wasn't right for the children to be laid out like game.

The soldier gave back Mingolla's papers. He was now all smiles, and—perhaps in the interest of solidifying Guatemalan-American relations, perhaps because he was proud of his work—he went over to the jeep and lifted the girl's head by the hair so Mingolla could see her face. "Bandida!" he said, arranging his features into a comical frown. The girl's face was not unlike the soldier's, with the same blade of a nose and prominent cheekbones. Fresh blood glistened on her lips, and the faded tattoo of a coiled serpent was centered on her forehead. Her eyes were open, and staring into them—despite their cloudiness—Mingolla felt that he had made a connection, that she was regarding him sadly from somewhere behind those eyes, continuing to die past the point of clinical death. Then an ant crawled out of her nostril, perching on the crimson curve of her lip, and the eyes looked merely vacant. The soldier let her head fall and wrapped his hand in the hair of a second corpse; but before he could lift it, Mingolla turned away and headed down the road toward the airbase.

There was a row of helicopters lined up at the edge of the landing strip, and walking between them, Mingolla saw the two pilots who had given him a ride from the Ant Farm. They were stripped to shorts and helmets, wearing baseball gloves, and they were playing catch, lofting high flies to each other. Behind them, atop their Sikorsky, a mechanic was fussing with the main rotor housing. The sight of the pilots didn't disturb Mingolla as it had the previous day; in fact, he found their weirdness somehow comforting. Just then, the ball eluded one of them and bounced Mingolla's way. He snagged it and flipped it back to the nearer of the pilots, who came loping over and stood

29

pounding the ball into the pocket of his glove. With his black reflecting face and sweaty, muscular torso, he looked like an eager young mutant.

"How's she goin'?" he asked. "Seem like you a little tore down this mornin'."

"I feel okay," said Mingolla defensively. " 'Course"—he smiled, making light of his defensiveness—"maybe you see something I don't."

The pilot shrugged; the sprightliness of the gesture seemed to convey good humor.

Mingolla pointed to the mechanic. "You guys broke down, huh?"

"Just overhaul. We're goin' back up early tomorrow. Need a lift?"

"Naw, I'm here for a week."

An eerie current flowed through Mingolla's left hand, setting up a palsied shaking. It was bad this time, and he jammed the hand into his hip pocket. The olive-drab line of barracks appeared to twitch, to suffer a dislocation and shift farther away; the choppers and jeeps and uniformed men on the strip looked toylike: pieces in a really neat GI Joe Airbase kit. Mingolla's hand beat against the fabric of his trousers like a sick heart.

"I gotta get going," he said.

"Hang in there," said the pilot. "You be awright."

The words had a flavor of diagnostic assurance that almost convinced Mingolla of the pilot's ability to know his fate, that things such as fate could be known. "You honestly believe what you were saying yesterday, man?" he asked. " 'Bout your helmets? 'Bout knowing the future?"

The pilot bounced the ball on the concrete, snatched it at the peak of its rebound, and stared down at it. Mingolla could see the seams and brand name reflected on the visor, but nothing of the face behind it, no evidence either of normalcy or deformity. "I get asked that a lot," said the pilot. "People raggin' me, y'know. But you ain't raggin' me, are you, man?"

"No," said Mingolla. "I'm not."

"Well," said the pilot, "it's this way. We buzz 'round up in the nothin', and we see shit on the ground, shit nobody else sees. Then we blow that shit away. Been doin' it like that for ten months, and we're still alive. Fuckin' A, I believe it!''

Mingolla was disappointed. "Yeah, okay," he said.

"You hear what I'm sayin'?" asked the pilot. "I mean we're livin' goddamn proof."

"Uh-huh." Mingolla scratched his neck, trying to think of a diplomatic response, but thought of none. "Guess I'll see you." He started toward the PX.

"Hang in there, man!" the pilot called after him. "Take it from me! Things gonna be lookin' up for you real soon!"

The canteen in the PX was a big barnlike room of un-painted boards; it was of such recent construction that Mingolla could still smell sawdust and resin. Thirty or forty tables; a jukebox; bare walls. Behind the bar at the rear of the room, a sour-faced corporal with a clipboard was doing a liquor inventory, and Gilbey—the only customer—was sitting by one of the east windows, stirring a cup of coffee. His brow was furrowed, and a ray of sunlight shone down around him, making it look that he was being divinely inspired to do some soul-searching.

"Where's Baylor?" asked Mingolla, sitting opposite him.

"Fuck, I dunno," said Gilbey, not taking his eyes from the coffee cup. "He'll be here."

Mingolla kept his left hand in his pocket. The tremors were diminishing, but not quickly enough to suit him; he was worried that the shaking would spread as it had after the assault. He let out a sigh, and in letting it out he could feel all his nervous flutters. The ray of sunlight seemed to be humming a wavery golden note, and that, too, worried him. Hallucinations. Then he noticed a fly buzzing against the windowpane. "How was it last night?" he asked.

Gilbey glanced up sharply. "Oh, you mean Big Tits. She lemme check her for lumps." A humorless smile nicked the corners of his mouth. He went back to stirring his coffee.

Mingolla was hurt that Gilbey hadn't asked about his night; he wanted to tell him about Debora. But that was typical of Gilbey's self-involvement. His narrow eyes and sulky mouth

31

were the imprints of a mean-spiritedness that permitted few concerns aside from his own well-being. Yet, despite his insensitivity, his stupid rages and limited conversation, Mingolla believed that he was smarter than he appeared, that disguising one's intelligence must have been a survival tactic in Detroit, where he had grown up. It was his craftiness that gave him away: his insights into the personalities of adversary lieutenants; his slickness at avoiding unpleasant duty; his ability to manipulate his peers. He wore stupidity like a cloak, and perhaps he had worn it for so long that it could not be removed. Still, Mingolla envied him its virtues, especially the way it had numbed him to the assault.

"He's never been late before," said Mingolla after a while.

"So what, he's fuckin' late!" snapped Gilbey, glowering. "He'll be here!"

Behind the bar, the corporal switched on a radio and spun the dial past Latin music, past Top Forty, then past an American voice reporting the baseball scores. "Hey!" called Gilbey. "Let's hear that, man! I wanna see what happened to the Tigers." With a shrug, the corporal complied.

". . . White Sox six, A's three," said the announcer. "That's eight in a row now for the Sox . . ."

"White Sox are kickin' some ass," said the corporal, pleased.

"The White Sox!" Gilbey sneered. "What the White Sox got 'cept a buncha beaners hittin' two hunnerd and some coke-sniffin' niggers? Shit! Every fuckin' spring the White Sox are flyin', man. But then 'long comes summer and the good drugs hit the street and they fuckin' die!"

"Yeah," said the corporal, "but this year . . ."

"Take that son of a bitch Caldwell," said Gilbey, ignoring him. "I seen him coupla years back when he had a trial with the Tigers. Man, that nigger could hit! Now he shuffles up there like he's just feelin' the breeze."

"They ain't takin' drugs, man," said the corporal testily. "They can't take 'em 'cause there's these tests that show if they's on somethin'."

Gilbey barreled ahead. "White Sox ain't gotta chance, man! Know what the guy on TV calls 'em sometimes? The Pale

Hose! The fuckin' Pale Hose! How you gonna win with a name like that? The Tigers, now, they got the right kinda name. The Yankees, the Braves, the—''

''Bullshit, man!'' The corporal was becoming upset; he set down his clipboard and walked to the end of the bar. ''What 'bout the Dodgers? They got a wimpy name and they're a good team. Your name don't mean shit!''

''The Reds,'' suggested Mingolla; he was enjoying Gilbey's rap, its stubbornness and irrationality. Yet at the same time he was concerned by its undertone of desperation: appearances to the contrary, Gilbey was not himself this morning.

''Oh, yeah!'' Gilbey smacked the table with the flat of his hand. ''The Reds! Lookit the Reds, man! Lookit how good they been doin' since the Cubans come into the war. You think that don't mean nothin'? You think their name ain't helpin' 'em? Even if they get in the Series, the Pale fuckin' Hose don't gotta prayer against the Reds.'' He laughed—a hoarse grunt. ''I'm a Tiger fan, man, but I gotta feelin' this ain't their year, y'know. The Reds are tearin' up the NL East, and the Yankees is comin' on, and when they get together in October, man, then we gonna find out alla 'bout everything. Alla 'bout fuckin' everything!'' His voice grew tight and tremulous. ''So don't gimme no trouble 'bout the candy-ass Pale Hose, man! They ain't shit and they never was and they ain't gonna be shit till they change their fuckin' name!''

Sensing danger, the corporal backed away from confrontation, and Gilbey lapsed into a moody silence. For a while there were only the sounds of chopper blades and the radio blatting out cocktail jazz. Two mechanics wandered in for an early morning beer, and not long after that three fatherly-looking sergeants with potbellies and thinning hair and quartermaster insignia on their shoulders sat at a nearby table and started up a game of rummy. The corporal brought them a pot of coffee and a bottle of whiskey, which they mixed and drank as they played. Their game had an air of custom, of something done at this time every day, and watching them, taking note of their fat, pampered ease, their old-buddy familiarity, Mingolla felt proud of his palsied hand. It was an honorable affliction, a sign that he had participated in the heart of the war as these men had not. Yet, he bore them no resentment. None whatsoever. Rather, it gave him a sense of security to know that three such fatherly men were here to provide him with food and liquor and new boots. He basked in the dull, happy clutter of their talk, in the haze of cigar smoke that seemed the exhaust of their contentment. He believed that he could go to them, tell them his problems, and receive folksy advice. They were here to assure him of the rightness of his purpose, to remind him of simple American values, to lend an illusion of fraternal involvement to the war, to make clear that it was merely an exercise in good fellowship and tough-mindedness, an initiation rite that these three men had long ago passed through, and after the war they would all get medals and pal around together and talk about bloodshed and terror with head-shaking wonderment and nostalgia, as if bloodshed and terror were old lost friends whose natures they had not fully appreciated at the time. . . . Mingolla realized then that a smile had stretched his facial muscles taut, and that his train of thought had been leading him into spooky mental territory. The tremors in his hand were worse than ever. He checked his watch. It was almost ten o'clock. *Ten o'clock!* In a panic he scraped back his chair and stood.

"Let's look for him," he said to Gilbey.

Gilbey started to say something but kept it to himself. He tapped his spoon hard against the edge of the table. Then he, too, scraped back his chair and stood.

Baylor was not to be found at the Club Demonio or any of the bars on the west bank. Gilbey and Mingolla described him to everyone they met, but no one remembered him. The longer the search went on, the more insecure Mingolla became. Baylor was necessary, an essential underpinning of the platform of habits and routines that supported him, that let him live beyond the range of war's weapons and the laws of chance, and should that underpinning be destroyed . . . In his mind's eye he saw the platform tipping, he and Gilbey toppling over the edge, cartwheeling down into an abyss filled with black flames. Once Gilbey said, "Panama! The son of a bitch run off to Panama."

34

But Mingolla didn't think this was the case. He was certain that Baylor was close at hand. His certainty had such a valence of clarity that he became even more insecure, knowing that this sort of clarity often heralded a bad conclusion.

The sun climbed higher, its heat an enormous weight pressing down, its light leaching color from the stucco walls, and Mingolla's sweat began to smell rancid. Only a few soldiers were on the streets, mixed in with the usual run of kids and beggars, and the bars were empty except for a smattering of drunks still on a binge from the night before. Gilbey stumped along, grabbing people by the shirt and asking his questions. Mingolla, however, terribly conscious of his trembling hand, nervous to the point of stammering, was forced to work out a stock approach whereby he could get through these brief interviews. He would amble up, keeping his right side forward, and say, "I'm looking for a friend of mine. Maybe you seen him? Tall guy. Olive skin, black hair, thin. Name's Baylor." He learned to let this slide off his tongue in a casual unreeling.

Finally Gilbey had had enough. "I'm gonna hang out with Big Tits," he said. "Meetcha at the PX tomorrow." He started to walk off, but turned and added, "You wanna get in touch 'fore tomorrow, I'll be at the Club Demonio." He had an odd expression on his face. It was as if he was trying to smile reassuringly, but—due to his lack of practice—it looked forced and foolish and not in the least reassuring.

Around eleven o'clock Mingolla wound up leaning against a pink stucco wall, watching out for Baylor in the thickening crowds. Beside him, the sun-browned fronds of a banana tree were feathering in the wind, making a crispy sound whenever a gust blew them back into the wall. The roof of the bar across the street was being repaired: sheets of new tin alternating with narrow patches of rust that looked like enormous strips of bacon laid there to fry. Now and then he would let his gaze drift up to the unfinished bridge, a great sweep of magical whiteness curving into the blue, rising above the town and the jungle and the war. Not even the heat haze rippling from the tin roof could warp its smoothness. It seemed to be orchestrating the stench, the mutter of the crowds, and the jukebox music into a tranquil unity, absorbing those energies and returning them purified, enriched. He thought that if he stared at it long enough, it would speak to him, pronounce a white word that would grant his wishes.

Two flat cracks—pistol shots—sent him stumbling away from the wall, his heart racing. Inside his head the shots had spoken the two syllables of Baylor's name. All the kids and beggars had vanished. All the soldiers had stopped and turned to face the direction from which the shots had come: zombies who had heard their master's voice.

Another shot.

Some soldiers milled out of a side street, talking excitedly. ". . . Fuckin' nuts!" one was saying, and his buddy said, "It was Sammy, man! You see his eyes?"

Mingolla pushed his way through them and sprinted down the side street. At the end of the block a cordon of MPs had sealed off access to the right-hand turn, and when Mingolla ran up, one of them told him to stay back.

"What is it?" Mingolla asked. "Some guy playing Sammy?"

"Fuck off," the MP said mildly.

"Listen," said Mingolla. "It might be this friend of mine. Tall, skinny guy. Black hair. Maybe I can talk to him."

The MP exchanged glances with his buddies, who shrugged and acted otherwise unconcerned. "Okay," he said. He pulled Mingolla to him and pointed out a bar with turquoise walls on the next corner down. "Go on in there and talk to the captain."

Two more shots, then a third.

"Better hurry," said the MP. "Ol' Captain Haynesworth there, he don't put much stock in negotiations."

It was cool and dark inside the bar; two shadowy figures were flattened against the wall beside a window that opened onto the cross street. Mingolla could make out the glint of automatic pistols in their hands. Then, through the window, he saw Baylor pop up from behind a retaining wall: a three-foot-high structure of mud bricks running between an herbal-drug store and another bar. Baylor was shirtless, his chest painted with reddish brown smears of dried blood, and he was standing in a nonchalant pose, with his thumbs hooked in his trouser

36

pockets. One of the men by the window fired at him. The report was deafening, causing Mingolla to flinch and close his eyes. When he looked out the window again, Baylor was nowhere in sight.

"Fucker's just tryin' to draw fire," said the man who had shot at Baylor. "Sammy's fast today."

"Yeah, but he's slowin' some," said a lazy voice from the darkness at the rear of the bar. "I do believe he's outta dope."

"Hey," said Mingolla. "Don't kill him! I know the guy. I can talk to him."

"Talk?" said the lazy voice. "You kin talk till yo' ass turns green, boy, and Sammy ain't gon' listen."

Mingolla peered into the shadows. A big sloppy-looking man was leaning on the counter; brass insignia gleamed on his beret. "You the captain?" he asked. "They told me outside to talk to the captain."

"Yes, indeed," said the man. "And I'd be purely delighted to talk with you, boy. What you wanna talk 'bout?"

The other men laughed.

"Why are you trying to kill him?" asked Mingolla, hearing the pitch of desperation in his voice. "You don't have to kill him. You could use a trank gun."

"Got one comin'," said the captain. "Thing is, though, yo' buddy got hisself a coupla hostages back of that wall, and we get a chance at him 'fore the trank gun 'rives, we bound to take it."

"But—" Mingolla began.

"Lemme finish, boy." The captain hitched up his gunbelt, strolled over, and draped an arm around Mingolla's shoulder, enveloping him in an aura of body odor and whiskey breath. "See," he went on, "we had everything under control. Sammy there . . ."

"Baylor!" said Mingolla angrily. "His name's Baylor."

The captain lifted his arm from Mingolla's shoulder and looked at him with amusement. Even in the gloom Mingolla could see the network of broken capillaries on his cheeks, the bloated alcoholic features. "Right," said the captain. "Like I's sayin', yo' good buddy Mister Baylor there wasn't doin' no harm. Just sorta ravin' and runnin' 'round. But then 'long comes a coupla our Marine brothers. Seems like they'd been givin' our beaner friends a demonstration of the latest combat gear, and they was headin' back from said demonstration when they seen our little problem and took it 'pon themselves to play hero. Wellsir, puttin' it in a nutshell, Mister Baylor flat kicked their ass. Stomped all over their esprit de corps. Then he drags 'em back of that wall and starts messin' with one of their guns. And—"

Two more shots.

"Shit!" said one of the men by the window.

"And there he sits," said the captain. "Fuckin' with us. Now either the gun's outta ammo or else he ain't figgered out how it works. If it's the latter case, and he does figger it out . . ." The captain shook his head dolefully, as if picturing dire consequences. "See my predicament?"

"I could try talking to him," said Mingolla. "What harm would it do?"

"You get yourself killed, it's your life, boy. But it's my ass that's gonna get hauled up on charges." The captain steered Mingolla to the door and gave him a gentle shove toward the cordon of MPs. " 'Preciate you volunteerin', boy."

Later Mingolla was to reflect that what he had done made no sense, because—whether or not Baylor had survived—he would never have been returned to the Ant Farm. But at the time, desperate to preserve the ritual, none of this occurred to him. He walked around the corner and toward the retaining wall. His mouth was dry, his heart pounded. But the shaking in his hand had stopped, and he had the presence of mind to walk in such a way that he blocked the MPs' line of fire. About twenty feet from the wall he called out, "Hey, Baylor! It's Mingolla, man!" And as if propelled by a spring, Baylor jumped up, staring at him. It was an awful stare. His eyes were like bull's-eyes, white showing all around the irises; trickles of blood ran from his nostrils, and nerves were twitching in his cheeks with the regularity of watchworks. The dried blood on his chest came from three long gouges; they were partially scabbed over but were oozing a clear fluid. For a moment he

38

remained motionless. Then he reached down behind the wall, picked up a double-barreled rifle from whose stock trailed a length of flexible tubing, and brought it to bear on Mingolla.

He squeezed the trigger.

No flame, no explosion. Not even a click. But Mingolla felt that he'd been dipped in ice water. "Christ!" he said. "Baylor! It's me!" Baylor squeezed the trigger again, with the same result. An expression of intense frustration washed over his face, then lapsed into that dead man's stare. He looked directly up into the sun, and after a few seconds he smiled: he might have been receiving terrific news from on high.

Mingolla's senses had become wonderfully acute. Somewhere far away a radio was playing a country-and-western tune, and with its plaintiveness, its intermittent bursts of static, it seemed to him the whining of a nervous system on the blink. He could hear the MPs talking in the bar, could smell the sour acids of Baylor's madness, and he thought he could feel the pulse of Baylor's rage, an inconstant flow of heat eddying around him, intensifying his fear, rooting him to the spot. Baylor laid the gun down, laid it down with the tenderness he might have shown toward a sick child, and stepped over the retaining wall. The animal fluidity of the movements made Mingolla's skin crawl. He managed to shuffle backward a pace and held up his hands to ward Baylor off. "C'mon, man," he said weakly. Baylor let out a fuming noise—part hiss, part whimper—and a runner of saliva slid between his lips. The sun was a golden bath drenching the street, kindling glints and shimmers from every bright surface, as if it were bringing reality to a boil.

Somebody yelled, "Get down, boy!"

Then Baylor flew at him, and they fell together, rolling on the hard-packed dirt. Fingers dug in behind his Adam's apple. He twisted away, saw Baylor grinning down, all staring eyes and yellowed teeth. Strings of drool flapping from his chin. A Halloween face. Knees pinned Mingolla's shoulders, hands gripped his hair and bashed his head against the ground. Again, and again. A keening sound switched on inside his ears. He wrenched an arm free and tried to gouge Baylor's eyes; but

39

Baylor bit his thumb, gnawing at the joint. Mingolla's vision dimmed, and he couldn't hear anything anymore. The back of his head felt mushy. It seemed to be rebounding very slowly from the dirt, higher and slower after each impact. Framed by blue sky, Baylor's face looked to be receding, spiraling off. And then, just as Mingolla began to fade, Baylor disappeared.

Dust was in Mingolla's mouth, his nostrils. He heard shouts, grunts. Still dazed, he propped himself onto an elbow. A short way off, khaki arms and legs and butts were thrashing around in a cloud of dust. Like a comic-strip fight. You expected asterisks and exclamation points overhead to signify profanity. Somebody grabbed his arm, hauled him upright. The MP captain, his beefy face flushed. He frowned reprovingly as he brushed dirt from Mingolla's clothes. "Real gutsy, boy," he said. "And real, real stupid. He hadn't been at the end of his run, you'd be drawin' flies 'bout now." He turned to a sergeant standing nearby. "How stupid you reckon that was, Phil?"

The sergeant said that it beat him.

"Well," the captain said, "I figger if the boy here was in combat, that'd be 'bout Bronze Star stupid."

That, allowed the sergeant, was pretty goddamn stupid.

"Course here in Frisco"—the captain gave Mingolla a final dusting—"it don't get you diddley-shit."

The MPs were piling off Baylor, who lay on his side, bleeding from his nose and mouth. Blood as thick as gravy filmed over his cheeks.

"Panama," said Mingolla dully. Maybe it was an option. He saw how it would be . . . a night beach, palm shadows a lacework on the white sand.

"What say?" asked the captain.

"He wanted to go to Panama," said Mingolla.

"Don't we all," said the captain.

One of the MPs rolled Baylor onto his stomach and handcuffed him; another manacled his feet. Then they rolled him back over. Yellow dirt had mired with the blood on his cheeks and forehead, hitting him with a blotchy mask. His eyes snapped open in the middle of that mask, widening when he felt the restraints. He started to hump up and down, trying to bounce his way to freedom. He kept on humping for almost a minute; then he went rigid and—his gone eyes fixed on the molten disc of the sun—he let out a roar. That was the only word for it. It wasn't a scream or a shout, but a devil's exultant roar, so loud and full of fury it seemed to be generating all the blazing light-and-heat dance. Listening to it had a seductive effect, and Mingolla began to get behind it, to feel it in his body like a good rock 'n' roll tune, to sympathize with its life-hating exuberance.

"Whoo-ee!" said the captain, marveling. "They gon' have to build a whole new zoo for that boy."

After giving his statement and letting a corpsman check his head, Mingolla caught the ferry to meet Debora on the east bank. He sat in the stern, gazing out at the unfinished bridge, this time unable to derive from it any sense of hope or magic. Panama kept cropping up in this thoughts. Now that Baylor was gone, was it really an option? He knew he should try to figure things out, plan what to do, but he couldn't stop seeing Baylor's bloody, demented face. He'd seen worse, Christ yes, a whole lot worse, guys reduced to spare parts, so little of them left that they didn't need a shiny silver coffin, just a black metal can the size of a cookie jar. Guys scorched and one-eyed and bloody, clawing blindly at the air like creatures out of a monster movie, but the idea of Baylor trapped forever in some raw, red place inside his brain, in the heart of that raw, red noise he'd made, maybe that idea was worse than anything Mingolla had seen. He didn't want to die; he rejected the prospect with the impassioned stubbornness a child displays when confronted with a hard truth. Yet he would rather die than endure madness. Compared to what Baylor had in store, death and Panama seemed to offer the same peaceful sweetness.

Someone sat down beside Mingolla: a kid who couldn't have been older than eighteen. A new kid with a new haircut, new boots, new fatigues. Even his face looked new, freshly broken from the mold. Shiny, pudgy cheeks; clear skin; bright, unused blue eyes. He was eager to talk. He asked Mingolla about his home, his family, and said, "Oh, wow, it must be great living in New York, wow." But he appeared to have some other reason for initiating the conversation, something he was leading up to, and finally he spat it out.

"You know the Sammy that went animal back there?" he said. "I seen him pitted last night. Little place in the jungle west of the base. Guy name Chaco owns it. Man, it was fuckin' incredible!"

Mingolla had only heard of the pits third- and fourth-hand, but what he had heard was bad, and it was hard to believe that this kid with his air of home-boy innocence could be an aficio-nado of something so vile. And, despite what he had just witnessed, it was even harder to believe that Baylor could have been a participant.

The kid didn't need prompting. "It was pretty early on," he said. "There'd been a coupla bouts, nothin' special, and then this guy walks in lookin' real twitchy. I knew he was Sammy by the way he's starin' at the pit, y'know, like it's somethin' he's been wishin' for. And this guy with me, friend of mine, he gives me a poke and says, 'Holy shit! That's the Black Knight, man! I seen him fight over in Reunion a while back. Put your money on him,' he says. 'The fucker's an ace!' "

Their last R and R had been in Reunion. Mingolla tried to frame a question but couldn't think of one whose answer would have any meaning.

"Well," said the kid, "I ain't been down long, but I'd even heard 'bout the Knight. So I went over and kinda hung out near him, thinkin' maybe I can get a line on how he's feelin', y'know, 'cause you don't wanna just bet the guy's rep. Pretty soon Chaco comes over and asks the Knight if he wants some action. The Knight says, 'Yeah, but I wanna fight an animal. Somethin' fierce, man. I wanna fight somethin' fierce.' Chaco says he's got some monkeys and shit, and the Knight says he hears Chaco's got a jaguar. Chaco, he hems and haws, says maybe so, maybe not, but it don't matter 'cause a jaguar's too strong for Sammy. And the Knight tells Chaco who he is. Lemme tell ya, Chaco's whole fuckin' attitude changed. He could see how the bettin' was gonna go for somethin' like the Black Knight versus a jaguar. And he goes, like, 'Yes, sir, Mister

Black Knight, sir! Anything you want!' And he makes the announcement. Man, the place goes nuts. People wavin' money, screamin' odds, drinkin' fast so's they can get ripped in time for the main event, and the Knight's just standin' there, smilin', like he's feedin' off the confusion. Then Chaco lets the jaguar in through the tunnel and into the pit. It ain't a full-growed jaguar, half-growed maybe. But that's all you figure even the Knight can handle.''

The kid paused for breath; his eyes seemed to have grown brighter. "Anyway, the jaguar's sneakin' 'round and 'round, keepin' close to the pit wall, snarlin' and spittin', and the Knight's watchin' him from up above, checkin' his moves, y'know. And everybody starts chantin', 'Sam-mee, Sam-mee, Sam-mee,' and after the chant builds up loud the Knight pulls three ampules outta his pocket. I mean, shit, man! Three! I ain't never been 'round Sammy when he's done more'n two. Three gets you clear into the fuckin' sky! So when the Knight holds up these three ampules, the crowd's tuned to burn, howlin' like they's playin' Sammy themselves. But the Knight, man, he keeps his cool. He is *so* cool! He just holds up the ampules and lets 'em take the shine, soakin' up the noise and energy, gettin' strong off the crowd's juice. Chaco waves everybody quiet and gives the speech, y'know, 'bout how in the heart of every man there's a warrior-soul waitin' to be loosed and shit. I tell ya, man, I always thought that speech was crap before, but the Knight's makin' me buy it a hunnerd percent. He is so goddamn cool! He takes off his shirt and shoes, and he ties this piece of black silk 'round his arm. Then he pops the ampules, one after another, real quick, and breathes it all in. I can see it hittin', catchin' fire in his eyes. Pumpin' him up. And soon as he's popped the last one, he jumps into the pit. He don't use the tunnel, man! He jumps! Twenty-five feet down to the sand, and lands in a crouch.''

Three other soldiers were leaning in, listening, and the kid was now addressing all of them, playing to his audience. He was so excited that he could barely keep his speech coherent, and Mingolla realized with disgust that he, too, was excited by the image of Baylor crouched on the sand. Baylor, who had

43

cried after the assault. Baylor, who had been so afraid of snipers that he had once pissed in his pants rather than walk from his gun to the latrine.

Baylor, the Black Knight.

"The jaguar's screechin' and snarlin' and slashin' at the air," the kid went on. "Tryin' to put fear into the Knight. 'Cause the jaguar knows in his mind the Knight's big trouble. This ain't some jerk like Chaco, this is Sammy. The Knight moves to the center of the pit, still in a crouch." Here the kid pitched his voice low and dramatic. "Nothin' happens for a coupla minutes, 'cept it's tense. Nobody's hardly breathin'. The jaguar springs a coupla times, but the Knight dances off the side and makes him miss, and there ain't no damage either way. Whenever the jaguar springs, the crowd sighs and squeals, not just 'cause they's scared of seein' the Knight tore up, but also 'cause they can see how fast he is. Silky fast, man! Unreal. He looks 'bout as fast as the jaguar. He keeps on dancin' away, and no matter how the jaguar twists and turns, no matter if he comes at him along the sand, he can't get his claws into the Knight. And then, man . . . oh, it was so smooth! Then the jaguar springs again, and this time 'stead of dancin' away, the Knight drops onto his back, does this half-roll onto his shoulders, and when the jaguar passes over him, he kicks up with both feet. Kicks up hard! And smashes his heels into the jaguar's side. The jaguar slams into the pit wall and comes down screamin', snappin' at his ribs. They was busted, man. Pokin' out the skin like tent posts."

The kid wiped his mouth with the back of his hand and flicked his eyes toward Mingolla and the other soldiers to see if they were into the story. "We was shoutin', man," he said. "Poundin' the top of the pit wall. It was so loud, the guy I'm with is yellin' in my ear and I can't hear nothin'. Now maybe it's the noise, maybe it's his ribs, whatever . . . the jaguar goes berserk. Makin' these scuttlin' lunges at the Knight, tryin' to get close 'fore he springs so the Knight can't pull that same trick. He's snarlin' like a goddamn chain saw! The Knight keeps leapin' and spinnin' away. But then he slips, man, grabs the air for balance, and the jaguar's on him, clawin' at his chest. For a

44

second they're like waltzin' together. Then the Knight pries
loose the paw that's hooked him, pushes the jaguar's head
back, and smashes his fist into the jaguar's eye. The jaguar flops
onto the sand, and the Knight scoots to the other side of the pit.
He's checkin' the scratches on his chest, which is bleedin'
wicked. Meantime, the jaguar gets to his feet, and he's fucked
up worse than ever. His one eye's fulla blood, and his hind-
quarters is all loosey-goosey. Like if this was boxin', they'd call
in the doctor. The jaguar figures he's had enough of this crap,
and he starts tryin' to jump outta the pit. This one time he
jumps right up to where I'm leanin' over the edge. Comes so
close I can smell his breath, I can see myself reflected in his
good eye. He's clawin' for a grip, wantin' to haul hisself up into
the crowd. People are freakin', thinkin' he might be gonna
make it. But 'fore he gets the chance, the Knight catches him by
the tail and slings him against the wall. Just like you'd beat a
goddamn rug, that's how he's dealin' with the jaguar. And the
jaguar's a real mess now. He's quiverin'. Blood's pourin' outta
his mouth, his fangs is all red. The Knight starts makin' these
little feints, wavin' his arms, growlin'. He's toyin' with the
jaguar. People don't believe what they're seein', man. Sammy's
kickin' a jaguar's ass so bad he's got room to toy with it. If the
place was nuts before, now it's a fuckin' zoo. Fights in the
crowd, guys singin' the Marine Hymn. Some beaner squint's
takin' off her clothes. The jaguar tries to scuttle up close to the
Knight again, but he's too fucked up. He can't keep it together.
And the Knight, he's still growlin' and feintin'. A guy behind me
is booin', claimin' the Knight's defamin' the purity of the sport
by playin' with the jaguar. But hell, man, I can see he's just
timin' the jaguar, waitin' for the right moment, the right move.''

Staring off downriver, the kid wore a wistful expression: he
might have been thinking about his girlfriend. ''We all knew it
was comin','' he said. ''Everybody got real quiet. So quiet you
could hear the Knight's feet scrapin' on the sand. You could
feel it in the air, and you knew the jaguar was savin' up for one
big effort. Then the Knight slips again, 'cept he's fakin'. I could
see that, but the jaguar couldn't. When the Knight reels sideways, the jaguar springs. I thought the Knight was gonna drop

down like he did the first time, but he springs, too. Feet first. And he catches the jaguar under the jaw. You could hear bone splinterin', and the jaguar falls in a heap. He struggles to get up, but no way! He's whinin', and he craps all over the sand. The Knight walks up behind him, takes his head in both hands, and gives it a twist. Crack!"

As if identifying with the jaguar's fate, the kid closed his eyes and sighed. "Everybody's been quiet till they heard that crack, then all hell broke loose. People chantin', 'Sam-mee, Sam-mee,' and people shovin', tryin' to get close to the pit wall so they can watch the Knight take the heart. He reaches into the jaguar's mouth and snaps off one of the fangs and tosses it to somebody. Then Chaco comes in through the tunnel and hands him the knife. Right when he's 'bout to cut, somebody knocks me over, and by the time I'm back on my feet, he's already took the heart and tasted it. He's just standin' there with the jaguar's blood on his mouth and his own blood runnin' down his chest. He looks kinda confused, y'know. Like now the fight's over and he don't know what to do. But then he starts roarin'. He sounds the same as the jaguar did 'fore it got hurt. Crazy fierce. Ready to get it on with the whole goddamn world. Man, I lost it! I was right with that roar. Maybe I was roarin' with him, maybe everybody was. That's what it felt like, man. Like bein' in the middle of this roar that's comin' outta every throat in the universe." The kid engaged Mingolla with a sober look. "Lotsa people go 'round sayin' the pits are evil, and maybe they are. I don't know. How you s'posed to tell 'bout what's evil and what's not down here? They say you can go to the pits a thousand times and see nothin' like the jaguar and the Black Knight. I don't know 'bout that, either. But I'm goin' back just in case I get lucky. 'Cause what I saw last night, if it was evil, man, it was so fuckin' evil it was beautiful, too."

CHAPTER THREE

Debora was waiting at the pier, carrying a picnic basket and wearing a blue dress with a high neckline and a full skirt: a schoolgirl dress. Mingolla homed in on her. The way she had her hair, falling about her shoulders in thick dark curls, made him think of smoke turned solid, and her face seemed the map of a beautiful country with black lakes and dusky plains, a country in which he could hide. They walked along the river past the town and came to a spot where ceiba tress with massy crowns of slick green leaves and whitish bark and roots like alligator tails grew close to the shore, and there they talked and ate and listened to the water gulping against the clay bank, to the birds, to the faint noises from the airbase that at this distance sounded part of nature. Sunlight dazzled the water, and whenever wind riffled the surface, it seemed to be spreading the dazzles into a crawling crust of diamonds. Mingolla imagined that they had taken a secret path, rounded a corner of the world, and reached some eternally peaceful land. The illusion of peace was so profound that he began to see hope in it. Perhaps, he thought, something was being offered here. Some new magic. Maybe there would be a sign. Signs were everywhere if you knew how to read them. He glanced around. Thick white trunks rising into greenery, dark leafy avenues leading off between them . . . nothing there, but what about those weeds growing at the edge of the bank? They cast precise

47

fleur-de-lis shadows in the clay, shadows that didn't have much in common with the ragged configurations of the weeds themselves. Possibly a sign, though not a clear one. He lifted his gaze to the reeds growing in the shallows. Yellow reeds with jointed stalks bent akimbo, some with clumps of insect eggs like seed pearls hanging from loose fibers, and others dappled by patches of algae. That's how they looked one moment. Then Mingolla's vision rippled, as if the whole of reality had shivered, and the reeds were transformed into rudimentary shapes: yellow sticks poking up from flat blue. On the far side of the river, the jungle was a simple smear of Crayola green; a speedboat passing was a red slash unzippering the blue. It seemed that the rippling had jostled all the elements of the landscape a fraction out of kilter, revealing every object as characterless as a building block. Mingolla gave his head a shake. Nothing changed. He rubbed his brow. No effect. Terrified, he squeezed his eyes shut. He felt like the only meaningful piece in a nonsensical puzzle, vulnerable by virtue of his uniqueness. His breath came rapidly, his left hand fluttered.

"David? Don't you want to hear it?" Debora sounded peeved.

"Hear what?" He kept his eyes closed.

"About my dream. Weren't you listening?"

He peeked at her. Everything was back to normal. She was sitting with her knees tucked under her, all her features in sharp focus. "I'm sorry," he said. "I was thinking."

"You looked frightened."

"Frightened?" He put on a bewildered face. "Naw, just had a thought, is all."

"It couldn't have been pleasant."

He shrugged off the comment and sat up smartly to prove his attentiveness. "So tell me 'bout the dream."

"All right," she said doubtfully. The breeze drifted fine strands of hair across her face, and she brushed them back. "You were in a room the color of blood, with red chairs and a red table. Even the paintings on the wall were done in shades of red, and . . ." She broke off, peering at him. "Do you want to hear this? You have that look again."

48

"Sure," he said. But he was afraid. How could she have known about the red room? She must have had a vision of it, and . . . Then he realized that she might not have been talking about the room itself. He'd told her about the assault, hadn't he? And if she had guerrilla contacts, she would know that the emergency lights were switched on during an assault. That had to be it! She was trying to frighten him into deserting again, psyching him the way Christians played upon the fears of sinners with images of fiery rivers and torture. It infuriated him. Who the hell was she to tell him what was right or wise? Whatever he did, it was going to be *his* decision.

"There were four doors in the room," she went on. "You wanted to leave the room, but you couldn't tell which of the doors was safe to use. You tried the first door, and it turned out to be a facade. The knob of the second door turned easily, but the door itself was stuck. Rather than forcing it, you went to the third door. It was cold, and it frightened you. The knob of the fourth door was made of glass and cut your hand. After that you just walked back and forth, unsure what to do." She waited for a reaction, and when he gave none, she said, "Do you understand?"

He kept silent, biting back anger.

"I'll interpret it for you," she said.

"Don't bother."

"The red room is war, and the false door is the way of your childish—"

"Stop!" He grabbed her wrist, squeezing it hard.

She glared at him until he released her. "Your childish magic," she went on. "The third door, the one that frightened you, that's Psicorps."

"Maybe I'm not frightened of it anymore."

"Bad side effects, remember?"

"What is it with you?" he asked. "You have some kinda quota to fill? Five deserters a month, and you get a medal?"

She tucked her skirt down to cover her knees, fiddled with a loose thread. From the way she was acting, Mingolla wondered whether he had asked an intimate question and she was

49

LUCIUS SHEPARD

framing an answer that wouldn't be indelicate. Finally she said, "Is that who you believe I am?"

"Why else would you be handing me this bullshit?"

"What's the matter with you, David?" She leaned forward, cupping his face in her hands. "Why . . ."

He pushed her hands away. "What's the matter with me? This"—his gesture included the sky, the river, the trees—"that's what's the matter. You remind me of my parents. They ask the same sorta ignorant questions." Suddenly he wanted to injure her with answers, to find an answer like acid to throw in her face and watch it eat away her tranquility. "Know what I do for my parents when they ask dumb-ass questions like 'What's the matter?' I tell 'em a story. A war story. You wanna hear a war story? Something happened a few days back that'll do for an answer just fine."

"You don't have to tell me anything," she said, discouraged.

"No problem," he said. "Be my pleasure."

The Ant Farm was a large sugarloaf hill overlooking dense jungle on the eastern border of Fire Zone Emerald; jutting out from its summit were rocket and gun emplacements that at a distance resembled a crown of thorns jammed down over a green scalp. For several hundred yards around, the land had been cleared of all vegetation. The big guns had been lowered to maximum declension and in a mad moment had obliterated huge swaths of jungle, snapping off regiments of massive tree trunks a couple of feet above the ground, leaving a moat of blackened stumps and scorched red dirt seamed with fissures. Tangles of razor wire had replaced the trees and bushes, forming surreal blue-steel hedges, and buried beneath the wire was a variety of mines and detection devices. These did little good, however, because the Cubans possessed technology that would neutralize most of them. On clear nights there was scant likelihood of trouble; but on misty nights trouble could be expected. Under cover of the mist, Cuban and guerrilla troops would come through the wire and attempt to infiltrate the tunnels that honeycombed the interior of the hill. Occasionally one of the mines would be triggered, and a ghostly fireball would bloom

50

in the swirling whiteness, tiny black figures being flung outward from its center. Lately some of these casualties had been found to be wearing red berets and scorpion-shaped brass pins, and from this it was known that the Cubans had sent in the Alacran Division, which had been instrumental in routing the American forces in Miskitia.

There were nine levels of tunnels inside the hill, most lined with little round rooms that served as living quarters (the only exception being the bottom level, which was given over to the computer center and offices); all the rooms and tunnels were coated with a bubbled white plastic that looked like hardened sea foam and was proof against antipersonnel explosives. In Mingolla's room, where he and Baylor and Gilbey bunked, a scarlet paper lantern had been hung on the overhead light fixture, making it seem that they were inhabiting a blood cell: Baylor had insisted on the lantern, saying that the overhead was too bright and hurt his eyes. Three cots were arranged against the walls, as far apart as space allowed. The floor around Baylor's cot was littered with cigarette butts and used Kleenex; under his pillow he kept a tin box containing a stash of pills and marijuana. Whenever he lit a joint he would always offer Mingolla a hit, and Mingolla always refused, feeling that the experience of the firebase would not be enhanced by drugs. Taped to the wall above Gilbey's cot was a collage of beaver shots, and each day after duty, whether or not Mingolla and Baylor were in the room, he would lie beneath them and masturbate. His lack of shame caused Mingolla to be embarrassed by the pimply-youth quality of the objects taped above his own cot: a Yankee pennant; a photograph of his old girlfriend, and another of his senior-year high school basketball team; several sketches he had made of the surrounding jungle. Gilbey teased him constantly about this display, calling him "the boy next door," which struck Mingolla as odd, because back home he had been considered something of an eccentric.

It was toward this room that Mingolla was heading when the assault began. Large cargo elevators capable of carrying sixty men ran up and down just inside the east and west slopes of the hill; but to provide quick access between adjoining levels, and also as a safeguard in case of power failures, an auxiliary tunnel corkscrewed down through the center of the hill like a huge coil of white intestine. It was slightly more than twice as wide as the electric carts that traveled it, carrying officers and VIPs on tours. Mingolla was in the habit of using the tunnel for his exercise. Each night he would put on sweat clothes and jog up and down the entire nine levels, doing this out of a conviction that exhaustion prevented bad dreams. That night, as he passed level Four on his final leg up, he heard a rumbling: an explosion, and not far off. Alarms sounded, the big guns atop the hill began to thunder. From directly above came shouts and the stutter of automatic fire. The tunnel lights flickered, went dark, and the emergency lights winked on.

Mingolla flattened against the wall. The dim red lighting caused the bubbled surfaces of the tunnel to appear as smooth as a chamber in a gigantic nautilus, and this resemblance intensified his sense of helplessness, making him feel like a child trapped within an evil undersea palace. He couldn't think clearly, picturing the chaos around him. Muzzle flashes, armies of ant-men seething through the tunnels, screams spraying blood, and the big guns bucking, every shell burst kindling miles of sky. He would have preferred to keep going up, to get out into the open where he might have a chance to hide in the jungle. But down was his only hope. Pushing away from the wall, he ran full-tilt, arms waving, skidding around corners, almost falling, past level Four, level Five. Then, halfway between levels Five and Six, he nearly tripped over a dead man: an American lying curled up around a belly wound, a slick of blood spreading beneath him and a machete by his hand. As Mingolla stooped for the machete, he thought nothing about the man, only about how weird it was for an American to be defending himself against Cubans with such a weapon. There was no use, he decided, in going any farther. Whoever had killed the man would be somewhere below, and the safest course would be to hide out in one of the rooms on level Five. Holding the machete before him, he moved cautiously back up the tunnel.

Levels Five, Six, and Seven were officer country, and though

52

the tunnels were the same as the ones above—gently curving tubes eight feet high and ten feet wide—the rooms were larger and contained only two cots each. The rooms Mingolla peered into were empty, and this, despite the sounds of battle, gave him a secure feeling. But as he passed beyond the tunnel curve, he heard shouts in Spanish from the rear. He peeked back around the curve. A skinny black soldier wearing a red beret and gray fatigues was inching toward the first doorway; then, rifle at the ready, he ducked inside. Two other Cubans—slim, bearded men, their skin sallow-looking in the bloody light— were standing by the arched entranceway to the auxiliary tunnel; when they saw the black soldier emerge from the room, they walked off in the opposite direction, probably to check the rooms at the far end of the level.

Mingolla began to operate in a kind of luminous panic. He realized that he would have to kill the black soldier. Kill him without any fuss, take his rifle and hope that he could catch the other two off guard when they came back for him. He slipped into the nearest room and stationed himself against the wall to the right of the door. The Cuban, he had noticed, had turned left on entering the room; he would have been vulnerable to someone positioned as Mingolla was. Vulnerable for a split second. Less than a count of one. The pulse in Mingolla's temple throbbed, and he gripped the machete in his left hand. He rehearsed mentally what he would have to do. Stab; clamp a hand over the Cuban's mouth; bring his knee up to jar loose the rifle. And he would have to perform these actions simultaneously, execute them perfectly.

Perfect execution.

He almost laughed out loud, remembering his paunchy old basketball coach saying, "Perfect execution, boys. That's what beats a zone. Forget the fancy crap. Just set your screen, run your patterns, and get your shots down."

Hoops ain't nothin' but life in short pants, huh, Coach?

Mingolla drew a deep breath and let it sigh out through his nostrils. He couldn't believe he was going to die. He had spent the past nine months worrying about death, but now when circumstances had arisen that made death likely, he had trouble

53

taking that likelihood seriously. It didn't seem reasonable that a skinny black guy should be his nemesis. His death should involve massive detonations of light, special Mingolla-killing rays, astronomical portents. Not some scrawny little fuck with a rifle. He drew another breath and for the first time registered the contents of the room. Two cots; clothes strewn everywhere; taped-up Polaroids and pornography. Officer country or not, it was your basic Ant Farm decor; under the red light it looked squalid, long abandoned. He was amazed at how calm he felt. Oh, he was afraid all right! But fear was tucked into the dark folds of his personality like a murderer's knife hidden inside an old coat on a closet shelf. Glowing in secret, waiting its chance to shine. Sooner or later it would skewer him but for now it was an ally, acting to sharpen his senses. He could see every bubbled pucker on the white walls, could hear the scrape of the Cuban's boots as he darted into the room next door, could feel how the Cuban swung the rifle left to right, paused, turned. . . .

He could!

He could feel the Cuban, feel his heat, his heated shape, the exact position of his body. It was as if a thermal imager had been switched on inside his head, one that worked through walls.

The Cuban eased toward Mingolla's door, his progress tangible, like a burning match moving behind a sheet of paper. Mingolla's calm was shattered. The man's heat, his fleshy temperature, was what disturbed him. He had imagined himself killing with a cinematic swiftness and lack of mess; now he thought of hogs being butchered and pile drivers smashing the skulls of cows. And could he trust this freakish form of perception? What if he couldn't? What if he stabbed too late? Too soon? Then the hot, alive thing was almost at the door, and having no choice, Mingolla timed his attack to its movements, stabbing just as the Cuban entered.

He executed perfectly.

The blade slid home beneath the Cuban's ribs, and Mingolla clamped a hand over his mouth, muffling his outcry. His knee nailed the rifle stock, sending it clattering to the floor. The Cuban thrashed wildly. He stank of rotten jungle air and cigarettes. His eyes rolled back, trying to see Mingolla. Crazy animal eyes, with liverish whites and expanded pupils. Sweat beads glittered red on his brow. Mingolla twisted the machete, and the Cuban's eyelids fluttered down. But a second later they snapped open, and he lunged. They went staggering deeper into the room and teetered beside one of the cots. Mingolla wrangled the Cuban sideways and rammed him against the wall, pinning him there. Writhing, the Cuban nearly broke free. He seemed to be getting stronger, his squeals leaking out from Mingolla's hand. He reached behind him, clawing at Mingolla's face; he grabbed a clump of hair, yanked it. Desperate, Mingolla sawed with the machete. That tuned the Cuban's squeals higher, louder. He squirmed and clawed at the wall. Mingolla's clamped hand was slick with the Cuban's saliva, his nostrils full of the man's rank scent. He felt queasy, weak, and he wasn't sure how much longer he could hang on. The son of a bitch was never going to die, he was deriving strength from the steel in his guts, he was changing into some deathless force. But just then the Cuban stiffened. Then he relaxed, and Mingolla caught a whiff of feces.

He let the Cuban slump to the floor, but before he could turn loose the machete, a shudder passed through the corpse, flowed up the hilt, and vibrated his left hand. It continued to shudder inside his hand, feeling dirty, sexy, like a postcoital tremor. Something, some animal essence, some oily scrap of bad life, was slithering around in there, squirting toward his wrist. He stared at the hand, horrified. It was gloved in the Cuban's blood, trembling. He smashed it against his hip, and that seemed to stun whatever was inside it. But within seconds it had revived and was wriggling in and out of his fingers with the mad celerity of a tadpole.

"*Teo!*" someone called. "*Vamos!*"

Electrified by the shout, Mingolla hustled to the door. His foot nudged the Cuban's rifle. He picked it up, and the shaking of his hand lessened—he had the idea it had been soothed by a familiar texture and weight.

"*Teo! Dónde estás?*"

Mingolla had no good choices, but he realized it would

be far more dangerous to hang back than to take the initiative. He grunted, *"Aqui!"* and walked out into the tunnel, making lots of noise with his heels.

"Dase prisa, hombre!"

Mingolla opened fire as he rounded the curve. The two Cubans were standing by the entrance of the auxiliary tunnel. Their rifles chattered briefly, sending a harmless spray of bullets off the walls; they whirled, flung out their arms, and fell. Mingolla was too shocked by how easy it had been to feel relief. He kept watching, expecting them to do something. Moan, or twitch.

After the echoes of the shots had died, though he could hear the big guns jolting and the crackle of firefights, a heavy silence seemed to fill in through the tunnel, as if his bullets had pierced something that had dammed up silence. The silence made him aware of his isolation. No telling where the battle lines were drawn . . . if, indeed, they existed. It was conceivable that small units had infiltrated every level, that the battle for the Ant Farm was in microcosm the battle for Guatemala: a conflict having no patterns, no real borders, no orderly confrontations, but which, like a plague, could pop up anywhere at any time and kill you. That being the case, his best bet would be to head for the computer center, where friendly forces were sure to be concentrated.

He walked to the entrance and stared at the two dead Cubans. They had fallen, blocking his way, and he was hesitant about stepping over them, half-believing they were playing possum, that they would reach up and grab him. The awkward attitudes of their limbs made him think they were holding a difficult pose, waiting for him to try. Their blood looked purple in the red glow of the emergencies, thicker and shinier than ordinary blood. He noted their moles and scars and sores, the crude stitching of their fatigues, gold fillings glinting from their open mouths. It was funny, he could have met these guys while they were alive and they might have made only a vague impression; but seeing them dead, he had catalogued their physical worth in a single glance. Maybe, he thought, death revealed your essentials as life could not. He studied the dead men, wanting to read them. Couple of slim, wiry guys. Nice guys, into rum and the ladies and sports. He'd bet they were baseball players, infielders, a double-play combo. Maybe he should have called to them, Hey, I'm a Yankee fan. Be cool! Meetcha after the war for a game of flies and grounders. Fuck this killing shit. Let's play some ball.

He laughed, and the high, cracking sound of his laughter startled him. Christ! Standing around here was just asking for it. As if to second that opinion, the thing inside his hand exploded into life, feeling and frisking about. Swallowing back his fear, Mingolla stepped over the two dead men, and this time, when nothing clutched at his trouser legs, he felt very relieved.

Below level six there was a good deal of mist in the auxiliary tunnel, and this implied to Mingolla that the Cubans had penetrated the hillside, probably with a borer mine. Chances were the hole they had made was somewhere close, and he decided that if he could find it, he would use it to get the hell out of the Farm and hide in the jungle. On level seven the mist was extremely thick; the emergency lights stained it pale red, giving it the look of surgical cotton packing a huge artery. Scorch marks from grenade bursts showed on the walls like primitive graphics, and quite a few bodies were visible beside the doorways. Most of them Americans, badly mutilated. Uneasy, Mingolla picked his way among them, and when a man spoke behind him, saying, "Don't move," he let out a hoarse cry and dropped his rifle and spun around, his heart pounding.

A giant of a man—he had to go six-seven, six-eight, with the arms and torso of a weight lifter—was standing in a doorway, training a .45 at Mingolla's chest. He wore khakis with lieutenant's bars, and his babyish face, though cinched into a frown, gave an impression of gentleness and stolidity: he conjured for Mingolla the image of Ferdinand the Bull weighing a knotty problem. "I told you not to move," he said peevishly.

"It's okay," said Mingolla. "I'm on your side."

The lieutenant ran a hand through his thick shock of brown

hair; he seemed to be blinking more than was normal. "I'd better check," he said. "Let's go down to the storeroom."

"What's to check?" said Mingolla, his paranoia increasing.

"Please!" said the lieutenant, a genuine wealth of entreaty in his voice. "There's been too much violence already."

The storeroom was a long, narrow L-shaped room at the end of the level; it was ranged by packing crates, and through the gauzy mist the emergency lights looked like a string of dying red suns. The lieutenant marched Mingolla to the corner of the L, and turning it, Mingolla saw that the rear wall of the room was missing. A tunnel had been blown into the hillside, opening onto blackness. Forked roots with balls of dirt attached hung from its roof, giving it the witchy appearance of a tunnel into some world of dark magic; rubble and clods of earth were piled at its lip. Mingolla could smell the jungle, and he realized that the big guns had stopped firing. Which meant that whoever had won the battle of the summit would soon be sending down mop-up squads. "We can't stay here," he told the lieutenant. "The Cubans'll be back."

"We're perfectly safe," said the lieutenant. "Take my word." He motioned with the gun, indicating that Mingolla should sit on the floor.

Mingolla did as ordered and was frozen by the sight of a corpse, a Cuban corpse, lying between two packing crates opposite him, its head propped against the wall. "Jesus!" he said, coming back up to his knees.

"He won't bite," said the lieutenant. With the lack of self-consciousness of someone squeezing into a subway seat, he settled beside the corpse; the two of them neatly filled the space between the crates, touching elbow to shoulder.

"Hey," said Mingolla, feeling giddy and scattered. "I'm not sitting here with this fucking dead guy, man!"

The lieutenant flourished his gun. "You'll get used to him."

Mingolla eased back to a sitting position, unable to look away from the corpse. Actually, compared to the bodies he had just been stepping over, it was quite presentable. The only signs of damage were blood on its mouth and bushy black beard, and a mire of blood and shredded cloth at the center of its

58

chest. Its brass scorpion pin was scarred and tarnished. Its eyes were open, reflecting glowing red chips of the emergency lights, and this gave it a baleful semblance of life. But the reflections made it appear less real, easier to bear.

"Listen to me," said the lieutenant.

Mingolla rubbed at the blood on his shaking hand, hoping that cleaning it would have some good effect.

"Are you listening?" the lieutenant asked.

Mingolla had a peculiar perception of the lieutenant and the corpse as dummy and ventriloquist. Despite its glowing eyes, the corpse had too much reality for any trick of the light to gloss over for long. Precise crescents showed on its fingernails, and because its head was tipped to one side, blood had settled onto that side, darkening its cheek and temple, leaving the rest of the face pallid. It was the lieutenant, with his neat khakis and polished shoes and nice haircut, who now looked less than real.

"Listen!" said the lieutenant vehemently. "I want you to understand that I have to do what's right for me!" The biceps of his gun arm bunched to the size of a cannonball.

"I understand," said Mingolla, thoroughly unnerved.

"Do you? Do you really?" The lieutenant seemed aggravated by Mingolla's claim to understanding. "I doubt it. I doubt you could possibly understand."

"Maybe I can't," said Mingolla. "Whatever you say, man. I'm just trying to get along, y'know."

The lieutenant sat silent, blinking. Then he smiled. "My name's Jay," he said. "And you are . . . ?"

"David." Mingolla tried to bring his concentration to bear on the gun, wondering if he could kick it away, but the sliver of life in his hand distracted him.

"Where are your quarters, David?"

"Level three."

"I live here," said Jay. "But I'm going to move. I couldn't bear to stay in a place where—" He broke off and leaned forward, adopting a conspiratorial stance. "Did you know it takes a long time for someone to die, even after their heart has stopped?"

"No, I didn't." The thing in Mingolla's hand squirmed toward his wrist, and he squeezed the wrist, trying to block it.

"It's true," said Jay with vast assurance. "None of these people"—he gave the corpse a gentle nudge with his elbow, a gesture that conveyed to Mingolla a creepy sort of familiarity—"have finished dying. Life doesn't just switch off. It fades. And these people are still alive, though it's only a half-life." He grinned. "The half-life of life, you might say."

Mingolla kept the pressure on his wrist and smiled, as if in appreciation of the play on words. Pale red tendrils of mist curled between them.

"Of course you aren't attuned," said Jay. "So you wouldn't understand. But I'd be lost without Eligio."

"Who's Eligio?"

Jay nodded toward the corpse. "We're attuned, Eligio and I. That's how I know we're safe. Eligio's perceptions aren't limited to the here and now any longer. He's with his men at this very moment, and he tells me they're all dead or dying."

"Uh-huh," said Mingolla, tensing. He had managed to squeeze the thing in his hand back into his fingers, and he thought he might be able to reach the gun. But Jay disrupted his plan by shifting the gun to his other hand. His eyes seemed to be growing more reflective, acquiring a ruby glaze, and Mingolla realized this was because he had opened them wide and angled his stare toward the emergency lights.

"It makes you wonder," said Jay. "It really does."

"What?" said Mingolla, easing sideways, shortening the range for a kick.

"Half-lives," said Jay. "If the mind has a half-life, maybe our separate emotions do, too. The half-life of love, of hate. Maybe they still exist somewhere." He drew up his knees, shielding the gun. "Anyway, I can't stay here. I think I'll go back to Oakland." His tone became whispery. "Where are you from, David?"

"New York."

"Not my cup of tea," said Jay. "But I love the Bay Area. I own an antique shop there. It's beautiful in the mornings. Peaceful. The sun comes through the window, creeping across the floor, y'know, like a tide, inching up over the furniture. It's as if the original varnishes are being reborn, the whole shop shining with ancient lights."

"Sounds nice," said Mingolla, taken aback by Jay's lyricism.

"You seem like a good person." Jay straightened up a bit. "But I'm sorry. Eligío tells me your mind's too cloudy for him to read. He says I can't risk keeping you alive. I'm going to have to shoot."

Mingolla set himself to kick, but then listlessness washed over him. What the hell did it matter? Even if he knocked the gun away, Jay could probably break him in half. "Why?" he said. "Why do you have to?"

"You might inform on me." Jay's soft features sagged into a sorrowful expression. "Tell them I was hiding."

"Nobody gives a shit that you were hiding," said Mingolla. "That's what I was doing. I bet there's fifty other guys doing the same damn thing."

"I don't know." Jay's brow furrowed. "I'll ask again. Maybe your mind's less cloudy now." He turned his gaze to the dead man.

Mingolla noticed that the Cuban's irises were angled up-ward and to the left—exactly the same angle to which Jay's eyes had drifted earlier—and reflected an identical ruby glaze.

"Sorry," said Jay, leveling the gun. "I have to." He licked his lips. "Would you please turn your head? I'd rather you weren't looking at me when it happens. That's how Eligio and I became attuned."

Looking into the aperture of the gun's muzzle was like peering over a cliff, feeling the chill allure of falling. It was more out of contrariness than a will to survive that Mingolla popped his eyes at Jay and said, "Go ahead."

Jay blinked, but he held the gun steady. "Your hand's shaking," he said after a pause.

"No shit," said Mingolla.

"How come it's shaking?"

"Because I killed someone with it," said Mingolla. "Because I'm as fucking crazy as you are."

Jay mulled this over. "I was supposed to be assigned to a

gay unit," he said finally. "But all the slots were filled, and when I had to be assigned here they gave me a drug. Now I . . . I . . ." He blinked rapidly, his lips parted, and Mingolla found that he was straining toward Jay, wanting to apply body English, to do something to push him over this agonizing hump. "I can't . . . be with men anymore," Jay finished, and once again blinked rapidly; then his words came easier. "Did they give you a drug, too? I mean I'm not trying to imply you're gay. It's just they have drugs for everything these days, and I thought that might be the problem."

Mingolla was suddenly, unutterably sad. He felt that his emotions had been twisted into a thin black wire, that the wire was frayed and spraying black sparks of sadness. That was all that energized him, all his life. Those little black sparks.

"I always fought before," said Jay. "And I was fighting this time. But when I shot Eligío . . . I just couldn't keep going."

"I really don't give a shit," said Mingolla. "I really don't."

"Maybe I *can* trust you." Jay sighed. "I just wish you were attuned. Eligío's a good soul. You'd appreciate him."

Jay kept on talking, enumerating Eligío's virtues, and Mingolla tuned him out, not wanting to hear about the Cuban's love for his family, his posthumous concerns for them. Staring at his bloody hand, he had a magical overview of the situation. Sitting in the root cellar of this evil mountain, bathed in an eerie red glow, a scrap of a dead man's life trapped in his flesh, listening to a deranged giant who took his orders from a corpse, waiting for scorpion soldiers to pour through a tunnel that appeared to lead into a dimension of mist and blackness. It was insane to look at it that way. But there it was. You couldn't reason it away; it had a brutal glamour that surpassed reason, that made reason unnecessary.

". . . And once you're attuned," Jay was saying, "you can't ever be separated. Not even by death. So Eligío's always going to be alive inside me. Of course I can't let them find out. I mean"—he chuckled, a sound like dice rattling in a cup— "talk about giving aid and comfort to the enemy!"

Mingolla lowered his head, closed his eyes. Maybe Jay

would shoot. But he doubted that. Jay only wanted company in madness.

"You swear you won't tell them?" Jay asked.

"Yeah," said Mingolla. "I swear."

"All right," said Jay. "But remember, my future's in your hands. You have a responsibility to me."

"Don't worry."

Gunfire crackled in the distance.

"I'm glad we could talk," said Jay. "I feel much better."

Mingolla said he felt better too.

They sat without speaking. It wasn't the most secure way to pass the night, but Mingolla no longer put any store in the concept of security. He was too weary to be afraid. Jay seemed entranced, staring at a point above Mingolla's head, but Mingolla made no move for the gun. He was content to sit and wait and let fate take its course. His thoughts uncoiled with vegetable sluggishness.

They must have been sitting a couple of hours when Mingolla heard the whisper of helicopters and noticed that the mist had thinned, that the darkness at the end of the tunnel had gone gray. "Hey," he said to Jay. "I think we're okay now." Jay offered no reply, and Mingolla saw that his eyes were angled upward and to the left just like the Cuban's eyes, glazed over with ruby reflection. Tentatively, he reached out and touched the gun. Jay's hand flopped to the floor, but his fingers remained clenched around the butt. Mingolla recoiled, disbelieving. It couldn't be! Again he reached out, feeling for a pulse. Jay's wrist was cool, still, and his lips had a bluish cast. Mingolla had a flutter of hysteria, thinking that Jay had gotten it wrong about being attuned: instead of Eligío's becoming part of his life, he had become part of Eligío's death. There was a tightness in Mingolla's chest, and he thought he was going to cry. He would have welcomed tears, and when they failed to material-ize he grew both annoyed at himself and defensive. Why should he cry? The guy had meant nothing to him . . . though the fact that he could be so devoid of compassion was reason enough for tears. Still, if you were going to cry over something as commonplace as a single guy dying, you'd be crying every

63

minute of the day, and what was the future in that? He glanced at Jay. At the Cuban. Despite the smoothness of Jay's skin, the Cuban's bushy beard, Mingolla could have sworn they were starting to resemble each other the way old married couples did. And, yep, all four eyes were fixed on exactly the same point of forever. It was either a hell of a coincidence or else Jay's craziness had been of such magnitude that he had willed himself to die in this fashion just to lend credence to his theory of half-lives. And maybe he was still alive. Half-alive. Maybe he and Mingolla were now attuned, and if that was true, maybe . . . Alarmed by the prospect of joining Jay and the Cuban in their deathwatch, Mingolla scrambled to his feet and ran into the tunnel. He might have kept running, but on coming out into the dawn light he was brought up short by the view from the tunnel entrance.

At his back, the green dome of the hill swelled high, its sides brocaded with shrubs and vines, an infinity of pattern as eye-catching as the intricately carved facade of a Hindu temple; atop it, one of the gun emplacements had taken a hit: splinters of charred metal curved up like peels of black rind. Before him lay the moat of red dirt with its hedgerows of razor wire, and beyond that loomed the blackish green snarl of the jungle. Caught on the wire were hundreds of baggy shapes wearing bloodstained fatigues; frays of smoke twisted up from the fresh craters beside them. Overhead, half-hidden by the lifting gray mist, three Sikorskys were hovering. Their pilots were invisible behind layers of mist and reflection, and the choppers themselves looked like enormous carrion flies with bulging eyes and whirling wings. Like devils. Like gods. They seemed to be whispering to one another in anticipation of the feast they were soon to share.

The scene was horrid, yet it had the purity of a stanza from a ballad come to life, a ballad composed about tragic events in some border hell. You could never paint it, or if you could the canvas would have to be as large as the scene itself, and you would have to incorporate the slow boil of the mist, the whirling of the chopper blades, the drifting smoke. No detail could be omitted. It was the perfect illustration of the war, of its secret magical splendor, and Mingolla, too, was an element of the design, the figure of the artist painted in for a joke or to lend scale and perspective to its vastness, its importance. He knew that he should report to his station, but he couldn't turn away from this glimpse into the heart of the war. He sat down on the hillside, cradling his sick hand in his lap, and watched as—with the ponderous aplomb of idols floating to earth, fighting the cross-draft, the wind of their descent whipping up furies of red dust—the Sikorskys made skillful landings among the dead.

CHAPTER FOUR

Halfway through the telling of his story, Mingolla had realized he was not really trying to offend or shock Debora, but rather was unburdening himself; and he further realized that by telling it he had to an extent cut loose from the past, weakened its hold on him. For the first time he felt able to give serious consideration to the idea of desertion. He did not rush to it, embrace it, but he did acknowledge its logic and understand the terrible illogic of returning to more assaults, more death, without any magic to protect him. He made a pact with himself: he would pretend to go along as if desertion were his intent and see what signs were offered.

When he had finished, Debora asked whether he was over his anger. He was pleased that she hadn't tried to offer sympathy. "I'm sorry," he said. "I wasn't really angry at you . . . at least that was only part of it."

"It's all right." She pushed back the dark mass of her hair so that it fell to one side and looked down at the grass beside her knees. With her head inclined, eyes half-lidded, the graceful line of her neck and chin like that of a character in some exotic script, she seemed a good sign herself. "I don't know what to talk to you about," she said. "The things I feel I have to tell you make you mad, and I can't muster any small talk."

"I don't want to be pushed," he said. "But believe me, I'm thinking about what you've told me."

"I won't push. But I still don't know what to talk about." She plucked a grass blade, chewed on the tip. He watched her lips purse, wondered how she'd taste. Mouth sweet in the way of a jar that had once held spices. And down below, she'd taste sweet there, too: honey gone a little sour in the comb. She tossed her grass blade aside. "I know," she said brightly. "Would you like to see where I live?"

"I'd just as soon not go back to Frisco yet." *Where you live*, he thought; *I want to touch where you live.*

"It's not in town," she said. "It's a village downriver."

"Sounds good." He came to his feet, took her arm, and helped her up. For an instant they were close together, her breasts grazing his shirt. Her heat coursed around him, and he thought if anyone were to see them, they would see two figures wavering as in a mirage. He had an urge to tell her he loved her. Though most of what he felt was for the salvation she might provide, part of his feelings seemed real, and that puzzled him, because all she had been to him was a few hours out of the war, dinner in a cheap restaurant, and a walk along the river. There was no basis for consequential emotion. Before he could say anything, do anything, she turned and picked up her basket.

"It's not far," she said, walking away. Her blue skirt swayed like a rung bell.

They followed a track of brown clay overgrown by ferns, overspread by saplings with pale translucent leaves, and soon came to a grouping of thatched huts at the mouth of a stream that flowed into the river. Naked children were wading in the stream, laughing and splashing each other. Their skins were the color of amber, and their eyes were as wet-looking and purplish dark as plums. Palms and acacias loomed above the huts, which were constructed of sapling trunks lashed together by nylon cord; their thatch had been trimmed to resemble bowl-cut hair. Flies crawled over strips of meat hung on a clothesline stretched between two of the huts. Fish heads and chicken droppings littered the ocher ground. But Mingolla scarcely noticed these signs of poverty, seeing instead a sign of the peace that might await him in Panama. And another sign was soon forthcoming. Debora bought a bottle of rum at a tiny store, then led him to the hut nearest the mouth of the stream and introduced him to a lean, white-haired old man who was sitting on a bench outside it. Tio Moíses. After three drinks Tio Moíses began to tell stories.

The first story concerned the personal pilot of an ex-president of Panama. The president had made billions from smuggling cocaine into the States with the help of the CIA, whom he had assisted on numerous occasions, and was himself an addict in the last stages of mental deterioration. It had become his sole pleasure to be flown from city to city in his country, to sit on the landing strips, gaze out the window, and do cocaine. At any hour of night or day, he was likely to call the pilot and order him to prepare a flight plan to Colón or Bocas del Toro or Penonomé. As the president's condition worsened, the pilot realized that soon the CIA would see the man was no longer useful and would kill him. And the most obvious manner of killing him would be by means of an airplane crash. The pilot did not want to die alongside him. He tried to resign, but the president would not permit it. He gave thought to mutilating himself, but being a good Catholic, he could not flout God's law. If he were to flee, his family would suffer. His life became a nightmare. Prior to each flight, he would spend hours searching the plane for evidence of sabotage, and upon each landing he would remain in the cockpit, shaking from nervous exhaustion. The president's condition grew even worse. He had to be carried aboard the plane and have the cocaine administered by an aide, while a second aide stood by with cotton swabs to attend his nosebleeds. Knowing his life could be measured in weeks, the pilot asked his priest for guidance. "Pray," the priest advised. The pilot had been praying all along, so this was no help. Next he went to the commandant of his military college, and the commandant told him he must do his duty. This, too, was something the pilot had been doing all along. Finally he went to the chief of the San Blas Indians, who were his mother's people. The chief told him he must accept his fate, which—while not something he had been doing all along—was hardly encouraging. Nonetheless, he saw it was the only available path and he did as the chief had counseled. Rather than spending hours in a preflight check, he would arrive minutes before takeoff and taxi away without even inspecting the fuel gauge. His recklessness came to be the talk of the capital. Obeying the president's every whim, he flew in gales and in fogs, while drunk and drugged, and during those hours in the air, suspended between the laws of gravity and fate, he gained a new appreciation of life. Once back on the ground, he engaged in living with a fierce avidity, making passionate love to his wife, carousing with friends, and staying out until dawn. Then one day as he was preparing to leave for the airport, an American man came to his house and told him he had been replaced. "If we let the president fly with so negligent a pilot, we'll be blamed for anything that happens," said the American. The pilot did not have to ask whom he had meant by "we." Six weeks later the president's plane crashed in the Darién Mountains. The pilot was overjoyed. Panama had been rid of a villain, and his own life had not been forfeited. But a week after the crash, after the new president—another smuggler with CIA connections—had been appointed, the commandant of the air force summoned the pilot, told him that the crash would never have occurred had he been on the job, and assigned him to fly the new president's plane.

All through the afternoon Mingolla listened and drank, and drunkenness fitted a lens to his eyes that let him see how these stories applied to him. They were all fables of irresolution, cautioning him to act, and they detailed the core problems of the Central American people who—as he was now—were trapped between the poles of magic and reason, their lives governed by the politics of the ultrareal, their spirits ruled by myths and legends, with the rectangular, computerized bulk of North America above and the conch-shell-shaped continental mystery of South America below. He assumed that Debora had orchestrated the types of stories Tio Moisés told, but that did not detract from their potency as signs: they had the ring of truth, not of something tailored to his needs. Nor did it matter that his hand was shaking, his vision playing tricks. Those things would pass when he reached Panama.

Shadows blurred, insects droned like tambouras, and twilight washed down the sky, making the air look grainy, the chop on the river appear slower and heavier. Tio Moíses's granddaughter served plates of roasted corn and fish, and Mingolla stuffed himself. Afterward, when the old man signaled his weariness, Mingolla and Debora strolled off along the stream. Between two of the huts, mounted on a pole, was a warped backboard with a netless hoop, and some young men were shooting baskets. Mingolla joined them. It was hard dribbling on the bumpy dirt but he had never played better. The residue of drunkenness fueled his game, and his jump shots followed perfect arcs down through the hoop. Even at improbable angles, his shots fell true. He lost himself in flicking out his hand to make a steal, in feinting and leaping high to snag a rebound, becoming—as dusk faded—the most adroit of the arm-waving, jitter-steeping shadows.

The game ended and the stars came out, looking like holes punched into fire through a billow of black silk overhanging the palms. Flickering chutes of lamplight illuminated the ground in front of the huts, and as Debora and Mingolla walked among them, he heard a radio tuned to the armed forces network giving a play-by-play of a baseball game. There was a crack of the bat, the crowd roared, and the announcer cried, "He got it all!" Mingolla imagined the ball vanishing into the darkness above the stadium, bouncing out into parking-lot America, lodging under a tire where some kid would find it and think it a miracle, or rolling across the street to rest under a used car, shimmering there, secretly white and fuming with home-run energies. The score was three to one, top of the second. Mingolla didn't know who was playing and didn't care. Home runs were happening for him, mystical jump shots curved along predestined tracks. He was at the center of incalculable forces.

One of the huts was unlit, with two wooden chairs out front, and as they approached, something about it blighted Mingolla's mood. Its air of preparedness, of being a little stage set. Just paranoia, he thought. The signs had been good so far, hadn't they? When they reached the hut, Debora took the chair nearest the door and invited him to sit next to her. Starlight pointed her eyes with brilliance. Visible inside the doorway was a sack from which part of a wire cage protruded. "What about your game?" he asked.

"I wanted to be with you tonight," she said.

That bothered him. It was all starting to bother him, and he couldn't understand why. The thing in his hand wiggled. He balled the hand into a fist and sat down. "What . . ." he began, and then lost track of what he had been about to ask her. He wiped sweat from his forehead. A shadow moved across the yellow glare spilling from the hut opposite them. Rippling, undulating. Mingolla shut his eyes. "What, uh . . ." Once again he forgot his subject, and to cover up he asked the first question that occurred to him. "What's happenin' here . . . between you and me? I keep thinkin' . . ." He broke off. *Christ, what an idiot thing to say! Too bold, man!* He'd probably just blown his chances with her.

But she didn't back away from it. "You mean romanti-cally?" she asked.

Nicely put, he thought. *Very delicate. Much better than saying, You mean are we gonna fuck?* Which was about the best he could have managed at the moment. "Right," he said.

"I'm not sure," she said. "Whether you go to Panama or back to your base, we don't seem to have much of a future. But"—her voiced softened—"maybe that's not important."

It boosted his confidence in her that she didn't have an assured answer. He opened his eyes. Gave his head a twitch, fighting off more ripples. "So what is important?" he asked, and was pleased with himself. *Very suave, Mingolla. Let her be the one to say it. Very suave, indeed!* He wished he didn't feel so shaky.

"Well, there's obviously a strong attraction."

Attraction? I guess so, he thought. *I wanna rip your damn dress off!*

"And," she went on, "maybe something more. I wish we had time to find out what."

Clever! Knocked the ball right back into his court. He tried to focus on her, had to close his eyes again, and saw Panama. White sand, cerulean water deepening to cobalt toward the

71

horizon. "What's it like in Panama?" he asked, then kicked himself for having changed the subject.

"I've never been there. Probably not much different from here."

Maybe he should stand up, walk around. Maybe that would help. Or maybe he should just sit and talk. Talking seemed to steady him. "I bet it's beautiful, y'know," he said. "Green mountains, jungle waterfalls. I bet there's lots of birds. Macaws, parrots. Millions of 'em."

"I suppose."

"And hummingbirds. This friend of mine was down there once on a hummingbird-collectin' expedition. Said there was a million kinds. I thought he was sort of a creep for bein' into collectin' hummingbirds. I didn't think it was very relevant to the big issues, y'know."

"David?" Apprehension in her voice.

"You get there by boat, right?" The smell of her perfume was more cloying than he remembered. "Must be a pretty big boat. I've never been on a real boat. Just this rowboat my uncle had. He used to take me fishin' off Coney Island. We'd tie up to a buoy and catch all these poison fish. You shoulda seen some of 'em. Like mutants. Rainbow-colored eyes, weird growths all over. Scared the hell outta me to think about eatin' fish."

"I . . ."

"I used to think about the ones that musta been down there too deep for us to catch. Giant blowfish, genius sharks, whales with hands. I'd see 'em swallowin' the boat, and . . ."

"Calm down, David." She kneaded the back of his neck, sending a shiver down his spine.

"I'm okay." He shrugged off her hand. Didn't need shivers along with everything else. "Lemme hear some more about Panama."

"I told you . . . I've never been there."

"Oh, yeah. How 'bout Costa Rica? You been to Costa Rica." Sweat was popping out all over his body. Maybe he should go for a swim, cool off. He'd heard there were manatees in the Río Dulce. "Ever seen a manatee?"

"David!"

She must have leaned close, because he could feel her heat spreading through him, and he thought maybe that would help, smothering in her heat, in heavy motion. Get rid of the shakiness. He'd take her into the hut and see just how hot she got. *How* hot *she got, how* hot *she got.* The words did a train rhythm inside his head. Afraid to open his eyes, he reached out blindly and pulled her to him. Bumped faces, searched for her mouth. She kissed back, and his hand slipped up to cup a breast. Jesus, she felt good! She felt like salvation, like Panama, like what you fall into when you sleep.

But then the feeling changed. Changed so slowly that he didn't notice until it was almost complete, until her tongue was no longer quick and darting in his mouth, but squirmed as thick and stupid as a snail's foot, and her breast was jiggling, trembling with the same wormy juice that had invaded his left hand. He pushed her off, opened his eyes. Saw crude-stitch eyelids sewn to her cheek. Lips parted, mouth full of bones. Blank face of meat. He got to his feet, pawing the air, wanting to rip away the film of ugliness that had settled over him.

"David?" She warped his name, gulping the syllables as if trying to swallow and talk at once.

Frog voice, devil voice.

He whirled around, caught an eyeful of black sky, spiky trees, and a pitted bone-knob moon trapped in a web of leaves and branches. Dark warty shapes of the huts, doors opening into yellow flame, with crooked shadow men inside. He blinked, shook his head. It wouldn't vanish, it was real. What was this place? Not a village, naw, un-unh! A strangled grunt came from his throat, and he backed away, backed away from everything. She walked after him, croaking his name. Wig of black straw, shining dabs of jelly for eyes. Some of the shadow men were herky-jerked out of their doors, gathering behind her. Croaking. Long-legged, licorice-skinned demons with drumbeat hearts, faceless nothings from the dimension of sickness. They'd be on him in a flash.

"I see you," he said, backing another few steps. "I know what you are."

73

"No one's trying to hurt you. It's all right, David," she said, and smiled.

She thought he'd buy that smile, but he wasn't fooled. It broke over her face the way something rotten melts through the bottom of a grocery sack after it's been in the garbage a week. Gloating smile of the Queen Devil Bitch. She had done this to him! Teamed up with the bad life in his hand and played witchy tricks on his head.

"I see you," he said again, and tripped. Stumbled backward, clawing for balance, and going with his momentum, came up running toward the town.

Ferns whipped his legs, branches slashed at his face. Webs of shadow fettered the trail, and the shrilling insects had the sound of a metal edge being honed. He ran out of control, bashing into trees, nearly falling, his breath shrieking. But then he spotted a big moonstruck ceiba tree up ahead, standing on a rise overlooking the water. A grandfather tree, a white magic tree. It summoned him. He stopped beside it, sucking in air. The moonlight cooled him, drenched him in silver, and he thought he understood the purpose of the tree. Fountain of whiteness in the dark wood, shining for him alone. He made a fist of his left hand, and the thing inside it eeled frantically as if it knew what was coming. He studied the mystic grainy patterns of the bark, found their point of confluence. Steeled himself. Then he drove his fist into the trunk. Bright pain lanced up his arm, and he cried out. But he hit the trunk again, hit it a third time. He held the hand tight against his chest to muffle the pain. It was already swelling, becoming a knuckleless cartoon hand; but nothing moved inside it. The riverbank, with its shadows and rustlings, no longer menaced him, transformed into a place of ordinary lights and darks. Even the whiteness of the tree seemed diminished.

"David!" Debora's voice, and not far off.

Part of him wanted to wait, to see whether she had changed for the innocent, for the ordinary. But he couldn't trust her, couldn't trust himself, and after a brief hesitation he took off running once again.

Mingolla caught the ferry to the west bank, thinking that he would find Gilbey, that a dose of Gilbey's belligerence would ground him in reality. He sat in the bow next to a group of five other soldiers, one of whom was puking over the side, and to avoid a conversation he turned away and looked down into the black water slipping past. Moonlight edged the wavelets with silver, and among those crescent gleams it seemed he could see reflected the broken curve of his life: a kid living for Christmas, drawing pictures, receiving praise, growing up mindless to high school, sex, and drugs; growing beyond that, beginning to draw pictures again, and then, right where you might expect the curve to assume a more meaningful shape, it was sheared off, left hanging, its entire process demystified and explicable. He realized how foolish the idea of the ritual had been. Like a dying man clutching a vial of holy water, he had clutched at magic when the logic of existence had proved untenable. Now the frail linkages of that magic had been dissolved, and nothing supported him: he was falling through the dark zones of the war, waiting to be snatched by one of its monsters. He lifted his head and gazed at the west bank. The shore toward which he was heading was as black as a bat's wing and inscribed with arcana of violent light. Rooftops and palms were cast in silhouette against a rainbow haze of neon; gassy arcs of bloodred and lime green and indigo were visible between them: fragments of glowing beasts. The wind bore screams and wild music. The soldiers beside him laughed and cursed, and the one guy kept on puking. Mingolla rested his forehead on the wooden rail, just to feel something solid.

At the Club Demonio, Gilbey's big-breasted whore was sitting at the bar, staring into her drink. Mingolla pushed through the dancers, through heat and noise and veils of lavender smoke. When he walked up to her, the whore put on a professional smile and made a grab for his crotch. He fended her off and asked if she'd seen Gilbey. She looked befuddled at first, but then the light dawned. "Meen-golla?" she said, and when he nodded, she fumbled in her purse and pulled out a folded paper. "Ees frawm Geel-bee. Forr me, five dol-larrs."

75

He handed her the money and took the paper. It proved to be a Christian pamphlet with a pen-and-ink sketch of a rail-thin, aggrieved-looking Jesus on the front, and beneath the sketch, a tract whose opening line read, "The last days are in season." He turned it over and found a handwritten note on the back. The note was pure Gilbey. No explanation, no sentiment. Just the basics:

I'm gone to Panama. You want to make that trip, check out a man in Livingston named Ruy Barros. He'll fix you up. Maybe I'll see you.

G.

Mingolla had believed that his confusion had peaked, but the fact of Gilbey's desertion wouldn't fit inside his head, and when he tried to make it fit, the rank and file of his thoughts was thrown into disarray. It wasn't that he didn't understand what had happened. He understood perfectly; in fact, he might have predicted it. Like a crafty rat who had seen his hole blocked by a trap, Gilbey had simply chewed a new hole and vanished into the woodwork. The thing that confused Mingolla was his total lack of reference. He and Gilbey and Baylor had triangulated reality, located one another within a coherent map of duties and places and events. Now that they both were gone, he felt utterly bewildered. Outside the club, he let the crowds push him along. Stared at the neon animals atop the bars. Giant blue rooster; golden turtle; green bull with fiery eyes. Great identities regarding his aimless course with dispassion. Bleeds of color washed from the signs, staining the air to a garish paleness, giving everyone a mealy complexion. Amazing, Mingolla thought, that you could breathe such grainy discolored stuff, that it didn't start you choking. It was all amazing, all nonsensical. Everything he saw struck him as unique and unfathomable, even the most commonplace of sights. He found himself staring at people—whores, street kids, an MP who was patting the fender of his jeep as if it were his big olive-drab pet—and trying to figure out what they were really doing, what

76

special significance their actions held for him, what clues they presented that might help him unravel the snarl of his own existence. At last, realizing that he needed peace and quiet, he set out toward the airbase, intending to find an empty bunk in some barracks. But when he reached the cutoff that led to the unfinished bridge, he turned down it, deciding that he wasn't ready to deal with sentries and duty officers. Dense thickets abuzz with crickets narrowed the cutoff to a path, and at its end stood a line of sawhorses. He climbed over them and soon was mounting a sharply inclined curve that appeared to lead to a point not far below the oblate silvery moon.

Despite a litter of rubble and cardboard sheeting, the concrete looked pure under the moon, blazing bright, like a fragment of snowy light not quite hardened to the material; and as he ascended he thought he could feel the bridge trembling to his footsteps with the sensitivity of a white nerve. He seemed to be walking into darkness and stars, a solitude the size of creation. It felt good and damn lonely, maybe a little too much so, with the wind flapping pieces of cardboard and the sounds of the insects left behind. After a few minutes, he glimpsed the ragged terminus ahead. When he reached it, he sat down carefully, letting his legs dangle. Wind keened through the exposed girders, tugging at his ankles. His hand throbbed and was fever-hot. Below, multicolored brilliance clung to the black margin of the east bank like a colony of bioluminescent algae. He wondered how high he was. Not high enough, he thought. Faint music was fraying on the wind—the inexhaustible delirium of San Francisco de Juticlan—and he imagined that the flickering of the stars was caused by this thin smoke of music drifting across them.

He tried to think what to do. Not much occurred. He picture Gilbey in Panama. Whoring, drinking, fighting. Doing just as he had in Guatemala. That was where the idea of desertion failed Mingolla. In Panama he would be afraid; in Panama—though his hand might not shake—some other malignant twitch would develop; in Panama he would resort to magical cures, because he would be too imperiled by the real to derive strength from it. And eventually the war would come

77

to Panama. Desertion would have gained him nothing. He stared out at the moon-silvered jungle, and it seemed that some essential part of him was pouring from his eyes, entering the flow of the wind and rushing away past the Ant Farm and its smoking craters, past guerrilla territory, past the seamless join of sky and horizon, being pulled irresistibly toward a point into which the world's vitality was emptying. He felt himself emptying as well, growing cold and vacant and slow. His brain became incapable of thought, capable only of recording perceptions. The wind brought green scents that made his nostrils flare. The sky's blackness folded around him, and the stars were golden pinpricks of sensation. He didn't sleep, but something in him slept.

A whisper drew him back from the edge of the world. At first he thought it had been his imagination, and he continued to stare at the sky, which had lightened to the vivid blue of a predawn darkness. Then he heard the whisper again and glanced over his shoulder. Strung out across the bridge about twenty feet away, a dozen or so children. Some crouched, some standing. Most were clad in rags, a few wore coverings of leaves and vines, and others were naked. Watchful; silent. They were all emaciated, their hair long and matted. Knives glinted in their hands. Recalling the dead children he had seen that morning, Mingolla was for a moment afraid. But only for a moment. Fear flared in him like a coal puffed alight by a breeze and died an instant later, suppressed not by any rational accommodation, but by a perception of these ragged figures as an opportunity for surrender. He had no desire to put forth more effort in the cause of survival. Survival, he had learned, was not the soul's ultimate priority. He studied the children. The way they were posed reminded him of a Neanderthal grouping in the Museum of Natural History. The moon was still graphite. Finally Mingolla turned back to face the horizon, now showing as a distinct line of green darkness.

He had expected to be stabbed or pushed, to pinwheel down and break against Río Dulce, its water gone a steely color beneath the brightening sky. But instead, a voice spoke in his ear. "Hey, macho!"

Squatting beside him was a boy of fourteen or fifteen, his swarthy monkeylike face framed by tangles of shoulder-length black hair. Wearing tattered shorts. Coiled serpent tattooed on his brow. He peered at Mingolla, tipping his head first to one side, then the other, perplexed: he made a growly noise, held up a knife. Twisted it this way and that, letting Mingolla see its keen edge, how it channeled the moonlight along its grooved blade. An army-issue survival knife with a brass-knuckle grip. Mingolla gave an amused sniff.

The boy lowered the knife and nodded as if he had expected such a reaction. "What you doin' here, man?" he asked.

Most of the answers that occurred to Mingolla demanded too much energy to voice. He chose the simplest. "I like the bridge," he said.

Again the boy nodded. "The bridge is magic," he said. "You know this?"

"There was a time I might have believed you," Mingolla said.

"Talk slow," said the boy. "Too fast, I can't understan'."

Mingolla repeated his comment, and the boy laughed. "Sure you believe it, man. Why else you here?" With a planing gesture of his hand, he described an imaginary continuance of the bridge's upward course. "That's where the bridge travels now. Don't have not'ing to do wit' crossin' the river, don't mean the same t'ing a bridge means. You know what I'm sayin'?"

"Yeah," said Mingolla, surprised to hear his own thoughts echoed by someone who so resembled a hominid.

"I come here," said the boy, "and I listen to the wind. Hear it sing in the iron. And I know t'ings from it. I see the future." He grinned, exposing blackened teeth, and pointed toward the Caribbean. "Future's that way, man."

Mingolla liked the joke. He felt an affinity for the boy, for anyone who could manage jokes from the boy's perspective, but he couldn't think of an appropriate means of expressing his feelings. "You speak good English," he said at last.

"Shit! What you t'ink? 'Cause we live in the jungle, we talk like animals? Shit!" The boy spat off the edge of the bridge. "I talk English all my life. Gringos, they too stupid to learn Spanish."

A girl spoke behind them, her voice harsh and peremptory. The other children had closed to within ten feet, their savage faces intent upon Mingolla, and the girl was standing a bit forward of the rest. Sunken cheeks, deep-set eyes. Ratty cables of hair hung down over her breasts. Her hipbones tented up a rag of a skirt, which the wind pushed back between her legs. The boy let her finish, then gave a lengthy response, punctuating his phrases by smashing the brass-knuckle grip of his knife against the concrete, striking sparks with every blow.

"Gracela," the boy said to Mingolla, "she wanna kill you. But I say some men they got one foot in the worl' of death, and if you kill them, death will take you, too. And you know what?"

Mingolla waited.

"It's the truth," said the boy. He clasped his hands, enlaced his fingers, and twisted them to show how firmly locked they were. "You and death like this."

"Maybe," Mingolla said.

"No, it's the truth," the boy insisted. "The bridge tol' me. Tol' me I be t'ankful if I let you live. So you be t'ankful to the bridge, 'cause that magic you don' believe, it save your ass." He dropped out of his squat, swung his legs over the end of the bridge. "Gracela don' care 'bout you live or die. She just goin' 'gainst me 'cause when I leave, she's goin' to be chief, and she's, you know, impatient."

The girl met Mingolla's gaze coldly: a witch-child with slitted eyes and bramble hair and ribs poking out. "Where you goin?" he asked the boy.

"I dream I will live in the south," said the boy. "I will own a warehouse full of gold and cocaine."

The girl began to harangue him again, and he shouted back.

"What's goin' on?" Mingolla asked.

"More bullshit. I tell Gracela if she don' stop, I goin' to fuck her and t'row her in the river." He winked at Mingolla. "Gracela she's a virgin, so she worry 'bout that firs' t'ing."

The sky was graying, pink streaks fading in from the east. Birds wheeled up from the jungle, forming into flocks above the river. The boy shook the hair from his eyes, sighed, and settled himself more comfortably. Mingolla saw that his chest was cross-hatched with ridged scars: knife wounds that hadn't received proper treatment. Bits of vegetation were trapped in his hair, and some were actually tied in place by pieces of twine: primitive adornments.

"Tell me, gringo," said the boy in a man-to-man tone of voice. "I hear in America there is a machine wit' the soul of a man. This is true?"

"I guess that's one way of lookin' at it," said Mingolla. "Yeah."

The boy nodded gravely, his suspicions confirmed. "I hear also America has builded a metal worl' in the sky."

"They're buildin' it now."

"And in the house of your president, is there a stone that holds the mind of a dead magician?"

"I doubt it," said Mingolla after due consideration. "But who knows . . . maybe."

The pink streaks in the east were deepening to crimson, fanning wider. Shafts of light pierced upward to stain the bellies of some low-lying clouds to mauve. Several of the children began to mutter in unison: a chant. They were speaking Spanish, but their voices jumbled the words, making it sound guttural and malevolent, a language for trolls. Listening to the chant, Mingolla imagined them crouched around fires in bamboo thickets. Bloody knives lifted sunward over their fallen prey. Huddled together in the green nights amid Rousseau-like vegetation, while pythons with ember eyes coiled in the branches above.

"Shit, gringo," said the boy. "This a weird motherfuckin' time to be alive." He stared gloomily down at the river; the wind shifted the heavy snarls of his hair.

Watching him, Mingolla grew envious. Despite the bleakness of his existence, this little monkey-king was content with his place in the world, assured of its nature. Perhaps he was deluded, but Mingolla envied his delusion, and he especially envied his dream of gold and cocaine. His own dreams had been dispersed by the war. The idea of sitting and daubing colors onto canvas no longer held any real attraction for him. Nor did the thought of returning to New York. Though survival had been his priority all these months, he had never stopped to consider what survival portended, and now he did not believe he could return. He had, he realized, become acclimated to the war, able to breathe its toxins; he would gag on the air of peace and home. The war was his new home, his newly rightful place.

Then the truth of this struck him with the force of an illumination, and he understood what he had to do.

Baylor and Gilbey had acted according to their natures, and he would have to act according to his, which imposed upon him the path of acceptance. He remembered Tio Moíses's story about the pilot and laughed inwardly. In a sense his friend—the guy he had mentioned in his unsent letter—had been right about the war, about the world. It was full of designs, patterns, coincidences, and cycles that appeared to indicate the workings of some magical power. But these things were the result of a subtle natural process. The longer you lived, the wider your experience, the more complicated your life became, and eventually you were bound in the midst of so many interactions, a web of circumstance and emotion and event, that nothing was simple anymore and everything was subject to interpretation. Interpretation, however, was a waste of time. Even the most logical of interpretations was merely an attempt to herd mystery into a cage and lock the door on it. It made life no less mysterious. And it was equally pointless to seize upon patterns, to rely on them, to obey the mystical regulations they seemed to imply. Your one effective course had to be entrenchment. You had to admit to mystery, to the incomprehensibility of your situation, and protect yourself against it. Shore up your web, clear it of blind corners, set alarms. You had to plan aggressively. You had to become the monster in your own maze, as brutal and devious as the fate you sought to escape. It was the kind of militant acceptance that Tio Moíses's pilot had not the opportunity to display, that Mingolla himself—though the opportunity had been his with Psicorps—had failed to display. He saw that now. He had merely reacted to danger and had not challenged or used forethought against it. But he thought he would be able to do that now.

He turned to the boy, thinking he might appreciate this insight into "magic," and caught a flicker of movement out of the corner of his eye. Gracela. Coming up behind the boy, her knife held low, ready to stab. In reflex, Mingolla flung out his injured hand to block her. The knife nicked the edge of his hand, deflected upward, and sliced the top of the boy's shoulder.

The pain in Mingolla's hand was excruciating, blinding him momentarily; and then as he grabbed Gracela's forearm to prevent her from stabbing again, he felt another sensation, one almost covered by the pain. He had thought the thing inside his hand was dead, but now he could feel it fluttering at the edges of the wound, leaking out in the rich trickle of blood that flowed over his wrist. It was trying to worm back inside, wriggling against the flow, but the pumping of his heart was too strong, and soon it was gone, dripping on the white stone of the bridge.

Before he could feel relief or surprise or in any way absorb what had happened, Gracela tried to pull free. Mingolla got to his knees, dragged her down, and dashed her knife hand against the bridge. The knife skittered away. Gracela struggled wildly, clawing at his face, and the other children edged forward. Mingolla levered his left arm under Gracela's chin, choking her; with his right hand, he picked up the knife and pressed the point into her breast. The children stopped their advance, and Gracela went limp. He could feel her trembling. Tears streaked the grime on her cheeks. She looked like a scared little girl, not a witch.

"Puta!" said the boy. He had come to his feet, holding his shoulder, and was staring daggers at Gracela.

"Is it bad?" Mingolla asked. "The shoulder?"

The boy inspected the bright blood on his fingertips. "It hurts," he said. He stepped over to stand in front of Gracela and smiled down at her; he unbuttoned the top of his shorts.

Gracela tensed.

83

"What are you doing?" Mingolla suddenly felt responsible for the girl.

"I'm going to do what I tol' her, man." The boy undid the rest of the buttons and shimmied out of his shorts; he was already half-erect, as if the violence had aroused him.

"No," said Mingolla, realizing as he spoke that this was not at all wise.

"Take your life," said the boy sternly. "Walk away."

A long powerful gust of wind struck the bridge; it seemed to Mingolla that the vibration of the bridge, the beating of his heart, and Gracela's trembling were driven by the same shimmering pulse. He felt an almost visceral commitment to the moment, one that had nothing to do with his concern for the girl. Maybe, he thought, it was an implementation of his new convictions.

The boy lost patience. He shouted at the other children, herding them away with slashing gestures. Sullenly, they moved off down the curve of the bridge, positioning themselves along the railing, leaving an open avenue. Beyond them, beneath a lavender sky, the jungle stretched to the horizon, broken only by the rectangular hollow made by the airbase. The boy hunkered at Gracela's feet. "Tonight," he said to Mingolla, "the bridge have set us together. Tonight we sit, we talk. Now, that's over. My heart say to kill you. But 'cause you stop Gracela from cutting deep, I give you a chance. She mus' make a judgmen'. If she say she go wit' you, we"—he waved toward the other children—"will kill you. If she wan' to stay, then you mus' go. No more talk, no bullshit. You jus' go. Understan'?"

Mingolla wasn't afraid, and his lack of fear was not born of an indifference to life, but of clarity and confidence. It was time to stop reacting away from challenges, time to meet them. He came up with a plan. There was no doubt that Gracela would choose him, choose a chance at life, no matter how slim. But before she could decide, he would kill the boy. Then he would run straight at the others: without their leader, they might not hang together. It wasn't much of a plan, and he didn't like the idea of hurting the boy; but he thought he might be able to pull it off. "I understand," he said.

The boy spoke to Gracela; he told Mingolla to release her. She sat up, rubbing the spot where Mingolla had pricked her with the knife. She glanced coyly at him, then at the boy; she pushed her hair back behind her neck and thrust out her breasts as if preening for her two suitors. Mingolla was astonished by her behavior. Maybe, he thought, she was playing for time. He stood and pretended to be shaking out his kinks, edging closer to the boy, who remained crouched beside Gracela. In the east a red fireball had cleared the horizon; its sanguine light inspired Mingolla, fueled his resolve. He yawned and edged closer yet, firming his grip on the knife. He would yank the boy's head back by the hair, cut his throat. Nerves jumped in his chest. A pressure was building inside him, demanding that he act, that he move now. He restrained himself. Another step should do it, another step to be absolutely sure. But as he was about to take that step, Gracela reached out and tapped the boy on the shoulder.

Surprise must have showed on Mingolla's face, because the boy looked at him and grunted laughter. "You t'ink she pick you?" he said. "Shit! You don' know Gracela, man. Gringos burn her village. She lick the devil's ass 'fore she even shake hands wit' you." He grinned, stroked her hair. " 'Sides, she t'ink if she fuck me good, maybe I say, 'Oh, Gracela, I got to have some more of that!' And who knows? Maybe she right."

Gracela lay back and wriggled out of her skirt. Between her legs, she was nearly hairless. A smile touched the corners of her mouth. Mingolla stared at her, dumbfounded.

"I not going to kill you, gringo," the boy said without looking up; he was running his hand across Gracela's stomach. "I tol' you I won' kill a man so close wit' death." Again he laughed. "You look pretty funny trying to sneak up. I like watching that."

Mingolla was stunned. All the while he had been gearing himself up to kill, shunting aside anxiety and revulsion, he had merely been providing entertainment for the boy. The knife seemed to be drawing his anger into a compact shape, and he wanted to carry out his attack, to cut down this little animal who had ridiculed him; but humiliation mixed with the anger, neutralizing it. The poisons of rage shook him; he could feel every incidence of pain and fatigue in his body. His hand was throbbing, bloated and discolored like the hand of a corpse. Weakness pervaded him. And relief.

"Go," said the boy. He lay down beside Gracela, propped on an elbow, and began to tease one of her nipples erect.

Mingolla took a few hesitant steps away. Behind him, Gracela made a mewling noise and the boy whispered something. Mingolla's anger was rekindled—they had already forgotten him!—but he kept going. As he passed the other children, one spat at him and another shied a pebble. He fixed his eyes on the white concrete slipping beneath his feet.

When he reached the midpoint of the curve, he turned back. The children had hemmed in Gracela and the boy against the terminus, blocking them from view. The sky had gone bluish gray behind them, and the wind carried their voices. They were singing: a ragged, chirpy song that sounded celebratory. Mingolla's anger subsided, his humiliation ebbed. He had nothing to be ashamed of; though he had acted unwisely, he had done so from a posture of strength, and no amount of ridicule could diminish that. Things were going to work out. Yes, they were! He would make them work out.

For a while he watched the children. At this remove their singing had an appealing savagery, and he felt a trace of wistfulness at leaving them behind. He wondered what would happen after the boy had done with Gracela. He was not concerned, only curious. The way you feel when you think you may have to leave a movie before the big finish. Will our heroine survive? Will justice prevail? Will survival and justice bring happiness in their wake? Soon the end of the bridge came to be bathed in the golden rays of the sunburst; the children seemed to be blackening and dissolving in heavenly fire. That was a sufficient resolution for Mingolla. He tossed Gracela's knife into the river and went down from the bridge in whose magic he no longer believed, walking toward the war whose mystery he had accepted as his own.

CHAPTER FIVE

At the airbase Mingolla took a stand beside the Sikorsky that had brought him to San Francisco de Juticlan; he had recognized it by the painted flaming letters of the words *Whispering Death*. He rested his head against the letter *g* and recalled how Baylor had recoiled from the letters, worried that they might transmit some deadly essence. Mingolla didn't mind the contact. The painted flames seemed to be warming the inside of his head, stirring up thoughts as slow and indefinite as smoke. Comforting thoughts that embodied no images or ideas. Just a gentle buzz of mental activity, like the idling of an engine. The base was coming to life around him. Jeeps pulling away from barracks; a couple of officers inspecting the belly of a cargo plane; some guy repairing a forklift. Peaceful, homey. Mingolla closed his eyes, lulled into a half-sleep, letting the sun and the painted flames bracket him with heat, real and imagined.

Some time later—how much later, he could not be sure—a voice said, "Fucked up your hand pretty good, didn'tcha?"

The two pilots were standing by the cockpit door. In their black flight suits and helmets they looked neither weird nor whimsical, but creatures of functional menace. Masters of the Machine. "Yeah," said Mingolla. "Fucked it up."

"How'd ya do it?" asked the pilot on the left.

"Hit a tree."

"Musta been goddamn crocked to hit a tree," said the pilot on the right. "Tree ain't goin' nowhere if you hit it."

Mingolla made a noncommittal noise. "You guys going up to the Farm?"

"You bet! What's the matter, man? Had enough of them wild women?" Pilot on the right.

"Guess so. Wanna gimme a ride?"

"Sure thing," said the pilot on the left. "Whyn't you climb on in front. You can sit back of us."

"Where your buddies?" asked the pilot on the right.

"Gone," said Mingolla as he climbed into the cockpit.

One of the pilots said, "Didn't think we'd be seein' them boys again."

Mingolla strapped into the observer's seat behind the copilot's position. He had assumed there would be a lengthy instrument check, but as soon as the engines had been warmed, the Sikorsky lurched up and veered northward. With the exception of the weapons systems, none of the defenses had been activated. The radar, the thermal imager, and terrain display all showed blank screens. A nervous thrill ran across the muscles of Mingolla's stomach as he considered the varieties of danger to which the pilots' reliance upon their miraculous helmets had laid them open; but his nervousness was subsumed by the whispery rhythms of the rotors and his sense of the Sikorsky's power. He recalled having a similar feeling of secure potency while sitting at the controls of his gun. He had never let that feeling grow, never let it empower him. He had been a fool.

They followed the northeasterly course of the river, which coiled like a length of blue steel razor wire between jungled hills. The pilots laughed and joked, and the flight came to have the air of a ride with a couple of good ol' boys going nowhere fast and full of free beer. At one point the copilot piped his voice through the onboard speakers and launched into a dolorous country song:

"Whenever we kiss, dear, our two lips meet,
And whenever you're not with me, we're apart.

When you sawed my dog in half, that was depressin',
But when you shot me in the chest, you broke my heart."

As the copilot sang, the pilot rocked the Sikorsky back and forth in a drunken accompaniment, and after the song ended, he called back to Mingolla, "You believe this here son of a bitch wrote that? He did! Picks a guitar, too! Boy's a genius!"

"It's a great song," said Mingolla, and he meant it. The song had made him happy, and that was no small thing.

They went rocking through the skies, singing the first verse over and over. But then, as they left the river behind, still maintaining a northeasterly course, the copilot pointed to a section of the jungle ahead and shouted, "Beaners! Quadrant four! You got 'em?"

"Got 'em!" said the pilot. The Sikorsky swerved down toward the jungle, shuddered, and flame veered from beneath them. An instant later, a huge swath of jungle erupted into a gout of marbled smoke and fire. "Whee-oo!" the copilot sang out, jubilant. *"Whisperin' Death* strikes again!" With guns blazing, they went swooping through blowing veils of dark smoke. Acres of trees were burning, and still they kept up the attack. Mingolla gritted his teeth against the noise, and when at last the firing stopped, dismayed by this insanity, he sat slumped, his head down. He suddenly doubted his ability to cope with the insanity of the Ant Farm and remembered all his reasons for fear.

The copilot turned back to him. "You ain't got no call to look so gloomy, man," he said. "You're a lucky son of a bitch, y'know that?"

The pilot began a bank toward the east, toward the Ant Farm. "How you figure that?"

"I gotta clear sight of you, man," said the copilot. "I can tell you for true you ain't gonna be at the Ant Farm much longer. It ain't clear why or nothin'. But I 'spect you gonna be wounded. Not bad, though. Just a goin'-home wound."

As the pilot completed the bank, a ray of sun slanted into the cockpit, illuminating the copilot's visor, and for a split second Mingolla could make out the vague shadow of the face

89

beneath. It seemed lumpy and malformed. His imagination added details. Bizarre growths, cracked cheeks, an eye webbed shut. Like a face out of a movie about nuclear mutants. He was tempted to believe that he had really seen this; the copilot's deformities would validate his prediction of a secure future. But Mingolla rejected the temptation. He was afraid of dying, afraid of the terrors held by life at the Ant Farm, yet he wanted no more to do with magic . . . unless there was magic involved in being a good soldier. In obeying the disciplines, in the practice of fierceness.

"Could be his hand'll get him home," said the pilot. "That hand looks pretty fucked up to me. Looks like a million-dollar wound, that hand."

"Naw, I don't get it's his hand," said the copilot. "Somethin' else. Whatever, it's gonna do the trick."

Mingolla could see his own face floating in the black plastic of the copilot's visor; he looked warped and pale, so thoroughly unfamiliar that for a moment he thought the face might be a bad dream the copilot was having.

"What the hell's with you, man?" the copilot asked. "You don't believe me?"

Mingolla wanted to explain that his attitude had nothing to do with belief or disbelief, that it signaled his intent to obtain a safe future by means of securing his present; but he couldn't think how to put it into words the copilot would accept. The copilot would merely refer again to his visor as testimony to a magical reality or perhaps would point up ahead where—because the cockpit plastic had gone opaque under the impact of direct sunlight—the sun now appeared to hover in a smoky darkness: a distinct fiery sphere with a steaming corona, like one of those cabalistic emblems embossed on ancient seals. It was an evil, fearsome-looking thing, and though Mingolla was unmoved by it, he knew the pilot would see in it a powerful sign.

"You think I'm lyin'?" said the copilot angrily. "You think I'd be bullshittin' you 'bout somethin' like this? Man, I ain't lyin'! I'm givin' you the good goddamn word!"

They flew east into the sun, whispering death, into a world

disguised as a strange bloody enchantment, over the dark green wild where war had taken root, where men wearing brass scorpions on their berets, where crazy lost men wandered the mystic light of Fire Zone Emerald and mental wizards brooded upon things not yet seen. The copilot kept the black bubble of his visor angled back toward Mingolla, waiting for a response. But Mingolla just stared, and before too long the copilot turned away.

THE GOOD SOLDIER

... I wish I had an army of a million guys like me,
I'd break the chains that bind the Beast
And pull the wings off Liberty.
I'd storm the Holy City and watch how long
The angels took to die,
Then bustin' into the Great Throne Room
I'd be surprised to find
That God ain't nothin' but an old gray man
Who can't remember why.

from "Marching Song"
—Jack Lescaux

CHAPTER SIX

Paths that lead to the most profound destinations, to moments of illumination or change, have nothing to do with actual travel, but rather negotiate a mental geography. And so the walk Mingolla took one day from the door of a hotel on the island of Roatán to a patch of grass where he sat cross-legged, hemmed in against a high concrete wall by a thicket of aguacaste bushes, was only the final leg of both a journey and a transformation that had encompassed a week of tests and five months of drug therapy, yet had covered scarcely any distance at all. Beside him, the bole of a palm was tipped half out of the dirt, exposing filaments of its root system, and the trunk curved up to a cluster of green coconuts, their slick dimpled hulls looking from below like the faces of evil dolls. Some of the fronds were dead, gone a tawny orange, and the burst wrappings of the newer fronds had unfurled into corkscrew-shaped lengths as gray and raveled as used bandages. Mingolla watched them shift in the wind, pleased by their slowness, by the twisting, coiling movements that seemed to mirror his own slowness, the drifty cast of mind that hid him from his trainer.

"Davy!" A bassy shout. "Quit playin' dese fool games!"

Two cashew trees stood up from the thicket, wrinkled yellow fruit tucked among spreads of dark leaves, and farther off, towering above the hotel, whose red tile roof was visible over the tops of the bushes, a ceiba tree drenched the under-

growth in a pool of indigo shadow; wherever sunlight penetrated the canopy, the air had a soft golden luminosity, and
insects hovering there glowed with the intensity of jewels in a
showcase.

"Don't vex wit' me, Davy!"

Fuck you, Tully!

From beyond the wall came the crash of surf piling in onto
the reef, and listening to it, wishing he could see the waves,
Mingolla thought it didn't seem possible he had been confined
for all those months. His memories of the time consisted of a
rubble of disconnected moments, and whenever he tried to
assemble them, to make of them a coherent measure, he could
not put together sufficient material to fill more than a few weeks
. . . weeks of needles slipping into his arm, faces blurring as the
drugs took hold, of fever dreams planing into a fevered reality,
of pausing by the pitted mirror in the hotel lobby and staring
into his eyes, not seeking any inner truth, just hoping to find
himself, some part of himself that had been left unchanged.

"Goddammit, Davy!"

Only one day was clear in his memory. His twenty-first
birthday . . .

"Okay, mon! Dat's how you want it!"

. . . Right after the plastic surgery. Dr. Izaguirre had cut off
the drugs so he could receive a call from his parents on a video
hookup in the hotel basement, and he had waited for the call
lying on a sprung sofa, facing a screen that occupied most of an
end wall. The other walls were paneled in plastic strips of
imitation maple, some of which had peeled away to reveal the
riverbed textures of mildewed wallboard, and in the dim track
lighting the overstated grain of the paneling showed yellow and
black like printed circuitry made of tiger skins. Mingolla pil-
lowed his head on the arm of the sofa, fiddling with the remote
control box, trying to map out what to say to his parents, but
couldn't get beyond, "Hi, how's it going?" He had trouble
calling them to mind, let alone designing intimacy, and when
the screen brightened to a shot of them in their living room,
sitting stiffly as if posing for a photograph, he continued lying
there, taking in his father's insurance executive drag of blue suit

and tie and stylishly long gray hair, his mother's worn face and linen dress, noticing how the flatness of the image made them seem elements of the decor, anthropomorphic accessories to the leather chairs and frilly lamp shades. He had no reaction to them: he might have been viewing a portrait of strangers to whom he had a chance blood connection.

"David?" His mother started to reach out to him, then remembered touch was impossible. She glanced at his father, who patted her arm, affected a bemused smile, and said, "We had no idea they'd made you look so much like a . . ."

"Like a beaner?" said Mingolla, annoyed by his father's unruffled manner.

"If that's your term of choice," his father said coldly.

"Don't worry. Little tuck and fold here and there, little dye job. But I'm still your all-American boy."

"I'm sorry," said his mother. "I knew it was you, but . . ."

"It's okay."

". . . I was startled at first."

"Really, it's okay."

Mingolla had not had high expectations for the call, yet he had wanted to have high expectations, to love them, to be open and honest, and now, seeing them again, understanding that they would demand of him a conversation to match their wallpaper, nothing more, his emotions went blank, and he wondered if he would have to dredge up old feelings in order to relate to them at all. They told him about their trip to Montreal. Sounds pretty there, he said. They spoke of garden parties, of yachting off the Cape. Wish I'd been there, he said. They complained about asthma, allergies, and they asked how it felt to be twenty-one.

"Tell ya the truth," he said, weary of stock responses. "I feel 'bout a thousand years old."

His father sniffed. "Spare us the melodrama, David."

"Melodrama." A burst of adrenaline set Mingolla trembling. "That what it is, Dad?"

"I should think," his father said, "that you'd want this to be a pleasant experience, that you'd at least try to be civil."

"Civil." For a moment the word had no meaning to

Mingolla, only a bitter, insipid flavor. "Yeah, okay. I was hoping we could talk to each other, but civil's cool. Fine! Let's do it! You ask how I've been, and I'll say, 'Great.' And I'll ask how's business, and you'll say, 'Not bad.' And Mom'll tell me 'bout my friends, what they're up to these days. And then if I'm real, real civil, you'll give a little speech 'bout how you're proud of me and all." He hissed in disgust. "There you are, Dad. We don't even have to go through it now. We can just sit here and fucking stare at each other and pretend we're having a pleasant experience!"

His father's eyes narrowed. "I see no point in continuing this."

"David!" His mother pleaded with him silently.

Mingolla had no intention of apologizing, enjoying his charge of anger, but after a long silence he relented. "I'm kinda tense, Dad. Sorry."

"What I fail to understand," his father said, "is why you insist on trying to impress us with the gravity of your situation. We know it's grave, and we're concerned about you. We simply don't believe it's appropriate to discuss our concern on your birthday."

"I see." Mingolla bit off the words.

"Apology accepted," said his father with equal precision.

For the remainder of the conversation, Mingolla fielded questions with a flawless lack of honesty, and after the screen had faded to gray, his anger also grayed. He lay punching the remote control buttons, flipping from car chases to talk shows and then to a haze of pointilist dots that resolved into a plain of bleached-looking ruins. He recognized Tel Aviv, remembered the ultimate bad omen of the city nuked on his birthday. The picture broke up, and he jabbed the next button. The ruins reappeared, the camera tracking past a solitary wall, twisted girders, and piles of bricks. Dark thunderheads boiled over the city, their edges fraying into silver glare; shards of buildings stood in silhouette against a band of pale light on the horizon, like black fangs biting the sky. There was no sound, but when Mingolla adjusted the fine tuning, he heard bluesy guitar chords, synthesizer, a noodling sax, and a woman's voice . . . obviously the voiceover from another channel.

98

". . . Prowler's latest, 'Blues for Heaven,' " she was saying. "Hope it ain't too depressin' for you music lovers. But, hey! Depression's all over these days, right? Just consider it a mood alternative . . . like a drug, y'know. Little somethin' to add texture to your usual upbeat feelin', make it all that much sweeter."

It had begun to rain in Tel Aviv, a steady drizzle, and the music seemed the aural counterpart of the rain, of the clouds and their fuming passage across the city.

"Prowler," said the woman. "The fabulous Jack Lescaux on vocals. Tell 'em 'bout the real world, Jack."

"Laney's in her half-slip, pacin' up and down,
chain-smokin' Luminieres, watchin' the second hand spin 'round.
I'm sittin' at the window, pickin' out a slow gray tune,
and two shadows walkin' east on Lincoln turn down Montclair Avenue.
'That mother he ain't comin' back,' says Laney. 'Y'can't trust him when he's broke.
I just know he took my money.' She blows a blue-steel jet of smoke.
I say, 'Take it easy, honey. Why don't you do some of my frost.'
She laughs 'cause life without the proper poison is a joke at any cost."

The song with its mournful disposition, its narrative of two junkies enduring a bad night, was like the voice of a ghost wandering the city, and it pulled Mingolla in, drew him along, making him feel that he—with his shattered memories and emotions—was himself half a ghost, and causing him to imagine that he would be at home among the spirits of Tel Aviv, able to offer them the consolation of flesh-and-blood companionship. There was a premonitory clarity to this thought, but he was too absorbed in the music and the city to explore it further. He saw that the ruins posed a dire compatibility for him, enforcing the self-conception that he was the ruin of a human being in whom a ruinous power was being bred.

"David." Dr. Izaguirre's voice behind him. "Time for your injection."

"Inna second . . . I wanna hear the rest of the song."

Izaguirre made a noise of grudging acceptance and walked in front of the screen. He was pale, long limbed, with a salt-and-pepper goatee, thinning gray hair, and a perpetually ardent expression: an aquiline El Greco Christ aged to sixty or thereabouts and fleshed out a bit, dressed in a starched guayabera and slacks. He peered at the ruins as if searching them for survivors, then pulled a pair of glasses from his pocket and fitted them to his nose with an affected flourish. All his gestures were affected, and Mingolla believed this reflected a conscious decision. He had the impression that Izaguirre felt so in control of his life, so unchallenged, that he had tailored the minutiae of his personality in order to entertain himself, had transformed his existence into a game, one that would test his elegant surface against the dulling inelegance of the world.

"Tel Aviv," said Izaguirre. "Terrible, terrible." He went back behind the couch and gave Mingolla's shoulder a sympathetic squeeze just as a flight of armored choppers flew out of the east over the city. It may have been this sight that triggered Mingolla's response, and perhaps Izaguirre's squeeze had a little to do with it, but whatever the cause, Mingolla's eyes filled, and he was flooded with a torrent of suddenly liberated emotions and thoughts, mingling shame over his behavior with his parents, irritation at Izaguirre's witness, and loathing for the self-absorption that had prevented him from relating to the tragedy of Tel Aviv in other than trivial and personal terms.

". . . rain is falling harder, makin' speckles on the walk,
blankets stuffed in broken windows glow softly in the dark.
An old bum his hands in baggies, slumps in a doorway 'cross the street,
his eyes are brown like worn-out pennies, got bedroom slippers on his feet.
Some wise-ass stops and says, 'Hey buddy! Know where I can get some rags like that?'
The bum keeps starin' into nowhere . . . he knows nowhere's where it's at."

Mingolla was overwhelmed by the desolation of the ruins and the song. The white blossoms lay in the dust like crumpled pieces of paper, the camera zoomed in on one to show how it was blackening from the radiation, and his identification with the place was so complete, he felt the white thoughts lying in the dust of his mind beginning to blacken as well. The vacancy of Tel Aviv was a sleet riddling him, seeding him with empti- ness, and he came to his feet, buoyed by that emptiness, gripping the sofa to keep from floating away.

"Don't you want to listen?" Izaguirre sounded amused.

"Naw, un-uh."

"Are you sure? We have time."

Mingolla shook his head no, continued to shake it, trying to get rid of all his nos, all his negatives, each shake more vehement, and when Izaguirre put an arm around him, he was most grateful, desperate to be led away from Tel Aviv and Prowler, ready now for his injection.

A crunching in the brush. Mingolla looked this way and that, thinking it must be Tully, but spotted a scrawny black man standing about twenty feet away: one of the islanders who inhabited the outbuildings. They had taken to following him around, retreating whenever he tried to confront them, as if he possessed some dread allure. The man slipped deeper into the thicket, and Mingolla relaxed, stretching out his legs. An alp of cumulus edged across the sun, transforming its radiance into a fan of watery light; wind flattened the tops of the bushes. Mingolla closed his eyes, basking in the warmth, in a heady sense of peace.

"You a damn fool, mon," said a rumbling voice above him.

He sat up with a start, blinking. Tully was a black giant, looming into the sky, hands on hips.

"A true damn fool," said Tully. "I wastin' my time teachin' you dat block, 'cause dere you sit, winkin' on and off like a fuckin' caution light. What you doin', mon? Daydreamin'?"

"I . . ."

"Shut your fool mouth. Now dis"—he tapped his chest—

"dis a good block. And dis ain't." As if a furnace door had been slung open, Tully's heat washed over Mingolla. "And dis what you doin'." The heat ebbed, vanished, flared again. "I should put my foot to you!"

The sun hung directly behind Tully's head, a golden corona rimming a black oval. Mingolla felt weak and weakening, felt that threads of himself were being spun loose and sucked into the blackness. Panicked, acting in reflex, he pushed at Tully not with his hands, but with his mind, and he was panicked still more by the sensation that he had fallen into a school of electric fish, thousands of them, brushing against him, darting away. Tully's fist swung toward him, but that electricity, and the attendant feelings of arousal and strength, was so commanding that Mingolla was frozen, unable to duck, and the blow struck the top of his head, knocking him flat.

"You ain't got de force to war wit' me, Davy." Tully squatted beside him. "But, mon, I just been waitin' for you to make dis breakt'rough. Now we can really get started."

Mingolla's head throbbed, grass tickled his lower lip. He stared at the tips of Tully's tennis shoes, the cuffs of his blue trousers. He struggled up, leaned against the wall, groggy.

"Caught me by surprise, mon, or I stay from bashin' you." Tully grinned, gold crowns glittering among his teeth, his good humor given the look of a fierce mask by the deep lines etched around his mouth and eyes. He was huge, everything about him huge, hands that could swallow coconuts, chest plated with muscle, and had about him an air of elemental masculinity that never failed to unsettle Mingolla. His hair was flecked with gray, his neck seamed, eyes liverish, but his arms—straining a white T-shirt—had the definition of a man twenty years younger. Above his left eye was a pink hook-shaped scar, startling in contrast to his coal-black skin, like a vein of some rare mineral. "Damn," he said. "You goin' to be somethin' special! You almost 'whelm me wit' dat touch."

Mingolla turned his gaze to the hotel roof, watched a string of pelicans flying above it, appearing to spell out a string of cryptic syllables.

"I know you wary, mon," said Tully. "You like a little boy,

and you got to be strong 'fore you go to facin' up to me . . . and dat's natural. Dese drugs, dey put you in a new world, and dat's a trial for anyone, 'specially somebody been t'rough it like you. But I for you, Davy. Dat you can count on. I just got to be hard wit' you, 'cause dat's how you goin' to get hard 'nough for dis new world.''

Mingolla's distrust must have showed in his face, for Tully let out a laugh as guttural and toneless as a lion's cough. "Dis t'ing 'tween you and me gettin' to be a bitch," he said. " 'Mind me of me and my father. Now dere was a harsh mon, lemme tell you. He come home drunk for he supper, and he say to me, 'Boy, you so ugly you make me lose my appetite. Get under de table! I no want to be lookin' at you while I chew.' And I don't do what he say, he put me under dat table!'' He gave Mingolla a friendly punch on the leg. "S'pose I tell you get under de table? What you goin' to do?''

"Tell you to fuck yourself,'' said Mingolla.

"Dat right?'' Tully scratched his neck. "Lessee if dat's de case. You stay outside tonight, Davy. Don't come back to de hotel. Stay out here and t'ink 'bout what's ahead.''

"How'm I supposed to know what's ahead?''

"Got a point dere. All right, I give you a glimpse of de future. Once you t'rough wit' trainin' dere will be a test. We be sendin' you to La Ceiba, and you goin' into de Iron Barrio and kill a mon wit' de force of your mind.''

The concept of killing as a test left Mingolla unmoved, but Tully's mention of the Iron Barrio drained him of belligerence.

"Stay clear of de hotel tonight, Davy." Tully stood, unkinked his back, twisting from side to side. "Study on how you goin' to deal wit' de Barrio wit'out my help. And if I catch you inside 'fore mornin', it will go hard for you. Dat much you don't need to study on.''

Tucked into a corner of the concrete wall was a tin-roofed shed that had once been a dive shop, and later that afternoon Mingolla entered it, intending to wait there until everyone was asleep and then sneak into the hotel. As he stepped through the door, a ghost crab scuttled from beneath the wooden table that centered the shed and vanished down a gap in the boards, leaving a trail of delicate slashmarks in the dust. Golden light slanted from rips in the tin, painting splotches of glare on the floor; dust motes stirred up by Mingolla's tread whirled in the light, making it appear that something was about to materialize in each of the beams. Resting on the table were four rusted air tanks, bridged by spans of cobweb and looking in the gloom like enormous capsules of dried blood.

Mingolla sat against the rear wall of the shed next to a stack of yellowed scuba diving magazines. To pass the time he leafed through one and was amused to discover ads for various of the island's resorts in the front pages. Pirate's Cove, Jolly Roger's, and such. Their buildings now abandoned, beaches cordoned by patrol boats, tourists driven off by the threat of rockets . . . though the island had never come under attack. Which was perplexing. Roatán was a logical target, being iso-lated, home to a CIA computer base, and well within range of rockets, bombs, or even an assault. The fact that there hadn't been an attack made no sense, but sense, he thought, was not something war made in any great quantity, and he supposed that some absurd reason underlay the island's security, some meshing of Marxist and capitalist irrationality, maybe a trade-off of immunities, an agreement to leave each other's computers alone in order to provide both sides with the capacity to mete out death and destruction along predictable lines. That he could have this thought, which seemed a very adult thought, the type of caustic and dispassionate judgment that people often charac-terize as symptomatic of a mature disinterest, was, he decided, a sign that he was on the mend, that he was growing inured to the corrosive passions of war, becoming capable of clear-sighted progress.

He turned to a photo spread of divers in red and yellow wet suits floating in a turquoise depth, lost among thousands of brightly colored fish. Something about the photograph struck him as familiar, and he recalled his experience with Tully earlier that day. That was how it had been: he had been a driver in Tully's mind, hovering in those electric depths, sur-rounded by the fish of his thoughts. And he was certain there had been a greater depth beyond. A place he imagined to be as labyrinthine as a coral reef, housing thoughts as intricate as sea fans.

Dusk made it impossible to read. Storm clouds blew in from the north, a freshet of rain spattering the roof; darkness slipped in under cover of the clouds, and moonlight filtered through the ripped tin, daubing the floors with lavender gray. Mingolla noticed a light fixture above the table. He went to the door, flipped a wall switch, and was surprised when the bulb flickered on, shining a white radiance into every corner of the shed. Moths began batting around it, casting a shrapnel of shadow over the walls. He sat back down and returned to reading, half-listening to the wind, the crashing on the reef. Then something creaked, and, glancing up, he saw a thin black woman standing at the door, wearing a threadbare dress that had bleached a pale indefinite brown. Alarmed, he reacted as he had with Tully, pushing toward her with his mind. Again that feeling of immersion, of power and arousal. But this time, meeting no resistance, he found himself swimming—it was the only word applicable—swimming in a pattern, a convoluted knot, and instead of penetrating an unknown depth as he had imagined, it seemed he was tunneling, that the stuff of the woman's thought was aligning around his pattern, hardening into form that he was dictating. He moved so rapidly, he was unable to trace the complexities of the pattern; however, satisfied at last by some intuitive criteria that it was complete, secure in this, he pulled back from the woman. An erection was ridging up his trousers.

The woman swayed, righted herself, gaping, apparently stunned. She was young—eighteen, nineteen—and cocoa skinned, with a dusting of freckles across her nose and cheeks; her face was pretty, with a cleverness of feature that reminded him of Debora, and framed by stubby dreadlocks. . . . He lost interest in the woman, puzzled by his use of Debora as a comparative after all these months. But then he realized that while she had not been foremost in his mind, she had been a subroutine in his thoughts, a place to which he had traveled in dreams, in idle moments. And he realized, too, that his knowledge of her had deepened: it was as if he had been carrying on a dialogue with her, assembling a portrait of her from clues implicit in her words, her smell, her manner.

"I been feelin' you come," said the woman in hushed tones.

Again Mingolla pushed toward her, aiming the desire he had been harboring for Debora, understanding as he did that desire had a shape he could feel . . . feeling it like a pitcher who, leaning in for his sign, grips the baseball behind his back, fingering the seams until he has found the proper position: an unconscious yet expert process. The woman's face went slack, her breath quickened.

"Been feelin' you come most all dis week," she said, edging closer. "You got so much power, mon!" She fondled a shell that was threaded on a string about her neck, painted with red and green designs.

"Who are you?" Mingolla asked, anxious, not really caring who she was, wanting an answer that might shed light on who he was becoming.

"I Hettie." She sank to her knees a body-length away. "De power full on you now. More power dan I ever felt, and praise God more de luck."

Mingolla's anxiety increased. "What're you talking 'bout?"

"De power bring de luck. Dat how it be always. De new ones come to power, and dey touch us fah to make dem safe."

He recalled his sense of security after completing the pattern.

"We keep you safe, too."

"Tell me 'bout the luck," he said.

She wetted her lips. "De luck ain't not'in' to talk on."

"Why not?"

"Talkin' liable to 'splain it 'way."

That struck a chord in Mingolla, putting him in mind of his ritual, how he had been reluctant to talk about it . . . except with Debora, in whom he had seen another configuration of luck. "Tell me," he said. "And I'll give you stronger luck."

A mixture of disbelief and glee melted up from Hettie's face, as if he had promised something both improbable and wonderful, like the promise of an afterlife. "You do dis fah me?"

106

"Yes."

She talked in a breathy whisper, fingering her shell, head bowed, offering a litany of explanation, describing lives bound by magical pattern, security guaranteed by the repetition of behavior, and Mingolla began to wonder about the similarity between Hettie's luck and his ritual of survival, the idiosyncrasies of the chopper pilots and of various other acquaintances back in Guatemala. All these behaviors shared the same delusionary character, and given that Hettie was essentially a test subject upon which fledgling psychics worked their changes, it could be that psychics were responsible in every instance, that the delusions were the product of their influence. He tried to dismiss this as paranoia, but found that he could not.

Hettie sat back on her haunches, silent, waiting for luck to be bestowed; her dress had ridden up, exposing the shadowy division between her thighs. Mingolla had no luck to give her, only desire, the one emotion he knew how to shape. Yet desire was powerful in him now. He was alive with it, alive with the power behind it. Everywhere he looked it seemed that the world was being enriched by the pressure of his vision. The weathered boards, the light beading silver on the cobwebs, the ruddy wood of the table, all these things seemed to shine brighter than before. Maybe, he thought, if desire was strong enough, it would effect luck. As he directed it toward her, he saw that luck, the feeling of being blessed with good fortune, also had a shape, and he incorporated that into the push of desire.

With an indrawn breath, Hettie arched her back, and, hands spread wide, caressed her belly, her breasts, pressing their rounds flat, kneading them. Watching her, Mingolla understood that his gift of desire and luck could have a return, that he could make love to her, that here among the moths and cobwebs he could commit an act of pure usage, almost of violence, of pleasure taken without toll or penance. And he was tempted. There was a peculiar tension in his body, a mingling of confidence and indecision, the way he had felt after receiving a pass at the top of the key, watching the waist of the man guarding him, not knowing whether to break right or left, leaning forward like a reluctant diver and letting gravity slowly take him, waiting until his opponent had seen—or thought he'd seen—a hint of direction, had shifted his weight in anticipation, placing himself at a disadvantage that would allow Mingolla to penetrate the lane. Hettie's head lolled, her hips lifted. Sweat beaded her upper lip, the hollow of her throat. Abandon had refined her looks to an animal delicacy, and Mingolla reached for her, thinking of Debora, her delicacy. But at that moment she cried out, went down on all fours, hips thrusting at nothing, crying out again, more softly, hoarsely, and in her mind there was flurrying as of a million fish responding to a danger sign, scattering, their space filled by a lazy current, a sluggish tingling wash.

Wind battered the shed, vibrating the tin roof. Hettie remained on all fours, staring dull-eyed at Mingolla through the fat coils of her dreadlocks. He was glad he hadn't taken her, because she was too easy a beast, because he wanted someone whose mind had not been walked through time and again. He got to his feet, and she followed him with her eyes; he moved around her to the table, and she turned her head, displaying no more emotion than a cow.

"Get up!" he said, irritated. But irritation gave way to pity, and when she stood, hands limp at her sides, he asked if she was all right.

"I . . ." She made a halfhearted effort at smoothing wrinkles on her dress. "T'ings dey comin' clear."

"What things?"

"T'ings of de luck."

Branches ticked the wall of the shed, a wave boomed on the reef.

"Better we find de others." Hettie came a step toward Mingolla, eyes wide, fidgeting with her shell. "Dis luck 'nough to make dem all catch a fire."

Silver-blue clouds scudded across the moon, and a seamless dark flowed over the hotel grounds. Then the moon sailed clear, and the grounds became a floating puzzle of light and shadow: the edges of fronds, sprigs of round leathery sea-grape leaves, bamboo stalks, all illuminated by swatches of moon-light, all bounded by toiling blackness, rustling, seething, a troubled noise audible above the whispery vowels of wind and sea. Hettie beckoned to Mingolla, saying, "Come, you follow!" Mingolla waved at her, picking his way cautiously through the thicket toward the hotel, its white stucco ablaze between the arching trunks of palms, the open windows black as caves. The thrashing of the pitch-dark foliage seemed to empower him: he felt he was growing stronger with every step, storing inside himself the wildness of the night.

They turned away from the hotel into thicker brush, a path choked with ferns and fleshy-leaved plants, and came to a large clearing of packed dirt surrounding a bungalow with board walls and a conical thatched roof. Candles flickered in the doorway, each point of flame centering an orange nimbus. "I bring dem fah you," Hettie said, and went inside the bunga-low, leaving Mingolla standing beside a palmetto. He was antsy and couldn't understand why. It must be the brilliance of the moon, the way it spotlit him, he thought, and to elude that silvery eye, he moved closer to the palmetto, entering the tickling embrace of its fronds.

One by one islanders emerged from the bungalow, nearly a dozen black men and women, old, young, uniformly under-nourished and ragged, all holding painted shells or some other fetish. Shadows collected in the folds of their clothing, in their wrinkles and eyesockets, giving them the appearance of walk-ing dead. Their silence seemed to be dimming the moon's wattage, muting the voice of the wind. Hettie urged them forward, but Mingolla did not let them get near, lashing out with his mind and halting their shambling approaches, tying inside their heads that intricate knot with which he had bound Hettie, and then firing them with good fortune, with other emotions whose shapes he was coming to know. They grunted as he struck, their eyes rolled and flashed with pure charges of moonlight; they muttered prayerfully, backing away, taking up positions at the perimeter of the clearing, fixing him with awed stares. Each exercise of power enlivened him, and when he had done he sat down in the dirt, calm at the center of their stares, but sensing himself the epicenter of a strange weather, a storm with impalpable winds that blew from a world just around the corner and passed without leaving a trace of damage, yet changed everything. He felt a need for normalcy, and spotting Hettie in the door of the bungalow, he called her over, asked her to sit. She lowered to her knees beside him, her hands clasped demurely in her lap.

"Where you live, Hettie?" he asked.

"I lives here."

"I mean before you came here . . . where'd you live then?"

The concept of "before" seemed to befuddle her, but at length she said, "My daddy have a little place out to Flowers Bay." Then, after a considerable pause: "He raise ponies."

"Yeah?" said Mingolla, thinking that ponies and Flowers Bay sounded idyllic. "Why'd you leave?"

"It were de ponies. Dem little children, dey wild! All de time tossin' dere heads, givin' you de duppy eye. Make me fearful to be 'mong dem."

One of the other islanders—a man sitting in the shade of a sea-grape bush—let out a keening wail and lifted his hands to the moon.

"Ponies ain't goin' to hurtcha," Mingolla said.

"Oh, yes! All t'ings be hurtful when dere duppy loose." Hettie brushed her fingers across his knee, a reassuring touch. "But you be too strong for de duppies, mon."

Her expression was in partial eclipse, half-moonlit, half-shadowed, impossible to read, but he detected in her a clouded regret, the trace of some sadness whose particulars she could no longer remember. He had wanted to talk with her, to pretend he was having an ordinary conversation with a pretty girl; but she was only the husk of a pretty girl, and there was nothing ordinary about either of them.

His thoughts turned again to Debora, and again he was confused by his fixation on her. He didn't believe he was in love with her, he didn't see how that could be possible. But this sort of thing, this long, almost unconscious study of another person, had once led him to fall in love, and he hoped that wasn't the case now. He had a low opinion of love, of its power to distract and injure, though he was forced to admit that distraction and injury were good teachers. The woman he'd loved was five years older than he, one of those pretty upper middle class housewives common to the better neighborhoods of Long Island, with a penchant for ceramic jewelry and denim skirts, for charitable works inspired by boredom with their husbands, always looking for a glimmer of excitement to brighten them, yet not really expecting anything, seduced by the role they had accepted into believing that their lives were ruled by a canon of mediocrity, that boredom was their lot. He had been teaching a sketching class at the Y, and two weeks after she had joined the class, they had begun an affair. Everything had been perfect at first, but as the affair progressed she had grown afraid, had tried to quantify love, to rank it against the security and stability of her marriage, and in the end she had broken it off with Mingolla, leaving him older, wiser, and his schoolwork neglected to such an extent that he had become eligible for the draft.

"Look like trouble lay he hand on you," said Hettie.

"It's nothing," he said.

Wind shredded the thatch of the bungalow, and smoky blue clouds drove across the moon, spreading a shadowy film through the air, a darkness that—as the clouds thickened—grew absolute.

"Trouble not find you here," said Hettie. "Here you safe wit' us."

He could hardly make her out, ebony against anthracite.

"Safe from war, from de duppies."

Safe, he thought. Safe in this eerie, lightless clearing, safe among dazed human relics, with the chaos on the reef sounding as final as artillery, and the wind howling a secret name.

Oh, yeah! He was safe all right!

"Safe from all t'ings," said Hettie.

As a reward for Mingolla's breakthrough, Dr. Izaguirre presented him with an autographed copy of *The Fictive Boarding House* by Juan Pastorín, Mingolla's favorite author. "I've

111

noticed you admiring it on my shelf," said the doctor, and Mingolla, who did not want to give Izaguirre credit for having been sensitive to him in any way, said that he had merely been curious, that he'd never heard of the book.

"It's a limited edition," said Izaguirre as they entered the hotel lobby, a long narrow room—essentially an expanded corridor—with tall windows ranging the eastern wall, and the western wall inset by a stairway and French doors that opened into a dining room. Vines and leaves scrolled the window-panes, admitting an effusion of gray light; velvety dust covered every surface. The carpet was indoor-outdoor runner brocaded with mildew, and above the dining room entrance was a painted menu listing the breakfast specials: faded misspelled words in English such as *hotcaks* and *freid potatas*. It was a place in which entropy appeared to have triumphed.

Beside the main door was a mirror, and beneath the mirror a bottomed-out rattan chair. Izaguirre dusted the chair with a handkerchief and sat; he pulled at his goatee, seeming to stretch the waxy stuff of his flesh. "What did you want to ask me?" he said.

In the light of day Mingolla was less certain of his theory concerning the effects of psychic manipulation on the troops in Guatemala, but he laid it out for Izaguirre.

"Yes, it's most unfortunate," Izaguirre said. "The electrical activity involved causes minor changes in the brain . . . especially in those subjects upon whom the psychic is working. But there's also a broadcast effect, and people in the immediate vicinity are affected as well. Delusionary systems are reestablished or enforced. Superstitions and so forth."

"Minor changes? You gotta be kidding!" Mingolla waved toward the grounds. "Those people out there are wrecked, and some of the people I knew in Guatemala weren't much better."

"The more frequent the encounters, the more extreme the effects." Izaguirre crossed his legs, imperturbable. "I sympathize with your reaction, but one has to look at the long result."

Mingolla walked over to the reception desk, laid down his book, and stared into the cobwebbed pigeonholes on the wall, unable to sort out his feelings. "So I guess I must not have been zapped too often."

"Often enough. For one thing, according to your debriefing you were likely subject to the wiles of a Sombra agent shortly before your departure from Guatemala."

"What's Sombra?"

"The Communist version of Psicorps. This woman was named"—Izaguirre tapped his forehead, encouraging memory—"Debora Cifuentes." He chuckled. "Here's an irony for you. Since trying to persuade you to desert, she herself has deserted, fled into the Petén. One of the people at headquarters suggested that if you came through training as well as we expect, we might send you to track her down. She's quite powerful, but we feel you'd be more than a match."

Mingolla was speechless with rage.

"Would you like that?" asked Izaguirre.

"Yeah," said Mingolla. "Yeah, that'd be all right." He paced beside the desk. "Y'know, I can't figure something out."

"Yes?"

"Why the hell all the fuss 'bout me, 'bout her. I mean all Psicorps does is sit around and try to guess when the next attack's coming. Crap like that."

"You and the Cifuentes woman are anomalies. There aren't more than thirty agents of your caliber in the world. You'll do more than make guesses." Izaguirre watched him pace. "You seem upset."

"I'm okay. Why didn't she just, y'know . . . blow me away or whatever?"

"She could have taken control of you, but that would have ruined your talent, and I assume she was trying to recruit you . . . not destroy you. It's troublesome for one psychic to exert a subtle influence over another. That sort of interaction strengthens the talents of both parties. It sets up a feedback system whose efficiency is related to the intensity of mutual focus. And since you had the greater natural talent, more room to grow, as she worked on you, you were gaining in strength more rapidly than she could have predicted. Thus the difficulty." He stood, walked toward Mingolla. "Surely something has upset you."

"It's not important."

"I'd like to hear about it anyway."

"That's too bad." Mingolla flipped open the book and looked at Pastorin's signature, a complex conceit of loops and flourishes.

"David?"

Mingolla slammed the book shut. "I thought I was falling in love with her." Then, sarcastically: "That probably had something to do with the intensity of our mutual focus."

"I wonder," said Izaguirre, his tone distant, abstracted.

Mingolla went over to a window. The jungly growth of the grounds stirred sluggishly beneath dark running clouds. "What 'bout the shit I was doing to those people last night?"

"What you called a 'pattern'?"

"Yeah."

"A paranoid mechanism." Izaguirre gave a delicate cough. "You simply struck at the woman, stunned her. It's a common enough first reaction. You already have quite a good grasp of how your talent operates. The shaping of emotion into a weapon and such. All you need is practice."

"Jesus," said Mingolla. "The shit with the pattern sounds like . . ."

"What?"

"I don't know . . . like something a wasp might do. Insect behavior."

"You're not concerned about your humanity?"

"Wouldn't you be?"

"I'd be delighted to learn my potentials transcended the human."

"Then why don't you take the fucking drugs?"

"I have . . . not intravenously. I've ingested them in their natural state. But I have no talent. I only wish I did."

"I thought the stuff was synthetic."

"No, it's a weed."

"Huh." Mingolla traced a design in the dust on the windowpane, saw that he had drawn a D, and wiped it out. "I want that assignment."

"The Cifuentes woman?"

114

"Right."

"I can't promise anything. You've still got six or eight weeks here ahead of you. But if she's still at large . . . perhaps." Izaguirre took him by the arm. "Get some sleep, David. You'll need it for tomorrow. I'll be starting RNA to bring your Spanish up to snuff, and Tully can hardly wait to put you through your paces."

Despite his anxieties, his alienation, Mingolla felt calmer. It struck him as odd that he should be soothed by Izaguirre's bedside manner, because at a remove, everything about the doctor grated on him.

"Oh, don't forget your book." Izaguirre retrieved the Pastorín book from the reception desk and handed it to him. "It's very, very good," he said.

The first story in *The Fictive Boarding House* told of two families who had feuded over the possession of a magic flower. Mingolla lost interest in it halfway through, finding it too mannered and concluding that all the members of the families were complete assholes. The title story, however, enthralled him. It detailed a strange contract made between an author and the residents of a boarding house in a Latin American slum. The author offered to educate the residents' children, to guarantee them lives of comfort, if in return the residents would spend their remaining days living out a story written by the author, one he would add to year by year, incorporating those events over which he had no control. Being in desperate straits, the residents accepted the offer, and though at times they balked and tried to break the contract, gradually their individual wishes and hopes were overwhelmed, subsumed into the themes employed by the story. Their lives had taken on almost mythic significance as a result, their deaths proving to be passionate epiphanies. Only the author, whose health had been ruined by the expenditure of energy necessary to script their lives, who had conceived of the project as a whimsy yet had realized it as a work of transcendent charity, only he had endured an ordinary life and ignominious extinction.

Sleepy, Mingolla closed the book, turned off his bedside

lamp, and settled back. Moonlight streamed in the window, bathing the walls in a bluish white glow, bringing up stark shadows beneath his writing desk and chair. Tacked to the walls were a number of sketches he had done during the months of drug therapy. They were unlike anything he had done before, all depicting immense baroque chambers of stone, with bridges arching from blank walls, ornate staircases leading nowhere, vaulted ceilings opening onto strange perspectives of still more outrageous architecture, and thronging the horizontal planes, hordes of ant-sized men, smudgy dots almost lost among the pencil shadings and lines. It made him uncomfortable to look at them now, not because of their alienness, but because he recognized the psychology underlying them to be his own, and he wasn't certain whether that psychology had been laid bare by the drugs or was the product of a transformation.

His eyelids drooped, and he thought of Debora, both with anger and with longing. Despite Izaguirre's revelations, his obsession had survived intact, and whenever he tried to apply the logic of recrimination, the fact of her betrayal was swept away by fantasy or by his insistence in believing that she must have had some real feeling for him. And so it was not at all surprising that he dreamed of her that night, a dream unusual for its lucidity. She was floating in a white void, clad in a gown of such whiteness that he could not see its drape or fold: she might have been a disembodied head and arms superimposed on a white backdrop. She was revolving slowly, tipping toward him, then away, allowing him to view her at every angle and each angle providing him with insights into her character, seeming to illustrate her resilience, her toughness, her capacity for devotion. There was no music in the dream, but her movements were so graceful, he had the notion they were being governed by an inaudible music that pervaded the void, perhaps a distillate of music that manifested as a white current. She drifted closer, and soon was near enough that—if the dream had been real—he could have touched her. She drifted closer yet, her limbs aligning with the position of his arms and legs, and in her pupils he saw tiny facsimiles of himself floating in whiteness. A keening noise switched on inside his head, and his desire for her also switched on; he wanted to shake off the bonds of the dream and pull her against him. Her lips were parted, eyes heavy-lidded, as if she, too, were experiencing desire. And then she drifted impossibly close, merging with him. He went rigid, terrified by a feeling of being possessed. She was inside him, shrinking, becoming as small as a thought, a dusky thought in a white dress wandering the corridors of . . .

He sat bolt upright in bed, sweating, breathing hard, and for a split second, confused by the moonstruck walls, he believed he had awakened in the white place of his dreams. Even after he recognized his surroundings, he couldn't escape the thought that she was in the room with him. The geometries of moonlight and shadow appeared to be describing the presence of an invisible form. He was alert to every creak, every quiver of shadow, every sigh of wind. "Debora?" he whispered, and when he received no answer he lay back on the bed, tense and trembling.

"Goddamn you!" he said.

CHAPTER SEVEN

Roatán was no tropical paradise. Though the barrier reef
was lovely and had once nourished more than a dozen resorts,
the interior consisted of low scrub-thatched hills, and much of
the coast was given over to mangrove. A dirt road ran partway
around the island, connecting the shantytowns of Coxxen Hole,
French Harbor, and West End, and a second road crossed from
Coxxen Hole to Sandy Bay on the north coast, where the hotel
was located: a curving stretch of beach that one moment could
seem beautiful and the next abysmally ugly. That, Mingolla
realized, was the charm of the place, that you could be walking
along on a beach of filthy yellow-brown sand, stepping carefully to avoid pig and cattle droppings, and then, as if a different filter had slid in front of the sun, you suddenly noticed the
hummingbirds flitting above the sea grape, the hammocks of
coco palms, the reef water glowing in bands of jade and turquoise and aquamarine, according to the varying depth and
bottom. Sprinkled among the palms were several dozen shanties set on pilings, their tin roofs scabbed with rust; jetties with
gap-boarded outhouses erected on their seaward ends extended
out over the shallows, looking at a distance to have the artful
crudity of charcoal sketches by Picasso.

It was along this beach that Mingolla learned control of his
power through daily lessons with Tully. The lessons were—as
Izaguirre had suggested—merely the practice of those things of

which he had become aware that first night in the shed, serving to augment his strength and the capacity to know the shape of his emotions; yet he believed he was learning another sort of lesson as well, a lesson in personal competence, in the shouldering of power, the acceptance of its virtues and the practical denial of its liabilities. Though Tully still unnerved him, he saw that his trainer's arrogance and forceful approach to life were qualities essential to the wielding of power; and though he continued to dream of Debora, to think of her in terms of longing, he came to view these dreams and thoughts in a grim light, to perceive her as a target.

One morning he and Tully sat floating in a dory just inside the reef. The tide was low, and iron-black coral heads lifted from the water like the parapets of a drowned castle, its crannies populated by whelks and urchins. Beyond the reef, the sea was banded in sun-spattered streaks of slate and lavender, and there were so many small waves, the water appeared to be moving in all directions at once. "I hate the goddamn sea," said Tully, and spat over the side. He leaned back in the stern, jammed a grease-stained baseball cap lower onto his ears; his skin was agleam with bluish highlights under the sun.

"Thought you used to be a fisherman," said Mingolla.

"Best on de island, mon. But dat don't mean I got to like de sea. Ain't not'in' but a motherfuckin' graveyard! Once dat come home to me, I never set foot 'pon her again. Look dere!" He pointed to another dory passing close to the shore, maybe fifty yards off. "Call de mon over, Davy."

Mingolla tried to engage the man's mind, but failed. "Can't reach him."

"Keep tryin' till you catch a hold." Tully propped his feet beside an oarlock, and the dory rocked. "Nosir! Once I seen de way of t'ings, I left de sea for good'n all."

"How come?"

The man in the dory shouted, waving at the shanties tucked among the palms. "Got silkfish, satinfish! Got reef snapper and blues!"

"How come?" Tully snorted. " 'Cause I were sixteen days stranded on dat graveyard sea. Dat were on de *Liberty Bell*, nice little craft. Tested hull, V-8. Had us some nice fish, too. 'Leven sacks kingfish, coupla sacks grouper.'' He shook his head sadly. "Sixteen days! And each one a longer day dan I have ever knowed. Drinkin' fish blood, watchin' men die crazy.''

The dory had come within twenty yards, and Mingolla made contact with its pilot, projecting amiability and curiosity into his mind. "Got him,'' he said as the man stopped rowing, shielded his eyes against the sun, and peered toward them.

"Not bad,'' said Tully. "Don't reckon I can do much better.''

Mingolla conveyed a sense of urgency to the man in the dory, wanting him to row faster.

"Sixteen days,'' said Tully. "And by de time dat shrimper fetch us in tow, wasn't but four of us left. The rest dey sun-killed or gone over de side.''

The man in the dory was bent over his oars, pulling hard.

"Towed us clear to Bragman Key,'' Tully went on. "Dat were an upful place, Bragman. Dey lodged us in a hotel and treat our fevers. Give us fresh fruit, rum. And dere were dis little gal who gimme special comfort. 'Pears she just couldn't stand to see me de way I was. We had us a time 'fore I left, me and dat gal. And I tell her I's comin' back for her, but I never did . . . I never did.'' Tully spat again. "I 'tended to, but when I get back to de island, everybody's makin' me out a hero, and I'm tellin' my story, drinkin'. I just loose track of dat gal. I 'grets it sometimes, but it probably for de best.''

The man shipped his oars, let his dory drift near, and caught hold of the stern. "How you be, Tully?'' he said. He was a wiry brown man in his thirties, with glittering black eyes, the skin around them seamed and puckered. His genitals protruded from one leg of his shorts, and sweat matted the curly hairs on his chest.

"Survivin','' Tully said. "Davy, dis my half-brother, Donald Ebanks.''

Mingolla exchanged nods with the man.

"What you catchin', mon?'' asked Tully.

Donald lifted the corner of a canvas, revealing a couple of dozen fish in the bottom of the dory, some turquoise, some red, some striped yellow and black, shining like a salad of oddly shaped jewels around the centerpiece of a long fish with black sides, a white belly, and needle teeth: a barracuda.

"How much for dat barra?"

Mingolla started to exert influence on Donald, trying for a free fish; but Tully kicked his ankle and said, "No, mon! Dat not how it goes."

"Why not?" said Mingolla.

"Take what you need, and give back what you can. Dat's de only way to be in dis world."

Tully's stare quailed Mingolla, and he looked down at Donald's fish, their gemmy sides pulsing with last breaths.

"I 'spect I take four lemps for de barra," said Donald.

"I 'spect so," said Tully with a laugh. " 'Spect you'd take more'n dat, and you find a big 'nough fool." He dug some wadded bills from his pocket. "Two lemps, mon. And don't be rude wit' me. Dat's a fat price, and you know it."

"You a bitch, Tully." Donald picked up the barracuda, heaved it into their dory. "Strip de shadow from my back, I give you de chance."

"Don't want your damn shadow, and if I did, I sure as hell not goin' to pay you two lemps for it." Tully handed over the money.

Donald regarded the bills dolefully, pocketed them, and without another word he rowed off toward shore.

"Sorry," Mingolla said. "Guess I shoulda figured him being your brother. . . ."

"Half-brother!" Tully snapped. "And dat don't have a t'ing to do wit' it. Son of a bitch ain't no friend of mine. Been tryin' to swindle me goin' on dese ten years. What I told you, dat's true for de world."

Mingolla studied the barracuda's doll eyes. "Didn't know you could eat barracuda."

"Can't all de time. You got to drop a crumb of de flesh on an anthill. If de ants take it, you can eat your fill. Fries up nice wit' plantain."

A northerly breeze sprang up, heavying the chop, stirring the palms along the shore, and the dory bobbed up and down.

"Don't take it to heart, Davy," said Tully. "You learnin'. Just take more time to be wise dan to be strong."

Misty night, the moon a foggy green streak between the palm fronds, and the surf muffled, sounding like bones being crunched in the mouth of a beast. Light spilled from the windows of a small frame church set back from the shore, and sweet African harmony spilled from it, too, resolving into a final Amen. Young boys in white shirts, blue trousers, and girls in frilly white dresses came down the steps, passing within thirty feet of the log where Tully and Mingolla were sitting, their voices liquid and clear; they turned on flashlights as they moved off into the dark, playing the beams onto the shallows, lacquering the black water.

"Dere," said Tully, indicating two teenage girls holding hymnals to their breasts. "De one on de left. But don't mess wit' de other . . . that my cousin 'Lizabeth."

"She's not tryin' to swindle you?" said Mingolla.

Tully grinned. "Don't be mouthin' me. Naw, dat 'Lizabeth's goin' to stay sweet 'long as I can help it. But dat Nancy Rivers, she been wit' half de island. You go on'n go crazy wit' her if you want."

Mingolla checked Nancy out: flat-chested, light-skinned, with a lean horsey face. He was not inspired to craziness, but nevertheless he touched her mind with desire. She glanced at him, whispered to Elizabeth, and after a second they walked over to the log.

"How de night, Tully?" Elizabeth asked.

"It's goin' all right," said Tully. "And you?"

"Not'in special, y'know." Elizabeth was sexy, tall, and had Tully's coal-black skin; her heavy-lidded eyes and pouting mouth and broad nose reminded Mingolla of statuettes he'd seen in displays of African folk art. Nancy elbowed her, and she performed the introduction.

Mingolla grunted, gouged a trench in the sand with his toe.

"Well," said Elizabeth after an uncomfortable silence. "Guess we'll be marchin'. You come see us, Tully."

"Dat I will."

The two girls ambled off, whispering, and Mingolla watched the roll of Elizabeth's hips. Tully shoved him, knocking him off the log. "What's wrong wit' you, mon? T'ought you was after some squint?"

"Not her, man . . . she's ugly."

"Shit! You got eyes 'tween your legs? C'mon!" Tully hauled Mingolla to his feet. "We goin' to de Hole. Dey got bitches dere will tie a knot in it for you!"

They returned to the hotel, where Tully changed into slacks and a rayon shirt with the silk-screened photo of a blonde in a bikini on the back. He broke out a bottle of rum, and they drank from it as they hurtled over the bumpy hill road in the hotel's Land Rover, swerving around tight corners, driving blind through patches of mist, past thatched farmhouses and banana plots, once nearly hitting a cow whose horns were silhouetted against the lesser blackness of the sky and faint stars. They seemed to be pulling the night along with them, to have the kind of delirious momentum that Mingolla associated with free-way flying, with speeding into nowhere, an angel in the backseat, a fortune in your veins, following the white lines to some zero point behind the horizon, the end of a black rainbow where the wrecked cars were piled to heaven and smiling corpses leaked golden blood. Tully sang reggae in a hoarse raucous voice, and Mingolla, not knowing the words, pounded a drumbeat on the dash. Then he sang a Prowler song: "Got see-thru windows, hyperventilation in my ride, and little Miss Behavior in a coma by my side . . ."

"What kinda hollerin' dat?" said Tully. "Dat ain't no damn song!"

And Mingolla laughed, knowing it was going to be a good time.

In Coxxen Hole, the yellow dirt streets were ablaze with glare from weathered shanties that perched on their pilings like ancient hens straining at empty nests, their slatboard shutters wobbling one-hinged, plastic curtains belling, rusted tin roofs curled at the edges. On the main street stood a two-story frame hotel, Hotel Coral, painted pink, with a light pole lashed to its second-floor balcony, and a cinderblock office building patrolled by Indian soldiers in camouflage fatigues. Between the offices and the hotel, a concrete pier extended out into the blackness of the sea; two stubby turtling boats with furled sails were moored at its extremity. Heat lightning flashed orange above the Honduran coast thirty miles away. Music blared from the shanty bars; fat women in print dresses and turbans to match waddled in stately pairs, staring down the black men—most as skinny as stick figures—who accosted them. Dogs skulked among the pilings, nosing at crab shells and broken bottles.

There was so much activity that Mingolla—accustomed to the peace of the hotel—became flustered and in order to escape the confusion went with the first prostitute who happened along. She led him into the back room of a large shanty whose sole designation as a bar was a hand-lettered sign nailed above the entrance that said FRENLY CLUB—NO RIOT. She stripped off all her clothes except her brassiere and lay down on a straw mattress that crackled like flames beneath her and held out her arms. She was mud colored, fat in the hips and thighs, with a face that might once have been pretty but had gone matronly and dull with—Mingolla thought—lack of expectation. For some reason her hopelessness aroused him. He tried to take off her bra, but she pushed his hands away. He squeezed her breasts, and she closed her eyes, enduring the pressure. He envisioned cancers or scars hidden by the brassiere, and he did not insist on her removing it. He fucked her quickly and hard, imagining that the drunken shouts from the bar were cheering him on. Her movements were mechanical, uninspired, and after he had rolled off, she wasted no time in pulling on her dress and sat on the mattress, lacing her tennis shoes. They hadn't exchanged a word since he had asked her price. He resented her indifference, and although he hadn't touched her mind during the act, now he made her sleepy. She yawned, passed a hand across her eyes.

"Little tired?" he said. "Why don't you get some rest?"

She pinched the bridge of her nose. "Can't," she said. "De room ain't paid for."

"I'll pay for it," he said. "Go to sleep."

"Why you do dat, mon?"

"I'll come back later and see you." He said this with menace, but she was too groggy to notice. She yawned again and flopped on the mattress. "Sleep tight," he said, and slammed the door behind him.

He paid the barman for the room, for a bottle of rum, and sat at a corner table, waiting for Tully, blinking against the light from an unshaded ceiling fixture. Red and black posters advertising local bands were taped to the board walls; a record player on the counter—unfinished planks laid over packing crates—ground out warped reggae tunes, their lyrics lost in the uproar. A black man was slumped face down across the table next to Mingolla's, and crowding the rest of the tables were thirty or so black men who looked on their way to joining him; they were waving dog-eared aces and queens, shaking their fists, shouting. Their eyes rolled, they spilled drinks on their shirts and jetted smoke from their nostrils. Scuffles broke out, were put down, and new scuffles broke out between the peace-makers. Mingolla slugged back shot after shot, trying for a level of drunkenness to suit the environment. But the noise became more and more aggravating. And it wasn't only the noise that bothered him, it wasn't merely a hangover of bad temper from the prostitute. His anger seemed funded by a less identifiable yet more poignant offense, and he wanted quiet in which to figure out what it could be. To that end he began to orchestrate calm, muting rages, soothing ruffled sensibilities, conjuring smiles in the place of frowns. Before long, the bar was a scene of hushed conversations and polite debates over misplays.

"I know de trey of clubs were played, Byrum," said a man nearby. "I 'member it were right 'fore Spurgeon lay de black queen." And Byrum, a grizzled old man in a captain's hat from which most of the braid had been worn, said maybe so, but he just couldn't recollect how the trey had sneaked into his hand.

Mingolla was delighted by the ease with which he had accomplished this, but was dissatisfied with the aesthetic result. What was needed, he thought, was not a sedate bridge-club atmosphere, but a diminution of the previous riot, a formal statement of its potential. He set the men at one table to laughing, those at another to weeping; then he sipped his rum, studying the effect and considering further changes. He kindled a shouting match between Byrum and another old man with a tobacco-stained prophet's beard, provoked them to point fingers and throw ineffectual punches over the shoulders of the men keeping them apart. The needle of the record player stuck, and Mingolla convinced the barman that everything was fine, left him smiling, nodding his head in time to the repeated scratchy phrase. By the time he had completed these adjustments, Mingolla's anger had faded. He sat contentedly, effecting decorative touches, modulating glee and despair, until the bar had acquired a theatrical atmosphere, that of a play set in the dayroom of an asylum, with the lunatics compartmentalized in different sections of the room according to the degree and character of their maladies.

"Goddammit!"

Tully came weaving his way among the tables toward Mingolla, scowling; he rested his fists on the back of a chair and said, "Mon, you crazy! You straighten dis out right now!" His fly was at half-mast, his shirt hung open, and he was having difficulty in focusing.

"I like it like this," said Mingolla.

An instant later he had an urge to comply with Tully, with his good friend and mentor, a man who had always been the caretaker of his best interests. He felt shame at having let him down. But recognizing the sudden onset of these feelings and the vagueness accompanying them to be symptomatic of Tully's influence, he shaped a wrecking ball of an emotion, of fear and insecurity, and launched it at Tully. Saw him wobble, catch the table for support. Tully fought back, and for a moment Mingolla could sense a border between them, a meeting ground of two streams of heat and electricity; but then that border crumbled, and Tully pulled back, slumped into the chair. Mingolla, too, pulled back. Had a sip of rum, smiled at Tully, who was rubbing his forehead with the heel of his hand.

"Straighten dis out," he said.

"Why should I?"

"Ain't everybody on de island your friend, mon? T'ink dere ain't spies 'round, t'ink dey ain't watchin' for signs?"

Mingolla parodied his accent. "Den better you get to straightenin', mon, 'cause I weary."

Tully glowered, then lowered his eyes, scraping at the label on the rum bottle with his thumbnail. All around them the bar began to regain its previous level of noise and discord. Card games back in full swing, record player fixed, voices raised in complaint. A tide of normalcy covering up Mingolla's folly. His pleasure at having defeated Tully ebbed. Tully's superiority had been a buffer, an assurance of protection; now that he was top gun, he felt leery and at risk.

"What de hell's crawled up your asshole, mon?" said Tully, leaning close. "And don't gimme no bullshit answer! Dis ain't your teacher axin' why you cut class, dis serious business."

"I don't know," said Mingolla sullenly.

"Damn, you better start knowin', Davy. You goin' to be meat on somebody's table, and you keep up dis messin' . . . understand?"

"Yeah, I guess."

"All dis crap have soured my stomach!" Tully shifted his chair, looking glum; he cocked an eye toward Mingolla. "You never take me if I been sober."

"Probably." Mingolla nudged the rum bottle toward him. "Have a drink."

Tully took a swig, wiped his mouth. "Probably! Ain't no probably 'bout it, mon!" He had another swig, sighed. "Better be headin' home soon."

"I wanna stay," said Mingolla. "All right?"

Tully chewed on the thought.

"I won't fuck up again."

"Can I trust dat?"

"Far as I know."

"Far as you know . . . huh!" Tully peeled away the rum label, wadded it. "Well, I got a little somethin' waitin' down de street, so I don't mind. What you goin' to do?"

"I got somethin' goin' here."

"Somethin' in de back room?"

127

"Uh-huh."

"What I tell you 'bout dese island girls? Dey work out de kinks or don't dey?"

"They're okay," said Mingolla.

"Aw, hell!" Tully levered up from the table. "You have your fun, mon. But just 'member . . . start messin' again, and it goin' to be your bones dat gets gnawed on, not mine."

Mingolla had intended to return to the prostitute with a vengeance, to make her crazy in sex and learn the awful secrets of her breasts; but his need for vengeful action had passed. She was still asleep. Curled up on the mattress, dress bunched around her thighs, a chubby, unlovely woman cornered by poverty and inanition: the grain of the silvery gray floorboards seemed a script spelling out her sad story. The bed was the only piece of furniture in the room, and not wanting to disturb her, Mingolla sat on the floor, listening to the shouts from the bar gradually subside into muffled chatter. It began to rain, a heavy downpour that drummed so loudly on the tin roof, he thought it would wake the prostitute. But she slept on under his spell, and the rhythms of the rain soon made him drowsy. His thoughts came and went one at a time, without logical attachments or chains of causation, like hawks circling an empty sky. Thoughts of Debora, of his power, of Tully and Izaguirre, of home and war. And from their isolation, their profound disunity, he concluded that a mind was not something grown or evolved, but was a mosaic, a jackdaw's nest of baubles and bits of glass between which lightning flickered now and again, connecting and establishing the whole for fractions of seconds, creating the illusion of a man, of a man's rational and emotional convictions. Years before, months before, he might have denied this conception, put forward a romantic conception in its stead. But the constituency of his mind, his jackdaw's nest, had changed, with war and prostitutes replacing home-cooking and girlfriends, and though a younger Mingolla would have rejected the bleakness of this self-knowledge, the current one found in it a source of strength, a justification for conscienceless action, for contempt of sentiment. Yet even this cold and contemplative stance was wedded to sentiment. He would have liked to curl up with the prostitute, to hold her. She was a fit consort for someone of his disposition. She would smell of clay and rain. His arms would gouge her malleable flesh, sink into her, merging with her substance, and they would dissolve in the rain, a brown fluid running out between the boards, puddling beneath the shanty, soaking into the earth and serving to hasten the hatching of insect and lizard eggs, sending forth a horde of mindless things to take their place.

He waked with a pale dawn light leaking through gaps in the shutter and went out into the bar. His head ached, his mouth felt dirty. He plucked a half-full beer from the counter and walked down the shanty stairs into the street. The sky was milky white, but the puddles of rainwater were a shade more gray, as if they held a soured residue; the slant of the roofpeaks looked askew and witchy. A dog slunk away from Mingolla as he headed for the center of town; crabs scuttled beneath an overturned dory, and a black man was passed out beneath one of the shanties, dried blood streaking his chest. Sleeping on a stone bench beside the pink hotel was an old man with a rifle in his lap. It seemed the tide of events had withdrawn, leaving the bottom dwellers exposed.

He walked down to the landward end of the concrete pier. The turtling boats had sailed, and the sky above the mainland had cleared to a pale aqua. He could see a chain of low smoky hills on the horizon. He had a swallow of warm beer, gagged, and spat it out; he tossed the bottle into the harbor, watched it float among oil slick and streamers of kelp, drifting back to clink against the barnacled concrete. Heaps of sudsy gray foam lifted on the swells, and just beneath the surface something stick-thin and opaque blew from its tubular mouth what looked to be a little ectoplasmic fog. The scents of brine and sweet rot on the offshore wind. Mingolla decided he felt pretty good, considering.

"See you made it, Davy!" Tully came up beside him. His eyes were bloodshot, and a chalky pallor suffused his skin.

"Rough night?" Mingolla asked.

"Dey all rough, you get my age. But I usually can find

129

some bitch be kindly to an ol' man." Tully flung a hand out toward the coast. "You checkin' out de Iron Barrio, huh?"

"What you mean?"

Tully pointed to the low-lying hills. "Dat dere's smoke from de Barrio. Breakfast fires, and maybe burnin' bodies. Dey like to hang de bodies on de roof and set dem afire."

"Oh," said Mingolla.

"Yeah, dey makes a big stink over dere every mornin'."

Mingolla squatted, tried to make out the definition of the smoke. Now that he knew what it was, it appeared to be wavering, betraying flashes of red, redolent of demonic activity. "This man I'm supposed to kill . . ."

"What 'bout him?"

"Who is he?"

"Some Nicaraguan name of de Zedeguí. Opolonio de Zedeguí. He one of Sombra's top agents, used to be a professor or somethin' 'fore de therapy." Tully hawked and spat. "Mon crazy to go try and hide heself in a prison."

"Why's he hidin' out?"

"Deserted, I 'spect. But de mon bound to be crazy, and he t'ink de Barrio goin' to keep him safe."

Mingolla gazed at the smoke, wondering what lay beneath it.

"You worried, Davy?"

"Some . . . but not as much as I thought I'd be."

"Dat's a good balance. You keep dat frame of mind, you be all right. Just don't be worryin' too much. Time you hit de Barrio, you goin' to be a dangerous mon." Tully grunted. "Hell, you a dangerous mon already."

Between lessons, Mingolla spent the hours reading and prowling the beach; occasionally Hetti or another of the derelicts would tag along, but he had grown tired of their attentions and worked to discourage this. Twice he ran into Tully's cousin Elizabeth on the beach, and once she shared her lunch with him, showing him how to eat cashew fruit by thumbing out the black seeds and sprinkling the sour pulp with salt. She seemed to like him, and he toyed with the idea of starting something

130

with her, but was reluctant to go against Tully. Weeks went by, and he grew bored and restless, now feeling as confined by the island as he had been by the wall around the hotel. His sleep was troubled by dreams of Debora, and whenever these dreams would wake him, he would put himself back to sleep by imagining scenarios of sexual vengeance.

One afternoon a couple of weeks before he was scheduled to leave for La Ceiba, Izaguirre gave him a final booster injection of the drug. The shot left him achy and nervous, the inside of his head tender-feeling; and that night, unable to sleep, plagued by flash hallucinations of unfamiliar streets and people's faces that melted away too quickly for him to identify, he wandered through the hotel, ending up in Izaguirre's office, which was never kept locked. It was a small room just off the lobby, outfitted with a desk, two chairs, a bookcase, and a filing cabinet. Mingolla sat in the doctor's chair and went through the files, too distracted to understand much of what he was reading, ignoring the typed material—the letters seemed to be scurrying around like ants—and concentrating on the marginalia penned in Izaguirre's florid script. He continued to have hallucinations, and when he ran across a note describing Izaguirre's concern that he might have given Mingolla too large a dosage in the booster shot, the hallucinations grew more vivid. He saw part of a mural on a pebbled wall, a woman's brown arm hanging off the edge of a mattress, rendered with a fey sensuality that put him in mind of Degas, and accompanying it, oppressive heat and the smell of dust and decay. This hallucination had the compelling clarity of a premonition, yet was so much more detailed than his usual premonitions that he became frightened. He stood up, felt queasy, dizzy, and shook his head. The walls darkened, whirled, brightened again, and he closed his eyes, trying to quell his nausea. Put his hand on the desk, and touched warm skin. Opened his eyes, saw a bag lady staring up at him from a curb, her fat cheeks webbed with broken capillaries, her nose bulbous, a scarf knotted so tightly under her chin, it warped her ruddy face into a knobbly vegetable shape.

"This ain't America," she said dolefully. "America wouldn't treat nobody like this."

Mingolla staggered, had an incoherent impression of orange sky, a night sky above a city, diseased-looking palm trees with brown fronds and scales on their trunks, and rain-slick asphalt reflecting nebular blurs of neon, and bars with glowing words above them. Sinewy music whose rhythms seemed to be charting the fluctuations of his nerves. Somebody bumped into him, said, "Whoops," an oily fat man with a moon face, sticking out his pink meat of a tongue on which a cobra had been tattooed, then smiling and mincing off to a world where he was beautiful.

"See what I tol' ya," said the bag lady.

Gaudily dressed crowds shuffling in and out of the low glass-front buildings, a history of the American perverse . . . Hookers in day-glo hotpants, leather boys, floozies in slit skirts, topless teenage girls with ANGEL stamped on their left breasts, and all the faces pale in the baking heat, characters in a strange language, circular dominoes with significant arrangements of dark eyes and mouths, borne along on the necks of fleshy machines, one thought per brain like a prize in a plastic egg, doing a slow drag down the devil's row of bars and sex shops and arcades, under the numinous clouded light, under the smears of red and yellow words melting into the air, their voices a gabble, their laughter a bad noise, the rotten yolk of their senses streaking the night, and Mingolla knew the bag lady was wrong, that this was most definitely America, the void with tourist attractions, the Southern California bottomland experience, and somewhere or everywhere, maybe lurking behind a billboard, was a giant red-skinned flabby pig of a Satan, his gut hanging over his tights, horny and giggling, watching through a peephole the great undressing of his favorite bitch, the Idea of Order. . . .

The bag lady shook her head in despair. "We need a new Columbus, that's what we need."

"Help out a vet," said a voice behind him, and Mingolla spun around to confront a weasly crewcut man on crutches, one-legged, wearing fatigues with a First Infantry Nicaragua patch, holding out a hand. In the darks of his eyes Mingolla saw the secrets of combat, the mysterious truths of shock.

"Hey," said the vet. "Hey! I know you, man! 'Member

132

me? The valley, man, the valley near Santander Jiménez.'' He hobbled a step forward, peering at Mingolla's face. "Yeah, it's you, man. You looked different . . . your hair was different or something. But yeah, I . . .''

"Un-uh.'' Mingolla backed away, feeling unbelievably tall, worried that he might scrape his head on the orange sky, get wet with that polluted color. "You got the wrong guy.''

"The fuck I do! You was there when I was hit, man. 'Member? The game with the beaner . . . y'gotta 'member the game!''

Mingolla stepped into the crowd, was carried away by their slow crush. He couldn't remember the man, but then he couldn't remember much of anything, and he was afraid some- one else might recognize him, someone with an ax to grind.

"You're a vet, huh?'' A woman, a beautiful, pale, black- haired woman with carmine lips and high cheekbones, enor- mous eyes, and the voluptuous body used to mold pornographic beer glasses displayed beneath a full-length gown fabricated of tiny black-lace serpents and filmy mesh, a woman with silkburns on her hips and probably a really keen tattoo . . . she took his arm and pressed close. "I'm Sexula,'' she said. "And I'm free to vets.''

That started him laughing, thinking about the GI Bill and benefits.

"Hey, fuck you, Jim!'' She pushed him away. "I'm just tryin' to be real, y'know. You some kinda faggot, get your ass over to The Boy's Room!''

"Faggot?'' Hilarity was peaking in him, graphing Himala- yas of unvoiced laughter. "Want me to show you my dingus, prove my point? Want me to unholster my—''

"I don't have to listen this shit! Maybe the other rides like it, man, but not me. I . . .''

"What you mean 'rides'?'' The unfamiliar term brought him down to earth, reminded him that he was lost, that he'd lost . . . who the hell was it? The crowd moved them up against a window.

"Rides, man!'' she said. "Like, y'know, this''—her gesture took in the street—"this here's the carnival, and I'm one of the

133

rides." She caught up his hand. "You okay, man? You lookin' pretty scorched."

Laughter was mounting inside him again. He took in the woman's body, incredible breasts, wild cherry nipples peeking from the twinings of black lace coils. Nice girl, he thought. A foreign student, no doubt. Working her way through junior college.

"What's in ya, man? Little too much frost?"

He remembered some more. "I'm looking for somebody . . . somebody's looking for me."

"You found her," she said. "C'mon, let's go see 'bout a room."

He could use some rest, a place to get his thoughts together. Out from under the orange sky. But he didn't trust her. He primed her for honesty, openness. "Why me?"

"Like I said, man, you're a vet . . . the town pays me for vets." She led him around the corner, through glass doors, along a carpet mapped with stains shaped like dark continents amid a burgundy sea, and into a narrow mirrored lobby at whose far end, hunched behind the reception desk, sat a gnomish old man with a beaked nose and tufts of white hair on the sides of his head reminiscent of goblin ears, and upon whose forehead the engraved word *finality* would not have been inappropriate. "Twenny for the room ya need drinks that's more," he said without punctuation, without looking up, and Sexula said, "He's a vet, Ludy."

Ludy squinted at Mingolla, who could feel cracks spreading across his skin from the power of that blood-webbed blue eye. "Ya gotcha card?" he asked.

"Uh . . . I was mugged," said Mingolla.

"Ain't gotcha card gotta pay the twenny." Ludy turned the page of a magazine, and peeping over the edge of the desk, Mingolla saw photographs of naked young boys in sexy yet playful couplings.

"Didn'tcha hear him." Sexula spanked the counter with her hand, calling Ludy back from gambols with pals named Jimmy and Butch and Sonny. "Man says he got mugged."

Ludy scowled, an expression that caused his eyes nearly to

vanish into folds of inflamed pink flesh, and said to her, "You wanna pay the twenny pay the twenny." He punctuated. "Don't wanna pay get the fuck out."

A tap on Mingolla's shoulder, followed by a girlish, "Excuse me."

Behind him stood a thin mousey girl of nineteen or twenty, whom Mingolla perceived to be at the peak of her good looks, poised between the incline of plainness and the decline of just plain ugly. Wearing jeans and a T-shirt bearing a rendering of the Last Supper and the legend THIS IS MY BODY, GIVEN FOR YOU. Toting a shopping bag. Her brown hair lusterless, her breasts with the conformation of upturned saucers.

"The gift of love can be a transcendent experience, but not if paid for," she said, her words sounding rote. "I want to give to you, brother."

"Get outta here," said Sexula.

The girl ignored her. "I am qualified to give you everything she might, and I can give you—"

"Give him a goddamn fatal disease, what with all the sleaze been poppin' you." Sexula took a little walk around the girl, shaking her head in exaggerated disgust.

"I can give you much more," the girl continued, swallowing back embarrassment. "Through the act of love, I can give you communion with our Lord and Master Jesus Christ, in . . ."

"These cunts come 'round sayin' that 'cause they're doin' it for God, it's pure," said Sexula. "But the truth is, they can't get laid 'less they give it away. They ain't nothin' but hips and a hole!"

Ludy laughed, a sound like something large and pulpy falling into an empty paper bag.

The girl's face worked. "Jesus Christ, in whose service I've . . ."

Sexula sneered. "Jesus got nothin' to do with it!"

That waxed it for the girl. "I don't care what you say about me, but you . . . you . . ." She hefted her shopping bag behind her back as if preparing to use it on Sexula. "What would you know 'bout Jesus? He's never laid his hands on you!"

"Man lays his hands on me," said Sexula with a wink to

Ludy, "and I give him that ol' time religion with a brand new twist."

"Please, don't go with her!" The girl's hands fluttered at Mingolla's chest. "The things I've seen the Lord do, the things that were done . . . the miracles! Miracles from ashes!"

Her speech grew more and more disconnected, her manner more pitiable, and Mingolla, suddenly concerned for her, touched her mind and listened to the static of her thought, a crackle of half-formed images and memories. . . .

. . . the filthiest thing, that's what I'll do, I'll do it no matter what, and it won't be like the basement, the light through cobwebs, it won't, through cobwebs on the cracked pane, gray like his heart, withered like his heart, and the pain right through me, bright, it had a color and bright, and I'll do it, I'll let him do it again, the pain so bright that God will notice, God will forgive, but not in the basement, not in the . . .

. . . what basement, what pain . . .

. . . is it you . . .

. . . what basement, what pain . . .

. . . it's you, it really is, oh God, thank you, yes . . .

. . . what basement, what pain . . .

. . . the basement, yes, in the homeless shelter, and I was asleep in the basement, warm, it was warm with the furnace, the heat from the furnace, and I woke up and he was on me, almost in me, and not the right place, the place no one should see, and it hurt so much . . .

. . . who . . .

. . . one of the old ones, so many old ones, and I couldn't see his face, just his hands on my shoulders, his yellow hands with one nail bruised, purple and black, like a claw, hooks in my shoulder forcing me down, my face in the dust, my tongue when I screamed tasting the dust, the ashes, and the furnace roaring, no one could hear me, except I could, I could hear my voice in the flames of the furnace, a voice singing in the flames, even with the pain it was singing, joyful, because there was so much to feel, and I wanted . . . is it you, really you, really . . .

. . . what did you want . . .

. . . the dust, to taste the dust again, but I couldn't he was pulling my hair, pulling back my head, bending me, breaking me, he said he'd kill me if I told, but I didn't want to tell, didn't want anyone to know, I wanted the dust in my mouth . . .

. . . why . . .

. . . to swallow back the pain, like cats when they're sick they swallow back the sickness, and they're better, they just don't let it lie there on the floor, they take it back inside and make it part of themselves, and when he'd gone I did it, I lapped up the dust like a cat laps up sickness until my tongue was gray, and . . .

. . . did the pain stop . . .

. . . yes, no, yes, for a while, but it's always there, always coming up again, always thick and gray forever, and I have to keep lapping up more and more, and is it you, really, please, please tell me, is it you . . .

. . .

. . . please oh please . . .

. . .

. . . is it you, I need your voice, I never knew the voice would feel so hot, is it you, tell me . . .

. . . yes . . .

. . . oh God take it away, please, give me a color bright without pain, please . . .

. . . yes . . .

. . . oh, oh, I . . .

. . . listen . . .

. . . I will, I will . . .

. . . picture the man who attacked you . . .

. . . I can't, I . . .

. . . he's old, jaundiced, his gray hair and ragged, his face a map of hollows and sorrows, of wrinkles and evils, his clothes are rags, his heart is rags, his teeth are gone, his gums are the color of blood, and his eyes are blue, watery, weepy, do you see him . . .

. . . yes, but . . .

. . . watch . . .

. . . he's . . . dissolving, cracking, cracks are spreading all over him, and his skin, it's flaking and . . .

. . . and what . . .

. . . light . . .

. . . watch . . .

. . . he's beginning to glow, to glow from inside the cracks, and the light . . .

. . . what's happening with the light . . .

. . . it's . . . coming into me, shining out in beams, shining into me . . .

. . . cleansing, pure . . .

. . . yes, and he's gone now, only light filling me . . .

. . . how do you feel . . .

. . . I don't know, different, I feel different . . .

. . . stronger . . .

. . . yes . . .

. . . strong enough to leave, to start over, to begin to live a new way, a new life . . .

. . . but where . . .

. . . you must leave . . .

. . . how . . .

. . . leave this place, you must leave now, soon, and find another place, a small town, the country, white houses and farms, and there you will be beautiful, you will open, a flower, your heart full, your body clean and sweet, and you will breathe new air, new thoughts, and love . . .

. . . love . . .

. . . love will take you, lift you, heal you, and you will forget the basement, the pain, you will forget it now, you will never think of it again, and when there is the beginning of that old pain, not the thought of it, only the beginning, the bad feelings, the fear, you will hear my voice and know that only the joy is real, do you feel the joy . . .

. . . yes, yes . . .

. . . and never listen to another voice, only his voice is real, is joy . . .

. . . I won't, I promise . . .

. . . and your beauty will be a perfume, a thought, a knowledge, a fire, and you will give only to one, to one who sees that beauty, whose touch will treasure you, whose heart

will know your heart, and when he comes to you, my voice will
confirm him, will feel your knowledge and will say his name . . .
   . . . love . . .
   . . . yes, love forever, love for now, and he will take you
deep and darling into the heartland, into a color bright and
painless . . .
   . . . love . . .
   . . . leave now, now, and seek your new home . . .
   . . . but . . .
   . . . I will be with you . . .
   . . . always . . .
   . . . yes, always, now go . . .
   . . . I'm afraid . . .
   . . . into light, go into light, into the promise of joy, go . . .

The girl backed away, her face perplexed but radiant. "I
. . . I've got to go." She smiled. "I'm sorry, I really have to."
Sexula laughed nastily.

"Here!" The girl reached into her shopping bag, took
something out, and pressed it into Mingolla's hand: a plastic
base atop which the holographic figure of a bearded man in a
white robe walked around and around, his hands clasped in
prayer. He thanked her, but she had already started for the
door, walking fast, breaking into a run as she pushed out into
the street.

Ludy said, "Don't got the twenny get outta the lobby."

Sexula rubbed against Mingolla, saying, "Ain'tcha got some
way of provin' you a vet?" And he remembered everything
now, his memory jogged by the exercise of power. He was lost,
lost in America, in sadness and confusion, and when he found
who he was looking for, although they had won, they would
still be lost, without plan or purpose, without even any understanding of what had been won. Ludy began demanding the
twenty, and Sexula told Mingolla that if he couldn't get it
together she was going to leave, because vet or not she wasn't
about to do it in no alley, and Mingolla stared through the glass
doors into the country of his birth, into an animated mural of
gaud and dissolution that seemed at once foreign and familiar,

into painted faces and unseeing eyes, wondering what to do, while the tiny Jesus circled constantly in his hand. . . .

. . . Izaguirre's office walls faded in, and Mingolla jumped up from the chair, still sick and feeling more lost than ever in the winded silence of the hotel. His thoughts whirled, trying to comprehend what had happened. It had been so real! The future . . . that's what it must have been. Yet there had been so much that smacked of hallucination. The way his thoughts had gone, the distortions. And the thing with the girl. Hearing her thoughts, answering them. But the most unbelievable thing had been his treatment of her. He'd recognized his paranoia and confusion. But that calm, compassionate soul, he hadn't recognized that person at all. No, it had to have been a hallucination. He'd tell Izaguirre about it in the morning, and . . . On second thought, maybe he'd keep it under his hat. Just in case it had been both a hallucination *and* real.

The sea was glowing streaks of aqua, light purple, and brown over sand, kelp beds, and muddy shallows. Combers bright as toothpaste broke over the coral heads, and beyond them, the water was choppy and dark. Crabs flexed their bone-white claws and scuttled from beneath a jetty into the kelp fringe at the margin of the shore; a crane stepped with Egyptian poise through a reflecting film of water overlying a sand bar. Roosters crowed, call and response. Skinks scurried into the beach vine. A fisherman in shorts and a red hard hat poled a dory past, heading for the channel. Tied to a coco palm, a spotted hog rooted in the mucky sand not far from a compound wall of green cinderblock inset with a wooden gate. And Mingolla sat on a palm stump about fifty feet seaward from the hog, holding a baby hummingbird in his hand. Bottle green with a ruby throat, barely the size of his thumb joint.

Angry voices from farther down the beach, where Izaguirre and Tully were arguing. ''. . . no reason,'' was all Mingolla could hear.

A live jewel in his palm, the hummingbird throbbed with life, with anxiety, its throat pulsing. Mingolla had searched for its nest, but with no luck. He wished he could do something for the hummingbird; he couldn't just leave it on the sand.

"Shit!" said Tully, waving his hand.

Izaguirre stood with his arms folded.

Mingolla wondered if he could calm the hummingbird down. He touched its mind cautiously, feeling the electrical contact as a tiny fire flickering at the edges of his thought, one that winked off abruptly. The hummingbird's throat had quit pulsing.

"All right, mon! You won't hear no more 'bout it from me!"

Tully came stomping up, dropped onto the sand beside him, and Mingolla closed his fist around the hummingbird. It was warm, its beak stabbing his palm. A shiver passed through him, the ghost of an emotion.

"Ever stop and t'ink dat dis damn war make no sense," said Tully grumpily.

Mingolla reached behind him, scooped a hollow in the sand, and gave the hummingbird a surreptitious burial.

"I mean here dere's war"—Tully swiped at the sand—"and here dere's none." He made another swipe next to the first one. "And damn fools are sendin' other damn fools to do t'ings nobody have any business doin'."

"What's the problem?" Mingolla asked.

"Dat Cifuentes squint was messin' wit' you. . . ."

"Yeah?"

"Dey goin' to send you after her, send you into de Petén to bring her back for interrogation." Tully sighed, exasperated. "I say to Izaguirre, 'Mon, dat's a waste of dis boy's talent. He got better t'ings he can be doin'.' But de doctor he say dat's how it goin' to be."

"That's fine with me," said Mingolla. "Just fine."

Tully looked at him askance. "Don't sound like you care much fah her."

"I care a lot," said Mingolla in a dead voice, watching grackles swoop out of the high sun like bits of winged matter blown from its core. A vulture landed with a crunch in a palm top.

"You gettin' strange, Davy," said Tully. "Gotta watch that."

"You ever hear words when you touch somebody's mind?" Mingolla asked.

"Words? Not'in' like dat . . . but I do hear 'bout one fella say he got words one time. Just a little bit. Why you axin'?"

"I had a dream 'bout it."

"What kinda dream?" Tully was more than a little interested.

Mingolla shrugged, thought back to his hallucination, wondering if his communication with the Christian girl had been evidence of something or just a fantasy. "Weren't you going to brief me on the Iron Barrio?"

Another sigh, and Tully pulled some papers from his hip pocket. "Yeah, all right. Dese here de plans, but 'fore you scan dem we better talk 'bout gettin' in. Ain't no big trick to that. De whores dat live dere . . ."

"Whores?"

"Oh, yeah. Lotsa people in de Barrio dey got family on de outside dat's hostage, and to earn some extra money, de prison guards dey send some of de women out to work the street. Dey know de women ain't goin' to be 'scapin' long as dere family have to pay de cost."

Voices behind them.

A squat black man and a small boy were walking from the compound gate; the man was carrying a machete and a pistol.

"Look like Spurgeon 'bout to slaughter he hog," said Tully. "Anyway, dere dis one whore . . . Alvina Guzman. De other prisoners treat her special 'cause her father Hermeto Guzman, de one who led de Army of de Poor up in Guatemala. Dey bot' heroes to people in de Barrio. So you hook up wit' her, and t'ings should go smooth."

The hog watched the man's approach, grunting softly as if expecting a treat. The man stopped half-a-dozen feet away and broke down the pistol.

"You won't have no trouble trackin' her. Most nights she be in one of de bars on La Avenida de la Republica."

Mingolla touched the hog's mind, found it strong, and hovered at its edges.

"We goin' to give you some drugs for to barter, for to . . ."

"Why? I can just take over whoever I need."

"Dat ain't always de best way. Y'can't take over every-body. And dem dat's watchin', dey might be gettin' suspicious 'bout how come you havin' such an easy time."

The man snapped the cylinder of the pistol into place, and the boy said something in a high piping voice.

"I won't 'vise you how to deal wit' it from dat point on. But gettin' in ain't a problem. You can handle de guards fine." Tully elbowed him. "Hey, mon! Listen up! T'ought you wanted dis briefin'."

A shot rang out, and Tully jumped. But Mingolla, who had been anticipating it, gave no sign of having heard.

The afternoon before he left for La Ceiba, Mingolla clo-seted himself in his room, intending to read awhile and fall asleep early. He read the title story of *The Fictive Boarding House* again, lingering over his favorite parts, the description of the building itself, with its ancient swimming pool whose wa-ters were so filthy that it looked like a lozenge of jade, and its owner, the old Korean man who sat in his wheelchair all day writing characters on strips of paper and tying them for luck to the vines in his garden, and the maid Serenita, the last survivor of the contract, whose final moments scripted the author's death. It was odd, he thought, that the same author could write two stories that had such opposite effects upon him, because the story about the two feuding families continued to rankle him. However, he managed to read it all the way through this time and was disgusted to find that the plot went unresolved. He tossed the book into his dufflebag, put a pillow over his face, and tried to sleep. But sleep did not come, and finally, giving up the idea, he went for a walk on the beach, watching sunset casting wild glitters over the sea, fading to a rippling line of gold drawn across the empurpled water within the reef. Darkness, and he sat down by the hotel wall, gazing up at the pale lumps of cloud cruising among the stars and whacking the sand with a stick.

"Best you not hit a toad wit' dat stick," said a girl's voice.

Elizabeth was walking toward him through the palm shadows, her white church dress aglow with striped moonlight, holding a hymnal. "Why not?" he asked.

"Dat a cassava stick," she said. "You hit a toad wit' it, and dey will run you off de island."

He laughed. "I'll try to avoid it."

"Not'in' funny 'bout it," she said. "Dis very thing have happen to Nadia Dilbert's boy last year. De toads spray milk at him, make he life not worth livin'."

"I'll be careful," he said, matching her graveness.

She came a few steps closer, and his eyes went to the cushy swell of her breasts backing the lace bodice.

"Where's your friend?" he asked.

"You mean Nancy? She off wit' some boy." She glanced behind her. "I guess I'll be . . ."

"Stay and talk a minute."

"Oh, I can't be late for church."

Mingolla opened her to the possibility of tardiness, projecting desire. "C'mon," he said. "Just a minute or two."

Her eyelids lowered, and she seemed to grow vacant, as if listening to an inner voice. "Well, a minute, maybe." She set her hymnal on the sand beside Mingolla and perched on it, careful not to soil her dress. She snatched a peek at him, then looked away, gone stiff, her breath quickening. "Tully," she said, "he tell me you be leavin' soon."

"Did you ask him 'bout me?"

"Oh, no . . . well, I did. But dat was for Nancy. She took wit' you."

"Uh-huh." Mingolla tracked the purple riding lights of a shrimper inching across the horizon. "Yeah, I'm leaving."

"Dat's too bad . . . you miss de carnival at French Harbor."

He looked at Elizabeth's beautiful face, her broad symmetrical nose and haughty mouth and sculpted cheekbones, a face that—if he were to draw it—would come off as registering an adult sensuality, but now seemed entirely youthful, eager yet under restraint; and he realized that he didn't want her, that he wanted to mark her, and by so doing to mark Tully. He wasn't sure why he wanted this. Despite their months together, Tully was an unknown quantity, hidden behind a front of braggadocio and crudity . . . though Mingolla suspected that the front was designed to disguise a simple and ingenuous self that Tully had long since rejected. And perhaps, Mingolla thought, what he really wanted was to establish his superiority by dismantling that front, revealing the fact that Tully cared about more than he would like to admit. It didn't matter. His wanting was reason enough.

"Elizabeth," he said, shifting, half-turning, resting a hand on her belly. She tensed, but didn't pull away, and as his hand moved to her breast, slipped up to finger loose a button, then two, she held her breath and arched against his palm. But when he began to slip the dress from her shoulders, she clutched at the material, holding the halves together. "I don't know 'bout dis," she said. "I don't know." He whispered her name, making it a charm, urging desire upon her, and grazed her neck, her cheek, with his lips. She threw back her head, released her hold on the dress, let his mouth find the upper slopes of her breasts.

"Ah, dat such a sweet feelin', Davy."

He lifted one breast free of the lace, its heft like a full wineskin, and admired its blackness agleam with sweat and starlight, tasted blackness on the nipple.

"Davy, oh Davy."

He was growing distant from her, distant even from his own desire. The stars, the mash of waves, this nubile island sophomore, it all smacked of some mixture of movie romance and high school follies, and he was beginning to get bored. More than bored. His very conception of evil mischief was at risk.

"Oh, God . . . Davy! You do dat so nice. . . ."

Christ, he thought, *let's remake the language of love, bring it into the world of intellect. When You Touch Me, My Self-Conception Dissipates, or at least a world of bad poetry, That Still Moment of Gladness After You Slip Inside, That Eyes-Closed Charge into Frenzy, and Later the Lights Beside Our Open Lips Are Senses Overused, or* . . . He had an idea! An inspirational idea. He scrambled up, helped her to stand. Stood close, hands on her hips. And pushed love into her mind, the shaped flow of all he had felt for his Long Island woman, for Debora. "Let's go in the water," he said. "I want to feel you close to me in the water." Amazing that she didn't puke, the sugar he'd injected into those words. But, no, she bought it a hundred percent, love translating stupidity into the meaningful. She wanted to be with him in the water, too. Whatever that meant to her. A trip to Paradise, a ride on the fabulous Sexmobile, a pass to some glandular Disneyworld. She undressed with her back to him, and the sight of her ass, the supple columns of her thighs, reinstituted desire. But he held to his course. They waded out holding hands, stepping on God only knew what manner of offal, hog guts, fish brains, a thousand grotesque possibilities, holding hands, and breasted into a shallow dive, and stroked to within twenty feet of the reef, near enough that the white starlit sprays came cold onto their skin, yet not so far out that they couldn't touch bottom. He pulled her close, kissed her deep, and the feel of her slippery hips, her nipples sliding across his chest, his cock gouging the cool rubber swell of her belly, once again kindled desire, causing him to consider having his cake and eating it, too. No, no! Stay with the plan. Unrequited and unconsummated. Her eyes glittered with fishy brilliance, her black mouth with its eel tongue poking out. Seeing her that way, he managed to disengage.

"Davy!" She tried to draw him back, but he eluded her, gliding farther away, until she was invisible against the dark wall of the reef.

"I don't know 'bout this," he said. "I don't know."

"Davy!" Panic in her shout.

He dived and stroked hard away, surfaced fifty feet away.

"Where you at, Davy! Don't be 'larmed!"

His laughter was drowned out by the surf, by a phosphorescent spray of water rising up like the teeth of a gigantic comb. He let the current carry him to the base of the reef and hid in a volute of rock, gripping a barnacled projection.

"Davy!" She was moving toward him. "You don't gotta be 'fraid, Davy! I love you!"

She passed within a few feet, calling, searching, and with the stealth of a shark, he ducked beneath the surface and swam underwater toward the shore. He could still hear her calling out to him as he dressed. Before long, fearing that he'd been swept out through the channel, she'd chance searching beyond the reef. "Davy, Davy!" she'd cry, bobbing off to Africa, her dark head sliding down the troughs between the waves, buoyed by love. Passing ships would toss life preservers, but she'd ask, "You seen my Davy?" and when they said no, she'd tell them to sail on, she wasn't going to stop until she found her man. He saw her washed up on Arab shores, wandering the deep forests, haunted, driven, ravished by terrorists, worshipped by multinational executives and sheikhs. "Who," they'd ask her, "is this Davy?" And she would sigh, she would weep, stare listlessly toward the Angel of the West, and the sheikhs would fume, knowing they could never really possess her, that this mysterious Davy had ruined her for all men, that one perfect moment had been marbled and set pedestal-high in memory, overshadowing all others, and that true love would never die.

CHAPTER EIGHT

The Avenida de la Republica in La Ceiba was a night street, wide and potholed, divided by a railroad spur belonging to the United Fruit Company. It ran along the waterfront between rows of stucco bars and rundown hotels, most of the latter painted a dark green, as if during some long-ago season of painting that color had been on special. The hotels had peaked roofs and rickety side stairs and interior courtyards where fat concierges held court at Formica tables, drinking Salvavida beer, joking with their friends, and bawling insults at the prostitutes who slept away the afternoons in the stuffy rooms. By day, the street was a scene of unparalleled torpor. Bits of cellophane and paper trash blew in the gutters, and there was little traffic apart from dogs, the occasional beggar searching for a doorway in which to sleep, and black-clad widows with corroded-looking skin, who would perch on the curbs, holding trays of cigarettes on their laps. From the docks beyond the seaward row of hotels came the constant grinding screech of metal under stress, and the heat was oppressive, every breath of wind filled with grit, rasping the skin like an animal's tongue: Mingolla noted with amusement that the prices in the hotels were five lempira for a room without extras, ten for a room with a woman, and twenty-five for one with an air-conditioner, thus firmly establishing the value placed upon coolness by the citizenry.

He chose an inexpensive third-floor room and spent the

afternoon going over the layout of the Barrio, which was situated several miles to the north, itself the size of a town, rumored to contain more than forty thousand souls, and studying photographs of Alvina Guzman and his target, Opolonio de Zedeguí. The Nicaraguan was a thin fit-looking man of middle years, with black hair, a high forehead, and skin the color of sandalwood. His sensitive features made it difficult for Mingolla to think of him as a formidable adversary, but then he doubted that his own photograph would strike fear into anyone, and he cautioned himself against overconfidence. At dark, he stowed these materials in a drawer and sat by the window, watching the street come to life. Prostitutes swarmed into the bars, packs of merchant seamen and dockworkers hard on their heels. Pushcart vendors sold ices and roasted shishkebobs of meat and onions on portable grills; children hawked candy and windup toys and necklaces of black coral. The pockets of the pool tables in the bars were blocked off and their felt surfaces used for dice games; the jukebox music seemed to be bearing up the shouts of winners on rich clouds of melody and rhythm. The entrances to the bars were wide and brightly lit, framing dancers and gamblers and brawlers, and it appeared to Mingolla that the street was the site of dozens of small theaters in which the same play was being performed.

At nine o'clock he walked two blocks south and entered the Cantina Las Vegas 99, the bar where Alvina Guzman plied her trade. He pushed through the crowd to the end of the counter and ordered a rum. Several men were ranged along the counter; the one nearest Mingolla favored him with a disconsolate stare, then went back to gazing into his glass. All the men at the counter were looking into their glasses, all gloomy, and Mingolla had the notion that if he were to imitate them, his thoughts would sail away at the speed of rum into some interior darkness. He engaged in a desultory conversation with the bartender, talking World Cup soccer and the weather, and critiqued the mural on the wall above the jukebox: sparkling dice and roulette wheels, playing cards and poker chips, each given the impression of enormity by the tiny people painted beneath them, their hands upflung in awe. Every couple of minutes he scanned the crowd for Alvina, and at last he picked her out. She was standing by the jukebox, feeding it a coin. A blocky, diminutive Indian woman with adobe-colored skin and full breasts and hips. Her black hair was woven into a single braid that fell to her mid-back, and her clothing—a white blouse and print skirt—showed signs of long usage. Like Hettie, her face conjured up Debora, not by its prettiness, for Alvina was not pretty, but by its impassivity. She stood unmoving, her squarish face without expression, and when a romantic ballad came on the jukebox, she began to dance alone, turning in tight graceful circles, her eyes fixed on the floor. Mingolla had been about to approach her, but held back, seeing in the dance, its sad abandon and its relation to the melodramatic Spanish of the lyrics, something he did not want to interrupt.

> "Today like yesterday just like tomorrow,
> I sit and watch the moon rise,
> the rumpled sheets frozen in its light
> like drifts of snow.
> At nine o'clock in the evening,
> only one cigarette left,
> and when I have finished smoking it,
> you will be a memory . . ."

Alvina looked lost when the record ended, as if she had awakened to find herself in another world. Mingolla beat his way through the crowd, put a hand on her arm, and her face seemed to drain of an energy whose presence he hadn't noticed before. "Ten lempira," she said.

"*Sí, pues,*" he said. "*Y por la noche?*"

"Your accent," she said. "It's Guatemalan."

"Yes, I'm from the Petén. San Francisco de Juticlan."

"I'm Guatemalan, too. From the Altiplano." Her interest flagged. "For the night it's fifty. You have a hotel?"

"It's nearby."

She took a step toward the door, then said, "I don't do the thing with my mouth . . . understand?"

Mingolla said that wasn't important.

150

They walked without speaking to Mingolla's hotel and up the stairs to his room. Inside was a cot, a chipped sink, a night table, and a ceiling fixture. The walls were dark green boards, striped with light showing through from the adjoining rooms, and from the room on the right came the sounds of strenuous lovemaking. Alvina started to unbutton her blouse, but Mingolla told her to wait.

"What is it?" she asked nervously.

"Sit down." He switched on the light. "I want to talk with you."

"Why?" Very nervous. "What do you want to know?"

"Please, sit down."

She did as he asked, but darted a glance toward the door.

"My name is David, and I know that you're Alvina Guzman."

"It's no secret," she said, affecting calm, but again looked at the door.

"I want your help," he said, infecting her with feelings of friendship and trust.

She lifted her hand as if to touch her face, but left the gesture uncompleted. "What help can I be? I'm a prisoner."

"I'm going into the Barrio."

"You don't need my help for that." She rested a hand on the pillow, then patted it again, testing its softness, its firmness, as if it were a very fine thing, indeed. "Why do you want to do this?"

"There's a man, a Nicaraguan named de Zeduguí. . . ."

"Never heard of him."

"He killed my family." Mingolla fleshed out the story, his desire for revenge, continuing to exert influence on Alvina, and explained that he wanted to pass himself off as her cousin and thus fall under the relative immunity accorded her family.

"A friend of mine, he may know this de Zeduguí." She looked at him with concern. "You may be tortured, and you'll probably never get out." In the adjoining room a prostitute gave a patently false cry of delight, and Alvina twitched her head toward the sound. "But if you insist on trying," she said. "I'll meet you at the Ninety-Nine just before three o'clock."

151

"What'll you do till then?"

"Work . . . the guards expect their money."

Muttered conversation from the next room, the sound of breaking glass.

"Here." He handed her a clip containing a thick fold of bills.

"This is too much," she said after counting it.

"It's not enough."

She raised no further objection, tucked the money into her blouse pocket, and sat with hands on knees, as stolid and glum as an idol. "Could I sleep until three?" she asked.

"Sure."

Her back to him, she unbuttoned her blouse, shrugged it off. Red weals of scar tissue crossed her shoulders, and when she slipped off her skirt, he saw that more severe scars figured her dimpled buttocks and thighs. The scars centered her for Mingolla, made clear her long history of hopeless striving and terror, of jungle hideouts and hard traveling. She folded her clothes at the foot of the bed and slid beneath the covers, sitting up, engaging Mingolla's stare. Her breasts were pendulous, the areolas large and brown. The pucker of an old bullet wound on her right shoulder.

"You've paid," she said.

He knew she was merely offering to fulfill a contract, and yet, aroused by his contact with her mind, he would have liked to make love to her. She wasn't attractive, but she was plain in the way history is plain, its contrivance lending the world a symmetry that implies hidden beauty; and it seemed to him that her impassivity was symptomatic of the quiet confidence with which beauty confronts the world. There was beauty in her, he thought, and the scars bore this out. However, he didn't want to use her: hers was not the sort of beauty he would feel comfortable using.

"You wear your scars well," he said.

This displeased her. "Some men like them."

"That's not how I meant it."

She continued to meet his eyes. "You haven't answered me."

"Yes, I have."

A fleshy smack in the next room, a cry that was not feigned.

"I'll turn out the light in a minute," Mingolla said.

He sat on the edge of the bed and opened the drawer of the night table, removing a knife, a calf sheath, and a largish packet filled with white powder. He tapped some of the powder onto the overfold of the packet and began dividing it into lines with the knife.

"What's that?" Alvina leaned in over his shoulder.

"Frost." He chopped at a granular lump. "It's like cocaine . . . stronger. Want some? You won't be able to sleep."

"No, not now. Aren't you going to sleep?"

"I don't want to be groggy at three."

He fitted a drinking straw to his nostril and snorted five fat lines in rapid succession. The skin on his forehead tightened.

"The guards will take that from you."

"We'll see," he said.

He did three more lines. His thoughts began an agitated dance, and he imagined blue-white crackles of electricity sparking at his temples. The drain was bitter at the back of his throat.

"Get some sleep now," he told her.

He extinguished the light and sat by the door. The lights were off in the adjoining room as well, and only a faint glow penetrated from the street, along with faint music and babble. Patches of shinier black like worn velvet appeared to be floating on the dark, and Mingolla wondered if—just as the chipped porcelain of the sink, the dinged cot, the splintered table—the darkness in cheap hotel rooms bore signs of previous occupancy. He thought about the Nicaraguan and was a little worried. Although he was stronger than Tully, and Tully was one of the best, he would be facing the Nicaraguan on his own territory . . . a dangerous territory. He would have to be very cautious. What most worried him was the Nicaraguan's craziness, the morbidity that must have prompted him to seek refuge in the Iron Barrio. Craziness was a variable for which he could not prepare, and he only hoped it would prove a weakness.

Alvina snored lightly. He made out the shape of her body, lying on her side, facing away from him. The frost had boosted his natural horniness, and he kept having to grapple with his erection, shifting it to a more comfortable position. He really would like to fuck her. To fuck history, do it doggy-style, kneeling and balls-deep in history's meat, overlooking its scarred plain and chunky ass. And he thought that was in essence what he was doing by working for Psicorps. Fucking the history of rebellion, of the Army of the Poor, of brutalized peasants and Indians. He was the bad guy now. This had crossed his mind before, but never with such immediacy, and fired by the exhilarating clarity of the frost, he pictured himself on a movie poster, MINGOLLA in flaming letters, his figure towering above burning villages and screaming hordes, mento-rays beaming from his eyes. Then he saw it from another viewpoint. Saw himself sneaking along a corpse-choked alley, hunting for a victim. He couldn't understand how he had come to this pass; he could perceive the events leading to it, but that alone explained nothing. It seemed to him that he must have been tricked, or that he had tricked himself, or . . . Alvina mumbled in her sleep. Damn, he wanted to fuck her! Not even fuck her, just be close to her, with someone. He was scared, and he wasn't ashamed to admit it. Anybody would be scared with the Barrio in their future. He would lie down next to her, that's all, lie down and hold her, feel his drugged heart slugging against her scarred back, and know that if she could survive horror and deprivation, he could make it, too. He needed that consolation, that creature comfort. He stripped, padded to the bed, and eased in beside her. She stirred but did not wake. But when he put an arm around her, inadvertently touching her breast, she looked at him over her shoulder, the whites of her eyes luminous. "Go back to sleep," he said. He couldn't help cupping the breast, letting the stem of the nipple slip between his fingers, making it stiff. His erection pronged her ass. Without a word, she cocked her knee, and he slid between her legs, rubbing back and forth, feeling her moisten. He worked a finger into her cunt, then two fingers, swirled them around, her muscles sucking him deeper, hips grinding. She must want him, he thought. In her mind they would be brother and sister in league against a Nicaraguan monster. And he wanted her, not just anyone, her, wanted her big Commie ass to milk him dry, wanted union and redemption and control. He flipped her onto her stomach, came to his knees behind her, and slipped in with a slick effortless motion, pushing inside until none of him was showing. He held her by the waist, liking the elevation, the combined sense of intimacy and distance. He withdrew a little, watched himself move in and out. He ran his hands along her flanks, molding them. Reached down and squeezed a hanging breast, forcing her face into the pillow. Not a sound from her, but that was guerrilla tactics, biting back their cries to keep their position secret, screwing under cover of midnight and ferns. He rode her hard, trying to drive sound out of her, trying to make her squeal, relishing the way her ass churned, forgetting to listen for her cries, and everything, fear and lust and drugs, balling up into a blazing knot, tightening and then unraveling into a thread of sweet languor, leaving him sweaty and gasping atop her.

She turned away after he withdrew, tension signaling her resentment. "I didn't mean . . ." he began.

"You paid," she said coldly.

He was ashamed, and he saw he would have to repair the damage done, shore up her trust, maybe establish affection. But he was also contented, pleased with himself, with his conquest of history. The repairs could wait, he thought; for now he wanted her to know exactly whom she was dealing with, even if he didn't know himself.

At three-thirty Mingolla and Alvina stood among a group of women—a couple of dozen at least—waiting for the bus that would transport them to the Barrio. Nobody spoke. The night was starless, moonless, and wind seethed in the grasses along the side of the road, pouring off the unfeatured blackness of the sea. Behind them lay a collection of huts, a true barrio, their thatch looking as bedraggled as molting feathers in the wash of light from their doorways. Headlights came from the north, swelled and resolved into a white schoolbus with neat black lettering above the windshield that read DEPARTMENT OF CORRECTIONS. The bus braked with a squeal, its door hinged open, and three short wiry men piled out, their pistols drawn. They wore street clothes, and red masks like those worn by wrestlers covered their heads. Mingolla saw that the masks were not merely red, but depicted flayed faces with anatomically correct renderings of muscle and tendon. Horrid things that made the men's eyes look glittery and false, their mouths becoming simple black holes each time they spoke. When they spotted Mingolla they cut him out from the milling women, pushed him down in the grass, and trained their pistols on him. "Wait!" he said, projecting camaraderie and trust. The pistols wavered, lowered.

"Who are you?" asked one of the men, helping him up.

Mingolla led the men aside, gave his name, and told them he was with the government, that he intended to work undercover in the Barrio, seeking intelligence from a certain prisoner. He asked their names.

"Julio."

"Martin."

"Carlito."

He asked if they would be on duty the next night, and they said yes; he told them to expect him to be among the women when it came time to drive them to work. He thought it strange that he could so easily work his will upon men with such fearsome visages, and his dominance made clear the petty resources of the evil that funded them. They hustled him onto the bus, and as he had instructed, they shoved him into the seat beside Alvina. "How did you manage it?" she whispered after the engine had kicked over.

"Bribes," he said.

She absorbed this and nodded. "You'll do well in the Barrio."

They drove for half an hour past coconut plantations and brush, then turned onto an unmarked road; the road widened into the plain of packed dirt that fronted the Barrio. Mingolla had seen aerial photographs of the place, showing it to be a single-story building with a roof of corrugated iron that spread across miles of defoliated jungle. Seeing the building at ground level was in some ways less impressive, for it had the appearance of a long warehouse atop which masked guards were posted—not an unexpected sight in Latin America; yet he felt rather than perceived its size, as if it possessed a gravity and atmosphere subtly different from the surrounding land. And closer, deeper within that sphere of influence, able to make out particulars, he understood the full menace of the prison. Spotlights swept over the roof from the nearby jungle, the beams causing the bloody masks of the posted guards to flare like matches, illuminating thick coils of smoke that twisted blue and ponderous like the tails of demons whose bodies were lost to sight in the heavens. Above the main gate—a sliding metal door—and also swept by the spotlights, the bodies of eight men and women were depended from crude gallows, all gashed and burned to such an extent that Mingolla couldn't believe any of them had survived to be hanged. Through the windows of the bus came a terrible smell compounded of charcoal cookery, smoke, the cloying mustiness of death, the sickly sweetness of people living cramped together, and God knew what else . . . a thousand smells blended into an evil perfume that made Mingolla gag. And as the bus pulled up to the gate, which was partway open, he heard a noise that—like the smell—was a combination of elements, of laughter and babble and screams, yet was remarkable neither for its constituency nor its whole, but for its rhythms, how it ebbed and faded with the inconsistent unity of jungle noise, of birds and insects obeying the designs and principles of an organic environment.

"Keep close," Alvina said as they were herded through the gate, and Mingolla caught up her hand. The gate grated shut behind them, stranding them in sultry heat and dimness, and their three guards disappeared into a door set into a side wall. Before them was another gate perforated with slits from which issued the noise and the smell and an orange glow: Mingolla felt as if he had been swallowed by a beast with metal jaws and fire in its guts. With a screech, the interior gate was hoisted, and they walked rapidly into the shadows on the right. They fetched up against a rough stone surface, and Alvina whispered, "Leon?"

"Who's with you?" came a raspy voice.

"My cousin . . . he's all right."

"Charmed," said the voice.

Mingolla acknowledged the greeting, but was mesmerized by the patterns of smoke and flame and shadow within the Barrio, a constant shifting of darks and lights so allied with fluctuations in the noise that it was several seconds before he could assemble a coherent image of the place. A forest of blackened beams supported the roof, lending perspective to what had at first seemed an infinite depth, and among the beams stood all manner of shelters: lean-tos, tents, huts, piles of brick hollowed by caves. The walls were the walls of small stucco houses with shuttered windows; in other parts of the Barrio, according to Mingolla's plans, were labyrinths of such houses, remnants of the town that had once occupied the land. Fires bloomed everywhere. Along the walls, in grills and oil drums. And the resultant light was a smoky orange gloom through which packs of prisoners shuffled, many with knives in hand.

"Bitch of a hometown, huh?" said Leon, emerging from the shadows. A middle-aged Indian almost as short as Alvina, with a seamed face and sunken cheeks and black bowl-cut hair. Despite the heat, his shoulders were draped in a blanket.

"This is the friend I told you about," Alvina said. "You can trust him to help you."

"Don't volunteer me for free." Leon grinned, revealing seven or eight rotting teeth tipped at rustic angles like gravestones.

"You'll be paid," said Mingolla.

Leon's face hardened in reaction to Mingolla's curtness. "What do you need?" And when Mingolla gave him de Zeceguí's photograph, he said, "I'll find him . . . we'll talk in the morning." He drew a knife from beneath his blanket. "You have a weapon, man?"

Mingolla unsheathed his own knife.

"Then let's go," said Leon.

During that walk across the Barrio, through zones of flame, patches of sticky-looking darkness, and layers of intolerable stench, Mingolla saw many memorable things, many things that beggared explanation; yet he asked no explanation, for though he grew sick at heart from seeing, he realized that the Barrio was its own explanation, a world with its own rules of right action and process of good and evil. The Barrio seemed to be displaying itself for him, offering him a sampling of its treasures. As he turned his head a frayed curtain would be drawn back from a lean-to, or a group of people gathered around an oil drum, silhouetted like ragged crows, would step aside, opening avenues of sight down which his eyes would travel toward some horrible or pitiful or—infrequently—beautiful sight or event. He saw gang rapes and beatings, a spectrum of the crippled and the diseased. He saw a man whose hand had been re-placed by a wooden stump in which a fork was embedded, and another man bearing a tray of mouse carcasses like tiny bloody candies. He saw two matronly women painting a design of crescents on an infant, and beyond them, a young woman crucified to a beam, her waxy breasts painted with this same design. Once a section of the roof was lifted, a noose dropped over the head of a sleeping man, and he was hauled up kicking and spasming by a handful of guards; and farther on, another section was lifted, and a barrel of water was poured onto some children who laughed and licked the droplets from one anoth-ers' skin. And the windowless one-room house shared by Alvina and her father provided a further instance of the Barrio's pro-cess. Chained to its door was a boy of about twelve armed with a machete; he appeared content to be chained and held out the lock to Leon, who opened it and gave him a mango. Then Leon bade them good night, reminding Mingolla of their meeting the next morning.

Inside, the walls were pale blue, flaking, inscribed with a decade of graffiti; the room was lit by thin candles and domi-nated by two mattresses, on one of which lay Hermeto Guzman: an ancient white-haired man with skin the reddish dark of raw iron, his bony frame scarcely making an impression on the sheet that was tucked around him. The smell of feces was strong, and Alvina spent the better part of an hour cleaning the old man, while Mingolla sat on the other mattress, leafing through a pile of paperback romance novels. Alvina didn't bother to perform introductions, and it was unclear whether the old man had seen Mingolla; but as she tipped up his head, helping him drink from a bottle of mineral water, he stared at Mingolla with eyes that were dark yet touched with light, stoic and alive. They seemed to be drinking him in with the same avidity as that with which he gulped down the water. The eyes made Mingolla feel young and unknowing, and he thought the old man's frail whisper must be commenting upon him.

"What's he saying?" he asked Alvina.

"He says the water tastes good . . . reminds him of a time back in the old days."

"Right after we killed that bastard Arenas." Hermeto struggled up, fell back. "Remember, Alvina?"

She soothed him, cautioned him to be quiet.

"She doesn't like me talking about the old days," Hermeto said.

"What's there to talk about?" she said roughly.

"The struggle," said Hermeto. "The struggle was . . ."

"The struggle!" Alvina pretended to spit. "All we did was die."

Mingolla felt sad for the old man. "I don't know," he said. "You . . ."

"No, she's right. We achieved nothing." Hermeto's voice rose in pitch at the end, making the sentence sound like a question, as if he couldn't believe it himself. "We thought we were fighting men, and because we killed so many, we thought we were winning. But we weren't fighting men. We were fighting tides . . . tides caused by two giants splashing the water thousands of miles away. We didn't have a chance."

"We didn't have a choice, either." Alvina opened a tin box, took out bread and cheese. "They were killing us."

The old man's voice became inaudible even to Alvina, and she asked him to repeat what he had said.

"My brother"—he made the sign of the cross—"may God deliver him."

Alvina stroked his hair.

He asked for more water, gulped it down. "But don't you remember that time, Alvina? Up in the Cuchumatanes?"

"Yes, I remember," she said wearily.

"They had us trapped in the high passes," he said to Mingolla. "We didn't have water, hardly any food. We could see the river down below, but we couldn't get to it. The sky was filled with the hum of helicopters. We were so thirsty, we ate the flowers of shrub palms, and everybody got cramps. Once we found a place where animals drank, a little pond filled with scum. Finally the helicopters left, and we staggered down to the river. It was such a strange day . . . thunder and mist. We looked like skeletons, but whenever the sun touched us we glowed like angels, our flesh almost transparent. Like angels throwing themselves into a river."

"You make it sound beautiful," said Alvina disparagingly.

"It *was* beautiful," said the old man.

She began feeding him crumbs of bread and cheese. Mingolla was glad for the interruption, because the old man's description had been hard for him to bear. He settled back against the wall, listening to the noise from outside, thinking about the struggle, the Army of the Poor; to banish thought he opened the packet of frost and snorted a quantity. He loaded a smaller packet with a supply for Leon, then lay down and closed his eyes. Through his lids the candle flames acquired a dim red value, and the bloodiness of the color started him thinking about Hermeto and Alvina. He realized that if he were to relax his guard, he would begin to sympathize with them, and his sympathy would be as ingenuous and ill-informed as his lack of concern. He had no way of understanding what it would be like to starve in the hills. The hardships he had endured seemed by comparison a privileged form of agony, and just knowing that made him want to pay some penance.

The candles were snuffed out, and Alvina lay down beside him. He edged away, afraid of contact, afraid she might contaminate him with principle and lead him down a risky path. She smelled of earth, of musky heat, and those smells and the action of the drug inflamed his desire. And as if she sensed this, she said, "If you want me again, you have to pay."

He couldn't frame a reply that would convey his mood, but at last he said, "I can get you out of here."

"No, you can't."

"But I can." He propped himself on an elbow, trying to see her in the dark. "I . . ."

"The government has my sister and her children. If we were to escape, they'd die."

"They could be located, they—"

"Stop it," she said.

They lay in silence, and the screams and gabble of the Barrio seemed to add a pressure to the darkness, squeezing black air from his lungs.

"I don't understand," she said.

"What?"

"You . . . I don't know you well, and I don't like you very much, yet I trust you."

"I'm sorry you don't like me."

"Don't feel put upon," she said. "I don't like most people."

Implicit in her statement, Mingolla thought, was a studied rejection of life, and he pictured how she must have been back in the days when politics was in the hills, when everything seemed possible: an ordinarily pretty Indian girl imbued with extraordinary zeal and passion. He wished he could help her, do something for her, and remembered the stack of romance novels.

"Do you like making love?" he asked. "I don't mean do you like . . . your work, but would you like it with someone you cared about?"

"Go to hell," she said.

"I'm serious."

"So am I."

"I could make you like it."

She laughed. "I've heard that before."

"No, really. Suppose I could hypnotize you, make you feel passion? Would you want me to do that?"

The mattress rustled as she turned to face him, and he

162

could feel her eyes searching him out. "Ten lempira," she said. "And you can make me crow like a rooster."

"That's not what I'm talking about."

She reached down, fondled his genitals. "Come on, man," she said bitterly. "Ten lempira. You'll forget all about the other girls."

Humiliated, he pushed her hand away.

"No?" she said. "Well, maybe when you're feeling better."

He was tempted to coerce her pleasure, but couldn't bring himself to do it, unable to shake the conviction that she was his superior.

"I don't understand," said Alvina after a while. "I just can't figure anything out anymore."

———————

Morning in the Barrio was different from night only in that when sections of the roof were lifted, chutes of gray light spilled in, and people stood beneath the open sky, risking mortal harm for a glimpse of freedom; otherwise the same smoky orange gloom prevailed among the black beams and fires. The center of the Barrio, where Leon and Mingolla sat in a shadowed niche, featured a row of stucco houses strung out across the width of the prison; and in one of them, a house with a white wall and black shutters, and an oil drum fire burning at its corner, lived Opolonio de Zedeguí. "See those four guys out front?" said Leon, inserting the tip of his knife into his packet of frost. "They're always there. His bodyguards. You'll have to do something to get rid of them. A diversion, maybe." He inhaled from the knife blade. His black eyes widened, his cheeks hollowed. "*Chingaste!* This is good stuff!"

The four men ranged in front of de Zeguí's house were young and well muscled, and Mingolla could tell from their slack attitudes that they were under psychic control. De Zeguí was being terribly incautious: these men might well have been the signal that had alerted American agents to his presence.

163

"If you've got more of this stuff, I know some guys who can help," said Leon.

"We'll talk about it later." Mingolla did a bladeful of frost and looked around. He was beginning to get used to the noise and the smell, and he wondered if the place was growing on him. He chuckled, and Leon asked what was funny. "Nothing," said Mingolla.

Leon laughed, too, as if "nothing" were a hilarious concept. Sharp lines spread from the corners of his eyes, making his reddish brown skin look papery. "So," he said after a silence, "you're her cousin, eh? Strange she never mentioned you. She talks about family all the time."

"She didn't know me," said Mingolla. "Different branch of the family."

"Ah," said Leon. "That explains it."

Mingolla had more of the drug. It was doing nice things to his head, but was tearing up his nose, and he thought he should start taking it under his tongue. Or stop taking it altogether. But he had become so used to being drugged, the indulgence seemed natural.

"I thought all her people lived around Cobán," said Leon.

"Guess not."

"Y'know," said Leon, "it's crazy you coming here just to kill this guy. In here, he's dead already."

"I suppose so."

"So what's your real reason?"

Mingolla saw that he would have to do something soon about Leon's suspicious nature, but he felt too loose and composed to want to bother with it now. "Let's get out of here," he said, coming to his feet.

They set off toward Alvina's, and Mingolla wondered if the place *had* grown on him, though more likely it was the drug that caused the Barrio to appear . . . not beautiful, exactly, but painterly. Everywhere were tableaux that had the inner radiance and important stillness he associated with the Old Masters. There, three men roughing up a woman, who was clawing, kicking, and all of them looking up as the roof above opened to admit a shaft of white sunlight that played over them, freezing and transfiguring the action. And there, almost lost in the shadow of a thatched lean-to, an old hag straight out of Goya, her ravaged face framed by a black shawl, staring with perplexed astonishment at a feather in her hand. And the whole of the place with its black divisions, its smoky orange segments of misery, leaping flames, and silhouetted imps, was a collection of pre-Renaissance triptyches. He could be like the guy who painted murals in the bombed villages, he could stay here forever and ensure immortality by memorializing a life of terror and deprivation. . . . A change in the noise, a wave of louder and more agitated noise rolling toward them, brought him alert. In the distance he saw a line of masked guards with whips and rifles driving a mob ahead of them.

"This way!" Leon grabbed his arm, yanking Mingolla toward the wall of houses. "We'll be safe in there."

Mingolla had a bad feeling. "Why there?"

"They're not hunting anybody . . . it's just a sweep." Leon pulled at him. "They always do it about this time; they never check the houses."

People were running in every direction, shouting, screaming, bright spears of sound that shattered at their peak, and Mingolla was slammed into a beam by someone's shoulder. Diseased flowers swirling, eddying around him, all the same kind, with patterns of black mouths and empty eyes and mottled brown petals like skin, a wilted vaseful of them washing down a drain. Forked twig hand clutching his arm, wrinkled mouth saying, Please, please, and being swept away. He fought toward Leon, but was thrown off course by the tidal flow of the mob. The guards were closing, he could see the patterns of bloody muscle on their masks, hear their whips cracking, and shouts of pain were mixed in now with those of panic. A little boy clung to his leg with the desperation of a small animal hanging onto a branch in a gale, but was scraped off as Mingolla beat a path through a clot of people stopping up the flow. The screams fed into the smoky light, making it pulse, making the flames leap higher in the oil drums, and Mingolla had the urge to lose control, to begin cutting with his knife and screaming himself. He wound up beside the door Leon had entered, wedged it open, and a teenage boy slipped past him into the dimly lit room . . . slipped past and cried out as a knife flashed across his neck. Leon's startled face peering out. Mingolla pushed inside and backhanded Leon to the floor, and Leon rolled up into a crouch, the knife poised. But he faltered, his expression growing puzzled, then woeful under Mingolla's assault of guilt and friendship betrayed. The knife dropped from his hand.

Mingolla bolted the door, kneeled beside the boy, and checked for a pulse; his fingers came back dyed with red. Leon had slumped against the rear wall and was weeping, his face buried in his hands. In the corner beside him, ringed by guttering candles, wrapped in blankets as gray as her skin, an old woman was trembling, staring fearfully at Mingolla. He snatched one of her blankets and used it to cover the dead boy. He picked up Leon's knife, squatted next to him. "Who are you working for?" he asked. Leon just sobbed, and Mingolla jabbed his leg with the knife, repeating the question.

"Nobody, nobody." Leon's Adam's apple bobbed, his voice broke. "I wanted the rest of the drugs."

Leon's treachery brought home to Mingolla the full extent of his foolhardiness. The manchild strolling around Hell, contemplating its aesthetic, playing ineffectual good Samaritan. He was damned lucky to be alive. *No more bullshit*, he thought. He'd finish his business and get out. Leon's tears glistened, he sobbed uncontrollably, and Mingolla intensified his assault, slowly elevating Leon's guilt to a suicidal pitch. He held the knife to the side of Leon's neck.

"No, please . . . God, no!" The old woman crawled toward him, dragging a train of blankets. "I'll die, I'll die!" Her voice articulated and decrepit, like a grating pain, like broken ribs grinding together. Her face a gray death mask with hairy moles, lumped cheekbones. Her death an accomplice after the fact to the dead thing of her life. Mingolla looked away from her, repelled, ready to cut Leon, full of cold judgment.

"It's not his fault," whined the old woman. "He's not responsible."

Mingolla had an answer for that, courtesy of Philosophy

166

101, but withheld it. "Whose fault is it, then?" he asked, pointing at the boy with the knife.

"You don't know," she said. "You don't know what he's . . ." A tear the size of a pearl leaked from one of her rheumy dark eyes. "The things they made him do, the awful things . . . but he fought back. Ten years in the jungles. Ten years living like an animal, fighting all the time. You don't know."

Leon's sobs racked his chest.

"Who are you?" Mingolla asked.

"He's my son . . . my son."

"Did you know he was going to do this?"

She didn't hesitate. "Yes, and you'd have done the same. All those drugs, so much money. You're no different from us."

"No," said Mingolla, pointing again to the boy. "I wouldn't have done this."

"Fool," said the old woman, and the screams and shouts from without, receding but still a measure of chaos, seemed to be echoing the word. "What do you know? Nothing, you know nothing. Leon . . . Oh, God! When he was seventeen, just married, the soldiers came to our village. They took all the young men and armed them with rifles and drove them in a truck to the next village, where the people were suing a big landowner. A real villain. And the soldiers ordered the young men to kill all the young women of that village. They had no choice. If they hadn't obeyed, the soldiers would have killed their women." She looked sadly at the gray walls as if they were explanations, reasons. "You know nothing."

"Forgive me," said Leon. "God, oh God, forgive me!"

"I know he tried to kill me," said Mingolla. "I don't care what made him this way."

"Why should I bother?" Leon's mother gazed at the ceiling, her hands upheld in supplication. "Let him take my son, let me starve. Why should I live any longer?" She turned a look of pure hatred on Mingolla. "Go ahead!" she shrilled. "Kill him! See"—she pointed a knobbly finger at Leon—"he doesn't care, either. What's it matter, life or death. In this place it's the same." She screeched at him. "I hope you live forever in this godforsaken hole! I hope life eats you away an inch at a time."

She tore at her blouse, ripping away buttons, baring the empty sacks of her breasts. "Kill me first! Come on, you devil! Kill *me*! Me!" And when he did nothing, she tried to pull his hand away from Leon's neck, to drive the knife into her chest. Her eyes as full of bright mad life as a bird's, her claw fingers unnaturally strong. Breath whistling in her throat. He shoved her down, and she lay panting, teeth bared, an old gray bitch-wolf gone into fear, gone beyond it into a kind of exultation, lusting for death. He didn't feel merciful toward her; mercy would have been inappropriate. She neither wanted nor needed it. He put her to sleep to rid himself of an annoyance. Withholding judgment on Leon, he settled in the far corner among the blankets . . . they even smelled gray.

To fend off weariness he did more frost. He rejected the idea of returning to Alvina's. There he would be drawn to listen to Hermeto's reminiscences, feel renewed appreciation for Alvina, and that would only weaken him. He would wait here until midnight and then take care of de Zeduguí. Take care of him in a straightforward fashion. No diversions, no tricks. He wanted a gunfight, a test of strength. Subtlety was not his forte, and he would be prone to bouts of foolhardiness until he gained more experience; he needed to reassure himself of the efficacy of brute force. A certain lack of prudence was corollary to the wielding of power, he thought; a credential of boldness. And if this attitude reflected a diminished concern for his survival, so be it: such a diminished concern would be an asset to a killer, for if one valued one's own life too highly, such a valuation would be difficult to dismiss in regard to other lives.

Leon's weeping began to perturb him, and he let him join his mother in sleep. He pulled out de Zeduguí's photograph, inspected it for clues. But that bland professorial face gave nothing away, unless its unreadability was itself a clue to subtlety. He hoped that was the case, that their struggle would be one of strength against subtlety: that would be the best proving ground of all. He dipped up more frost with the edge of the photograph. The drug was a solid form in his head, a frozen vein of electricity that soon began to prevent any thought aside from a perception of its own mineral joy. Mingolla's nasal membranes burned, his heart raced, and he sat unmoving. He gazed at a spot on the wall, his resolve building into anger, like a warrior envisioning the coming battle, living it in advance, yet for the moment secure amid hearth and home, with his dogs sleeping at his feet.

It began to rain shortly before six o'clock, a hard downpour that drummed like bullets on the iron roof, drowning out every other noise. All over the Barrio, sections of the roof were being lifted, allowing tracers of rain to slant through the orange gloom, the separate drops fiery and distinct. People cast off their rags and danced, their mouths open, their torsos growing slick and shiny, and others caught the water in buckets, and others yet dropped to their knees, their hands upheld to heaven. Fires hissed and burned low. Smoke fumed, and a damp chill infiltrated the air. There was a general lightening of mood, a carnival frenzy, and, taking advantage of it, Mingolla strolled up to the oil drum fire at the corner of de Zeduguí's house and joined three old men who had gathered around it, convincing them that his presence was expected and welcome; out of the corner of his eye, he studied the four guards flanking de Zeduguí's door. He blocked, becoming invisible to the uncommon senses of the man he intended to kill, and thought how best to deal with the guards.

The old men were roasting snakes that had been pierced by lengths of wire; the snakes were crisp and blackened, their eyes shattered opaque crystals, their jaws leaking thin smoke, and underlit by the fire, the men's faces were made into cadaverous masks of shadow and glowing skin. They offered Mingolla a portion of the meat, but he suggested instead that they share their bounty with the guards. This struck the three as a marvelous idea. Why hadn't they thought of it themselves? They extended whispered invitations, and de Zeduguí's guards hurried over. When the guards slumped to the ground, put to sleep by Mingolla's exertions, the old men expressed consternation, worrying that the meat might be tainted; but Mingolla reassured them and urged them to drag the guards off behind a pile of rubble, where they might rest more comfortably. That done, the old men returned to their snakes, paring slices of meat, tasting, and declaring that the snakes could use another turn, all as if nothing unusual had happened.

Five minutes later, de Zeduguí came to stand at his door. He wore jeans and a green shirt with the sleeves rolled up, and he was more slender than Mingolla had assumed; his hair had grown long, falling in black curls to his shoulders, and his dark face was composed. He, too, was blocked, but on noticing the absence of his guards, he let the block slip. His heat was strong, but not as strong as Tully's, and this gave Mingolla the confidence to let his own block slip. De Zeduguí sought him among the men gathered by the oil drum and spread his hands in a show of helplessness; then he beckoned, and Mingolla, committed to a concept of forthright challenge, walked over to his side. The drumming of the rain seemed to be issuing from within his body, registering his rush of adrenaline.

"I've been expecting you," said de Zeduguí in a soft, cultured voice.

Mingolla said nothing, afraid that speech, that any interaction would undermine his determination.

"I knew they'd eventually send someone, and I knew it would be someone strong. But you"—de Zeduguí's smile was thin and rueful—"it seems they've adopted a policy of overkill." He rubbed his jaw with his middle finger as if smoothing away some imperfection. "You *have* come to kill me?"

Mingolla maintained his silence.

"Yes, well . . ." Again de Zeduguí held out his hands palms up. "I promise you I won't resist. Even if I did, I wouldn't have a chance . . . I'm sure you're aware of that." He gave a nervous laugh. "So unless you're in a rush, why don't you come inside, let me have a last smoke, some wine. I'm a stickler for the formalities, and I've always been of the opinion that a man's death should be an occasion of rigorous formality."

Nothing was going as Mingolla had imagined. De Zeduguí's surrender had disconcerted him, and he could not help sympathizing with the man.

"Nobody's hiding in there," said de Zeduguí. "Check through the window if you want."

Mingolla went to the window, flung open the shutter, and peered inside. Cot against the rear wall, cushions on the floor in the opposite corner, and hung from a ceiling hook, a kerosene lamp that shed an unsteady orange glow. Stacked on the floor were canned goods, bottles, and a large number of books. Everything was very clean.

"All right," said Mingolla. "Let's go."

Once inside, de Zedeguí turned the lantern flame down to a crescent, throwing the room into near darkness. "Don't be alarmed," he said. "No tricks. I prefer it dark." He picked up a wine bottle and sat on the cot. "I won't offer you anything, I've no wish to compromise you. As a matter of fact, I've been impatient for you to arrive."

"You want to die?" Mingolla asked, taking a seat on the cushions.

A match flared, the coal of a cigarette was puffed into life, and de Zedeguí lay back, merging with the shadows. "Not exactly. It's just that I no longer care to be who I am."

Mingolla felt disadvantaged, realizing that he had enlisted in the problem of de Zedeguí's existence; he wondered if he could go through with the act.

"You may reach the same conclusion someday," de Zedeguí went on. "You're no different from me."

The rain was slackening, the drumming dwindling away, and the brutal music of the Barrio was regaining dominance. "What made you come here?" Mingolla asked.

"I understood that I had become a criminal," said de Zedeguí. "I should have understood it long ago, but I was too"—he laughed—"too much in love with my criminality to recognize it as such. But when I did, I wanted to be at the heart of the law, subject to its lessons, its wise institutions. As I told you, I'm a stickler for formality."

"Penance?" said Mingolla.

"Justice. Of course justice has always been confused with punishment. Men have exerted their creativity to contrive just punishments for ages. Did you know, for instance, that an author named Bexon once proposed an entire tableau of penitential heraldry? He suggested that condemned prisoners be brought to the gallows dressed in red or black, that parricides should wear black veils and embroidered daggers, and the shirts of poisoners be decorated with serpents. Astonishing! What would it matter to me the color of my shirt at death? I merely want the justice my crimes demand, and now"—he toasted Mingolla with the bottle—"now you've come."

"If you feel so strongly, why didn't you kill yourself?"

"You haven't been listening. I want justice, and I would certainly be more merciful than you." De Zeduguí had a long swallow of wine. "There's no point telling you anything. You're too young, too inexperienced. But when you reach Sector Jade, you'll understand . . . though perhaps you won't care. Most of us don't."

"Sector Jade? What's that?"

"You'll find out soon enough," said de Zeduguí. "And I doubt you'd believe me now."

"I can make you tell me."

"Why don't you? I'll tell you why. Because you're feeling sorry for me . . . or if not sorry, you're feeling something. And you've been so stripped of feeling by the process that birthed you, you want to hang on to any feeling, no matter how inconsequential. But in the end you'll do your duty. You're a creature of power, and now you're too enamored of its usage to understand the damage"—his voice grew strained—"the horrid self-inflicted damage you will incur."

Mingolla, angered by de Zeduguí's description of him, was made afraid by the passion embodied by this last statement.

De Zeduguí threw himself off the cot, and Mingolla tensed. But the Nicaraguan only paced back and forth, passing from shadow into dim light and back. He stubbed out his cigarette. "Prisons . . . fascinating subject. Books have been written on the psychology of their construction. Bentham, for example. The Panopticon. A marvelous design! A circular building with a tower at the center of an interior courtyard, and the tower has wide windows that face the inner wall of the ring, and the cells in the ring are backlit so they can be viewed from the tower like thousands of little stages. And of course the watchers in the tower, they're hidden from the eyes of the prisoners. Their invisibility guarantees order. Who's going to try to escape when they're being watched all the time? The Panopticon is similar to the carceral concept being developed in Sector Jade, though not half so effective. But the truth of the matter is that Sector Jade is a joke . . . the joke power has played on itself." He shook his forefinger. "Wait till you get there! You won't believe what's going on! The little family feud this war involves. The Madradonas and the Sotomayors."

"I've heard those names before," said Mingolla, plumbing his memory. "In a story I read . . . I think."

De Zedeguí laughed. "It's no story, believe me. You'll find that out." He continued to pace, planting his feet forcefully as if stamping out small fires, and his words came in impassioned bursts. "Did you know that confession was once considered a primary form of justice? Men declaring their guilt from the gallows. 'Oh, Lord! Forgive my execrable deed, my lamentable sin!' Here in Honduras we keep the tradition alive. Rustlers are photographed holding strips of beef, their guilt published in the press. Myself, I once saw two murderers supporting the body of their drowned victim. What a horrible sight! His eyes were like hardboiled eggs, all white and bulging . . . the little children who passed by were probably afflicted for life. But who would believe my confession? What evidence should I hold?" He flung the wine bottle against the wall, and the splintering glass wired Mingolla's nerves. "We're living in the Dark Ages! The countryside's beset with pillories and gibbets and wheels. A fiesta of punishment! And I helped to . . ." He stopped pacing, stood by the door. "I think you should go ahead now, I really do."

Mingolla lowered his head, defeated. The Nicaraguan was insane, pathetic, his sensibility scoured raw by guilt, and there would be no battle, no gunfight. To kill him would be an act of extermination.

"What are you waiting for?"

"Let it alone, all right," said Mingolla.

"Oh, have I touched your soul?" said de Zedeguí in a tone of mock concern. "Dredged up some scrap of humanity? Having a little trouble with our motivation, are we? Here, I'll help you." He walked over to Mingolla and kicked him hard in the thigh.

Mingolla cried out, grabbed the injured spot.

"Want more motivation?" said de Zeduguí. "All right." He spat in Mingolla's face.

Revolted, yet restraining a reaction, Mingolla wiped his cheek on his sleeve.

"What control!" De Zeduguí clapped his hands. "Why, you're a remarkable likeness of the human! But"—he dropped his voice to a nasty whisper—"you and I both know you're not. Come on, asshole! All that power crawling around in there, all that sick wormy juice, and you've never really used it. You know you want to . . . so come on! Here I am! Blind me with your lightnings!" He broke into a giddy laugh that went sky high and kicked Mingolla in the hip.

"Dammit!" Mingolla rolled away, came up into a crouch, his eyes narrowed in a hateful squint.

"Marvelous!" said de Zeduguí. "The hound snarls, his eyes redden!"

Mingolla's anger was building to critical, fed by the self-loathing that de Zeduguí was making him feel, and he thought how appropriate it would be to return the favor. The Nicaraguan spat once again, catching Mingolla with the spray. "It's so amusing to stand here and see you trying to pretend you're a real boy, when you're nothing but a filthy little spider about to spew poison on one of his weaker brothers." Another kick. "Don't hold back! Just think of the ecstasy that murder will bring, your thoughts arrowing into me . . . what's that the Americans say? Fucking with my mind. What a perfect phrase! And that's what you'll be doing, coming all over yourself as you fuck my mind to death. How you can stand waiting? Or is this just the foreplay, the anticipation?"

He aimed another kick, but as he drew back his leg, Mingolla struck with all his power, with power he'd never known he had, sending waves of self-loathing at de Zeduguí. The Nicaraguan stumbled back into the shadow beside the door, and Mingolla heard a steamy hiss, a whimper that went higher and higher like a teakettle on the boil. De Zeduguí clapped his hands to his head and staggered through the door, swayed, a black mad figure against the orange murk, then turned the corner, with Mingolla following behind.

The three men were still grouped around the oil drum fire, and lurching, out of control, de Zeduguí pushed them aside. He stood beside the drum, shaking violently, then gripped the edges of the drum with both hands. The metal must have been superheated, yet he gave no cry. One of the men started toward him, his knife drawn, but before he could cut, de Zeduguí—with the formal precision of a deep bow—ducked his head into the drum. The glow reflected on the interior of the drum brightened by half, and when de Zeduguí straightened, his head was burning, his shirt was burning, foot-high flames licking up from his scalp like weird reddish orange hair marbled with threads of black. Shouts, the rustling of voices, many voices rolling away as swiftly as wind through a forest, spreading the news. For a moment Mingolla thought de Zeduguí would survive, that he would jam his hands in his pockets and stroll casually off into the Barrio. But then he toppled, sparks flying out on impact, and was soon blocked from view by the curious and those trying to remove his shoes and watch.

Mingolla couldn't gather his thoughts and was briefly afraid that they had been sucked down the drain of de Zeduguí's death, whirled away into some garbage heap of stale brainwaves. He backed into the house and felt calmer in the dark room. It was early . . . what was he going to do with all that time? Somebody peeped in the door, and he yelled at them. He dug out the packet of frost, was horrified to see de Zeduguí's smiling photograph inside it; he sailed it away into the corner, and sat on the cot. Scooped up the white powder with his knife, shoveled it in. Too fast, spilling powder on his knees, the floor. He nicked his nose with the blade. *Calm down*, he told himself; *it wasn't your fault*. He hadn't wanted de Zeduguí to stick his head in the fire. He didn't know what he had wanted. For the man to keel over, sudden and painless. Yeah, that would have been acceptable. He did more frost. More. Shoveling it in faster, blood mixing with the powder on the blade, forming a crust. God, he was ripped! Dazzles like stars, like miniature burning heads, floating on the dark, and his heart doing poly-rhythms. Painless. That's what he'd wanted. *Sure, right,* he said. *You were glorying in the possibilities of violence, pictur-ing skulls split by pitchfork thoughts, and you didn't give a crap about the guy. Well, so what? The guy was into death, wasn't he? A little more frost? Why, certainly. Couldn't hurt. Painless, in fact. Like that nosebleed you got, man?* Christ, he hadn't noticed. All over his damn mouth, his chin. In Hell, he wrote in his mental diary, Mingolla was afflicted by a nosebleed and avoided serious involvement; he neither drank the water nor sampled the cuisine, and . . . *Shut up! Why don'tcha make me! Blow an ugly thought into my brain, and whoosh! I'm all aflame. Stop it!* Whoosh, crackle. *Did you catch that smell? Worse than those fucking snakes! Better snort that shit on the blade, man, or you're gonna drop it, the way you're shaking. Yeah, that's it. Do a little more . . . little more. See how it shuts down the voices, the memories? Smoothing everything out. Wiring shut the mouth of the brain with stitches of blue-white electricity, and soon there won't be anything except cool blue-white sparkling silence. But you know what, David, Davy, Dave, Mister Mingolla, you know what?*

No, what?

Even that'll be damning.

On the drive back to La Ceiba through the moonless dark, Mingolla sat in front with the guards, with Carlito, Martín, and Julio. He avoided looking at Alvina, who was a few rows back, and instead studied the masks of the guards. It seemed he was beginning to be able to read them, to assign expression to the maps of bloody tendon and muscle. He hated the masks, but that was not indicative of any specific grudge or attitude. Hate was coming to be something he kept in a secret compartment, something statistical and impersonal, yet a signal of his identity, like a license to carry a gun. He listened to the guards joking about the banalities of their lives, the funny things they'd wit-nessed back at the Barrio, and he made a decision. It was only fair, he thought. Eye for an eye, and like that.

The bus stopped on the edge of town, and the whores

walked off in a body toward the lights of the Avenida de la Republica. Mingolla sat with his head down, waiting for motive to surface, for anything that would create a reason to act: he was that empty. "Don't you have to report?" one of the guards asked.

Mingolla saw the three anonymous faces turned his way. "There's danger," he said, backing up the statement with emotional evidence. "Get off the bus." He told them to leave their rifles, picked one up, and unchecked the safety.

Wind poured off the sea in a cold unbroken rhythm, sweeping through the roadside grass, pebbling his arms with gooseflesh. The guards huddled to the right of the door, their shirttails flapping, hugging themselves against the chill. Their faces were puzzled twists of tendon, confused alignments of muscle. "You mustn't be seen," Mingolla told them. "Lie down in the grass, and I'll let you know when the danger's passed."

Two of them moved off into the grass, but one asked, "What sort of danger?"

"Terrible danger," said Mingolla, wielding more influence. "Hurry now! Hurry!"

They lay down in the grass, hidden from sight, and he felt they had fallen from the earth, plummeted in a long dark curve. Why was he doing this? he wondered. What difference did it make? Whose moral imperative did it serve? Blackness everywhere he turned. Black sea, black grass, black air. Only the bus was white, and that was a lie. One guard poked up his head, and that little red face with its surprised hole of a mouth punctuating the turbulent black poem of the winded grass . . . it irritated Mingolla. "Get down!" he cried. "Get down!" And opened fire. The bursts barely audible above the wind. He raked the grasses until the clip was exhausted. He took the gun by the barrel and slung it toward the sea. He listened. Nothing, no moans, no screams. The mortal silence was astounding in its depth. All that had once been alive might now be dead. He liked it like that. The silence touched his heart with a cold snaky kiss, and he wondered if he should inspect the bodies. Check for breath. Nope, he thought; no need. He scented the air. Briny and clean. He'd done his duty, done it well. He could have stayed there forever, serene with accomplishment, but at last he climbed back into the bus and drove into town.

He strolled along the Avenida de la Republica, peering into the bars, feeling distant from the music and laughter, immune to the atmosphere. He bought a lime sno-cone from a vendor and sucked at ice chips as he walked, smiling at everyone, shaking his head at the kids who pushed black coral jewelry into his face. A whore stumbled out of a bar, bumped him, and he caught her around the waist to keep her from falling. She was skinny, with light freckled skin, reminding him of Hettie, and she was very drunk. He helped her back to her hotel, keeping a grip on her waist, and when they reached the door, she asked if he wanted to go upstairs.

"Wish I could," he said. "I've got an appointment."

"Well"—she patted her hair into shape, smiled foggily—"you very nice to gimme a hand."

"My pleasure," he said, and sauntered off.

At the end of the street was a public square with tall hibiscus bushes at the corners, flowering pink and red. Coconut palms looming along concrete paths that crossed at diagonals, stone benches, a central fountain like a stone lily. Facing the square was a large white stucco church with two tiers of steps leading up to its brightly lit facade. Mingolla chose a bench near the fountain, did some frost for alertness, enough to put an extra shine on the splashing water. Clumped in the shadow of a hibiscus farther down the path was a group of shoeshine boys. Chattering, smoking cigarettes. Their kits were decorated with mosaics of broken glass, and to Mingolla they looked like midgets with diamond-studded satchels. He wished he had a cigarette; he had never smoked, but recalling friends who did, he thought that this seemed the perfect time for a cigarette, the sort of significant lull during which a smoke is helpful in focusing one's thoughts. He did a tad more frost, instead. The shoeshine boys watched with interest, but showed no sign of going for the police. Not that he cared. He could handle the police. He got a nice drain off the frost and kicked back, crossing his legs, thinking that he had overreacted to de Zeduguí's death. Still, he realized a certain amount of reaction was inescapable. He would be better prepared in the future. He would go to the Petén, take care of Debora, and after that . . . well, after that the future would take care of itself.

The faint drift of music from the bars brought back nights on a Florida beach with an old girlfriend, the car door left open so they could hear the radio while they made out on the sand or screwed in the shallows. You could walk out a hundred yards and only be in up to your thighs. Tepid, calm water. Lighted buoys winking like fallen stars. Kids drinking in the other cars, throwing bottles to smash against the sea wall. These thoughts cheered him. He had come through a bad time, but it was behind him now, and he had his memories back. All of them. He did a bladeful of frost to celebrate, and suddenly felt that he was David Mingolla, David fucking Mingolla, the guy he had nearly lost track of, the guy of whom great things had been predicted, his old self again . . . only more so.

FIRE ZONE EMERALD

. . . According to tradition, the abuse that led to the war between the Madradonas and the Sotomayors was the abduction of Juana Madradona de Lamartine by Abimael Sotomayor in the year 1612, but can one explain away centuries of bloodshed and malfeasance by the emotional reactions to this single act? Can one assign blame for the Slaughter of the Children in Bogota in 1915, or the bombing of the Sotomayor compound in Guatemala City in 1949 to the excesses of a man three centuries dead? No, the feud between the families was—like all great conflicts—nurtured by a lust for power, the power contained within an innocuous-looking weed that grew only in a valley west of Panama City divided by the border of their adjoining estates.

from *The War Between the Madradonas and the Sotomayors*
—*Juan Pastorín*.

CHAPTER NINE

O n their last night together in the Petén, Santos Garrido told Mingolla a story. It was an act neither of camaraderie nor of instruction, merely the answer to a casual question; but because of events that followed shortly thereafter, Mingolla came to assign it more than a casual meaning.

For three days they had been hiking through the jungle, leaving behind the village of Sayaxché, once a staging area for Cuban infantry, but now—the fight having moved north along the Mexican border—reverted to the sleepy unimportance of a stopover for the peddlers who traveled the Rio de la Pasión, selling tin lanterns and bolts of cheap cloth and striped plastic jugs. Mingolla's previous experience of jungle had been limited to strolls through the fringe surrounding the Ant Farm, and this, the heart of the rain forest, surprised him by the hardships levied upon those who entered it. They walked along narrow paths of brown clay crossed by tiny grooves, the trails of leaf-cutter ants, and whenever Mingolla stopped to catch his breath, the ants would swarm up his legs and bite; because Garrido—his guide—would not wait for him to pick them off, he would beat at them as he went, creating deep bruises on his thighs. They encountered mattes of dead vines from which clouds of stinging flies and mosquitoes would rise, buzzing in Mingolla's hair, invading his nose and mouth. They plunged down rocky defiles, crawling beneath toppled tree trunks, home to centipedes and spiders that dropped onto their necks. The heat was

overwhelming at first. Mingolla's mosquito repellent was sweated
off in minutes, and he would have to wash with water in which
Garrido had dissolved cigar tobacco, his theory being that
nicotine was the most effective of all repellents . . . a theory
that Mingolla to his own satisfaction disproved. But as they
moved deeper into the Petén, it became cooler, clammy and
dripping. Every leaf he brushed against left a wet print on his
clothing, and even the cries of the monkeys sounded liquid. He
began to notice the beauty of the jungle. Green light, green
shadow. Cathedral pillars of giant figs and ceibas upholding a
vaulted canopy, their boles furred with orange club moss, and
butterflies with six-inch wingspans dappling their trunks. Prows
of limestone bursting from the jungle floor, netted in vines, like
petrified schooners saved from sinking into a long-vanished
lake. Everywhere was the litter of war, and this added to nature
a curious inorganic beauty. A combat helmet with a cracked,
cobwebbed faceplate lying in a hollow like a strange egg; the
rusted turret of a minitank protruding from a stand of bamboo,
draped in flowering epiphytes; an un-exploded missile so overgrown with scale and algae that it seemed a vegetable produc-
tion, as if the jungle had mimicked the creatures of war, giving
birth to a creature that could pass among them.

That third night, Mingolla and Garrido set up camp beneath a high limestone shelf, stringing their hammocks between
three sapodilla trees, making a meal of cold beans and tortillas.
Garrido was a wizened yet hale man in his early sixties, his hair
still black and his dark brown skin underlaid with a rosy tint.
The only words he had addressed to Mingolla had been by way of
caution or direction, and it was clear that he did not think much
of Mingolla either as a colleague or as a man. Mingolla was untroubled by this opinion; in his eyes Garrido was merely a tool.

He spent the hour after dinner cleaning his machine pistol;
then he took out a packet of frost and got high. Moonlight filtered
through the canopy, puddling silver over the limestone and the surrounding foliage, and it looked like they were sitting in a fold of
black cloth imprinted with an abstract design. Insects and frogs
started an eerie chorus that had the sound of music made by hollowed bamboo and bubbling water. Mingolla paused to listen,
balancing a heap of white powder on the tip of his knife.

"Why do you take that?" Garrido asked.

Mingolla inhaled, tipped back his head to let the frost drain. "It makes things sharper." He gave a brittle laugh. "And it keeps off the bugs."

"Are you an addict?"

"I have a slight dependency."

Garrido was silent for a bit. "When we set out," he said finally, "I didn't think I understood you. I thought you were different from the other Americans I've guided. Why, I asked myself, does this young man hunt with such zeal? I sensed something in you that doesn't accord with this sort of hunt. But I was wrong. You're the same as the others. You look at things the same way."

"And how's that?"

"Without emotion."

Mingolla's sniff was partly to clear his nose, partly a reaction: to be emotionless seemed to him an ideal.

"As if," Garrido continued, "emotion were an impediment to your master plan."

"Why are you telling me this?"

"It's best to make plain where one stands when going into dangerous territory."

"You saying you won't back me up?"

"Simply defining the limits of my responsibility."

The music of the jungle was growing louder, closing in around them, and Mingolla imagined the darkness to be a trillion open throats ringing the camp. "Why bother?" he asked.

Garrido fingered a cigar from his shirt pocket and lit up. The coal illuminated his mouth and the glints of his eyes. "Once a friend and I found a jade cup in an unexcavated mound. A Mayan cup. Our fortunes were made. But I wanted it all for myself, and I ran off with it. Later I learned that my friend had died of the fever . . . without money for medicine. Since then I've been honest with my companions. Honesty prevents that sort of misunderstanding."

He said this with a degree of feeling, and Mingolla tried to see his expression, but could not. "What 'bout the cup?"

"It was stolen . . . by an American."

"Which explains why you don't like us." Mingolla dug into the packet of frost again.

185

"That's not it. I understand Americans, and it's hard to care about anything you understand."

"It must really be a chore for you," Mingolla said, "walking around so fulla crap all the time. I know it is for me. I know when I look inside myself and see all the ridiculous crud and opinion I think are wise, it makes me fucking sick to realize I ever bought any of it. But then the next minute, there I go spouting it all over again." He inhaled from the knife, spat mucus. "Excuse me. It's just that when I hear major bullshit like 'I understand Americans,' I tend to get amused. 'Specially when it's followed up with, 'It's hard to care 'bout anything you understand.' I mean that's very deep. That's, y'know, like philosophy."

"Perhaps you're right," said Garrido. "But what I've said tonight is true enough for you and me."

"Whatever."

Maybe, Mingolla thought, inhaling again, he would stay up all night and grow full of jungle profundity like Garrido. "So why you work for us if you don't like us?"

Garrido blew smoke and coughed. "I'll tell you a story."

"Oh, boy!" said Mingolla. "Lemme grab the popcorn! What's it called?"

"I've never given it a title," said Garrido, an edge to his voice. "But I suppose you could call it 'The Conquistador's Ghost.' "

"Sounds spooky!" Mingolla leaned forward, making a dumb show of attentiveness. "I'm all fucking ears."

"This is my only answer," said Garrido stiffly. "Do you want to hear it or not?"

"Sure do . . . I mean there's nothin' on TV, right?"

Garrido sighed, exasperated. Insects swarmed in haywire orbits around the coal of his cigar, flashing whitely across the glow.

"Once not long ago," he began, "there was a hunter, a Mayan like myself, who lived in a village not far from the ruins of Yaxchilán. Every morning he would rise before dawn, breakfast with his wife and son, and head out into the jungle with his rifle. He would hunt all morning, tracking tapir and deer, avoiding the trails of the jaguar, and when the sun was high he would find a place to rest and eat his lunch. Then he would have a siesta. One afternoon he fell asleep in the shade of a buried temple, and he was waked by the ghost of a Mayan

186

king, his ancestor, a man wearing a red cloth about his waist and a necklace of gold and turquoise.

" 'Help me!' cried the king. 'My enemy pursues me!'

" 'How can I help?' asked the hunter; he had no idea what manner of assistance he could render against an enemy immune to bullets and blows . . . so he concluded the enemy to be, for no one can harm a creature of the spirit world except another similar creature.

" 'You must let me lay my hand on your brow,' said the king. 'When I have done this, you will fall into a dream, and I will enter it and hide therein.'

"The hunter was pleased to be of service to his ancestor, for he was a man who honored tradition, who had great regard for the old Mayans. He let the king lay a hand on his brow and immediately fell into a dream of a palace with labyrinthine corridors and rooms with secret doors. The king passed down one of the corridors and vanished from sight. The dream faded, and other, more ordinary dreams took its place.

"Not long thereafter the hunter was waked by a white man dressed in a suit of armor with gold filigree, riding a black horse with fiery eyes and steam spouting from its nostrils. The ghost of a conquistador. 'I know you have hidden the king,' he said in a voice like an iron bell. 'Open your mind to me, and I will follow him.'

" 'No,' said the hunter. 'I will not.'

"The conquistador's ghost drew his sword and swung it in a mighty arc that shivered the trees and left a trail of smoke in the air. But the Indian was not afraid, willing to die for the security of his traditions. When the conquistador's ghost saw his lack of fear, he sheathed his sword, leaned down, smiled, and said in a voice like honey, 'I will give you a golden coin if you but let me enter.'

"Now this sorely tempted the hunter, for he was poor, his home a hut of thatch and brushwood, and though he provided his family with enough to eat, like all men he sought to improve the lot of his loved ones. But he resisted temptation and once again refused. His face twisted in rage, the conquistador's ghost reined his horse hard, making it rear, and galloped off, dwindling to a point of darkness that flashed as red as a star in the instant it disappeared.

"The hunter was pleased with himself, and that night he played happily with his child and embraced his wife with fervor, certain that his assistance to the king would bring him great good fortune. But the next day as he took aim at a deer, he heard a pounding as of iron-shod hooves, and out of no-where appeared the conquistador's ghost, riding straight at the deer and sending it leaping away into the cover of the brush. Laughing wildly, the ghost reined in his horse and vanished in the same manner he had the previous day. The hunter did not sight another deer and returned home empty-handed. There was food in his larder, however, and he was sure his luck would improve. But for two weeks thereafter, each time he made to kill his quarry, be it deer or tapir or agouti, the conquistador's ghost would ride out of nowhere and give the alarm. Doggedly, the hunter persisted, but by the end of two weeks his wife and child had become ill from lack of food and he had grown desperate. He had no lunch to carry with him on his hunts, but he continued his habit of siesta, and on the fifteenth day after he had helped the king, the conquistador's ghost waked him from a dream of skulls and said in a voice like ashes, 'Let me enter, or I will haunt your days until your family dies of starvation.'

"The hunter saw that he had no choice, and he let the conquistador's ghost touch his breast with his sword, at which point he fell into the dream of the labyrinthine palace. The ghost galloped down the corridor, and when the hunter waked he found a gold coin lying in his palm. His first impulse was to throw the coin away, but remembering the plight of his family, he took the coin and bought food. That night it did his heart good to see the color return to their cheeks as they lay with full bellies under the stars, but he felt shame over what he had done, and he wondered if he would ever feel otherwise.

"The next afternoon he dreamed again of the palace, and to his amazement the king came to the front of the dream, begged to be released, and told him the secret of opening the doors of a dream. The hunter was delighted to have this chance to atone for his weakness and did as the king instructed. But moments later the conquistador's ghost galloped from the depths of the palace and demanded exit. Gleeful, the hunter locked the doors of the dream and went about his business. But during his siesta the following afternoon, he fell into a nightmare of such vivid torment that under ordinary circumstances he would have waked screaming. He did not wake, however. Demons flayed his skin, insects with steel pincers fed each other morsels of his flesh and tweaked his exposed nerves, and still he slept on. And in the background of the dream he saw the conquistador's ghost looking on and smiling, resting his arms on the pommel of his saddle. At last the ghost cantered forward and said in a voice like ice, 'Give me passage, or I will make you dream your own death.' And again having no choice, the hunter opened the doors of his dream and let the ghost sally forth.

"When he waked he found another golden coin in his palm, and he was so unnerved that he went to the nearest cantina and drank himself insensible. He understood that he had been chosen by the spirits as the ground on which to fight their ancient battle, and he could only hope this particular engagement would be brief. But the next afternoon the king once again begged entry to the hunter's dream, and when a brief time later the conquistador's ghost came into view, the hunter complied with his demands and, his heart full of remorse, accepted another golden coin. First months, then years went by. The hunter constructed plots against the conquistador's ghost, but for each the ghost had a remedy. He grew wealthy due to the daily payments, and his family's future now assured, he considered suicide. But his moral imperatives had been seduced by comfort, and he reasoned that if it were not he whose dreams served as the battlefield, it would be some other: how could he burden anyone else with this terrible conflict?

"Then one day as the king fled the dream, he said to the hunter, 'Friend, thank you for your years of service. I am leaving now to find a new dream, for the conquistador has delved all the secrets of the palace and I can no longer elude him.'

"Stricken by guilt, the hunter asked forgiveness, but the king told him that there was nothing to forgive, that the hunter had provided him with the best hiding place he had ever had. He sprinted off into the jungle, and soon the conquistador's ghost emerged from the dream. He, too, spoke to the hunter.

" 'Of all the hunts I have known,' he said in a voice that rumbled like a volcano, 'yours has provided the most intriguing of all. I am sorry to see it exhausted.'

"The hunter trembled with hate, but limited himself to saying, 'I am grateful I will never have to lay eyes on you again.'

"The ghost's laughter filled the sky with dark clouds. 'You are an innocent, my friend. That which is fallow will one day be fertile again, and that which is valueless will grow to be priceless. Sooner or later you will dream a new dream, and we will return to have our sport within it.'

" 'Never!' said the hunter. 'I would rather die.'

" 'Die, then,' said the conquistador's ghost in a voice of flame. 'Perhaps your child will have the gift of dreams.'

"The hunter was staggered by this possibility, and knew that he would do anything to spare his child this doom.

"Again the ghost laughed, and lightning flashed across the sky, its forked values defining the thousand forms of terror in the language of the gods. 'Here!' The ghost tossed a golden coin studded with emeralds at the hunter's feet, a coin worth a decade of its usual payments. 'I commission you to build me a new dream, one more elaborate than that of the palace. When I return it had better be ready.' And with that the ghost rode off in pursuit of the king, its steed leaving a trail of hoofprints from which an ineffable smoke arose, signs clear enough so that any spirit peering down from the heavens might take note of them and follow."

Garrido butted his cigar, making a nest of sparks on the limestone. He seemed to be waiting for a response.

"Coulda used a hair more dialogue," said Mingolla. "But not bad."

Letting out a hiss of disgust, Garrido pulled himself up by his hammock rope. "Good night," he said. He slipped into the hammock and pulled the mosquito netting over his head.

Despite himself, Mingolla had been impressed by the story,

although his secondary reaction had been to consider asking Garrido why he hadn't simply said, "For the money." But he realized this would have been unfair. He would have liked to question Garrido further, for it had occurred to him that not only were there a great many things he did not understand, but there well might be a great many other things to whose very existence he had been blind. He gave thought to cultivating Garrido's friendship, but after reflection decided against it, feeling that friendship would blur his judgments, and that the argument between them would in the long run prove more entertaining than any conversation generated by an accord.

He managed to get to sleep despite the frost, though sleep was hardly restful, a tapestry of anxiety dreams, and when he was awakened by a bright light shining in his eyes, he wondered if he had cried out and disturbed Garrido. "What is it?" he asked, shielding his eyes, his hand tangling with the mosquito netting.

"Son of a bitch!" said a voice with a hillbilly twang. "This ol' beaner talks American."

"I am American." He struggled up. "What the fuck's going on?" Something jabbed him hard in the chest, shoving him back; through the white mesh, he saw a rifle barrel and a hand holding a flashlight.

"Sure looks like a beaner," said somebody else.

"I'm an agent . . . a spy. Who are you people?"

"We own this place, man," said the hillbilly voice, loaded with menace. "And you trespassin'."

A chill washed away the dregs of Mingolla's drowsiness, and he pushed with his mind; but rather than meeting mild electrical resistance and enforcing his will, he was flung back, repelled: it was as if he had been riding in a car, had stepped out while it was still moving, and instead of running smoothly along, had been flipped up into the air. He tried again, achieved the same result.

"That's a disguise, huh?" said the hillbilly. "How we gonna tell for sure? Lotsa Cubans do real good American. Maybe we scrape 'way a little bitta that color, see what's under it."

A chorus of dopey-sounding laughter.

"Whyn't ya do like them ol' war movies, Sarge? Ast him questions 'bout baseball and stuff?" Another voice.

"Yeah!" Hillbilly. "How 'bout that, friend. S'pose you tell us who plays centerfield for the Chicago Bears."

"Your pal in disguise, too?" Still another voice.

"What you guys want?" Mingolla tried to push the rifle barrel away. "Lemme up!"

"Guess his buddy's a beaner for real," said the hillbilly. "Go 'head and do him."

A burst of automatic fire.

Mingolla stiffened. "Garrido?"

"He answers ya, man," said the hillbilly, "and I'm gettin' outta here."

"You crazy motherfucker!" Mingolla said. "We're . . ."

The rifle punched harder into his chest. "You ain't outta the woods yo'self, boy. Now you wanna answer my question?"

Mingolla suppressed an urge to scream, to heave up from the hammock. "What question?"

" 'Bout who plays centerfield for the Bears."

Snickering.

"The Bears play football," said Mingolla.

"Well, I'm convinced! Take a reg'lar American to know that," said the hillbilly amid renewed laughter. "Trouble is"—the humor left his voice—"we don't cotton that much to Americans, neither."

Silence, insects chittering.

"Who are you?" Mingolla asked.

"Name's Coffee . . . Special Forces, formerly 'tached to the First Infantry. But y'might say we seen the light an opted outta the military. You gotta name, boy?"

"Mingolla . . . David Mingolla." He thought he knew them now, and to make sure he asked, "What do you mean, 'seen the light'?"

"The light's holy in Emerald, man. Y'sit under the beams what shine through the leaves, let 'em soak into ya, and they'll stir truth from your mind."

"That right?" Mingolla pushed again, and again achieved nothing.

"Think we're nuts, don'tcha?" said Coffee. "You 'mind me of my ol' lieutenant. Man used to tell me I's crazy, and I say, 'I ain't ordinary crazy, lieutenant sir. I'm crazy gone to Jesus.' And I'd tell him 'bout the kingdom we was gonna build. No machines, no pollution. Y'gonna thrive here, David, if you can pass muster. Learn to hunt with a knife, track tapir by the smell. Hear what weather's comin' in the cry of a bird."

"How 'bout the lieutenant?" Mingolla asked distractedly, trying to gain a purchase in Coffee's mind. "He learn all that?"

"Y'know how it is with lieutenants, David. Sometimes they just don't work out."

The mosquito netting was flung back, and he was hauled from the hammock, forced to his knees, a rope cinched about his wrists. He saw the shadowy cocoon of Garrido's hammock in the indirect glow from the flashlight: it looked to be bulged down lower than before, as if death had weighed out heavier than life. He was yanked upright, spun around to face a gaunt rack of a man with rotting teeth and blown-away pupils; an unkempt beard bibbed his chest, and dark hair fell in snarls to his shoulders. He was holding the flashlight under his chin so that Mingolla could see his grin. Behind him stood his men, all of a cut, bearded and thin, smaller than their leader. Their fatigues holed, rifles outmoded.

"Pleased to meetcha, David," said Coffee, lowering the flashlight. "You up for a little night march?"

"Maybe he should pop a couple?" said one of the others.

"Yeah, maybe." Coffee dug into his pocket, then shone the flashlight into his palm, illuminating two silver foil bullets. "Ever do Sammy?"

"Listen," said Mingolla. "I've got—"

Coffee drove a fist into his stomach, bending him double. Only the fact that someone was holding the rope around his wrists prevented him from falling. He couldn't breathe for several seconds, and when he had recovered sufficiently to breathe through his mouth, Coffee grabbed his chin and straightened him. "That's the first lesson," he said. "Y'answer when you spoke to. Now y'ever done Sammy?"

"No."

"Well, don't get all anxious . . . it's purely a joy and a triumph." Coffee held up one of the ampules. "Just breathe in deep when I pop it, y'hear. Or else I'm gonna give ya 'nother lesson." He crushed an ampule between his thumb and forefinger, and Mingolla inhaled the stinging mist. "Here comes number two," said Coffee cheerfully.

The world was sharpening, coming closer. Mingolla could see the spidery shapes of monkeys high in the canopy, backed by rips of moonlight, framed in filigrees of black leaves; he heard a hundred new sounds, and heard, too, how they knitted the darkness into a comprehensible geography of rustling ferns and scraping branches. The wind was cool, its separate breezes licking at him, feathering his hair.

"I love to watch the first time," said Coffee. "God, I love it!"

Mingolla felt disdain for Coffee, and his disdain manifested in a rich, nutsy laugh.

"Feel like you lookin' down from the mountaintop, don'tcha? Don't you trust that feelin', David. Don't figger on runnin' off or takin' me out." Coffee grabbed Mingolla's shirt, pulled him face to face. "I been up in Emerald for two years now, and I can tell when a fly takes a shit. Far as you concerned, I'm lord of the fuckin' jungle!" He released Mingolla with a shove. "Awright, let's go."

"Where we going?" Mingolla asked.

"Questions?" Coffee went face to face with him again, and madness seemed to be flying out of his enlarged pupils, a vibration beating around Mingolla's head. "Y'don't ask questions, y'do what ya told." Coffee relaxed, grinned. "But since you new, I'll tell ya. We goin' to the light of judgment, gonna decide whether or not y'run with the pack." He shouldered his rifle. "Hope that eases your mind."

The man holding Mingolla's rope gave it a jerk, and he fetched up against Garrido's hammock; he recoiled from it, and the man said, "Ain'tcha never seen a dead beaner?"

A chemical fury was building in Mingolla, a furious perception of new involvements of honor and character. He wrenched the rope loose from the man's grip, and when the man jabbed at him with his rifle, he brushed the rifle aside and, moving with uncommon swiftness, kicked the man's legs out from under him. "I'll kill your ass!" he said. "Touch me again, I'll kill your ass quick!"

"My, my," said Coffee from behind him. " 'Pears we gotta tiger by the tail." His tone was mirthful, sardonic, but when Mingolla turned, he saw in the configuration of Coffee's grin a kind of harsh appraisal, and realized he had made a mistake.

Every half-hour as they walked, the men beside Mingolla would pop ampules under his nose, and the inside of his head came to feel heavy with violent urges, as if his thoughts had congealed into a lump of mental plastique. He tried to influence the men, using all his power, but without success. Even had influence been an ordinary problem, his concentration was not what it should have been. The roughness of the terrain commanded a measure of his attention, and the generic mystic-warrior personality supplied by the drug tended to decry the concept of influence as lacking in honor. Rather than continuing his efforts, he concocted intricate escape plans with bloody resolutions. The sharpness of his senses was confusing—he spent a good deal of time identifying odors and sounds—and the initial burn of the drug was of such intensity, he became convinced that many of his perceptions were hallucinations. He had trouble believing, for instance, that the drumbeat issuing from his chest was his heartbeat; nor could he accept that the high-pitched whistlings in his ears were the cries of the bats that flashed like Halloween cutouts through the moonbeams. And so when he first sensed Debora's presence, he disregarded it. But the impression remained strong, and once, straining toward the darkness from which the impression seemed to derive, he was positive that he had brushed the borders of her mind, feeling the telltale arousal of electrical contact, and feeling also a mental coloration that—though he'd had no previous experience of it, at least on a conscious level—he recognized as hers. After that one contact she either blocked or moved beyond range. What was she doing? he asked himself. Tracking him? If so, did she know his assignment? Then why hadn't she ambushed him? Maybe, he thought, she had never been there at all.

They came to a large circular clearing overgrown with ferns, ringed by giant figs and mahogany trees: the canopy here was less dense, and the clearing had the look of an aquarium bowl filled with pale milky fluid at the bottom of which strange feathered creatures were stirring in a feeble current. Man-shaped objects were affixed to the tree trunks, but the dimness masked their exact nature. Mingolla was thrown onto the ground and left in the care of a single guard, while the rest—fifteen in all—sat down in the middle of the clearing. The guard forced two more ampules on Mingolla, and he lay on his back in a silent fury, working at the ropes. The subdued voices of the men, the insects, and the soft wind fused into a hushed clutter of sound, and it increased his fury to think that he should be subject to any judgment conceived in this muddled place.

"Ain't gon' do ya no good to slip them ropes," said the guard. "We just run ya down." He was a balding man with a full reddish brown beard and a triangular piece of mirror hung around his neck. "Naw, ol' Sarge ain't gon' let ya 'scape. He been waitin' onna sign for a long time, and 'pears to me you it."

Mingolla redoubled his efforts. "Maybe I ain't the sign he's been expecting."

The guard laughed derisively. "Sarge don't 'spect nothin'. He just reads 'em when they come. Ain't nobody better'n Sarge at readin' sign."

"I am," said Mingolla, hoping to play on the guard's delusions. "That's why I've come . . . to instruct, to give direction."

The guard laughed again, but shakily; he lifted his piece of mirror and reflected moonlight into his face.

Mingolla had just begun to make headway with the ropes when Coffee walked over, dismissed the guard, and squatted beside him. He sucked on his teeth, making a whiny glutinous sound, and said, "Ever think much 'bout the Garden of Eden, David?"

Coffee's wistful tone—as if he were regretting original sin—

took the edge off Mingolla's anger and left him at a loss for words.

"Read this article once't," Coffee went on. "Said the Garden was somewheres in the Anartic. Said they found all these froze-up berries and roots from thousands of years ago. They figgered once't the Serpent did his business with Eve, the life force drained outta the place, and everything turned to ice. Reckon that's so?"

"I don't know." Mingolla tried to influence Coffee and failed. It seemed the drugs added a spin to the electrical activity of the brain, one with which he couldn't synchronize even when under the influence himself.

"Yeah, me neither. Can't believe nothin' y'read in the papers. Like all the horseshit they print 'bout politics." Coffee popped an ampule, sucked in the mist. He glanced toward the clearing. Only three men remained sitting there.

"Where the rest of your men?" Mingolla asked, leery.

"Scoutin' 'round." Coffee cracked his knuckles. "Yeah, the stuff they print 'bout politics . . . Man! Pure horseshit! Gotta dig out the truth for yo'self. Half of them First Ladies was guys wearin' dresses. Y'can see that just by lookin'. Ugly! I mean if you was president, wouldn't you have yo'self somethin' better for a wife than one of them ol' bags? Yessir, them presidents was all queers . . . members of a secret queer organization."

"I didn't know that," said Mingolla, making another fruitless effort at mental contact.

"Wouldn't 'spect ya' to know. Come to me as a revelation. That's the only sorta knowledge y'can trust." Coffee's profound sigh seemed the result of understanding the wide world and its great trouble. "Ever have a revelation, David?"

"Depends what you mean by 'revelation.' "

"If y'have to figger what it means, y'ain't never had one." Coffee scratched his beard. "Y'believe in anything . . . like a higher power?"

"No," said Mingolla. "I don't."

"Oh, yes y'do, David. You a man with a plan, a man what's too busy schemin' to stop and figger things out. That's when the revelations come, when you stop." Coffee gazed out at the clearing again, his Lincolnesque profile set off by the pale light. "That's what y'believe in, David. In not stoppin', in not believin'."

The three men in the clearing were as still and silent as prophets at their meditations, shadows in a milky globe, and the mystical quality of the scene convinced Mingolla for a moment that Coffee's assessment had been accurate, that inspiration was to be had at the center of the light.

"Last man with a plan to come 'round Emerald was me," Coffee said. "Way it looks from here, I can't judge ya 'cause you a judgment on me. I ain't been too clear in my mind lately, been slackin' in my work. 'Pears you sent to test me, and I welcome the test."

"What kinda test?"

"Fang and claw, David. Fang and claw." Coffee took a handful of ampules from his pocket and heaped them on the ground. "There's your ammo, man. Roll on over, now, and I'll cut ya loose."

"Wanna tell me what's going on?"

Coffee turned Mingolla over, sawed at the ropes with a knife. "I'm comin' for ya in the mornin', when the light's strong. Gonna take ya out, David."

Mingolla's stomach knotted. "What if I kill you?"

"You a test, David, not a challenge."

Mingolla sat up, rubbing his wrists, looking at Coffee. The moonlight brightened, and he felt it was illuminating more than their faces and clothes, enforcing honesty like a shared attitude. He thought he could see Coffee's truth, see him leaning against a gas station wall at some hick crossroads, top dog in a kennel of curs, sucking down brews and plotting meanness, and it seemed to him that though Coffee was misguided, insane, he had at least come to an honorable form of meanness. He wondered what Coffee could see of him. "What 'bout weapons?" he asked.

"Like I said." Coffee held up his hands. "Fang and claw." He gestured at the men in the clearing. "The boys'll make sure nobody gets illegal, and the rest is spread out in case anybody runs." With a show of weariness, he got to his feet, and from

Mingolla's perspective his head appeared to merge with the canopy, making him look as tall and mysterious as the trees. "See ya in the mornin'," he said.

"This is bullshit, this crap 'bout a test!" said Mingolla, his fear breaking through like a moon escaping cloud cover. "You just need to kill somebody, to prove something to your men."

Coffee kicked a fern, moved off. "Why's a car engine work, man? 'Cause ya turn the key in the ignition? 'Cause sparks fly from the generator? 'Cause you 'membered to gas up? 'Cause some law of physics says so? Naw, it's 'cause of all that and a million things more we don't know nothin' about." He strolled farther off, becoming a shadow among shadows. "Ain't no such thing as cause and effect, ain't but one law means shit in this world." His voice came from utter darkness and seemed the sum of all the dark voices issuing from beyond the clearing. "Everything's true, David," he said. "Everything's real."

Coffee had left sixteen ampules, and feeling irritable and nauseated, symptoms he could trace to the packet of frost back at his camp, Mingolla popped a couple right away. A rain squall swept in, and after it had passed, to Mingolla's ears the plips and plops of dripping water blended into a gabbling speech; he imagined demons peeping from beneath the leaves, gossiping about him, but he wasn't afraid. The ampules were doing wonders, withdrawing the baffles that had been damping the core of his anger. Confidence was a voltage surging through him, keying new increments of strength, and he smiled, thinking of the fight to come: even the smile was an expression of furious strength, of bulked muscle fibers and trembling nerves.

Dawn came gray and damp, and birds set up a clamor, began taking their first flights, swooping over the heads of the three men in the clearing. The underbrush looked to be assuming topiary shapes. Violet auras faded in around ferns, pools of shadow quivered. Mingolla saw that the manlike objects affixed to the tree trunks were combat suits: ten slack, helmeted figures, each featuring some fatal rip or crack. Though he concluded that the suits might be equivalent to notches on Coffee's belt, he was undismayed. The drugs had added a magical

199

coloration to his thoughts, and he pictured himself moving with splendid athleticism, killing Coffee, becoming king of that dead man's illusion and ruling over the Lost Patrol, robed in ferns and a leafy crown. But the battle itself, not its outcome, that was the important thing. To reach that peak moment when perfection drew blood, when you muscled aside confusion and—as large as a constellation with the act, as full of stars and blackness and primitive meaning—you were able to look down on the world and know you had outperformed the ordinary. This was the path he had been meant to take, the path of courage and character. A mystic star shone through a rent in the canopy, marooned in a lavender streak above the pink of sunrise. Mingolla stared at it until he understood its sparkling message.

The light brightened, and butterflies flew up from the brush, fluttered low above the ferns. There were, Mingolla thought, an awful lot of them. Thousand upon thousands, an estimate he kept elevating until he reached the figure of millions. And he thought, too, that it was unusual for so many varieties to be gathered in one place. They were everywhere in the brush, perching on leaves and twigs, as if a sudden spring had brought forth flowers in a single night: some of the bushes were completely hidden, and the trunks were thick with them. Now and again they would rise from one of the bushes in a body and go winging in formation about the clearing. Mingolla had never seen anything like it, though he'd heard how butterflies would congregate in such numbers during the mating season, and he guessed that this was something similar.

Beams of sun angled into the clearing from the east, so complexly figured with droplets of moisture that they appeared to embody flaws and fracture planes, like artifacts of golden crystal snapped off in midair. The three men stood and took positions at the rim of the clearing. Apprehension spidered Mingolla's backbone, and he popped two ampules to clear his head. Then, tired of waiting, he walked to the center of the clearing, his nerves keyed by every shift of shadow, every twitching leaf. Clouds slid across the sun, muting the sky to a platinum gray; a palpable vibration underscored the stillness.

Less than a minute later, Coffee came jogging toward him from the east, a grin splitting the wild thatch of his beard. Mingolla had expected formalities, but Coffee broke into a run, and he barely had time to brace himself before the man hurtled into him, his head catching Mingolla in the side and knocking him to the ground. He went with the fall, rolling out of it and up to his feet; he circled away, amazed by the fluidity of his movements, and though his ribs ached from the impact, he laughed in delight.

"Aw, David!" Coffee balanced on one hand and a knee, still grinning. "I hate to rob ya of this joy." He hopped to his feet, held both fists overhead as if squeezing power from the air.

Laughter bubbled out of Mingolla. "You too crazy to live anymore, man. This ain't a test. . . . I'm here to relieve you of command."

"Are ya, no shit?" Coffee dropped into a crouch.

"Come to me inna dream," said Mingolla. "Your soul ascending into the light, your body all maggoty and hollow."

Coffee gave his head a good-natured shake, pawed at a butterfly that fluttered into his face. "I love ya, David. Swear I do." He stared admiringly at Mingolla. "Wish there's another way."

He lunged, swung his left fist, catching Mingolla on the cheekbone, rocking him; a second blow landed flush on the mouth, but he managed to keep his feet. His head spun, pain spiked his gums. He spat blood and the fragments of a tooth.

"See what I'm sayin', David?" Coffee flexed his left hand, swiped at some butterflies that danced before his eyes; two others had settled atop his head, like a bow tied in his stringy hair. "Just a matter of time."

He charged again, ducked Mingolla's looping right, and nailed Mingolla twice to the head, knocking him down; he planted a kick in Mingolla's ribs, the same spot he'd rammed with his head. Mingolla yelped, crawled away, and was flattened by another kick. Coffee hauled him to his knees, slapped him lightly as if to gain his attention.

"Well, David," he said. "It's cryin' time."

A couple of dozen butterflies were preening on Coffee's scalp—a bizarre animate wig—and others clung to his beard; a great cloud of them was circling low above his head like a whirlpool galaxy of cut flowers. Coffee noticed those in his beard, and with a befuddled look, he swiped at them. Two more perched on his brow. Ignoring them, he threw a punch that landed on the side of Mingolla's neck with stunning force. Threw another that clipped his jaw. He cocked his fist for a third punch. Mingolla fought to retain consciousness, but darkness was flittering at the edges of his vision, and when his head thudded against the ground, he blacked out.

He came around to cap-pistol noises, to a sky that was a hallucinatory blur of color. Reds, blues, yellows. He couldn't figure it out. Something odd lurched past, turning, staggering. Mingolla sat up, watched the thing reeling about the clearing. Matted with delicate wings, man-shaped, yet too thick and bulky to be a man. It screamed, tearing at the clotted wings tripling the size of its head, pulling off wads of butterflies, and then the scream was sheared away as if the hole had been plugged. Butterflies poured down in a funnel to thicken it further, and it slumped, mounded, its surface in constant motion, making it appear to be breathing shallowly. It continued to build, accumulating more and more butterflies, the sky emptying and the mound growing with the disconnected swiftness of time-lapse photography, until it had become a multicolored pyramid towering thirty feet above, like a temple buried beneath a million lovely flowers.

Mingolla stared at it, disbelieving yet also terrified that it would fall on him, bury him under a ton of fragile weights. The cap-pistol noises were coming more frequently, and a bullet zipped into the ferns beside him. He went flat, whimpered at the pain in his ribs, and belly-crawled through the ferns. Blight-dappled fronds pressed against his face, slid away with underwater slowness. It seemed he was burrowing through a mosaic of muted browns and greens into which even the concept of separateness had been subsumed, and so he didn't notice the boot until his hand fell upon it: the rotting brown boot of a man lying on his stomach, holed at the ankles and with vines for laces. Several butterflies perched on the heel. He inched closer, spotted a rifle stock protruding from a mound of butterflies. Carefully, afraid to touch them, he pulled the rifle to him. About a dozen butterflies came with it, clinging to the barrel and the clip. One fluttered onto his hand, and he squawked, shaking it off. Then he eased around the body and into the margin of the jungle.

The firing had become sporadic, and bullets were no longer striking near. Mingolla dragged himself behind a fallen tree trunk. He popped an ampule, had a resurgence of energy, but still felt like shit. His ribs were on fire, and the lumped bruises on his face were heavy and sick-feeling, full of poison. He spat more blood, probed with his tongue at the hole where his tooth had been. Then he turned onto his back, thinking about Coffee under all those butterflies, throat stuffed with their prickly legs, ticklish wings. He looked through a screen of brush at the clearing. Butterflies everywhere, a storm of them whirling and whirling. They'd be coming for him soon. And that was all right. He lay drained and thoughtless, watching the butterflies, not really seeing them, seeing instead the afterimages of their flights, streaks of color that lingered in the air. Time seemed to collapse around him, burying him under a ton of decaying seconds.

Something snapped in the brush to his left, and a man stumbled out of the cover. The red-bearded man who had stood guard over him. He'd lost his little piece of mirror. Dirt freckled his cheeks, bits of fern ribboned his hair. A survival knife dangling from one hand. He blinked at Mingolla. Swayed. His fatigues were plastered to his ribs, and a big bloodstain mapped the hollow of his stomach. His cheeks bulged: it looked as if he wanted to speak but was afraid more than just words would come out. "Jesus," he said sluggishly. His eyes rolled back, his knees buckled. Then he straightened, appeared to notice Mingolla, and staggered forward swinging the knife.

Mingolla tried to bring the rifle up and found that the stock was pinned under his hip. But somebody else got off a round. The bullet pasted a red star under the man's eye, stamped his features with a rapt expression, and he fell across Mingolla's ribs, knocking the breath from him. Shouting in the distance. Mingolla heaved the man off, his eyes squeezed shut against the pain. The effort mined a core of dizziness inside him. He resisted it, but then realizing that there was nothing attractive about consciousness, nothing he cared to know about the some-one in charge of death and butterflies, he let himself go spiral-ing down past layers of darkness and shining wings, darkness and mystical light, and a memory of pain so bright that it became a white darkness wherein he lost all track of being.

CHAPTER TEN

Lantern light washing shadows from a tin roof, fanning across a dirt floor, shining over walls of palmetto thatch, the fronds plaited into a weave like greenish brown scales. Smell of rain and decay. A wooden chair and table were the only furnishings aside from the pallet on which Mingolla lay, his ribs taped, jaw aching. And something bright was strung on the ceiling. Ribbons . . . or paper dolls. He rubbed his eyes, squinted, and made out hundreds of butterflies clinging to the roof poles, their wings stirring gently. He kept very still. He heard a man and woman speaking outside. Their words were unintelligible, but he thought he detected an accent in the man's voice. German, maybe. A second later, the man entered the hut. He wore dark slacks and a blue polo shirt, and radiated an unnatural measure of heat. Mingolla pretended to be asleep.

The man sat at the table, gazed thoughtfully at Mingolla. He was thin but well muscled, his short blond hair shot through with gray, and he had a cold ascetic handsomeness that in association with the accent called to mind evil SS officers in old war movies. One of the butterflies descended, perching on his knuckles. He let it walk across the back of his hand, then with a flick of his wrist, as if loosing a falcon, cast it aloft. " 'Transparent forms too fine for mortal sight,' " he said. " 'Their fluid bodies half-dissolv'd in light.' " He watched the butterfly alight on a roof pole. "And yet they can be quite formidable, can they not?"

Mingolla kept up his pretense.

"You are awake, I think," said the man. "My name is Nate, and you, I'm told, are David."

"Who told you that?" asked Mingolla, giving it up.

"A friend of yours . . . one who is convinced you are *her* friend."

"Debora?" Mingolla shrugged up, winced at a shooting pain in his side. "Where is she?"

Nate shrugged, an economic gesture, the merest elevation of his shoulder. " 'Fluttering like some vain painted butterfly from glade to glade along the forest path.' Matthew Arnold, from *The Light of Asia*." He smiled. "You know, I believe I could construct an entire conversation from quotations about butterflies."

Mingolla pushed his mind toward Nate, began to exert influence, and several dozen butterflies flew down from the ceiling, fluttered in his face.

"Please don't," said Nate. "There are a great many more outside."

There was something peculiar about Nate's mind, a dominant pattern in the electrical flux unusual for its complexity and resistance to influence; it seemed to Mingolla that the pattern was weaving a mesh too fine for his own mind to penetrate. He was fascinated by it, but didn't want to risk further exploration. "It was you back at the clearing, wasn't it?" he said.

Nate looked at him with disapproval. "That was a bad job . . . very bad. But she says you're worth it."

The thing to do, Mingolla thought, would be to buddy up to Nate, gain his confidence. "You've obviously been through the therapy," he said. "How'd you wind up here. You desert?"

"Not at all," said Nate. "Psicorps considered me a failure. I wasn't able to achieve any effect until after my release. To tell you the truth, I doubt the therapy had much to do with the development of my abilities. I was close by Tel Aviv when it was destroyed, and not long afterward I began to show some signs of having power. A product of my anger, I'm thinking." He stared up at the roof poles. "Butterflies. Hardly an appropriate tool for anger. Now if I'd managed an affinity with tigers or serpents . . ." He broke off, studied his clasped hands.

"What was it like?" Mingolla asked.

"What was what like?"

"Tel Aviv." Mingolla injected sympathy into his words. "Back in the States we heard about the suicides, the apathy."

"The bomb is a powerful symbol, powerful beyond its immediate effects. To see it . . . I can't explain it." He made a gesture of dismissal and glanced up at Mingolla. "Why are you hunting Debora?"

Mingolla didn't think he could lie successfully. "Things have changed," he said.

"Indeed, more than you know."

"I'll talk to him now," said Debora.

She was blocked, standing at the door, an automatic rifle under one arm, and seeing her, all Mingolla's preparations for this moment went skying. Of course the circumstances were different from those he had planned, but he had the feeling that even if everything had been as expected, his reaction would have been the same. It seemed his obsession was feeding on the sight of her, absorbing the loose fit of her jeans, the hollows in her cheeks, her hair—long uncut—falling to her waist, and composing of these elements a new portrait of obsession, a portrait of a leaner, more intense Debora. Her dark eyes reminded him in their steadiness of Hermeto Guzman's, and the clean division of white blouse and dusky skin reminded him of his dream of possession. Only after he had satisfied himself that she was more or less as he remembered did his resentments surface, and even then they were not vengeful, but the weaker, wistful emotions of a betrayed lover.

Nate gave her his chair and, with a cautionary look at Mingolla, went outside, followed by a leaf storm of butterflies. Debora laid her rifle on the table and said, "Your disguise isn't bad, but I liked you better as an American."

"So did I," he said, and, after a silence, asked, "Why'd you save me? How'd you know I was coming?"

She glanced at him, looked away. "It's complicated. I'm not sure how much I want to tell you."

"Then why are we talking?"

"I'm not sure about that, either."

Mingolla felt a bewildering mixture of anger and desire. "Are my ribs broken?"

"Just bruised, I think. I couldn't do much for your mouth. You'll have to be careful . . . keep it clean."

"You patched me up?"

"There wasn't anyone else. Nate's not much of a doctor."

"Yeah, but he's good with butterflies."

"Yes." Sadly.

"What's he alla 'bout, anyway?"

"He used to be a journalist." She had another quick look at him. "And he's going with me to Panama."

"Panama, huh?"

She nodded, toyed with the trigger guard of the rifle.

"Why don't you explain what's going on?"

"I can't trust you."

"What am I gonna do . . . overwhelm ten zillion fucking butterflies?"

"Your mind's very strong," she said. "You might be able to do something."

"We're going to have to talk sometime."

"Maybe."

A dozen intents were colliding in his head, running into one another, bouncing off, like cartoon policemen trying to grab someone who had just vanished into thin air; and what had vanished, he realized, what kept materializing in different parts of the room, shouting, "Hey, over here!" and causing another collision, was his basic intent regarding her . . . which was something he didn't care to confront and so made vanish time and again. But at the core of every intent was the tactic or the urge toward seduction. She lifted her head, and in the flickering light he thought he detected a scurrying of dark shapes behind her eyes, as if her purposes, too, were in collision.

"You shouldn't be suspicious of me," he said, and understanding how ludicrous that statement was, yet that he had meant every word, he laughed. "Look, I've been pretty fucked up. I, uh . . ."

"I know how it is," she said. "Believe me, I know what they can do to you."

That hadn't been his meaning, but he went along with her. "Yeah." He let a couple of seconds leak away. "Why'd you desert?"

She continued to examine the trigger guard. "I learned things that made me realize what I was doing was a lie. That made the revolution meaningless."

Mingolla thought about Alvina and Hermeto. "The struggle," he said, and gave a dismal laugh.

"There's nothing funny about it!" She smacked the rifle stock against the table.

"I guess not. It's just pathetic the way people keep ramming their heads into a brick wall."

Her face tightened. "And what would you do?"

"It's not my business. I got roped into this war."

"But not into Psicorps."

"That's true, but if I had a choice now, I would desert. I'm tired of killing, of people trying to kill me." He was borne away into memories of Coffee, de Zeguí, and the rest, and understood the full measure of their deaths. He felt he had been stripped of some armor that had enabled him to withstand the aftereffects of what he'd done. "I just wanna get outta here."

"Back to America!" She made the prospect sound obscene.

"What's wrong with that?"

"Nothing . . . if you can live with what you've seen, if you stuff your knowledge of oppression under a pillow and go back to painting little pictures." She snatched up the rifle and stood. "I can't take this. We'll talk tomorrow."

"What can't you take?"

"Your self-absorption," she said. "Your ability to look away from whatever offends your eye. I'm beginning to think it's a national characteristic."

"It's not my war."

Her turn to laugh. "Oh, yes it is! But you have to decide whose side you're on." She paused in the doorway and—her back toward him—said, "I was going to let the soldiers kill you."

"Why?" he said after a silence.

"You were after me. You might have killed me."

"How'd you know I was tracking you?"

"It doesn't matter."

She started through the door.

"What stopped you?" he called after her. "What the hell stopped you?"

Seconds later, fluttering ribbons of butterflies convoyed Nate into the hut. They settled on the roof poles, and with similar precision, Nate settled on the edge of the chair. His eyes probed Mingolla, and he gave a satisfied nod. "I'm thinking it will be all right now."

Distracted, wishing he hadn't acted like such an asshole with Debora, Mingolla said, "What's that?"

"Everything." The simplicity of the answer seemed to exploit a simplicity in Nate's features that Mingolla hadn't noticed before. He held up a hand, and two butterflies drifted down to decorate his forefinger. " 'Twixt purple shadow and gold of sun,' " he said, " 'two brown butterflies lightly settle, sleepily swing.' "

The village, a fly-swarmed Indian place littered with dung and mango rinds, was strung out along a bend in a jade-green river and consisted of about thirty huts, all less grand than Nate's. The high walls of vegetation hemming it in against the river were a weave of lush greens, and by contrast the huts were made of blackened poles lashed together with rotting twine; they were wrecked-looking, pitched at every angle like the remnants of unsuccessful bonfires. Pale smoke trickled from holes in the roofs, and the way the plumes were attenuated and pulled apart by the breeze, drifting into invisibility, they appeared to be responsible for the gradual whitening of the sky. Hammocks were strung inside the huts, plumped full, with children's faces peeping over the sides; chickens and pigs wandered in and out of doors. Except for a few flattened cans and sun-bleached beer labels on the ground, it might have been a settlement of the Dark Ages.

Mingolla strolled through the village, hunting for Debora, and unable to find her, he stood on the bank, watching the sun burn off streamers of ghost-gray mist. Nate joined him, butterflies clumped in patches on his trousers, others circling above. For want of anything better to do, Mingolla tried to strike up a conversation. "Debora tells me you're a journalist," he said.

"I was," Nate said.

"Uh-huh," Mingolla said after waiting a reasonable length of time for more detail. "A correspondent?"

Nate seemed to return from a mental vacation. "Yes, I was a war correspondent. An occupation with little focus these days."

Weary of puzzles, Mingolla didn't attempt to unravel the statement. "What's your last name? Maybe I've read your stuff."

"Lubove."

Mingolla sounded the name, heard a familiar resonance. "Shit! You're the guy did the articles on the guy who paints the ruins . . . the War Painter!"

"Yes."

"You ever find out who he is?"

"I learned he was Scandinavian. A Dane. But as to his specific identity, no luck there. Have you seen his work?"

"Just stuff on the news and photographs. Did they manage to save any of it?"

"Not to my knowledge. His boobytraps are most ingenious. Who would have thought that the profession of curator would have become so hazardous?"

"Yeah, I saw one of the murals blow up on TV." Mingolla kicked at a clump of mud, listened to it plop into the water. "Why're you and Debora going to Panama?"

"She'll tell you when she's ready."

"Where is she?"

"Busy," said Nate. "She asked me to accompany you this morning."

"She said we were gonna talk."

"Then you will . . . but not this morning." Nate waved toward the jungle. "I thought we'd go for a walk and visit a friend of mine."

"Terrific!" Mingolla threw up his hands. "Let's pack a lunch! Make a picnic out of it!" Butterflies eddied before his face. "Right," he said. "We'll go for a walk."

They set out along a trail that ran downhill through dense growths of bamboo and palmetto, and Mingolla asked whom they were going to visit.

"God," said Nate.

Mingolla inspected him for signs of insanity, then wondered if a walk was the jungle equivalent of taking someone for a ride.

"Actually, it's only a computer," said Nate. "But he makes an intriguing case for his divinity."

"A computer . . . what kinda computer?"

"An experimental model in one of your helicopters. It was shot down by a Russian missile, and the pilot was killed. But the missile didn't explode, just penetrated the computer deck. The computer cannibalized the missile for parts and repaired itself. According to it, this syncretic process gave birth to the incarnation."

"And you buy that?"

"Not an easy question to answer," said Nate. "For a long time I believed only in the god that rose over Tel Aviv one morning. But now, well . . . why don't you judge for yourself."

By the time they reached the crash site—a sizable ferny hollow ringed by granite boulders—the sun was fully up, and in the fresh morning light it had the look of a place touched by divinity. The helicopter was slim, black, cigar shaped, and had not fallen to earth, but was suspended about twenty feet above the floor of the hollow by a webbing of vines and shattered branches; with its crack-webbed cockpit eyes and buckled rotors, it showed in semisilhouette against the low sun like a mystical embryo, the unborn child of a gigantic alien race. The rents in the canopy caused by its passage had grown back, and blades of greenish gold light played over the metal surfaces, alive with refracted dust and moisture, shifting with the action of the breeze. Epiphytes fountained from the rotors, dripping crimson and lavender blooms, and butterflies appeared to materialize from the dazzles on the cockpit plastic, glowing flakes of white gold. At certain angles it was possible to see the skeleton of the pilot still strapped into his harness, but this reminder of death did not detract from the beauty of the hollow, rather effected a formal signature like a cartouche at the bottom of a painted scroll. It seemed less a geographic location than the absolute moment of a place, a landscape that brought to mind the works of Jan van Eyck, a mystic pastoral scene where at any second springs might burst from the rock and birds acquire the power of human speech.

They stood atop a boulder from which they could look down into the hole punched by the Russian missile ten feet below, at the glittering blue and green telltales of the computer inside the chopper. "What happens now?" Mingolla asked, and Nate put a finger to his lips.

"Good morning, Nate," said a dry amplified voice from the helicopter. "Are you feeling well?"

"Quite well, thank you."

"And David," said the computer. "It's good to meet you at last."

Though Mingolla assumed that the computer's identification was based on sensor readings, on information received from Debora and Nate, he was disconcerted by the cool immensity of the voice. "It's mutual," he said, feeling foolish. "How's it going?"

"Kind of you to ask," said the computer. "To tell you the truth, things are shaping up nicely. I expect we will soon have a resolution to the war, and . . ."

Mingolla laughed. "Really?"

"I take it, David, that you have been apprised of my nature and doubt my authenticity."

"You take it right."

"And what do you think I am?"

"A freak accident with a voice."

The computer emitted a mellow chuckle. "I've heard less apt definitions of God, although perhaps none less flattering. Of course the same definition might be applied to man."

"I won't argue that," said Mingolla, beginning to appreciate the computer's affability.

"Aha!" said the computer. "I believe I may be dealing with a practicing existentialist, a man who—in the vernacular— plays philosophical hardball, denying sentiment except when it coincides with his notions of romantic fatalism. Am I correct?"

"Don't you know?"

"Most assuredly, I do know. But this is a conversation, David. And I doubt you would find it entertaining were I to insist on omnipotence and infallibility. Besides, the times do not require these proofs."

"What do they require?"

"Me," said the computer. "No more, no less. Are you

213

interested in a summary of my function? I wouldn't want to bore you."

"Please," said Mingolla, thinking that by its urbanity, the computer had imbued this eerily beautiful place with the genteel atmosphere of a drawing room.

"It's quite simple. God appears now and again in highly visible incarnations . . . when the times call for such. However, most periods require only a token appearance, and this period is typical."

"It's hard to think of God as a token figure," Mingolla said.

"We've already established, David, that God is not a subject upon which you are expert."

"He has you there." Nate gave Mingolla a chummy elbow to the ribs, sending him reeling in pain. "Oh, I'm sorry!"

"No serious damage, I trust?" said the computer.

"I'm all right." Mingolla sat down on the edge of the boulder. Below him, the bank of lights underwent a rippling change, looking like a sudden shift in alignment among the stars of a distant galaxy.

"As I was saying," the computer went on, "most periods require only minimal intercession on my part to set things right. The work done in such times goes unnoticed, and mine, aside from a brief flurry of notoriety, will leave no historical record. The appearance of Jesus and Buddha were necessary pyrotechnics. But for the most part"—another chuckle—"I work in mysterious ways."

"And what is your work?"

"It has been completed. The copilot of this helicopter, a young man named William, was traumatized by the crash. It was my task to heal him, to educate and prepare him for the important work upon which he is now engaged."

"His absence seems pretty convenient," said Mingolla.

"Proof was Jesus's evangel, not mine. I demand faith of no one other than William, and William can do nothing other than practice faith. Your faith, David, is immaterial. My work is done, and soon I must go to meet my fate . . . a most ignominious fate, yet suitable to the age."

"Care to say what that is?"

"Certainly. After the war a businessman from Gautemala City will stumble over me in the course of a hunting trip, and thinking me a curiosity, he will have me transported to his home. He will attempt to exploit me, never realizing he has the genuine article in his possession, and will generate the wrath of the Church, which in turn will incite the masses. One day a mob will break into the businessman's home, kill him, and destroy me. The glory of my Assumption will be obscured by an electrical fire."

"If you know the future," Mingolla said, stifling laughter, "maybe you'd like to tell me what the next year or so has in store."

"There is no purpose in disclosing your future."

"Uh-huh, right."

"However, there is a purpose to your being here. I want you to come inside me."

Mingolla looked into the hole, at the banks of winking lights; a thrill ran across the muscles of his shoulders. "Why?"

"Don't be alarmed," said the computer.

"I'm not alarmed, I just don't see the point."

"The point will be made manifest. I'm not trying to prove anything, David. I simply feel that a brief intimacy between us will benefit you in the days ahead."

"It's up to you," said Nate. "But I've found it quite restful."

"You've been inside?"

"A number of times."

Mingolla looked again at the hole and decided it would be stupid to give in to nervousness. "Why the fuck not?"

Nate lowered him by the arms, released him after he had gained a footing. The chopper shifted, vines creaked, and vegetable debris rained down. Mingolla dropped to his hands and knees, crawled over to the hole, and went in headfirst, carefully negotiating the sharp peels of metal. He slid to the end of the deck, positioned himself against the computer facing.

He had expected that—despite its protestation to the contrary—the computer would attempt his conversion; but there was only silence, and though he felt stupid sitting there, he didn't want to create the impression that he was afraid by

215

crawling back out. The air was cool, drier than the outside air, like an expression of the computer's voice, and as Nate had said, it was restful inside the chopper, with the blinking lights and the faint whine of the power system and the edges of the hole framing a ragged circle of greenish gold light like an opening into Eden. From this vantage it was hard to believe that in that light lived loonies and jaguars and poisonous snakes. And maybe that was the truth of the computer's delusion, of all religious delusion: that if you were to limit yourself to such a narrow view, hold within yourself a ray of greenish gold light, a pocket of cool dry air, you might cultivate an innocence that to some extent would repel the violence of the world. Maybe if he had been armored with faith instead of power he could have avoided much that had come to harrow him. He folded his arms, closed his eyes, letting himself steep in the peace of the dead chopper and its deluded oracle, the image of God appropriate to the age. His thoughts idled. Memories of the Barrio, the Lost Patrol, and the Ant Farm flitted past like scenes from a damaged print of an old silent film, their colors faded, the exaggerated displays of their characters redolent of an antiquated school of acting, and he saw in every instance how irredeemably wrong his own actions had been.

"That should be enough, David." The computer's voice seemed to surround him. "If you start back to the village now, I think you'll find that Debora is available."

Mingolla started to ask how the computer knew Debora's business; but then he understood that whether it was a matter of reasoning or innate knowledge, *his* judgment was unimportant. Willing to accept this much of delusion, he crawled out from the dark computer deck and let himself be hauled up into the light.

Debora was waiting by the river, and he had the idea from her pose—sitting with knees drawn up, chin resting on her folded arms—that she had been waiting for some considerable time. She was unblocked, shedding heat in waves like the radiation from an open fire, and when she glanced at him, he detected strain in the unnatural steadiness of her gaze. He noticed that her loss of weight had added a sculptural quality to the shape of her face, making it a more suitable framework for her sensual features. Her beauty had been the main focus of his dreams and fantasies, and she *was* beautiful, albeit less so than his memories of her; yet considering her now, he perceived a bright particularity of which beauty was only a small part. The movements of her body, the black curls hanging over the front of her blouse like the tail feathers of exotic birds, the way the wind pressed the fabric against her breasts: these things were more significant and precious in their familiarity than the fact of her good looks. He rebelled against this perception, trying to resurrect his sense of outrage and betrayal; but he was beginning to realize that didn't matter anymore, that whatever the reasons underlying the attraction, he wanted to immerse himself in it, to wash away the stains he had accumulated since he had left her.

She invited him to sit, but when he did she shifted her position, creating a wide space between them. He gazed out at the jungle fringing the opposite bank. The sun was an explosive white glare whitening the sky, causing the greens of the vegetation to appear a single livid, overripe color. Birds with scythe-shaped wings made low runs across the treetops; a silver arc and splash out on the river. "Are we gonna talk?" he asked.

"Yes." She let the answer stand.

The bank fell away sharply, and below Mingolla's feet the surface of the water was figured with eddies forming around the slick brown tips of a submerged branch; black flies hovered above them, and shadowy fingerlings darted in the green murk of the shallows. Farther along the bank a row of tree ferns leaned out over the river, their stalks ten or twelve feet long, their plumy fronds nodding: the nodding gave them the semblance of an animal vitality, and they seemed to be signaling their approval of all that passed before their strange eyeless heads, measuring the peace of Fire Zone Emerald.

"All right," said Mingolla finally. "I'll start. You told me you learned stuff that made what you were doing meaningless. What was it?"

She drew a line in the clay with her forefinger. "There's another war being fought. A war within a war."

217

His impulse was to ridicule her, but her glumness was convincing. "What sorta war?"

"Not really a war," she said. "A power struggle. Between two groups of psychics, I think."

Maybe she was crazy after all. "How'd you find out 'bout it?"

"My superiors told me. That's how they work. They build you up, give you power, watch how you handle it. And when they think you're so involved with the power that all you want is more, they admit you to their"—her voice quavered—"their goddamn fraternity! They tell you a little at a time, they give you clues to see how you'll react. Well, they told me too damn much!" She looked at Mingolla, anguish in her face. "I believed in the revolution. I gave it everything . . . everything! And there isn't any revolution! There isn't even a counterrevolution! It's all camouflage."

Mingolla remembered Tully's outburst about the war not making sense, remembered de Zedegui's cryptic statements. He told Debora about Tully, and she said, "That's it! That's how they begin, by seeding doubt. And next they tell you about special operations, drop hints about underlying purposes. Then they present the whole picture . . . nothing specific, because they still don't trust you. Nobody trusts anybody. That's the one verity. Everything is suspect, everyone's after power. And no one gives a damn about anything else. The cause is a joke!" She looked at him again, calmer now. "Do you know why I deserted, the final straw? It was because of what they told me about you."

He waited for her to go on.

"They said you were going to be assigned to kill me. I know how the training goes, how isolated you are. Never more than a couple of other people around. If you'd been given an assignment, only your trainer and the person in charge of the therapy would know about it, and that meant that one of them had to be in league with one of my superiors. With all the other information I had, I realized that what was really going on must be so elitist, so complicated and filled with intrigues, I'd never figure it out . . . not while I was still involved in it."

Mingolla kept his eye on the eddying water, watching strands of dark scum being spun loose from a clot of mud caught on the tip of the submerged branch. "It's hard to swallow," he said. "But I've heard some things, too."

"There's more," she said. "Amalia knows it."

"Amalia?"

"She's another clue. A little girl. She's in my hut. Sleeping. That's all she does now." Debora rubbed the back of her neck as if the subject were making her weary. "That's why I rescued you. I'm not strong enough to wake her anymore. I need your help."

"That's all . . . that's the only reason?"

"Why else would I? You were hunting me." She said this with defiance, but he could hear the lie.

"Not now . . . I'm not hunting you now."

"No, but that isn't by choice."

"Debora," he said. "I was just . . ."

She jumped up, walked a couple of paces off.

"I wasn't thinking clearly," he said.

The wind veiled her mouth with a sweep of dark hair; behind her, three old shirtless Indian men were sitting beside one of the huts, staring at them with fascination. "Do you want to help or not?" she asked harshly.

"Sure," said Mingolla. "That's what I want."

Amalia was a chubby Indian girl of twelve or thirteen, with a psychic's heat and a melanin deficiency that had dappled her reddish brown skin with pink splotches; in the candlelit gloom of Debora's hut the splotches looked raw and vivid, like scars made by poisoned flowers pressed to her face. She lay with one arm hanging over the side of a hammock and wore a dirty white dress imprinted with a design of blue kittens. Her breathing was deep and regular, her eyelids twitched, and according to Debora she had been asleep for almost a week.

"She just ran down," Debora said. "Like a windup toy moving slower and slower. Then she stopped. But even before that she wasn't right. I thought she was retarded. She'd lie there and stare at the walls and make noises. Then she'd have violent spells . . . break things and scream. Once in a while she'd be lucid, and I could get her to talk. She talked about Panama, about a place she called Sector Jade . . . she said everything was being decided there. A lot of what she said sounded rote, like pieces of poems and stories she'd memorized."

The last of Mingolla's doubts vanished. "I've heard stuff about Sector Jade."

"What did you hear?"

"Just the name, and that it was important."

A starved-looking cow stopped by the door and looked inside the hut, its ripe smell filtering in. Its mottled red-and-white skin was sucked in over its cheekbones like a caved-in map, and its unpruned horns had grown into circles that almost met its eyes. It snorted, then moseyed off.

"What else did she say?" Mingolla asked.

"She'd talk about where she used to live. With one of 'the others,' she'd say. She said she was one of his 'broken toys.' I asked what she meant by 'the others,' and she said they were like us, but not as strong . . . though they were stronger in some ways. Because they were hidden, because they couldn't be detected."

Flies droned in the thatch, a chicken clucked. It was hot, and sweat burned in the creases of Mingolla's neck. He breathed through his mouth. "It's weird," he said. "When I was in therapy, I never worried about failures or fuck-ups with the drugs . . . even though they gave me an overdose once. I just assumed everything was fine. Beats me why I leapt to that assumption, but I did."

"You think that's what happened to Amalia . . . a failure with the drugs?"

"Don't you?"

"Maybe. But she might not have been sound before they gave them to her."

"Either way, it's not a pretty picture."

"I should warn you," Debora said. "She's strong . . . very strong. And her thoughts are chaotic."

He glanced at her, held her eyes. Her skin was almost the same shade of ashen brown as the air, and for an instant the eyes appeared to be disembodied, floating toward him. She moved back, nervous, and put a hand on the hammock ropes.

"I'll give it a shot," he said.

Chaotic was too mild a term to describe the process of Amalia's thoughts; they seemed a fiery shrapnel spraying around inside her skull. The electric sensation was overwhelming, and the subsequent arousal shocking in its suddenness. "Jesus Christ!" he said.

"Can't you do it?" Anxiety in Debora's voice.

"I'm not sure." He rubbed his temples; the pain there was more an inflammation than an ache.

After several tries he became acclimated and began to project alertness and well-being. Though painful and dizzying, his contact with Amalia's mind proved instructive. He was beginning to understand that what he had perceived as random flux was in fact an infinity of patterns, most of them so minimal that they tended to obscure one another; and he found that what he was doing intuitively was reinforcing certain of them, channeling his energy and strength along their course. Some of Amalia's patterns were—like that one of Nate's—powerful, easily perceived, and the longer he worked on her, the more dominant these grew. However, half an hour went past, and he still had not been able to wake her.

"I could be here all day," he said to Debora. "Why don't we work on her together?"

Debora frowned, plucked at the hammock ropes. "I guess it's worth a try," she said. She ducked under the ropes and stationed herself on the opposite side of the hammock. "All right."

Mingolla's attention was focused on Amalia, on the boil of her thought, and at first he failed to notice the presence of a new and more controlled electrical flow, one whose borders kept withdrawing from his own. When he did notice it, he mistook it for one of Amalia's patterns and pushed toward it with all his strength. At the moment of contact he had an impression of two streams of crackling energy knitting together, entwining, tightening, forming a kind of liquid knot that grew more and more complex, twisting in and out of itself, and his focus became limited to completing that knot, to contriving its ultimate expression, until even that intent was absorbed into a blaze of sexuality: like a man clutching a live wire, his thoughts sparking, conscious only of the voltage pouring through him. And then he found himself staring at Debora, unsure of who had broken the circuit and of how it had been accomplished. She looked terrified, her mouth open, breathing labored, and appeared on the verge of bolting from the hut. He wanted to say something to calm her, to stop her, because he saw that a barrier between them had been eliminated. He saw this very clearly, and he believed he had also seen down to the core of their mutuality; he didn't understand what he had seen—its shape was as complicated as the knot they had created—but the fact that he could see it at all debunked the notion that his feelings for her had been manufactured. Enhanced, maybe. Their progress sped up, hurried along. But not manufactured. He believed she saw this, too.

"Debora?" Amalia's voice, weak and whispery.

Her eyes were open, and she thrashed about as if being swallowed by the hammock.

"How do you feel?" Debora leaned down to her, stroked her hair.

Amalia stared at Mingolla. Though not in the least pretty, asleep she had embodied a youthful healthiness; now a sullen energy had gained control of her features, and she looked to be a fat little prig of a girl, the one with whom nobody wants to play.

"Why do you love him?" she asked Debora. "He does evil things to people."

"He's a soldier, he has to do bad things sometimes. And I *don't* love him."

"You can't fool me," Amalia said. "I know!"

"Think what you like," said Debora patiently. "Right now we want you to tell us more about Panama."

"No!" Amalia twisted onto her side, facing toward Mingolla, her dumpling belly netted by the hammock mesh. "I want to play with you."

"Please, Amalia. We'll play later."

Mingolla started to exert his influence on her, but the instant he touched Amalia's mind, a pattern he hadn't noticed, one that must have been buried beneath the surface, began flowing back and forth, creating an endless loop that seemed to be threading through his thoughts, fastening itself to them with stitches of bright force. A point of heat bloomed in the center of his forehead, grew into a white-hot sun of pain filling his skull. He felt the jolt of a fall, heard Debora crying out. The pain dwindled, and he saw Amalia sitting up, skewering him with a look of piggy triumph.

"I want him to play, too," she said.

"We'll both play with you afterward," said Debora. "After you tell us about Panama."

"*You* play with her." Mingolla pushed himself up. He gingerly touched the back of his head, found a lump. Then, alarmed by Amalia's scowl, he backed toward the door.

"Don't hurt him," said Debora.

A sly smile spread across Amalia's face. "Say you love him, and I won't."

Debora cast a grim look toward Mingolla.

"Say it!" Amalia insisted.

"I love him."

"And you'll keep loving him forever and ever, won't you?"

"Yes."

"Can I have something to eat afterward?"

Mingolla almost laughed at the greediness that came across Amalia's face, it was so comically extreme an expression.

"I'll cook you chicken and rice," Debora said. "I promise."

"All right!" Amalia lay back in the hammock, arms folded across her immature breasts. "What do you want to know?"

"Tell us 'bout Sector Jade," said Mingolla.

She glared at him, then turned her eyes to the ceiling. The innocence of sleep seemed to possess her once again. She remained silent for a long moment, and Mingolla said, "Is she . . ."

"Shh!" Debora waved to him to quiet. "She'll tell us."

"Into . . ." Amalia wetted her lips. ". . . Vanished . . . all vanished beneath . . . as smooth as stone, like a sector of jade

223

amid the bright tiles, and he imagined that they would never reappear, that they were traveling an unguessable distance to a country beneath the shell of the world to which Panama was affixed like a curious pin on a swath of blue silk, and there, in that faraway country, the blood knot would be unraveled and the peace would be forged." Her intonation grew firmer. "Not the peace that passeth understanding, no, this would be a most comprehensible peace, one purchased with banknotes of blood and shame, with the coinage issued by those who at last have realized that what is fair in war must be incorporated into the tactics of peace, and from this issue would be established an unnatural yet stable order, a counterfeit of salvation, which is in itself a counterfeit of hope, and once . . . and once . . ." She sighed, lapsed again into silence.

"I've heard that before . . . those words." Mingolla couldn't jog his memory.

"Where?"

"It'll come to me. Ask her about 'the others.' "

This time there was a longer pause after Debora had put the question, but when Amalia began to speak it was with more certainty.

". . . Only the latest incidence in the centuries-long feud, which was called by the Madradonas the War of the Flower, this euphemistic characterization exemplary of their tendency to embroider reality. Now Diego Sotomayor de Cabrillo, whose niece had been violated, was not slow to take his vengeance, yet went about it in typical Sotomayor fashion, preferring to concoct an ornate and subtle reprisal rather than initiating an immediate strike. He was at the time a man of great influence in the government of Panama, and using his high office, he sent against the Madradonas an army of tax assessors and other civil servants, by this harassment seeking to occupy their attention while he prepared his plot. From the populace of Barrio Clarín he selected a witling tool, a handsome young boy with a shred of the natural ability, whose brain had been damaged by a fall in his infancy, and from this stone of a child he constructed over the years a weapon of sublime elegance, supplying him with the gifts of poetry and song, making of him a pretty toy that would be sure to delight Serafina, the youngest daughter of his nemesis, and burying in the deepest labyrinth of the boy's thought a violent potential to be triggered by the sight of her naked body . . ."

"Son of a bitch!" Mingolla pounded a fist into his palm.

"Don't!" Debora bent over Amalia, who appeared to have dropped off into a deep sleep. "You can't interrupt her. She just stops if you do. Damn! Now we'll have to wake her again."

"It's okay. She said enough." Mingolla went to the door, stood looking out at the lethargic activity of the village. Women rolling cornmeal on wooden flats, sleepy children lolling in hammocks, pigs waddling and snooting. "It's like you were telling me. Clues. Izaguirre was giving me clues."

Debora joined him in the doorway. "I don't understand."

"What she calls 'the others,' they're characters in a story about two families who're addicted to this plant that gives them mental powers. They can influence people like we do, but it takes them a long time to get the job done. They're weak." He gave a rueful laugh. "But they're hidden. Their power isn't detectable."

"Are you sure?"

"Wake her ass up again, milk her dry, and head the fuck away from Panama."

"That wouldn't do any good. She always uses the same quotes. It's probably all she's been programmed to say. I just never understood the part about the families." She looked up at Mingolla, seemed startled by his proximity, and walked off toward the river.

"Where you going?" he called.

She didn't break stride. "For a walk . . . to think."

He caught up to her, fell into step. "I'll go with you."

"No." She paused beside a hut in whose doorway two naked little girls were playing, flattening cakes of mud between their hands. "I'd rather be by myself."

"We've got more to talk about."

"I think we've covered everything."

"We haven't covered you and me."

"That's a dead issue."

225

"Bullshit! I know damn well what you feel."

She took a step back, not in fear, but as if she needed distance in order to see the whole picture. "I'm sorry," she said coolly. "I may have misled you. There's . . ."

"Uh-uh. You . . ."

". . . absolutely no chance of a deeper relationship between you and me."

"You can't deny what you feel."

"That's exactly what I intend to do."

Her voice had risen in volume, and the two little girls were gazing at them in awe.

"Sure, you save my life and tell me it's 'cause I can help you with Amalia. Then we wake her and you say she's already told you everything she knows. You didn't need my help. So why'd you save me?"

"I felt responsible," she said. "I got you into this."

"Be real. It didn't take Amalia saying you loved me to make it true."

Anger notched her brow. "If you think I'm going to let emotion control me, then you don't know me. The revolution, that's . . ."

"There isn't any revolution," he reminded her.

"Maybe not. But I'm going to learn what's happening, and nothing I feel for you is going to get in the way."

"I don't believe I'm hearing this shit," he said. "I mean you musta got this dialogue from a bad movie. 'Forgive me, Manuel. But until all wrongs are righted, my heart belongs to the cause.' "

She slapped him hard on the cheek, slapped him again, coming at him with a flurry that stung both sides of his face. He grabbed her wrists, and when she tried to knee him, he shoved her away. "You bastard!" she said, standing with her hands clawed, staring at him like a madwoman through strands of hair. "Stupid bastard!" Then she spun on her heel and strode off, disappearing behind one of the huts.

He clenched his fists, needing to hit something, but found only air. The little girls watched him, big-eyed and solemn. "Take my advice," he said. "Grow up to be lesbians."

They exchanged stares and giggled.

"I'm serious," he told them. "It's got to be easier than this shit." He ambled toward the river, rubbing the sting from his cheeks, looking at the hut behind which Debora had vanished. "I love you, too," he said.

CHAPTER ELEVEN

Some days it seemed he was moving through a vacuum, an airless gray created by his lack of purpose, and other days it seemed he wasn't moving at all, that life was flowing past beneath a projection of rock upon which he had been stranded. He had nothing to do, nowhere to go. He had come to the end of purpose, and though the frustration caused by Debora's rejection had acted to shore up his feelings for her, she was a problem he had no energy to solve; he thought she might be right about the comparative values of commitment and emotion, and he envied her capacity for denial, because seeing her every day drove him to distraction. Whenever their paths crossed he would—like a vampire anticipating a hot feast—relish every detail of scent and dewy fever; he would imagine himself following her to Panama, saving her life, and receiving infinite gratification. He had the idea that she was delaying her departure, that she was having trouble putting him behind her; but while this augured well for his chances with her, he knew that to take advantage of those chances he would have to endure more war, and he doubted he was capable of endurance. The memories of the dead men in his wake were weights bracketed to his heart, holding him in place. He could feel them. They were solid and fundamental restraints. And even more solid, more fundamental, was the idea that he was a pawn in a centuries-old feud. He wasn't sure he believed that to be the case: spoken out loud it had the ring of fantasy. Yet each time he added up the elements of his experience, it seemed clear that fantasy and truth were in union. He saw that the feuding families in Pastorin's stories, the playful way he had been maneuvered, and much of the war were imbued with a common character, a whimsical arrogance, and this enforced his belief. Belief made him angry, and anger made him eager to explore the perversity that underlay the war. But anger and eagerness were outfaced by his spiritual exhaustion, and so he did nothing.

He went often to the hollow, occasionally accompanied by Nate Lubove. Sunsets were the best time. The shafts of light bathing the chopper would burn red and orange through the canopy, kindling fiery glints from the cockpit, scalloping the black metal with gleams, and the huge silhouette would take on the aspect of an evil Easter egg waiting for a monster child to reach down and snatch it. Mingolla would feel that the light was congealing around him, armoring him in orange and black, and he would think darkly romantic thoughts concerning solitary adventures and high purpose. Whenever the computer addressed him, he would refuse to respond: he didn't want its solace or companionship. Its skeleton pilot and divine mechanical voice seemed to him emblems of the fraudulence of the war, and he sat beside it only to remind himself of this state of affairs.

Now and then he tried to engage Nate in conversation, and for the most part Nate begged off. Always a minimal soul, he was growing more minimal, less inclined to both speech and action, content to watch his butterflies, and Mingolla, who, like him, sensing a resonance between them, chalked up his taciturnity to a brooding nature. Once, however, Nate did talk to him, telling stories about the wars he'd covered. Afghanistan, Kampuchea, Angola. He'd come to be a war tourist, spending his days in luxury hotels talking to other bored correspondents, comparing the current conflict with the various back-fence wars they'd seen, filing sentimental human interest pieces and getting drunk with ex-presidents while mortar fire chewed the surroundings into ruins.

"I've never experienced a war like this, though," he said, kicking his heels against the boulder. "It's insane. And the most insane part of it is in Panama."

"You've been there?" Mingolla asked.

"Yes, a year ago. The place was a puzzle. Most of the city went on as usual, but one barrio—Barrio Clarín—was barricaded from the rest. The official word was that it had been quarantined, but no one could tell you what disease had caused the quarantine. It was impossible to get clearance to enter it, but we heard things. Rumors of pitched battles in the streets. And stranger rumors yet. They sounded ridiculous, but you kept hearing them over and over, and you couldn't help but pay attention to them."

"Tell me," said Mingolla.

"There's not much to tell. Just that people said there were some sort of negotiations going on in Barrio Clarín, something to do with the war. That's all. I have no verification of it, of course. But I saw some things that, uh, while they weren't verification, they did tend to lend substance to the rumors. For instance, I saw the doctor who managed my therapy entering the barrio. It was at a distance, but I could never mistake Izaguirre for anyone else."

"Izaguirre!"

"Do you know him?"

"He was in charge of my therapy, too."

"You were in Mexico City, then?"

"No," said Mingolla. "Roatán."

"Hmm." Nate looked down at the chopper. "The doctor gets around, doesn't he?" He let out a pained sigh. "Well, I suppose it must all come clear in Panama."

"What . . ." Mingolla began, wanting to question Nate further about Izaguirre, but Nate cut him off.

"I'm so terribly weary of all this blood, this confusion," he said. "It seems my life has been nothing but blood and confusion. The other day I was trying to remember something pleasant out of all my times at war, and I could only recall one thing that struck me as of moment. Such a small thing, too. Yet because it's unique, I suppose I've magnified it."

Mingolla asked Nate to tell him, impressed by the fact that he could recall anything pleasant of war.

"It was the summer of '89, Afghanistan," said Nate. "The Bamian Valley. Do you know it?"

"No."

"It was beautiful. There were dust storms to the south, and the sunsets . . . Unbelievable! Violent red and yellow skies, the colors melting before your eyes, and the hills black against them. Like a prehistoric landscape. There was a boy, a young boy, he'd lost his leg to a Russian mine, and he'd lost his voice, too. Or at least he wouldn't talk to anyone. Not even me . . . though he was curious about me because of my blond hair. They were all curious about that. I had with me a thumb piano. Do you know this? A little wooden box, hollow, with metal strips for keys. Twelve keys, I think. You strike them with your thumbs, and they make a brittle tinkling music. An African instrument. The boy was fascinated. I was not so good a player, you understand. I only used it to accompany my thoughts, my reveries. And when I saw the boy's interest in the instrument, I gave it to him." Nate yawned, leaned back on an elbow. "I taught him how to strike the keys, and he would sit for hours with it on his lap. Of course I was occupied with other matters. Russian fighters would launch rocket strikes at our positions, and I was working with a film crew, shooting the battles. So for a time I forgot the boy and the thumb piano. Then one night I was walking on the perimeter of the camp. Beautiful night." Nate slumped lower, resting his head on his arm. Blinked sleepily. His speech grew slurred, slower. "Stars, more stars than you see down here, because the air was so clear. A sickle moon, cold and silver. Cool air. A night of clarity. And I came across the boy sitting on a rock looking out over the valley. He was playing the thumb piano. His shoulders hunched, his face intent upon the instrument, a shadow against the stars and the dark blue sky. God, how he played! So fluent, so expressive! He'd outstripped the limits of the twelve notes. Cold rippling arpeggios that seemed to be making the stars dance, with simple melodies stated above them. Poignant melodies, sad

231

melodies. It had power, the music. Power like Bach, even though it had no great amplitude or range. For a moment I wasn't sure it was the boy playing. I thought he must be a spirit, that if I moved closer I would discover he was a creature of shadow without eyes or mouth or any feature. The war was in the music, the strength of the people." Nate sat up straighter, drew a deep breath. "They weren't an admirable people, you see . . . though much was made of their nobility, their fighting spirit. They were murderers and thieves, many of them. For example, I spoke to one man who told me that years before he'd learned that young travelers were selling their blood to hospitals in Kabul. He'd been inspired by this to ambush travelers going through the Khyber Pass. He'd cut their throats and store their blood in leather sacks. And when he had collected what he assumed to be a fortune in blood, he'd taken the sacks to Kabul. The blood was rotten, of course, and he'd been terribly distressed when the hospital wouldn't buy it. Now he thought the whole thing absurd, that it had been a big joke on him. That was how a lot of them were. But whatever was good about them, it was in that music the boy played. The purity of their determination, their love of the land. I"—another yawn—"I still hear it sometimes. It seems to be playing in my nerves. When I'm sleepy, like now."

He appeared to doze off for a couple of seconds, and Mingolla, astonished by how much this reminded him of Amalia, shook him awake.

"You okay?" he asked.

"The humidity," said Nate. "I've never gotten used to the humidity down here. I'm always having drowsiness."

"You looked sick or something."

"No, it's only the humidity. The heat doesn't trouble me . . . but in Israel it's dry, you understand."

Mingolla wasn't convinced, but let it pass. "What's it like in Israel these days?"

"I have no idea. It's been years since I was there . . . years." Nate stared at a far-off point in the canopy. "I can hardly remember it."

Ordinarily Mingolla would have passed off this last comment as well, but there had been an anxious undertone to Nate's voice that made it seem a matter of real concern. He asked Nate what he did remember, and Nate, uncomfortable with the question, muttered something about inflation and militance, and refused to discuss the subject.

"I don't get much pleasure from remembering it," he said, and Mingolla, guilty over having pressed him, said he could understand that.

Returning from the hollow one evening, he noticed a trail leading south away from the village yet angled toward the river, and on impulse he set off down it. The trail was densely overgrown, running for the most part uphill, and by the time he reached a thicketed bluff overlooking the river, he was sweaty and begrimed. Twilight had blended water and jungle into a gray medium, and mist was forming in mid-stream; but full dark was still a half-hour off, and Mingolla thought he would have a swim. He threaded his way down the bluff and was about to push through the wall of brush bordering the bank, when he spotted Debora. She was buttoning her dress, and he had a glimpse of her high small breasts before white cotton closed them in. Her hair was wrapped in a towel, and after she had done all her buttons, she removed the towel and let the hair spill over her back. She sat on the bank, legs dangling over the edge. Beside her stood a tent, its peak outlined against a band of pink light that showed above the treeline on the far side of the river. Mingolla stood a minute considering the possibilities, realized there was just one, and pushed through the brush.

She started at the noise, turned toward him. He had expected her to react violently, but she only said, "What are you doing here?"

"Walking," he said. "I didn't know this was your place."

"I stay here some nights. There's a hot springs."

He sat next to her. The water below was crystal clear, bubbling from a limestone cavity, and he could make out tiny fish darting over a pebbled bottom. "How hot is it?"

"Too hot to touch at the source. But farther out it's just warm. You should try it."

Her solicitude made him think he could talk to her, but he found he had nothing much to say. He felt her eyes on him.

"I'll be leaving soon," she said, her voice icy.

The action of the springs made a racy turbulent sound that was audible above the rush of the current.

"Do you want to come with me?"

Startled, he tried to catch her eye, but she had turned away.

"It'll be easier with someone else along." She gave a twitch of her head as if she wanted to look at him but was fighting the urge. "It's up to you."

Her shirt was molded to the wet curve of her ribcage, and he could see tension there, tension in her cabled neck, the stillness of her head.

"Well?" she said.

"I don't have the strength for it anymore."

"That's not true," she said. "You're just tired . . . like how you get after you've been hiking, and when you lie down, your muscles ache and you don't think you can go on. But once you do, you're all right again."

"You have Nate," he said. "He'll share the load."

"I know, but . . ."

"But it's not the same, right? Why don't you be honest, why don't you tell me the real reason you want me along?"

He traced the line of her jaw, and she shivered—an all-over shiver, the way a colt reacts to something unfamiliar in the wind—but she didn't pull away. "Because I want you, because I want to make love with you . . . is that what you want me to say?"

"If it's true." He moved his hand to her shoulder, lower, felt her heartbeat. The band of pink in the west had deepened to crimson, widened, its shape like a flame blown back in a strong wind, and the curve of her cheek held a red sheen.

"Of course it's true. I can't hide it, I've never been able to hide it. Maybe that is part of the reason, but it's the smallest part."

234

"Because it's suspect, because everything is suspect." He heard the seductive challenge in his voice.

"Yes."

"The only way it won't be suspect is if you learn to trust it."

"I . . . I don't know."

"Then why do you want me along? You think we're going to be buddies or something? That it?"

"No . . . I . . ."

"You have to trust it, you have to trust something."

"I want to," she said. "I do, but I can't."

He turned her, his hands went to her waist. "Why not?"

Her words came in a fragmented rush. "It's just never been good, not with . . . and . . . I want to . . . I want for it . . ."

He slipped one hand up under her shirt, and she caught her breath, holding very still.

"No," she said weakly.

"I love you," he said, inching his hand higher. "And you love me."

"I'm trying not to," she said.

"What for?"

His thumb nudged the swell of her breast, rubbed slowly back and forth, a sleepy rhythm. Her head drooped to the side as if her attention had been attracted by a faint sound on the far bank, and he kissed the angle where her neck and shoulder joined. The cool green taste of the river and the warmth of her skin mixed on his tongue. Like a hypnotist, he locked on to her eyes as he undid her blouse. She made a sound that started to be a rejection but died in the back of her throat. He spread the halves of the blouse, bent to her breasts, nuzzled them, kissed their tips, teasing the nipples hard. When he took one in his mouth, worked it gently with his teeth, she shuddered and put her hands on the back of his head, guiding him.

"Wait," she said. "Wait."

But he was through waiting and drew her down on the bank, his hand moving to her belly, lower, feeling the softness beneath her jeans, knowing she was open, ready.

"Wait!"

235

This time she shrilled it, and dismayed, startled, wondering if he'd hurt her, he let her go. She rolled away from him, stood, holding her blouse closed. "I can't," she said. "I don't even know you."

That could be argued, he thought, but why bother? He sat up, his balls aching. He was puzzled, though not by her reaction. Women were always making this mistake, discovering in the middle of things that they weren't prepared for you to touch them here or there or somewhere, leaving you doubled over in pain. No, he was just generally puzzled. Looking at the bubbled surface of the spring, it seemed he was staring down through the strata of his various conditions. Blue-balled, on a riverbank at sunset, in the midst of a rain forest, the midst of war, surrounded by lunatics and Indians, in Guatemala. And binding it all together the strange web of his relationship with this woman. He wondered why he wasn't more puzzled.

"You're right," he said. "Let's just skip it." He turned to the far bank, and when he looked back a minute later, he found that she had gone.

Darkness sifted in, the moon was still down, and not wanting to negotiate the trail without a flashlight, he crawled into the tent. It had her smell, and that made him feel isolated among the night cries and the slop of the river. Too bad the tent wasn't equipped with a phone. He'd make some calls. His parents, of course. Just for the sake of getting oriented to the American wavelength, a dose of salt and Nutra-Sweet. Hi, Mom, hi, Dad, here I am with gun and camera in Mangoland, the war's no worse than a Disney Tru-Life Adventure narrated by a noble voice, and I'll be home soon with souvenirs, bye, Mom, bye, Dad. And then, then maybe he'd give Sparky's a buzz, his hometown hangout. He could picture it. Sparky the old fart scuttling crabwise for the phone, saying, "Yeah, whatcha want?" and he'd say, "Hey, Spark. It's David Mingolla calling from Guatemala." And Sparky would repeat the name a couple of times and say, "Sure . . . Davy! Cheeseburger plate and a lemon Coke, right? How the hell are ya?" he'd say with false heartiness, recalling what a big shot Mingolla's father was, and Mingolla would say, "I'm kicking ass down here, Spark. Refrying them beaners, y'know." Because Sparky was a hardcore patriot and why get into it? Then he'd ask who was around, and Sparky would say, "Well, nobody you'd know, what with your crowd split up and all." And maybe he'd bag calling Sparky's, he didn't need a reminder that those days were gone. Who else could he call? Light bulb switching on overhead. Yeah! He'd call up Long Island Woman. Give her a chill and a thrill. What was today? He counted on his fingers. Friday. Damn! They'd be out for a pizza and a movie, their idea of a hot date, and home around midnight for a bout of uninspired sex. Four times a week, regular as sin. Less would be unsalubrious. He remembered the first time they'd made love, how just as they were about to do the deed, she'd drawn back and said in a cool clinical voice, "At home we always do it on our sides. That way neither of us has to bear the other's weight." He'd been amazed by her sexual naïveté, yet knowing this about her had given him a sense of mastery, and maybe that had been responsible for his loving her. You didn't need much of a reason for love; that had been proved again with Debora. And it might be that lack of knowledge was a stimulant to emotion, that things were most alluring when they were not quite real. . . . Naw . . . he'd bag that call, too. He needed to talk to Debora. In a way, she hung on to revolution with the same avidity that Long Island Woman had hung on to marriage. But there was some hope for her. He'd buzz her on the jungle hotline. "Listen," he'd say, and hold out the phone to catch the electric message of the night, the crickets and frogs with glowing eyes, the red-skulled monkeys with vibratory tongues, the black magic birds with tympany beaks, and she would tune in to what they were saying separately and unanimously, saying in music, saying in code, in clicks and squeals and arcs of iridescent noise, There is no reason There is no reason There is no reason, and she would be mesmerized, and she would understand, and she would give up her fear.

———————

Mingolla awakened from a dream of suffocation, unable to breathe the stale heated air inside the tent. He crawled out, stood and stretched. It had rained during the night, rinsing the sky of clouds, and the sun was fierce on the river, adding a shimmering glaze to its jade finish. Blue-and-silver fish were nudging pebbles along the bottom of the hot springs. It looked inviting. He could, he thought, get into nudging pebbles, hunting for tiny bugs in the silt. He stripped and waded in, quickstepping away from the scalding current that bubbled from the bank. The limestone bank extended about ten feet out, and at its edge the water was only inches deep over a smooth bottom. He kneeled, splashed himself, and tilted his face to the sun, his thoughts going with the race of the current. Something splashed near shore, and he turned toward the sound. Saw Debora standing in the water, undoing her blouse, her jeans folded on the bank. Water beads glistened on her thighs, in her black pubic brush. She shrugged off the blouse, held it crumpled in front of her, then tossed it next to the jeans. For a moment her body seemed inset into the greenery, a keyhole opening onto a tawny desert place.

His senses ran out of him, coiling around her. She was a little thick-waisted, her breasts so small in contrast to the fullness of her hips that they looked immature, and this gave her a sexy childlike allure. She kneeled facing him, her expression tentative, a dozen expressions trying to be one, and he thought he must look much the same, because now he was insecure, afraid of making mistakes with her.

"I couldn't . . ." she said. "I had to."

He wasn't sure what specific uncertainty she was trying to put behind her, but to smooth over her confusion he kissed her, met her tongue, and slid a hand along her inner thigh. She eased into the touch, and his finger slipped between her legs, found her open; she shifted forward, letting his finger penetrate, and he understood that she didn't want to wait, she wanted to rush past the beginning, to know everything. He lifted her astraddle him, and her head resting on his shoulder, her hair striping his vision, she guided him into place, worked herself down until he was all the way inside. To be held that way, her warmth enclosing him, gripping him, it was, Jesus! so good, so good, he was melting in her, dissolving in that perfect fit. He could feel a clean untroubled face breaking through his old mask of war and anger, the shards falling away into the flood of the sun, the daze of bright water. Everything was melting, the jungle and the river running together, slick with heat and brilliance, greens and blues washing into a unity of light that penetrated his eyelids. She began to tremble, her nails pricking his back, and just the trembling nearly brought him off.

He needed to move but they were angled wrong. Supporting her with one hand, he tipped her backward until her hair fanned across the water; he planted his free arm on the bottom to bear their weight. Her legs locked around his waist, inching him deeper, and he came, all the bad days, the longing, loosed in a heart-stopping pour that left him wobbly and gulping for breath. But he stayed hard, wanting her again. Sweat trickled down his back like molten cracks spreading; salt drops stung his eyes. His planted arm began to ache with the awkwardness of the position, but then as if it had connected with limestone muscles, the ache subsided. She worked her hips, grinding, pushing, building her moment. It was quick for her, too. Her belly tensed, she gave a sharp cry and clawed at his shoulders. Then she relaxed, mouth going slack, eyes closed against the glare. He pulled out, eased back in. So good, that silky muscle. Good like Jesus, like everything calm and sweet at once. A single word began sounding over and over in his head, *Debora, Debora, Debora*, but that wasn't it, not her name, her name was only a translation of the real word, which meant much more, secret kingdoms of meaning, of mastery and giving. He looked down at her. At the tendrils of black hair floating on jade, the dreamy eastern face. He saw where they joined. He wished he could say something, tell her something, but he was leery of words . . . words spoken out loud had the weight of evidence, they could be held against you, and even though they'd become lovers, there was still distrust between them. But it was all right, all right for now. He gazed out past her head across the shimmering water toward the tree line, and as he moved again, as it became all right forever for a moment, he caught a flash of the way it had been after they'd mowed down the jungle around the Ant Farm: the full-bore immensity and silence of the light, the clear innocent air above palms blackened like matchsticks, the cracked red earth leaking steam, and how they'd walked through the dead land, crunching the scorched, brittle stalks underfoot, unafraid, because all the snakes in hiding were now just shadows in the cinders.

They lay on their sides in the warm flow of the springs, and looking at the far bank, at the diminutive crowns of the trees, Mingolla felt they had grown enormous, that they were two exhausted giants newly surfaced from a deep. Debora threw back her head, and at that precise instant something silver streaked across the top of the sky; a worry line creased her brow. He pulled her to him, but she drew back and said, "No . . . the tent. Let's go in the tent." And coming to her feet with a splash, she outran him to the bank.

With the flap closed, sealing them into a confine of half-dark and air as still as a held breath, he felt more alone with her, strangely more alive. Her body was aglow with dampness, her eyes were gleams. He knelt between her legs, bent lower and tasted her. Tasted her, exploring the folds of her cunt, lapping at her, imagining honey smearing his mouth. She hardly moved for a minute or so, but he could tell how she'd wanted this, how known and gloried in it made her feel. Her hips bucked, her legs clamped his head. Breath was knocked out of her in hoarse gasps. The muscles of her stomach bunched, and she wrapped her hands in his hair, holding him immobile, as if were he to take his mouth away or do anything more, she would break into pieces. Afterward he lay beside her, kissed her, and she said, "I can taste myself . . . I thought it'd be horrible to taste myself."

"And it's not?"

"No, because I can taste you, too."

The demureness in her voice aroused him, and he entered her again. And this time, obeying an impulse, he pushed into her mind as well, reestablishing that blazing mental circuit they'd experienced with Amalia. His body was galvanized, his movements seemed to be conforming to the twists and turns of the electric knot they were weaving inside each other's heads, and from that point on he was aware of what was happening only during lapses in the connection. He would find himself battering at her, pinning her wrists above her head, or that she had mounted him and was raking his chest with her nails. Hours of this, on and on into the night. Brutal, sweaty, animal sex. He knew he should be worn out, but every renewal of the mental contact restored him, kindled in him a sensation of thrilling strength and vitality.

Toward dawn, with gray light hanging in the folds of the tent flap, Debora went outside, returning a few minutes later, her body damp from the river, carrying a cloth and a full canteen. She sponged off his chest, his groin, and then, setting the canteen aside, she took him in her mouth. She was a shadow bending to him, the act veiled by the fall of her hair, and because she had caught him by surprise, he was at first less aware of his responses than of hers. Fingers digging into his thigh, the pressure of her mouth. She was sweetly inexpert, too gentle with him, learning as she went, but his thoughts went with her hesitant movements, and it was fine, lovely, the concerned delicacy of those thoughts, the fleeting memories of other more expert women, the messages he tried to send, urging to do it this way, oh yeah, Jesus, that's it, and worries that she wouldn't like it when he came, he wanted her to like it, and then his regard of her was subsumed into dominance and need, the need to flood her, fill her, purient images of her lips, his cock going in, hollowing her cheeks, mixed in with the sensation of her tongue curling around him, and he saw flashes in the dark air, and he followed them with his eyes, with the thrusting of his hips, with all his wish, all his muscled intent, his hips bridging to meet her mouth, and said, "Debora, Christ!" and laid his hand on the back of her head, guiding her the last bit, going blank and rigid into light, into a nervy flare of pleasure that was a greater fulfillment than all the previous violent ones. She nestled close, smiling a bright prideful smile, and kissed him, bringing his own salt taste to his mouth. She whispered something.

"I didn't hear," he said.

"Nothing."

He was certain she had whispered, "I love you," and was happy that words were becoming accessible to them, that trust was building; but at the same time he was put off by the claim implicit in the words, frightened by their power, and he began once more to wonder who she was, this stranger whom love made seem so familiar, and why they were here and what they were going to do.

The most intriguing thing about their lovemaking was not the intensity of their mental contact—Mingolla realized that he'd been expecting something of the sort—but was its aftermath, the sense of strength and vitality it brought to them. He recalled what Izaguirre had said about a mutuality of focus between two psychics acting to increase their powers, and to test the truth of this, he went with Debora to visit Amalia again. They each awakened her with only the slightest of efforts, and when she attacked Mingolla, he repelled her without difficulty. Amalia did not take defeat well. She peered fearfully at them over the edge of the hammock, the pink splotches on her face glowing like radium in the gloom of the hut, and wept. Debora tried to comfort her, but Mingolla's interest was more clinical, and he worked to shore up the less dominant patterns of her mind, fueling them with his strength, curious as to what she might be able to tell them about her past.

"I don't remember," she said defiantly when he asked about her therapy. But he could tell she was lying and urged her to comply.

"There were lots of us," she said. "In a big house."

"Boys and girls like you?" Debora asked.

"No one's like me," said Amalia.

"I mean were they . . . sick?"

"Broken," she said, and the word seemed to resonate beyond the walls of the hut, as if every broken thing were responding to her signal.

Mingolla framed another question, but before he could ask

it, Amalia began to speak. ". . . And the light of the Beast that had been loosed was the light of reason for the Madradonas and the Sotomayors, and they met in the city of Cartagena to contrive a peace, and when they went forth from the city unified in purpose and over the years insinuated themselves into the seats of the mighty, preparing for the consolidation of the world into a single nation. But not all were of this accord. Passions still ran high among the youth of the families, and they continued to murder and rape, to swindle and defraud, as had the countless generations that preceded them, and so it was determined that . . . that they, too . . . they, too, should . . ."

Amalia slumped in the hammock, the patterns of her mind in utter disarray, beyond Mingolla's capacity to restore. For a moment the only sound was the creaking of the hammock ropes, and to Mingolla, feeling desolate, realizing that he and Debora were trapped in a circumstance beyond their control or comprehension . . . to Mingolla the creaking of the ropes opened into a vision of a room with softly glowing walls, the light issuing from almost imperceptible cells embedded in pattern of magenta swirls on the wallpaper, and he was lying on a bed in a motel, furnished with a chrome desk beneath a wide mirror, and matching chairs of chrome and mauve upholstery, the decor achieving an effect both sterile and gaudy. Water running in the bathroom. A click, the bathroom door opening, and Debora came in drying her hands on a towel. Wearing a T-shirt and panties. He'd never gotten used to the changes plastic surgery had made in her face, and each time she reappeared after an absence—no matter how brief—he would fail to recognize her for a second, would have to seek out the old planes and lines, blur the new regularity of her features and find the exotic asymmetry that had first attracted him. Only her subdued manner was familiar, the way she moved around the room, keeping close to the walls like a cat exploring, eyes down, withdrawn. She fingered a dial beside the door, dimming the lights, and lay next to him.

"How you doing?" he asked.

"I'm still not used to it here," she said. "There's so much . . ."

"So much what?"

"Everything. Food, light, coolness. Anything you want."

"It's the land of silk and money. We do not want for the luxuries."

"I don't like it," she said.

Years before, he would have made a joke of her asceticism, but they had gone beyond jokes, beyond any sort of lightness.

"Won't be much longer," he said. "After tomorrow . . ." He left the rest unspoken; they both knew about tomorrow.

They made love in the cool dry room, and yes, there was heat, and yes, there was joy, and there was that electric fusion of minds, yet it was no longer love they made, it was something less and something more, a ratification of their commitment and an exercise in power, an erotic calisthenics that bred in them a core dispassion that—like love—was its own reason for being. After they had done, their power was as palpable and bristly as ozone in the room, and with only a slight effort, Mingolla reached beyond the walls to engage the mind of a harried businessman on his way to shuffle papers over a drink at the motel bar, to worry about sales techniques, to ponder the morals of the waitresses . . . and the minds of passing motorists, dazed by the lights of Love City in the distance, scattered across a tawny strip of desert like stars whose constellate figure has abdicated to a better sky, and Mingolla plucked the thoughts from their heads, his own thought ranging over them, as strong as God in contrast to their firefly frailty, tuning in the trillion-watt wastage of the American West. . . . *Jerk-off motherfucker, cut in on me like that, I'll drive this iron up your asshole . . . If I brake real hard, it'd jack her through the goddamn windshield, and serve her ass right for whimperin' alla time, goddamn bitch has to pee every fifteen minutes . . . God, let not the wickedness of the world, let the wickedness, let not . . .* in that mind the image of God a pearly sexual light, a pernicious denial . . . and wordless drones of thought, a static crackle of imagery and wants and hopes as feckless and ill-informed as a child's, memories as random as a wash of transmission during a thunderstorm, and nowhere a mind of true strength or substance.

Not within range, anyway.

In the pale glow that came through the drapes, Debora looked worried, and he asked if she was thinking about the next day.

"No . . . about the day after. About what we'll do then."

"We'll be okay."

"I know," she said, and turned away from him.

They awakened before dawn and ate breakfast in the diner next to the motel, a place called—according to its three-tiered neon sign—EAT VERNA'S TEX-MEX DELICIOUS. They had eggs-over-easy and bacon and toast and coffee, and sat in a booth of red vinyl sparkles, staring out through their reflections at the highway, the torrent of headlights and sleek dream machines westering, whispering toward the false dawn of Love City, piloted by men and women who wanted a good time then salvation and still believed this was possible, and thought maybe an immersion in the lingerie department of life would silver their hopes and streamline their wishes and send them home to boredom all chromed and supercharged with the horsepower of sexy experience. They lingered over their empty plates. No reason to hurry. Izaguirre wasn't going anywhere, secure with his guards and his walls. There were no other customers, and when the waitress brought the check, she leaned on the booth and said, "You folks goin' or comin'?"

"Coming," said Mingolla.

"This your first time to Love City?"

"Uh-huh."

She nodded, a skinny fortyish woman with lines of sad wisdom on her face and rainbow stripes in her frizzy baby-chick-colored hair, an aging hillbilly punkette who had come late to a regretful morality, her disguise completed by a starched green uniform. "Ain't nothin' there you two couldn't work out by yourself . . . if you take my meanin'," she said. "Don't get me wrong, now. I ain't preachin' 'gainst L.C. God knows, I let it all wallow there a time or two. It's just it don't make nobody happy. Don't make 'em sad, neither. It just sorta *is* . . . like everything else, y'know. So what's the point?"

Debora murmured agreement; her response seemed casual, but Mingolla sensed between her and the waitress a woman-to-woman exchange to which he wasn't attuned.

"Where you folks comin' from?" the waitress asked, affecting deep interest.

"Mexico," said Mingolla. "And Honduras before that." Made paranoid by the question, he checked her mind for signs of tampering and found her to be a mundane original.

"Mexico!" The way she said it, Mexico might have been something at the end of the boulevard of dreams, the distant glow of paradise. "Y'know, I sell Mex jewelry here"—she hooked her thumb toward the display case beneath the cash register; it was filled with cheap onyx and silver—"and Mex food. Hell, I even had me a Mex boyfriend. That was 'fore the war, y'understand. But I never been down there. Always wanted to go. See the pretty boys and the lizards on the beaches and all. The ruins, too. Always wanted to see them ruins."

Perky, feeling intimate with them now that she'd disclosed her heartfelt wish, she asked if they wanted more coffee . . . on the house. She brought the pot, poured, and plunked herself down beside Debora. She inquired about their backgrounds, said "uh-huh, uh-huh," in response to their minimal answers, impatient, eager to tell *her* story, the story she got to tell once every slow-predawn-while, the story that made her believe she'd lived that day.

"This ol' place probably looks pretty nothin' to you folks," she said. "But believe me, you can see a thing or two here. The idea of gettin' their Charlie doctored in Love City brings some strange 'uns thisaway."

"Oh?" said Debora with polite interest. She glanced guiltily at Mingolla, and he checked his watch. They had time, and it would be okay to sit and listen and pretend for a little while that they weren't going anywhere special, to have that much normalcy.

"You wouldn't believe some of 'em," said the waitress. And she told them about a man and a most unusual dog, and then about two women who'd looked as alike as two beans, pretty ol' girls, y'know, like starlets, blondes, they was blondes, and it was surgery made them so alike, they'd told her about it, how they was eye-dentical down to their moles, and they'd had their voices altered so they could harmonize even when they just talkin', not singin' or nothin', they sounded buzzy and high-pitched together like a coupla birds who'd learned to speak English. It had been a real treat hearin' them order the same thing simultaneous, waffles and cream and bacon, that's what they'd had, and they'd done all this surgery just to make a big splash in Love City.

Mingolla tuned the waitress out, watched Debora, and realized that she was watching him. He seemed to connect with her as he had back in San Francisco de Juticlan, to all of a sudden notice her, know her, and for a moment it seemed to him she was looking through younger eyes, seeing the kid he had been. It was such a clean feeling, that startled recognition, it confused Mingolla . . . and that was also part of the moment, part of the past, because he had long since learned to deny confusion. The moment was gone almost before it had existed, and he knew better than to try to hang on to it. It was simply there on occasion, one of their minor resources. He found it amusing that Izaguirre—in his guise as divinity—had told them the moment would always be a salvation. They hadn't believed him; what he'd said had sounded too fanciful to be true . . . though now Mingolla realized that he'd been talking about a matter of basic psychology. He wondered if the fact that Izaguirre had brought it up was evidence that he had planted the idea in them, that he was still manipulating them. Everything remained suspect. But whatever its nature, the moment *did* save Mingolla. He began to listen to the waitress, to like her, to see the good thing she wanted to be, the sweet ineptitude underlying her wishes, and he joined in the conversation, joined with all his heart, putting aside who he was and what he had to do, and they talked on into the gray morning, with dirty clouds piling up like seafoam on the horizon, they spoke of common sorrows and touched each other's hands, they told lies and believed them, they made a passion of forgetting and they laughed.

Mauve streaked the eastern sky, a couple of truckers came into the diner, leaking cigarette smoke like steam, braying for

247

coffee and steak. The waitress bawled the order out to the kitchen, brought more coffee, and sat back down, still full of stories. But more customers pushed in through the glass doors, all as gray as the sky with fatigue, itchy with highway dirt, their underwear ridden up into their crotches from hours of sitting, and the waitress had to go back to work. Mingolla and Debora waited, hoping she'd have another break, but she kept getting busier and busier. They walked to the register, stood with money in hand, and at last she slopped steak and eggs in front of another trucker, and rushed up breathless to collect her bill. She told them to drop back, tell her how they'd liked L.C., and she'd sure enjoyed meeting them, wasn't it funny how you could meet up with some people, perfect strangers, and next thing y'know you'd be like old friends talkin'? They promised to stop by again, tipped her big, and waved so-long. Then they went back to the motel and transferred the automatic rifles to the car. . . .

Confused, wanting to reject what he was beginning to understand, Mingolla went out of the hut and stood taking in the dreary particulars of the village. Sunlight glittered on the thatch, still wet from last night's rain; the puddles pocking the yellow dirt were leaden like pools of mercury. A man and a chicken passed each other on the street, the Indian heading for the jungle, the chicken toward the riverbank where it would hunt worms in the narrow margin of bright green grass. Mingolla recognized all the elements of the scene, knew their names and functions; yet there was a lack of coherence about it, and he came to realize that this incoherence stemmed not from any inherent wrongness in the village, but from the wrongness of his presence. He glanced back at Debora, who was tending to Amalia. Nothing incoherent about her.

Panama.

He remembered a brochure portrait of white skyscrapers and an aquamarine harbor, with Barrio Clarin somewhere behind, labyrinthine and silent.

It suddenly seemed right that he should go to Panama. More than right. It seemed he had a moral imperative, and studying Debora, he wondered if one side-effect of love was that it gave you a moral peg upon which to hang your fear and turned unacceptable risks into causes. Or maybe his desire to go was fueled by the sense of desolate triumph that had accompanied his vision, maybe he just needed a victory, any victory, and now believed one could be gained. No, he thought. He didn't believe that. Despite what he'd seen, he had the feeling that the future was never assured, no matter how clear your view of it.

Debora came out of the hut, shook her head when he asked about Amalia, and they walked toward the bank. The river was high from the rains, and the edge of the bank was mucky; they sat on an overturned canoe, and she began to talk distractedly of her home, her childhood in a wealthy barrio of Guatemala City, where the houses had fountains and walls topped with broken glass. He knew Panama was foremost on her mind, but now that they were lovers, she was less willing to make demands on him, less sure of what she wanted.

He listened to her happily; he didn't want to dwell on anything serious, and he enjoyed learning about her life. But a source of greater pleasure were the things he himself had told her over the past days, memories he hadn't believed consequential, but that seemed integral to the person he was becoming with her. The summer he'd spent on his uncle's farm in Nebraska, for instance. He'd been fascinated by the corn. He'd never thought of it as other than yellow ears dripping with butter, but standing in the midst of a cornfield he'd discovered that the plants were odd creatures with leaves that cut like stiff paper and white roots so powerful that you couldn't pull them from the soil. And you could hear them grow. The thick end of each leaf where it met the stalk would emit a soft quacking sound, this sometimes caused by the wind shifting them, but also when there was no wind, no motive force whatsoever. So much green around him, it had made him claustrophobic. And then there was the winter his great-grandmother had died. Cancer. He'd been going on twelve, and he had taken turns with his mother and grandmother caring for her. His father not disposed to such ministrations. Tumors hard in her neck. He'd had to massage her. Her muscles so tight, she'd felt like a rock with just a flicker of life beneath. Teeth grinding, eyelashes growing inside her lids, adding to her hurt. Eyes as hopeless and empty as crossed-out circles. He remembered her good times. Never talking much, order spreading around her in the form of baked goods and surfaces suddenly clean. She'd married a stunt flier, a guy who'd flown through barns and brought whiskey in from Canada. But she'd remembered none of that, gone inside to nothing. Once he'd stopped massaging her, and her hand had shot out, grabbed him, holding him tightly, and that night he'd dreamed about trying to kill a tiger with a spear. A beautiful young tiger with sleek muscles. It hadn't moved quickly, but very intelligently, and he'd seen it was trying to show him things as he killed it. Later he'd realized that the tiger's muscles had the same hardness as the tumors in his great-grandmother's neck.

The sluggish current carried bits of vegetable debris to nudge and clutter against the bank, and watching them be sucked beneath the murky green chop, Mingolla came to a decision.

"Debora," he said, breaking in. "When you wanna start?"

She looked up, uncomprehending.

"For Panama," he said.

Her face remained blank, but after a second a thin smile surfaced and she gave him a hug. It was a weak, sheltering hug, and in concert with the smile it seemed she was accepting him into the arms of her sadness.

"It'll take me a few days to get things ready," she said, and then, after a pensive silence, she asked why he'd changed his mind.

"Does it matter?"

"No, I'm just curious."

He knew she wanted to hear that it was because of a commitment to truth and justice, or some shit; but he couldn't lie. "Because of you, because I can't let you go alone."

She took his hand, toyed with his fingers, and finally, in a little-girl voice, shy and somewhat perplexed, she said, "Thank you."

Two days before they left, Mingolla visited the computer. Though he had rejected it, he at least wanted to acknowledge its existence with a farewell, for it had played a part in his coming to terms with many things. Debora scoffed at the idea, her rationality offended, but she went along to humor him. It was late afternoon when they reached the hollow, and the blades of golden light skewering the chopper were so defined by dust and moisture, they looked like transmuted chords of music, the sort of light that accumulates above organs and choir stalls in vast cathedrals. The skeleton of the pilot looked gilded and smiling, and the computer's voice seemed the implementation of a rich silence, of words saved up for centuries.

"You have my blessing for your journey," it said.

"This is ridiculous," said Debora.

"You're wrong," the computer said. "Lovers need blessings. Their rectitude is not enough to counter the loveless process of the world. They must depend on the strength of the moment, and if they do, then they are blessed. Look around you. A machine has become the Host. Light has been transformed into something rarefied. Even death has been transfigured. What you see here is an ordinary beauty made extraordinary by a moment that has outlasted its advent. And that is the best definition of love, the one most pertinent to you in your peril. Your moment lingers. You have hauled yourself up onto it and are living upon it even now. Sooner or later you will be pulled down, but that height is always there for you. Always reachable, always offering salvation. What the heart makes, the mind cannot destroy."

Debora made a disparaging noise.

"You believe me," said the computer. "But you don't want to hear your beliefs spoken by the unbelievable something you think I am."

The vines holding the chopper creaked, the light trembled, as if a mighty thought had troubled the innermost structures of the hollow.

It was approaching twilight when at last they headed back to the village. Birds were roosting, monkeys chattering, the beams of light withdrawing from the jungle floor. From the boulders ringing the hollow the trail wound downhill, narrowing into an archway of low-hanging branches, a leafy tunnel that curved west and opened onto a glade of palmettos and sapodillas. At any time of day the glade was lovely, but as they came out of the archway, they discovered that it had been made more lovely by the presence of millions of butterflies perched on every twig and frond. There was so much color and pattern that for a moment Mingolla failed to notice Nate standing on the opposite side of the glade, himself flowered with butterflies; some were swirling around his head, forming into a cloud through which his cold unreadable face could now and again be glimpsed.

"Nate!" Debora's voice was sharp with panic, and Mingolla, already deep into panic, probed at Nate, but to no effect. That peculiar pattern he had encountered on his first day in the village resisted his efforts, creating a fluctuating barrier he was unable to penetrate.

More butterflies eddied up, the cloud filling the glade, and Debora pulled at Mingolla, broke into a run back toward the hollow. He glanced behind him and saw that the archway was choked with a flurrying tide of butterflies, a tide of flowers flooding a green tube, making a whispery rustle that chilled him and weakened his legs. They reached the boulder that overlooked the chopper, and poised on the brink, butterflies streaming about her head, Debora shouted, "Jump!" They jumped together, and Mingolla landed in a crouch, fell forward. Spotted Debora slipping off the side of the chopper, which was swaying violently. He caught her arm. Butterflies were batting at his mouth, his eyes, and he swatted them away. He dragged Debora toward the hole punched by the missile and followed her inside, slicing his hand on the ragged edge. He slid past the blinking telltales to the dark end of the computer deck and began prying at the cockpit hatch. Debora joined him, straining at the rusted metal, working her fingers into the crack of the seal. Butterflies everywhere. Light touches on his face and hands. He spat them off his lips. His heart was doing a fancy dribble against his chest wall. The hatch squealed open, and they wedged through, forcing it shut behind them. Several dozen butterflies had poured into the cockpit, and in a frenzy, Mingolla went about killing them, crushing them against the plastic bubble, stopping them, squeezing them into a glue of broken wings. Once he had killed them all, he leaned against the copilot's chair, gazing at the skeleton, its ribcage protruding from the shreds of a flight jacket. The skull was parchment yellow, blotched with brown; dessicated tendon strings adhered to the corners of its mouth, lending the grin a grotesque silliness. Mingolla had the notion that the pilot was about to tell a joke; then a blue butterfly fluttered up in an empty eyesocket, and the expression of the skull was altered toward the sinister. With a shriek, Mingolla backhanded the skull, knocked it off the neck to roll on the floor; white dust puffed from the splintered spinal column.

Breathing hard, he turned to Debora. She had sagged down against the hatch, her knees drawn up, resting her forehead. "We're okay," he said. "We're okay now."

The light dimmed, dimmed with such suddenness that Mingolla wheeled around to learn the cause. Thousands of butterflies were massing on the crack-webbed plastic, obscuring the reddened light with a matte of wings and brittle bodies. Like looking at a puzzle of butterflies laid on a red table, with a few pieces missing. The missing pieces filled in rapidly, and the cockpit grew dark, only a faint effusion of reddish glow filtering through the overlapping wings. He could sense the enormous weight accumulating on the plastic, and moments later he began to hear scratchy sounds of strain, the bubble giving way.

"C'mon!" He groped for Debora, plucked at her shoulder. "Find Nate! Stop him!"

He flung out his mind, made immediate contact with Nate, and focused his fear into a knife that pried at his defenses. But even when Debora added her strength to his, that resistive pattern disrupted their attempts to penetrate it. The creaking had intensified, sharp bits of plastic dusted Mingolla's face, and he felt the tonnage above them as a pressure on his chest, a crushing weight that was forcing air out of him. Desperate, he tried merging with the defensive pattern, and—a triangular chunk of plastic fell from above, striking his cheek—he found that he could. Wings rustling, prickly legs stalking his forehead; he bit down on something that crunched, spat it out. The edge of his fear flowed in complicated loops and arcs, stitching along Nate's pattern with the rapidity of a sewing machine, and he added all his strength to the flow, accelerating it. Debora's mind joined his, and the signature knot of their involvement threaded itself into the pattern, overwhelming it, drawing it into a bizarre three-way connection of pain and sexuality. Then a scream from beyond the cockpit, and with the suddenness of a spell being broken, the connection was dissipated.

Butterflies lifted from the plastic; the dying light streamed in between the mattes of crushed bodies and wings that remained, stippling the floor with shadow. Through a gap, Mingolla saw Nate's blond head lying on the boulder above, and felt his mind roiling in the sluggish tumble of unconsciousness. Butterflies settled in Debora's hair as she leaned on the pilot's chair, shaking, and dozens more were eddying inside the cockpit, but Mingolla had no energy left to deal with them; he watched them batting around the headless skeleton, some fluttering out the new rent in the bubble, their colors flamed by the sunset, drifting higher and higher like glowing ash, until they became invisible against a lacework of black leaves and crimson sky.

They climbed up from the chopper to the boulder where Nate was lying. He was wearing a sidearm, and Mingolla removed the gun from its holster. Then they set about waking him. His mind had lapsed into a disarray similar to Amalia's, but apparently their strength had grown over the last days, for they managed the job with ease. The patterns of Nate's thoughts—again, like Amalia's—kept unraveling, but Mingolla was able to restore them when they did. He saw that it would be no problem to reverse the process, to weaken and dissolve the patterns of a healthy mind, and he wondered if this was what had happened to Nate. Soon Nate sat up and looked around blearily; he smoothed down his hair.

"I, uh . . ." He pinched the bridge of his nose. "I'm not sure what went wrong."

"You tried to kill us," said Mingolla. "Remember?"

"Of course, yes. But I was only supposed to watch, to assist you." He stared down at the chopper. "Always so many mistakes."

"What do you mean 'mistakes'?" Debora asked.

"Can I be of assistance?" asked the computer.

It seemed to Mingolla there was urgency in the computer's voice, and ignoring it, he repeated Debora's question.

"They are skillful, very skillful," said Nate. "It takes them a long time to control someone, but they've had centuries of practice. The thing is, though, they're careless. They rely too much upon their power, and that makes them prone to sweeping tactics, the grandiose. They tend to neglect minor details . . . details that would be obvious to you and me."

" 'The others,' " said Mingolla. "That who you mean?"

Nate spotted the gun in Mingolla's hand and reached for it. "Let me have it, please."

"You're kidding!"

"You must," Nate said. "He will find me, use me again."

"I really believe I can help him," said the computer.

"Do you know what it's like to be almost nothing?" said Nate. "To see things that aren't there, obey voices in your head." His eyes darted about, and he wrung his hands, growing more agitated by the second. It was not good to watch; it appeared he was winding himself up, his springs coiling tighter and tighter.

"Who's using you?" Debora asked.

"Izaguirre." Nate made a grab for the gun, but Mingolla knocked his hand away. "Please! It's been years since I've felt this clear. I may not have another chance."

"Tell us about Izaguirre," said Debora. "Then we'll help you."

"All right." Nate rested a hand on the boulder, laid it there with precise care as if he wanted to know it, to draw its coolness inside. "All right, I'll trust you."

Darkness fell, moonlight inlaid the black metal of the chopper with gleams, and Nate talked calmly, steadily, his head thrown back, eyes lidded, like an enraptured saint. He told them he'd suffered a breakdown during therapy, and afterward had spent a long confinement in a house with other damaged recruits. Somewhere in the States, he thought, but he wasn't sure.

"Izaguirre was in charge," he said. "In fact, he was the only one of the families in residence."

"The families?" Mingolla said. "That stuff Amalia said . . . it's true?"

"Oh, yes. Izaguirre would tell us stories about the families, the feud. He'd shake his head as if it were weighing upon his soul, but he enjoyed the stories, and I think he relished their bloody past. It was in the way he embellished them. He made horror sound elegant." Nate cast an eye toward the gun. "Such a strange, moody place . . . that house. You must be careful. There were dangerous people there. Izaguirre's toys, his weapons."

It was all coming together for Mingolla. The clues, Nate and Amalia, and Pastorín's stories. Izaguirre was behind everything . . . if that was his name, and it probably wasn't. Sotomayor and Madradona. His arrogance would demand he use real names in the story. He must have subverted Pastorín. And maybe he *was* Pastorin. The author's penchant for privacy was notorious, and now that Mingolla thought about it, he'd never seen a photograph of the man.

"What did he have planned for us?" he asked.

"I'm not sure. I was supposed to watch you, protect you. But something went wrong."

"Did he say anything 'bout us getting stronger? Anything 'bout a mutuality of focus making us strong?"

"Actually," said the computer. "I'd forgotten that."

They all turned to the chopper.

"I simply thought it would be amusing to send you after Debora," the computer went on. "I have a fondness for irony. And I'm glad I did send you. No one has ever been able to defeat Nate until now. His malfunction has made clear how valuable you two will be. We look forward to your arrival."

"Izaguirre," said Mingolla. "You motherfucker!"

The computer gave forth one of its easy chuckles. "Hello, David. Surprised to see me?"

"Not really." Mingolla stood and looked down at the chopper, wishing Izaguirre were there in person. "Where are you?"

"Don't be annoyed, David. I have nothing but good wishes for you and Debora. As to where I am, you'll see me in Panama."

"What makes you think we'll go to Panama after all this?"

"Where else can you go? You're both deserters, so you can't go home. And besides, you want to learn about Panama. You want to find out what's there, don't you?"

"Why don't you just fly us there now?" Debora asked.

"Ordinarily I might," said the computer. "However, I think in your case it would be wise to gauge your strength. The trip will provide you with tests, and I for one will be most interested in seeing how you cope with them."

"You're nuts!" said Mingolla. "You're playing games with us, with everyone."

"Not at all," said the computer. "I'm merely being cautious."

"What *is* going on in Panama?"

Silence, the black web of vines stretched taut by the enormous bulk of the chopper. Mingolla felt its size and power within him, felt that his body, too, was a web holding a black shape, a potential that Izaguirre in his arrogance might not suspect. If he could hide that potential, if Debora could hide hers, they just might have a surprise for Izaguirre.

"Please," Nate said, gesturing at the gun.

"If you leave Nate here," said the computer, "I'll have someone look after him."

"No!" Nate jumped to his feet. "I won't go back."

"Calm down, Nate," said the computer. "It's not as bad as all that."

Debora held out her hand to Mingolla. "Give me the gun."

Appalled, he said, "What're you going to do?"

She said nothing, but continued to hold out her hand.

"You don't have to," said Mingolla. "Maybe . . ."

"Give it to her!" said Nate. "You have to!" He had a sick, eager look; Debora's expression was resigned.

"If it has to be done, I'll do it," Mingolla said.

"There's no need to *do it* at all," the computer said. "Nate is overstating the horrors of his service. He'll be well cared for, I promise."

"Well cared for?" Nate stepped to the edge of the boulder, his fists clenched. "Yes, I'll be well cared for! I can sit in a room all day without a thought to trouble me. And when I'm waked . . . hah! When I'm waked I'll be so grateful to have you twist me . . . to let you . . ." He appeared to have lost the train of thought and stared at the chopper. Insects fizzed out in the dark scrub beyond the ring of boulders.

Debora took the barrel of the gun. "Wait for me in the glade."

Reluctantly, Mingolla turned the butt loose, and with a final look at Nate, he walked down the archway of leaves and stood in the feathery shadow of a palmetto. It gave him a strange feeling to think of Debora killing someone, especially by this method of mercy killing cum execution. He tried to excuse her in terms of her guerrilla experience; he wanted her to be virtuous. Minutes passed, and he became worried that something bad had happened, that Nate had managed to get the gun away from her. He started back toward the hollow, and at that moment the gunshot sounded. Monkeys screaming, a thousand dark wings beating overhead. A few seconds later Debora came through the archway, the gun tucked into her belt. He wanted to comfort her, but she walked past without comment, moving so quickly through the sparse brush that he had trouble keeping up with her.

They spent their last day in Emerald packing a canoe with

provisions and weapons, and finalizing their plans for the journey. By river to the Petén Highway. Bus to the town of Réunion. Then on foot through jungle to the Rio Dulce south of San Francisco de Juticlan, and thereafter by boat downriver to Livingston. They gave Amalia—who had wandered into the village shortly after Debora's arrival, likely directed that way by Izaguirre—into the hands of a young childless widow; they had little hope that Izaguirre would fail to reclaim her, but at least she would be well taken care of in the interim. Then they paddled the canoe to the hot springs, where they would spend their last night.

The early evening was a quiet time. Debora sat on the bank, morose, dangling her legs, touching her toes to the scalding water as if testing her threshold of pain. Mingolla sat beside her, cleaning the rifles, thinking of the days ahead. He gazed south down the river. The darkness looked thicker there, a black gas welling toward them, and he thought he could sense the precise articulation of their journey, the uphills and downhills, the ducking-into-covers, the sprinting away from this or that danger; it seemed his thought was a wind going out of him, coursing over the shapes of land and event. Once in a while they talked, mostly about nothing, asking if one or the other was hungry, thirsty, sleepy. On only one occasion did they have a real conversation, and that occurred after Debora asked Mingolla what he was thinking.

"Not much . . . just 'bout the apple trees in my backyard. Back home, y'know."

"I would have thought you'd be thinking about the trip."

"I was, but just then I was remembering pruning the apple trees, sawing off the dead limbs."

"I've never seen an apple tree."

"They're kinda neat. I never thought much about 'em 'till I had to work with 'em. You spend hours cutting at something, and you start noticing things."

"Like what?"

"Like when the sawdust gets hot, it smells like hot apples."

"What else?"

He mulled it over. "When there's a long branch that's

259

dying, and it has a choice where to bring out a new leaf, it always puts the leaf right at the end, right at its tip."

She dabbled her toes in the water. "Nate was like that."

"How do ya mean?"

"Just something he said before . . ." She pursed her lips, stared at her hands. "I wish," she said after a long pause, "that I could really believe he wanted to die, that it wasn't just madness."

"I think it was both."

"No," she said. "It was just madness."

"Then why'd ya do it?"

"He might have tried to hurt us again."

"That's a good enough reason."

"It always has been before, but . . ." She kicked the surface of the water, sent spray flying. "I'm feeling too much," she said, glancing at him as if in accusation. "I don't want this— you and me—to make me weak."

He tried to jolly her. "Seems to me it's done just the opposite."

She looked puzzled, and he explained he was talking about their increased strength.

"That's not what I meant!" She kicked the water again. "I meant what feelings do to your resolve."

"When you kill somebody, you should feel something." He told her about the Barrio and de Zeduguí, what his lack of feeling had done to him, and after he had finished, she said, "He was right. We are creatures of power. But we're not in control of anything. Izaguirre's in control, or else somebody's controlling him."

"Probably," he said. "And it's for sure we've been manipulated. But that doesn't mean that we can't have some control." He laid the rifle on the bank, put an arm around her. "I keep thinking about what Nate said."

"What?"

" 'Bout how they always made mistakes, how they were skillful but careless. There's this haphazard character to everything that's happened. I've noticed it in myself, the way I acted in the Barrio. I assumed I'd blow through everything, that I was

260

in complete command, and I ended up taking stupid risks, almost getting killed. And I can see it in the shit that's been done to me. Like the time Izaguirre gave me that booster shot and then worried after the fact whether he'd given me too much. It's in the stories, in their playfulness. The chopper's a perfect example. I mean what a fucking waste of energy it was to set that up. It wasn't necessary, it was a conceit, a chance for Izaguirre to play God. These people have been doing the drug for centuries, and that character's engrained in them. They're powerful but they're fuck-ups. And if we can just stay cool, if we don't trust anybody but each other, maybe we'll catch them off guard. Maybe we'll be their biggest fuck-up of all. I really feel that's true."

She said nothing.

"Really," he said. "It's more than a feeling."

"I hope they're not fuck-ups," she said. "I hope whatever they're doing, it's something that'll change things."

"You mean . . ."

"I don't care who's running things down here," she said, "as long as it isn't the American Chamber of Commerce in Guatemala City. Or United Fruit, or Standard Fruit, or the Banco Americano Desarrollo. Or some other American company. If Izaguirre is working against them, then I want to work with him."

She had thrown off her despondency and seemed on the verge of anger; Mingolla didn't want to argue.

"Yeah, well . . . whatever. But let's be careful? Let's not start trusting people before we're damn sure about them. Okay?"

"Okay," she said. "But we're going to have to trust somebody eventually, and I hope it can be Izaguirre's people."

Starlight laid a sheen on the river, picking out the eddies. Wind drove off the mosquitoes, and Debora and Mingolla spread their sleeping bags outside the tent and lay down. Close to him, her features looked softer than usual, more girlish, and when he touched her breasts, her breath came quick and warm on his cheek. Despite their intimacy, he felt estranged from her, too full of trepidation about the journey to lose himself, and he explored the shapes of her breasts, her hips, her cunt, trying to

261

find in his knowledge of her body a truer knowledge of mind and soul, some fact of topography that would confirm the good news of his emotions, that would explain her and justify the risk he was taking. Arousal, however, was the only result. Her skin felt like the starlight, smooth, coated with a cool emulsion. As he lowered between her legs, fenced by her long thighs, she arched her neck, staring up into the sky, and cried out, "God!" as if she had seen there some mysterious presence. But he knew to whom she was really crying out. To that sensation of heat and weakness that enveloped them. To that sublimation of hope and fear into desire. To the thoughtless, self-adoring creature they became, all hip and mouth and heart. *That* was God.

CROSSING THE WILD

Men are weeds in this region.

—Thomas de Quincy

CHAPTER TWELVE

Ruy Barros was a bad man. Everybody in the town of Livingston would testify to this. Consider, they'd say, that Ruy has often been seen wearing watches and gold chains resembling those once belonging to his passengers. Consider, too, that his wife embarked upon one voyage heavy with child and returned with neither a big belly nor an infant. Does this not suggest that Ruy, who has no patience with the weak and infirm, found the child a nuisance and cast him over the side? Is this not borne out by the fact that his wife left him shortly thereafter and went to live with her family in Puerto Barrios? And consider the woman with whom he has since taken up, a slut with a mystic rose in place of her eye of wizardly power. Should proof be needed of his evil nature, consider his cargoes. Cocaine, deserters, antiquities. No, they told Mingolla, you would do well to take passage on another boat . . . though the *Ensorcelita* is the only boat in the harbor that will bear you to Panama, and who but God knows when another will present itself. It might be best, señor, for you to rethink your travel plans.

The men and women who offered these warnings were Caribes, who dwelled in white casitas, who swam in a tiered waterfall in the green hills above the town, and the peacefulness of their lives in such close proximity to the battle zone was a perfect evidence of the war's artificial character. From their words Mingolla had conjured a piratical image of Ruy Barros—

grizzled, scarred, tattooed, with gold teeth—and the *Ensorcelita* was a battered old fishing tub that might well have belonged to such a character: a forty-footer with a dark green hull, four cramped cabins belowdecks, and a refrigerated storage compartment aft. Its wheelhouse, which was canted about five degrees out of true, had not been painted in many years, yet retained a yellow stippling that from a distance lent it a polka-dotted gaiety. The decks were strewn with rags, greasy machine parts, coils of rope, holed gas cans, and much of the planking was speckled with dry rot. But while Ruy's personality accorded with the dilapidated state of the boat, his appearance did not. He was a gangly hollow-chested man in his late twenties, with fashionably cut black hair lying flat to his neck, and a lean horsey face that—despite its homeliness—showed evidence of breeding and struck Mingolla as familiar. Maybe because Ruy's handsome face reminded him of Goya's court portraits of dour, long-nosed, thick-lipped dukes and marquesses.

On the morning they boarded, a chill overcast morning with banks of fog crumbling out to sea, Ruy met them at the rail with a refined bow whose effect was dispelled by his greeting. "I told you seven o'clock," he said. "What you think, man? This a goddamn taxi? My other passenger, he been on board for a fuckin' hour."

Mingolla was about to ask, What other passenger, when a huge black man hove into view from behind the wheelhouse and came toward them, beaming. Gray flecks in his crispy hair, wearing a red baseball cap and jeans and a T-shirt stretched by his muscular arms and chest. Hook-shaped pink scar above one eye. Mingolla couldn't believe it was Tully, but then, accepting the fact, he whipped out the automatic that had been tucked under his shirt.

"Put that bitch away!" said Ruy, backing.

Tully stood his ground. "You lookin' strong, Davy. And feelin' strong, too. Dat I can tell." He gave Debora the once-over. "Dis dat Cifuentes woman, huh? She fah from unsightly, mon."

"What're you doing here?" said Mingolla.

"Same like you, mon. Panama!" The way Tully sounded

the name, it had a ring of destiny, of great deeds in the offing. "I been puttin' two and two toget'er, and Panama de sum I 'rive at."

Ruy had backed to the door of the wheelhouse and was about to slip inside; Mingolla told him to stay put.

"Who's he?" Debora asked; she had her own gun out.

"Davy never tell ya 'bout Tully Ebanks?"

Tully came a step closer, and Mingolla, realizing he didn't need the gun, tucked it back into his waistband. "Be wise, Tully," he said. "I can handle ya, no problem."

"I been ever knowin' dat, Davy. Weren't it me sayin' you was goin' to be somethin' special? I seen dis moment from de back-time. And I still fah you, mon."

"Uh-huh, sure."

Ruy started into the wheelhouse again, and Mingolla cautioned him. "I'm gonna start this motherfucker up," Ruy said. "You bastards wanna kill each other, go 'head. I got the fog to worry 'bout." He ducked into the wheelhouse, and a moment later a grumble vibrated the hull, black smoke spewed from the stern.

"You gonna shoot me, Davy?" Tully asked, and grinned.

"I might," said Mingolla. "Tell me why you're going to Panama."

"Ain't nowhere else to go. Must be a fool, took me so long to figure t'ings out."

"What things?"

"T'ings I been hearin' . . . from Izaguirre and de rest. It alla sudden start makin' sense."

Mingolla picked his way through the debris on the deck and confronted Tully from an arm's length away. Tully grinned down at him, his seamed face as massive as an idol's. Then his grin faded as Mingolla pushed into his mind, brushing aside his defenses and influencing him toward honesty. He asked Tully again his reasons for traveling to Panama, and Tully gave back a fragmented tale of clues, hints, things overheard, all leading to the same conclusions that Debora and Mingolla had reached.

"Christ God Almighty!" said Tully afterward, staring at him in awe. "What de fuck happen wit' you?"

267

"Practice," said Mingolla. From his brush with Tully's mind he had gained an image of greed and strength, and underlying that, an essential good-heartedness that had been weakened by drugs and power. He thought he could trust him, but he was having trouble sorting out his feelings for him: an amalgam of camaraderie and antagonism.

"Listen, Davy." Tully adopted a conspiratorial tone. "We got to talk, mon. Work somet'ing out 'bout dis Panama trip. 'Cause I'm feelin' it's gonna be deep down there. We gonna need each ot'er."

"Yeah, we'll talk." Mingolla turned to Debora. "He was my trainer, he's okay."

She dropped her gun into a tote bag, favored Tully with a suspicious stare, then went forward. The *Ensorcelita* rattled and lurched in the gray chop, leaving Livingston behind. "I hate dis fuckin' sea," said Tully, staring out over the water. "Damn, I hate it!" He moved close to Mingolla and draped an arm about his shoulders. "Been too long, ain't it, Davy?"

Mingolla muttered agreement, but shook off Tully's arm. "What you wanna talk about?"

"Well . . ." Tully leaned on the rail, adopted a stern tone. "To start wit' you might wanna tell me 'bout why you messed wit' my 'Lizabeth."

Mingolla didn't place the name at first. "Oh, yeah . . . I don't know, man. I was pretty loose back then. Sorry."

"Mon, dat little girl be cryin' for a month 'bout you."

"I told ya I was sorry," Mingolla said, irritated. "What you want me to do, go back to the island and fix her?"

"I coulda done dat. But I lef' her the way she was . . . figured dat her feelin's keep off de ot'er flies. Naw, I just wantin' to know if your conscience been vexin' you."

"Not a lot," said Mingolla. "I've been busy."

"You always did enjoy actin' hard," said Tully. "And now you hard fah true. But dere's good in ya, mon. Dat's clear."

"I don't need my character analyzed, man. Tell me what you got in mind . . . y'got something in mind, don't ya?"

Ruy came out of the wheelhouse to stand beside Debora, who was looking back at the receding town.

"Yeah, I got somethin' in mind," Tully said. "Back when I was fishin', I spend some months in Panama. Got to know de country some. 'Case t'ings go sour down dere, dere's dis place I know up in Darién. Kinda place where a mon can lose heself."

Ruy was talking, gesturing wildly, and his hand flicked across Debora's breast, causing her to jump back.

Mingolla brushed past Tully and, kicking garbage aside, stalked toward Ruy. "You better watch where you put your fuckin' hands, man!"

"It was an accident, David." Debora stepped between him and Ruy, and Ruy smiled, shrugged.

"Don't get excited, *hombre*," he said. "I got my own woman. Hey, Corazon! C'mere!"

A woman popped her head up from the hatch that led to the cabins. Ruy beckoned, and she came up onto the deck. She was a little plump, but sexy nonetheless, with Indian coloring, regular mestizo features, and long black hair weaved into a single braid. She radiated a psychic's heat, and in her left eye was the holograph of a dewy rose floating against a starless night.

"Yeah," said Ruy. "I need a squeeze, Corazon she gimme one." He waggled a finger at her. "Open it up."

Corazo dropped her eyes and started undoing the buttons of her blouse.

"Don't do that," Mingolla said.

But Corazon didn't stop.

"You tell your woman what to do," Ruy said. "Not mine."

The blouse fell open, Corazon's heavy breasts spilled out.

"Let's go," said Mingolla, guiding Debora toward the hatch.

Behind them, Ruy's voice was filled with amusement. "C'mon back and give her a squeeze, man! Y'don't know what you missin'!"

They sailed close to the shore, avoiding the cordon of warships that fortressed the deep water. The overcast held, and whenever the sun pierced the clouds, its vague light layered the sea with a flat uniform shine, making it seem they were crossing an ocean of fresh gray housepaint. The only event to break the monotony of the voyage was Ruy's ongoing attempt to seduce Debora. Each time she came on deck, he would pin her against the rail and regale her with testimony to his revolutionary zeal, tell stories about his villainy in service of the cause. When Mingolla asked if she wanted him to put a stop to this, she said, "He's crude, but he's harmless. And he's really not so bad. At least his political conscience is genuine." Her attitude was at odds with Mingolla's: *genuine* was the last word he would have used to describe Ruy, and besides, he was mightily offended by Ruy's treatment of Corazon.

His initial impression of her had been that she was more than pretty, but he subtracted from that impression the exotic bauble embedded in her eye. You were drawn first to look at the eye, only then at the rest of her, and it seemed that the surreal beauty of the rose had created an illusion of beauty, that she was in reality quite ordinary. This secondary impression was enhanced by her doglike obedience to Ruy's whims. Once, for instance, he had her dress in black pumps and an evening gown, pile her hair high and fix it with glittering jeweled pins that resembled bunches of tiny flowers, and set her to scrubbing the decks, a chore that took her most of the night and left her dress in tatters. She went about with her head down, rarely speaking to anyone, and would flinch at the sound of Ruy's step.

But one night as Mingolla walked along the companionway belowdecks, heading for his cabin, he heard Corazon's voice coming from Tully's door, which was cracked an inch open. "No, I don't feel nothin'," she was saying.

"Hell you don't," Tully said. "Can't fool me 'bout dat."

Through the door, Mingolla saw Corazon standing by Tully's bunk, wearing only panties. Lantern light flashed off the rose in her eye.

"Why you want me to feel?" she said. "Feelin' don't mean nothin'. I don't wanna feel."

"Dat's horseshit," said Tully. "Dat's just how Ruy want you to be . . . he like you to be dat way. And for some reason I can't unnerstan', you t'ink dat's upful."

"I have to go." She shrugged into her blouse.

Tully, hopeless-sounding: "You be back?"

Mingolla didn't wait for the answer, ducking into the vacant cabin next door. When he heard Corazon's footsteps retreating, he crossed to Tully's door and pushed on in. "You're playing with fire, man," he said. "We don't need trouble with Ruy."

"Ain't gonna be no trouble," said Tully, lying back on his bunk. "And if dere is, den we fix he head for him."

"I just as soon not scramble the brains of a man who's sailing reef waters," said Mingolla.

"Don't be worryin'." Tully heaved a forlorn sigh. "Mon know alla 'bout me and Corazon. Fact it were his idea, her comin' to me. He like to have her tell 'bout how it is wit' ot'er men." He slammed his fist into the mattress.

"What's the matter?"

The lines on Tully's face appeared to be etched deeper than before, like cracks spreading through his substance. "Damn fool, me," he said. "To get taken wit' some squint at my age . . . 'specially one dat ain't even taken wit' herself." He made the muscles of his forearm bunch and writhe, watched their play. "She enjoy t'inkin' 'bout herself like she a doorstop or somethin'. And the damn t'ing is, I know she feel fah me, 'cept she won't 'mit it."

"Maybe she doesn't feel anything," Mingolla suggested. "Maybe you're kidding yourself."

"Naw, she feel it all right. She just shamed by the feelin'. Goddamn women, dere feelin's is most all de power dey got, so dey likes to go fuckin' 'round wit' 'em, y'know. See how fuckin' twisted dey can make 'em, and den get a mon all cotched up in dem." He hit the mattress again. "Can't figger how she got dat way."

"Could be Ruy's doing."

"I don't t'ink so. De woman been t'rough de therapy, she got no reason to bow down to Ruy. Naw, ut strike me she been like dis awhile." Tully held up his fist to the light, examined it: like an alchemist inspecting a strange root in the rays from his alembic. "But, mon, I could have fun fah a few minutes alone wit' dat son of a bitch."

271

"That wouldn't be real smart," Mingolla said. "We need him right now."

"What 'smart' got to do wit' anyt'ing?" Tully glowered at Mingolla. "You t'ink it's smart de way you carryin' on wit' dat Cifuentes woman? T'ink dat don't 'fect your judgments?"

"Least she's not spoken for."

"Naw, but Ruy he gotta yearnin' fah her."

"He's just flirting."

"Dat not what Corazon say, she say de mon have fall hard."

"Then that's his tough luck."

Tully snorted, stared at the ceiling. "You sure as shit still gotta lot to learn, Davy."

Mingolla perched on the edge of the bunk. "So tell me 'bout Panama, man. This place you talking 'bout."

"Dat'll keep."

"What you got better to do . . . brood?"

Tully said nothing for several seconds, but finally sat up. "Guess you gotta point. All right, I tell you. Dere's dis little village name of Tres Santos up in de Darién Mountains. Here"— he grabbed pencil and paper from the table by the bunk—"I draw a map." He kept talking as he drew. "It 'bout four, five hours from Panama City . . . less dere's mist. Den you could be a week gettin' dere. Or maybe you take de coast road 'long de Pacific and come at Tres Santos from de west. Less mist dat way."

"What's there?" Mingolla asked.

"Not'in' 'cept Indians. But in case t'ings go to hell in Panama City, Tres Santos be a good place to start a run."

"Shit, they'd find us there."

"Dat's true . . . Tres Santos open to the sky. But from dere you can cotch a trail dat lead into de cloud forest. And once you up in de clouds, you can't be stayin' dere, neither. But you can hide your tracks. De Indians dey be helpful and you say to dem my name. Dey show you de secret ways, and no matter who will follow, you take dem ways and you will be far away 'fore de dogs can trace your scent." He held up the paper, studied it. "Dere . . . you hang on to dat 'case t'ings don't work out in Panama."

272

Mingolla tucked the map into his shirt pocket. "What were you doing up in the mountains? Thought you were fishing."

"I were fishin' all right . . . fishin' under de meanest mot'erfucker dat ever put on a braided cap. We hit Colón, mon, I were over de side and runnin' fah he cut the engines. Had me a time, too. Dat Darién some wild country."

"What's it like?"

"Most of it just wilderness, but de cloud forest now, dat's somet'in unusual fah true." Tully folded his arms behind his head. "Dere's villages up dere where de sun never comes . . . even on de brightest day dere's mist, and the air look like it fulla some kinda shiny atoms, y'know. And when you see a mon walkin' toward you, wit' de mist swirlin' 'round him and de sun givin' him a halo, it make you t'ink you gone to Jesus. And it's quiet. Every sound's muffled by de mist, and you cannot judge de distances 'tween t'ings. You get de feelin' dat de place is made of mist, and dat de distances is always changin'. You will hear wings beatin' and see only shadows, and de jungle 'pear like it movin' slow, all de vines writ'in and twistin' like snakes. And dere's brujos. Witch men. You can see dere fires in de night, bloomin' out in de solitudes, in de high places. Hear dere chantin'. And when de chantin' cease, dere may come a black dog strollin' t'rough de village, a dog dat belong to nobody, and dey say if you look in he eye, den you will learn of de mysteries."

A cold uneasiness had stolen over Mingolla as Tully spoke, but he denied it and merely said that the place sounded interesting.

"Oh, it dat all right. But dat ain't why I told you 'bout it." Tully propped himself on an elbow and stared at Mingolla. "I got a feelin' dat you gonna come dere someday, and dat's de reason fah I make de map."

"I s'pose I might get up that way," Mingolla said, affecting casualness.

"Dat ain't my meanin', Davy," said Tully. "You know what I'm talkin' 'bout. I got me a real deep feelin'."

It wasn't until the second week of the voyage that Mingolla

entered into another conversation with Ruy. He had been sitting beside Debora, who was sunning herself in a pale leakage of light through the overcast, watching the blackish green line of the Honduran coast, when Ruy came out of the wheelhouse carrying a cassette player and sat down by the door; he lit a cigarette and switched on the player. The volume was low, but Mingolla recognized Prowler's rhythms and Jack Lescaux's vocal style. He moved along the rail to within twenty feet of Ruy and pretended to be studying the shore, pleased to hear something familiar in all this foreign emptiness.

". . . a big red moon had squirted straight up from hell,
and under it, I spotted my friend Rico,
who was not my friend, then, owin' me twenty,
and I chased after him, yellin' as we ran away . . .
from that electric sun of midnight flashin'
Twenty-Four-Hour Topless Girls! Girls! Girls!
Yeah . . . Twenty-Four-Hour . . ."

"Like that music, man?" said Ruy, cutting the volume. "I do."

Mingolla said it was okay.

"Bet the little lady down there, she like it. Maybe I invite her over to have a listen. She look so sad, I bet it cheer her up."

"I doubt it." Mingolla turned a baleful eye on Ruy.

"That Debora, she's a nice little lady," said Ruy expansively. "Real nice! She tell me you in love, but I know that's the crap you gotta hand 'em to make 'em do de backstroke."

Mingolla hardened his stare but said nothing.

"Love!" Ruy sniffed and flipped his cigarette over the rail; he shielded his eyes from the glare and peered toward Debora. "Yeah, she sure is nice. I'm tellin' ya, man, this ain't casual with me. I'm really feelin' somethin' for her. I'm thinkin' ol' Ruy can put a smile on her face."

"All you done so far is bore the hell outta her."

"Then maybe I try harder." Ruy squinted up at him. "Tell ya what, we make a trade, okay? I'll send Corazon to your cabin tonight, and you lemme see what I can do for the little lady."

Disgusted, Mingolla turned away.

"Hey, you gettin' the best of the deal, man," said Ruy. "That Corazon, she got tricks that'll notch your pistol."

Something occurred to Mingolla, something he'd been intending to ask Ruy about. "You remember a guy named Gilbey?" he said. "Short blond guy 'bout my age. He traveled with you 'round eight or nine months ago."

"Gilbey," said Ruy. "Naw, uh-uh."

Mingolla searched his face for a hint of a lie. "You'd remember this guy. He was surly, y'know . . . had a bad attitude. Wouldn't take shit from anybody."

"What you think?" said Ruy with menace. "I dump him over the side?"

"Did you?"

"You been talkin' to them dumb cunts back in Livingston, that it?" Ruy climbed to his feet, adopted a challenging pose. "Listen, friend. I ain't a nice guy, I'm a fuckin' criminal! But I don't throw nobody over the side 'less they begging for it."

"Maybe Gilbey begged for it."

"Then I'd remember him."

"How 'bout your baby, you remember your baby, don'tcha?"

Ruy spat at Mingolla's feet. "My baby's born dead, man. I get rid of it 'cause my woman she can't stand to be 'round it."

"If you say so."

"That's what I say. Those bullshit savages back in Livingston, what they know 'bout Ruy Barros. What they know 'bout my work for the cause. I work my butt off for the cause, I do things nobody else got the belly for."

"That right?"

"Yeah, that's right." Ruy went chest-to-chest with Mingolla. "But what's a fuckin' gringo like you know 'bout shit. You . . ."

Mingolla gave Ruy a push. "How you know I'm American?"

Ruy grinned. "Debora, she tell me."

"That's crap," said Mingolla. "How'd you know?"

"Huh! Ruy Barros, he can smell a fuckin' gringo. That's a nice paint job, man, and you got the language down . . . but you walk gringo, you act gringo, and the things you say is gringo. And you don't see that the cause is for all the people.

275

For priests, murderers, whatever." He shook his fist at the sun. "*La Violencia!* Lemme tell ya, man. This war ain't gonna end 'till we win it."

Despite himself, Mingolla was impressed by Ruy's vehemence, by the honest zeal it appeared to embody.

"You don't unnerstan' nothin', gringo," Ruy continued. "And that's why me and the little lady gonna work things out. 'Cause in her heart she know I unnerstan' her."

The time had come, Mingolla decided, to stake out his claim. "You talk a lot, man. I like that. Guys who talk a lot, that's all they're up for."

Ruy rubbed his chin, his long face grew thoughtful. "You sayin' you can take me, man?"

"Absolutely." Mingolla gestured at Debora. "And y'know what? She can take ya, too. You ain't a threat at all, beaner. So set it out, give it a shot."

Ruy's shoulders tensed as if he were preparing to throw a punch, but he must have thought better of it. He hitched up his pants, scowled at Mingolla, and went into the wheelhouse. Mingolla picked up the cassette player, held it up to show Ruy, who looked away, attending to the business of steering. Then he walked back to the stern, turning up the volume of a ballad.

"Come and live with me . . .
Aw, girl, there ain't no better place for you,
'cause you just hangin' on
to somethin' old when your mind is onto somethin' new.
Listen to that jukebox pla-ay-ay,
one of them sad ol' Sentimental Journey tunes,
somebody's singin' 'bout, Hey, girl,
I guess it wasn't meant to be for me and you . . .

But though you say we're through,
I guess it all depends upon your point of view,
'cause when I look into your eyes,
I can see clear through ya and don't ya know . . .

You Can't Hide Your Love From Me

You Can't Hide Your Love From Me
Well, y'can run but . . .
You Can't Hide Your Love From Me
Y'ain't no mystery, lady . . ."

"What's that?" said Debora, frowning at the player as Mingolla sat beside her.

"Prowler . . . like it?"

"It's all right."

"It's old," he said. "From four or five years ago. And not typical. They do mostly uptempo stuff. I'll find something else."

"No, I'm starting to like it." She leaned into him.

". . . that stranger over there,
sittin' all alone, so sad and blue,
he's playin' solitaire and losin' bad,
drinkin' gin and feelin' sad 'bout missin' you.
But don'tcha see, somewhere in his heart
he knows there's still a trace
of lovelight in your eyes tonight
and foolish dreams you can't deny
each time you look his way . . ."

"What were you and Ruy talking about?" she asked.

"Nothing."

"You sounded angry."

"He's an asshole."

". . . he don't believe in fate,
and to win at solitaire
you just lay the red queen down
upon the diamond ace,
y'can't lose that way and . . .

"You Can't Hide Your Love From Me . . ."

Debora's hair drifted into his face, and it seemed he was breathing her in with the same rhythm as that of the swells

277

lifting the *Ensorcelita*. Seaweed floated on the swells, clumped reddish brown beard-lengths with black bean-shaped seeds. The sun beat down, wedging silvery between the clouds, and a dark bird wheeled above the shore, then dived and vanished into the palms.

"I guess he is," she said.

"What?"

"Ruy . . . an asshole. But I still think he means well."

"Meaning well doesn't matter when you're that much of an asshole."

>"Come on, girl!
>Can't ya find it in your heart
>to take a chance,
>and see if there's a world where we
>could live and never have to take
>a backward glance?
>Maybe I'm a dreamer, maybe I'm a fo-oo-ool,
>or maybe I'm just a lonely man,
>but maybe I've got the answers to
>all those questions that are troublin' you . . .
>All ya gotta do is ask . . ."

Ruy poked his head out of the wheelhouse, glaring at them, his lean cruel face a badge of enmity, a reminder of all they had endured, all they were going toward. But Mingolla felt so content, so removed from the world of trials and disasters, that—not stopping to think how Ruy might take it—he grinned and gave him a cheerful wave.

The next day they were stopped by a patrol boat, but it was no big deal. Ruy paid a bribe, and they went on their way, sailing along the Honduran littoral. However, they spent the day after that moored in a deep cove, and Ruy informed them that they would be traveling at night for a while; he claimed he was "illegal" in this part of Honduras and didn't want to risk being spotted by the militia. He continued to pursue Debora, and although his pursuit was somewhat more circumspect,

Mingolla believed it had become more intense, more driven. From watching him, from further information that Debora had passed to Tully, he realized that as a byproduct of his confrontation of Ruy, Ruy's feelings had acquired validity, and he thought this involved a conscious decision on Ruy's part, that he had elevated simple lust to an obsessive level, as if the idea of the unattainable had inspired a passion.

To avoid Ruy, he and Debora kept to their cabin, and as a result they engaged more and more in their fierce mental communion. There was tangible proof that their powers were still increasing, but even had there been no proof Mingolla would have known it. Standing in the bow one night, at the extreme end of a road of rippling gold light that stretched across the black water to the newly risen moon, he felt as he had on the riverbank their last evening in Fire Zone Emerald, that he could look past the horizon and grasp the essence of the days to come; this time the feeling was freighted with clarity, and he believed that were he to exert the slightest effort, he might launch himself into another vision. But he was afraid of visions, of visionary knowledge. He wanted to inhabit this long ocean-going moment and never arrive anywhere, and so he restrained himself from testing his strength.

A further consequence of their retreat was that they gained new insights into each other. Though the things Mingolla had already learned about Debora implied the existence of a complex personality, he saw now that her growth had been interrupted by the war, her complexity channeled into the simple pragmatism of the revolutionary; her incarnation of the revolutionary spirit was childlike, capable of aligning everything she perceived into rudimentary categories, black and white, pro and con, and whether she continued to grow would depend on how much longer her natural processes were constrained. He sensed a similar inhibition in himself, but pictured his process as being less constrained than trained into specific patterns of growth, the way Japanese gardeners bind the limbs of trees to make them spread crookedly and sideways.

The smell of gasoline was always thick in the cabin, and they could feel the vibration of waves against the hull. There

279

were two bunks, no lights, and the close quarters and darkness acted to enforce intimacy. One night as they lay together, Debora's buttocks cupped spoon-style by Mingolla's hips, he started to turn her onto her stomach, to enter her from behind, and inside his head he heard a shrill, *No!* Heard it clearly, enunciated in Debora's voice. The message was so sharp and peremptory, it stimulated him to answer in kind, *What is it? What's wrong?*

"I heard you," she said, shifting to face him.

"I heard you, too. Let's try it again."

After several minutes they gave it up.

"Maybe it didn't happen," she said.

"It happened, and it'll happen again. We just can't push it."

The grinding of the engine, the mash of waves shouldering the hull. Debora settled against him, and he put an arm around her. "What *was* wrong?" he asked. "What'd I do?"

"It's not important."

"If you don't wanna tell me . . ."

"No, it's not that. It's just that things are so good for us, I don't want to spoil it by bringing up the past."

The pitch of the engines dropped to an articulated grumble, and Ruy shouted.

"Maybe I should tell you," she said. "Maybe it'll explain why I was so reticent with you at first."

"Back in Emerald?"

"Yes . . . you see there were a lot of reasons I didn't want to get involved with you like this, and one was I was afraid it wouldn't be any good between us."

"You mean sex?"

She nodded. "It hadn't ever been good for me, and I thought nothing could change that, not even being in love. But it is good, and I keep getting scared it won't last."

"Why?"

"Because it's so perfect . . . the way you fit me, how you touch me. And everything before was so imperfect." She turned away as if embarrassed. "When they brought us in for interrogation . . . the government . . ."

"Your family?"

"Yes." She let out a sigh. "When they brought us in, I knew they'd rape me. That's what they always do. I prepared for it, and every day that passed, every day it didn't happen, I grew more afraid. I thought they must be saving me for something special, some special horror. Finally this man came to see me. Major Armangual. He was very young to be a major, and not too bad-looking. He spoke politely, softly. He made me feel hope. He explained that he'd interceded on my behalf with the government, and that he'd take me out of prison that same day if I'd cooperate with him. I was sure that cooperation included sex, but I didn't care. The prison was awful. Other women screaming all the time, bodies being carried past my cell. And I thought if I was out, I might be able to help my family. So I told him, Yes, I'd do anything. He smiled at that and said I wouldn't have to do much at all, that his requirements were limited and specific. Just some office work."

Debora gave a tired-sounding laugh, plumped up the pillow beneath her head. "It was the weekend, and he was off duty, so we went back to his house. A fancy house in Zone One, near the big hotels. There was a pool, maids. He installed me in a room on the second floor, and I expected him to come to me that night. But no such thing. I ate dinner with him, and afterward he said he had papers to go over and suggested I get some sleep. The whole weekend was like that. It was as if I were a houseguest. I considered trying to escape, but the grounds were patrolled by dogs, and I still hoped I could do something for my family . . . even though I didn't have much hope left." Her voice faltered, steadied. "Monday morning I rode to work with him. He was in the air force, and he had an office at the airport. Do you know Guatemala City?"

"Not well."

"There's a small military airport across from the civilian one, and that's where the office was. All morning I sat in the reception room with his aide, staring at the walls. Around noon the aide brought me a sandwich and a soda. I ate, waited some more. I was beginning to think the major just wanted me to sit there and look nice. Then about two o'clock he came to his door and said, 'Debora, I need you now.' Just the way he'd ask a secretary in to take dictation, just that offhanded tone. I went into the office, and he told me to take off my underwear. Still very polite. Smiling. I was afraid, but like I said, I'd prepared for this, and so I did what he asked. He told me to get down on my hands and knees beside the desk. I did that, too. I shed a few tears, I remember, but I managed to stop them. He pulled out a tube from his drawer, some kind of jelly, and . . . and he lubricated me. That was almost the worst part. And then he dropped his trousers and came inside me from behind, the way you . . .''

"I'm sorry," said Mingolla. "I didn't . . .''

"No, no!" Debora's hands fluttered in the dark, found his face, cupped it. "Sometimes I want you to do that, but . . .'' She sighed again. "Let me tell the whole story.''

"All right.''

"I thought he'd make love to me roughly. I'm not sure why. Maybe I figured that his good treatment had been to lull me, to undermine my preparation. But he didn't. For a long time he didn't even move. Just kneeled behind me, inside me, his hands on my hips. There was a bottle of whiskey on his desk, and after a couple of minutes he had a drink from it. Then he moved a little, but only a few times. He had another drink, moved some more. It went on like that for about a half-hour. Then somebody knocked on the door. The major yelled for them to come in. It was another officer. He looked at me, but didn't seem surprised by what was going on. After that first look, he didn't pay any attention to me, just discussed business with the major, something about scheduling, and then he left. It kept on like this for the rest of the afternoon. The major having a few drinks, moving now and again, conducting business. At the end of the day he pulled out of me and masturbated. He didn't insist I watch, he didn't seem to care what I was doing. He finished, wiped it up with a rag. Then he drove me back to his house, and that night over dinner he treated me as if I were his houseguest again.''

Mingolla rested his head on her shoulder, bitter, wishing he could take the memory from her.

"It was the same every workday," she said. "In the beginning I felt relieved that he wasn't hurting me, but before long

. . . I don't know how to explain what I was feeling. Humiliation was there, the fact that I was being used like a piece of furniture. Guilt that it wasn't worse. The feeling of being a nonperson. Sometimes I'd hate myself for not hating it worse than I did, and sometimes I'd almost enjoy it. I'd have a sense of being freed by it, that once he was inside me I'd go floating off into some other universe, invisible, made different, unique. Then I'd worry that he'd get tired of me and put me back in prison. I remember once when I was worrying about that, I started to make love to him, to take an active part . . . you know, to give him a better time. But he didn't want that. He reprimanded me, told me to hold still or he'd punish me. My feelings for him changed, too. Back and forth. One day I'd be repelled by him, I'd dream about killing him. And the next day I'd be thankful that he was sparing me from worse. I'd actually look forward to the office, to the chance to prove myself to him. I'd make bright conversation at dinner, bring him presents. For a while I was actually in love with him, at least I felt something like love. And I think that's why he finally released me, I think my attachment to him didn't suit his needs. I was terribly distracted, close to a breakdown, and I'd begun to tell him how I felt. Trying to widen our range of communication. I guess I thought he'd be interested. Like a scientist, you know. I thought he might want to take notes on the disintegration of my personality. But he wasn't interested. God knows what did interest him."

She was silent a long time, and Mingolla asked what had happened.

"One morning I was waiting for him, and two soldiers came instead. They drove me out of town, north toward Antigua. I knew they were going to kill me, throw my body in a barranca. But they just dropped me off by the side of the road. I felt lost, I didn't know what to do. I walked back and forth, laughing and crying. I didn't realize they'd left me off at a bus stop until the bus pulled up. I got on the bus . . . it seemed the only choice. I never saw the major again. Two years later, after I'd gone through the therapy, I tried to find him. But I learned he was dead. Assassinated."

"Did you want to kill him?"

"There was more to it than that. I think I wanted to understand what he'd been trying to do with me . . . if it wasn't just a matter of his own perversity. I'm not sure what I would have done to him. Probably killed him . . . I don't know."

The engines had slowed, and Mingolla could hear the bubbling of the *Ensorcelita*'s wash; he was grateful for the sound, because its sudden incidence alleviated the need for speech. Minutes went by with no communication between them other than touches. Debora's breathing grew deep and regular. Then she said, "Make love to me."

"I thought you were asleep."

"I was . . . but I was dreaming we were making love."

"Aren't you too sleepy?"

"Maybe, but we can try."

He pulled her close, kissed her. Her response was tentative at first, and he wondered if she was testing herself against the bad memory. Soon, though, she lost herself in the foreplay. But when he entered her, she lay motionless beneath him and he started to withdraw.

"I want you to finish," she said.

"You're too sleepy."

"No, it's good. Sometimes when I don't move I can feel you more. I like that."

He felt irrationally aloft, distant from her, and this gave him an inarticulate concern; but then concern vanished as he heard her voice call to him in the quiet of his mind.

Once she had fallen asleep he lay back, listening to the engines. Something was bothering him, and he realized that he still felt distant from her. He knew if he were to turn and embrace her, the distance would vanish, and he would feel drifty, at peace. But knowing that changed nothing. He had the idea that his insights into her were somehow in error. As were her insights into him. It seemed to him that they had become shifty characters to each other, that their mode of honesty— these sudden bouts of revelation and confession—were smokescreens. Not that they were lies, but rather that by being framed so dramatically they became less than truths, a means of obscuring some truth that perhaps they themselves didn't understand. That must be it, he decided. That they didn't understand themselves well enough to practice honesty . . . or else they were frightened of self-discovery. Self-discovery was an unpleasant chore. He could look back a mere matter of weeks and see what an idiot he had been. Like in Emerald. His role of hard-ass creep, his lovesickness. Roles poorly conceived and poorly acted. And God only knew what sort of idiot he was being now. He turned onto his side, facing away from her. Their problems likely had something to do with how they had begun; though for the most part he had been able to put that behind him, it was always there beneath the surface, always a cause for doubt. He sighed, and the sigh coincided with an enormous swell lifting the *Ensorcelita*, and for an instant he felt that the coincidence of tide and breath would carry them in a gravitiless arc beyond Panama to a dark country where silent cowled figures with burning eyes awaited their arrival. He turned onto his back again, causing Debora to stir and mumble. He tried to resurrect his train of thought, but it no longer seemed important. None of it mattered, none of it had real weight. He lay awake a long time, unable to think of anything that did.

The engines broke down the next night while Ruy was attempting to impress Debora with the fervor of his revolutionary convictions, with his inside information concerning secret matters. The moon, almost full, hung low above the coast, and they were close enough to shore that Mingolla could make out the separate crowns of palms silvered by its light. Ruy was leaning against the wheelhouse door, and inside, visible through his opaque reflection, Corazon stood at the wheel. She turned toward Mingolla, her left eye glinting redly. He tried to read her face, and she held his gaze without a hint of challenge, as if willing to let him learn all he could.

"Yeah," Ruy was saying. "Don't matter to me if the revolution's dead. I start it all over myself if I have to, unnerstan'? And anyway"—he shook a finger at Debora—"why you keep tellin' me that shit 'bout it's dead? You think that, why you goin' to Panama? You runnin'? Naw, that's not it! You and this Yankee come on board, act like you gonna kill this black man, and then the next minute you actin' like old friends. It don't make sense. You got some kinda plan. A fool can see that. And lately there's been too many strange motherfuckers headin' for Panama. Gotta be somethin' big happenin' down there."

"How you figure?" Mingolla asked.

"I told ya, lotsa strange fuckers travelin' these days." Ruy fingered a cigarette from his shirt pocket. "Wonder what' goin' on."

"You don't know what you're talking about," said Debora. "People have been running to Panama since the war began."

"Not this kinda people." Ruy cupped a match, lit up. He threw back his head and blew smoke, affording Debora a view of his sharp profile.

With every gesture, he was—Mingolla thought—projecting the image of the Romantic Smuggler, layering it with his Zorro-like commitment. The pose was laughable, but Mingolla was coming to believe that Ruy knew this, that he was using the image to disguise a real commitment. He had been operating too long in dangerous waters to be the buffoon he pretended, and besides, Mingolla had a bad feeling about him, about his whole act.

"Yeah," Ruy said, tapping the side of his nose. "I been smellin' somethin' funny for a while now. Been hearin' things, too."

"You fulla shit, mon." Tully, perched on the rail, turned his head; the moonlight washed over half his face. "Ain't nobody be tellin' a chump like you nothin'."

Ruy ignored him. "This one man I carry south, he don't think mucha me. And that's good, 'cause when a man don't think mucha you, he ain't cautious." He blew smoke toward Tully. "So he say to me, 'Ruy, there's more to this war than meets the eye.' And I say, 'Yeah? What you mean?' I'm pretendin' I ain't really interested, y'know. 'Well,' he says, 'I probably shouldn't be talkin' on this, but the peace is comin' soon, and Panama is where it's comin' from.' And I say, 'Wow! Peace, man! That's fuckin' terrific!' And the man's all puffed up 'cause of how he's astoundin' me, y'know. 'Oh, yeah,' he say. 'People I know, they workin' on the peace right this second. Negotiatin', y'understan'.'"

Ruy folded his arms, cocked his head, and from that pose,

286

the pose of a bemused lecturer pausing to consider the effect of his words, Mingolla recognized the man of whom Ruy reminded him. It should, he thought, have been obvious to him from the beginning. All Ruy's little clues had been designed to give himself away.

"Anyhow," Ruy went on, "I start pressin' this man . . . not so he'd notice, y'unnerstan'. Just workin' on him. And he tells me that, yeah, dey workin' on a peace in Panama, but dere's fightin' still. Armies in the streets. I ask him who's fightin', and he act like it's a big secret, like he's really doin' me a favor by tellin' me, y'know, and he say he ain't clear on the whole story, but he give me a name and say this name got a lot to do with it." He put on a sly smile, swept all of them with a glance. " 'Sotomayor,' he say to me. 'You 'member that name. Sotomayor. That name, it's the key to everything.' "

Mingolla met his eyes, and though Ruy was not smiling, Mingolla could sense his secret amusement. He was about to call Ruy, to demand an accounting; but at that moment the engines stopped.

"Fuck!" Ruy threw down his cigarette, flung open the door to the wheelhouse. "What'd you do?"

"Nothin'," said Corazon. "I don't do nothin'. It just stop."

Ruy stomped forward, heaved off the hatch of the engine compartment; he put his hands on his hips and stared down into the darkness. "Corazon!" he bawled. "Bring the flashlight!"

Corazon went forward with a flashlight, and Ruy grabbed it, lowered himself into the compartment. The rest of them gathered around Corazon. Below, Ruy swept the beam across a maze of grease-smeared metal. He held the beam steady a second, then banged the side of the compartment. "Son of a bitch! Motherfucker!"

"Can't you fix it?" Debora asked.

Ruy banged the wall again, hauled himself back onto the deck. "Take parts to fix this cunt! And I ain't got no parts." He looked as if he were about to throw the flashlight, but only smacked it against his hip. "Man, this some real fuckin' shit!"

"Look like we gonna have to put into port," said Tully.

Ruy's face was wild, the muscles knotting at the corner of

287

his mouth. "I told ya, I'm illegal 'round here. They blow my fuckin' head off if they catch me."

"Run up the sail," Mingolla suggested.

"Sure, man! That way we be right off Truxillo come day-break, and that son of a bitch Dominguez, he be smilin' ear to ear when he see the *Ensorcelita*. Shit!" Ruy clutched his fore-head. "What the fuck am I gonna do?"

"You can't fix it for sure?" Mingolla asked.

"Ain't you listenin', man?" Ruy spun around to face him, his fists balled.

"Den we got no choice but to 'bandon dis washtub," said Tully. "I go look fah somethin' to wrap de guns."

Ruy shoved him. "We ain't abandonin' shit, man!"

Tully knocked him against the side of the wheelhouse and engulfed his throat in a one-handed chokehold. "Don't be 'busin' me, mon. Got dat?" He gave Ruy a squeeze, and Ruy's eyes bugged. "Now you wanna stay wit' de ship, dat's fine. We don't need you."

Mingolla looked at the shore, at the shadowed hills rising inland. "What's out there?"

"Too many fuckin' soldiers," said Ruy, massaging his throat. "That's what."

"Olancho," said Tully. "Mountains, jungle. Dat's where de war begin, but dere's no fightin' now. Hard to say what's out dere."

"Maybe there's a way," said Ruy. "If we can get past the checkpoints, then maybe I can get you to Panama. And maybe I can get financin' for another boat."

"We do fine by ourselves, mon," Tully said.

"Fuck you will!" But Ruy moved away from him. "You be lost 'fore you go ten miles. But there's ways I know. Military roads, old contra trails. 'Fore I got the *Ensorcelita* I used to travel that route."

Mingolla stared out at the coast, then at Ruy. It might be best, he thought, to hold back on calling Ruy, see what he had in mind. "Are those ways still open?"

"Oh, yeah," said Ruy. "But we need a truck or somethin'. Maybe one of them off-road vehicles. Won't be hard to find somethin'. Lotsa these farmers 'round here, they fix up their trucks with extra gas tanks so they can go huntin' in the hills."

"How long will it take?" Debora asked.

"Depends what we get into," Ruy said, sidling up to her, solicitous. "But I tell ya one thing. Time we come to Panama, we gonna have a few stories to tell."

Two miles from where they came ashore, tucked in among the ranks of coconut palms, stood a copra plantation: tall wooden racks for drying coconut fiber; three tin-roofed sheds in which the product was stored; and a long ranch-style building of whitewashed stone with a red tile roof. This last served as living quarters and office for the owner, Don Julio Saldivar. Parked around the corner of the building was a venerable Ford Bronco with an auxiliary gas tank welded into the luggage compartment. Don Julio met them at the door with an automatic pistol in hand, but Mingolla persuaded him to amiability and generosity, telling him that they were government agents on secret assignment. The plantation owner offered him use of the Bronco, camping equipment, and offered Debora, whose clothes had been lost during the swim to shore—no lifeboat on the *Ensorcelita*—the old clothes belonging to his daughter who was off at the university in San Pedro Sula. Mingolla had Ruy and Tully check out the Bronco, and sat with Don Julio in the kitchen, a cramped room with an old-fashioned gas stove and a motel icebox and photographs of Don Julio standing over a variety of slaughtered game animals decorating the pebbled white walls. Don Julio set about drawing a map of the coastal hills, tracing the roads that would lead them away from the checkpoints.

"What's here?" Mingolla asked, indicating a section on the map where the roads vanished. "You haven't marked anything down."

"There's nothing to mark," said Don Julio. "Just ghosts and jungle."

He was short and paunchy, in his late fifties, mahogany-skinned, and dressed in baggy shorts and a guayabera unbuttoned to display his smooth chest; his head was massive, jowly, and his thick black hair was frosted at the temples. The stern prideful lines of his face put Mingolla in mind of his own father, and from the prideful blustery way Don Julio spoke of his daughter's devotedness Mingolla got the idea he was lying, that his daughter really hated him. Don Julio's conversation veered into politics. He patted his gun, vowed eternal vigilance against the Red Menace: there was something more than a little pathetic about the combination of his machismo, his self-portraits with dead jaguars and tapirs, and the emptiness of his house. He spoke of his youth. He'd owned a ranch in the Petén. It had been a chore, he said, to keep the guerrillas off the land, but he'd managed. And, oh, what a man he'd been for the ladies! His Cadillac, his nights at the Guatemala City discos. Was there a town in all the world as fine as Guatemala City? Mingolla withheld comment. He himself had spent three days in the city. One night he had been standing in a pachinko parlor on Sixth Avenue, a major downtown artery, playing the machines; he had been lost in playing, and when he had turned around to get more change, he had discovered that not only was the parlor empty, but that Sixth Avenue, which moments before had been thronged with crowds and traffic, was completely deserted. He'd run all the way back to his hotel, and none of the Guatemalans there had wanted to talk about what was going on. Guatemala City, to Mingolla's mind, was brimstone country. Death squads patroling in their unmarked Toyotas, sirens and distant gunfire, and up in Zone 5, where people lived in houses built of tires and mud, young boys dreamed of making rich men bleed.

"I warned my friends about the Reds," said Don Julio, returning to his favorite topic. "Once I took some of them down to the beach in Tela . . . you know Tela?"

"No," said Mingolla.

"Nice little town up the coast," said Don Julio. "Government people vacation there in the summers. But that didn't stop the Commies from making their mark. Defacing the walls with slogans. Anyway, I took my friends down to the beach. These friends, they were liberals"—he made an obscenity of the word—"they believed in freedom of speech! Pah! And I pointed out the slogans on the walls of the bars. Look, I told them. Now that communism has spread to the grassroots, all its fine philosophy has been reduced to these misspelled words. Stupid passions

290

like the ones aroused by a soccer match are invading the political process. Up with Liberty! Down with Injustice! As if poverty and disease were something you could stamp out by a score of two to nothing. Aren't the lessons of history plain, I asked them. Just consider Nicaragua. They invited in the Cubans, and now the whole country's nothing but an armed camp of goose-stepping snitches and assassins. And what's the revolution done for the poor? The only difference is that nowadays when they crap on the streets, they do it single-file and sing songs about brotherhood." Don Julio sighed. "But they wouldn't listen, and you see what happened. Six years of hell." He patted Mingolla's arm. "Thank God for men like you and me. Communists know better than to come around us, they know what they'll get."

Debora entered the room in time to hear these last words, and she shot Don Julio a venomous look. She had on a gray skirt and a print blouse, and unmindful of her hostility, Don Julio said, "You look breathtaking, señorita! Lovely!"

She let the comment pass. "The car's ready."

"You're leaving so soon?" Don Julio stood. "What a pity! I get so little company since my wife died. Ah, well." He pumped Mingolla's hand. "I'm proud to have made your acquaintance, and I'll pray for the success of your mission."

He stood in the door waving as they went around the corner. Dawn was breaking, and in its gray light the beach was revealed to be foul with animal wastes and coconut debris, the tidal margin heaped with piles of foam and clumps of seaweed that at a distance had the appearance of dead bodies cast up by the surf. The *Ensorcelita* was a dark stain bobbing beyond the breakwater.

Mingolla opened the driver's door, then realized he had forgotten the map. "Forgot something," he said. "Be right back."

Ruy, sitting in the back beside Corazon and Tully, looked as if he were about to say something; then turned away.

The front door was open, and as Mingolla entered he heard Don Julio talking in the kitchen, saying in a dull monotone, "I have a message for him."

291

Mingolla moved cautiously into the kitchen. The plantation owner was speaking into a wall phone, his back to the door.

"Yes," he said. "They have just left."

"Put the phone down," said Mingolla.

Don Julio whirled around, his left hand going to his holster, and Mingolla struck at him, expecting an easy victory. But as he penetrated Don Julio's mind, he was stunned by the emergence of a powerful pattern. A frail tide of emotion washed over him, a seepage of anger, and it seemed that the pattern— which he perceived as a serpentine form of crackling silver— was breeding its double inside his skull, influencing his thoughts to glide in a slow hypnotic rhythm. It was so easy just to go with the pattern, to loop and loop, to let his head nod and wobble, to listen to the droning that came to his ears from within his head, a shrill oscillating sound like the whine of a nervous system on the fritz. And maybe that's what it was, maybe it was, maybe that's . . . He saw Don Julio's hand slipping toward his holster, and tried to shake himself alert. But the seductive rhythms of the pattern were all through him, lulling him, convincing him of his security. Don Julio, moving very slowly as if submerged in thick syrup, unsnapped the holster. Mingolla took a feeble step toward him, stumbled, and whacked the side of his head hard against the wall; the pain blinded him for a moment, but acted to disperse the pattern, and before it could be reestablished, he generated a charge of fear. Don Julio staggered backward, and Mingolla kept up the assault, sending waves of fear, of loathing at being touched so intimately by a strange mind. The plantation owner whimpered and fell in a heap, his eyes rolling back.

Mingolla picked up the phone and listened.

"Hello," said a man's voice through long-distance static. "Hello."

"Who is this?" Mingolla asked.

"Why, David! Congratulations! You must have passed your test."

"Izaguirre?"

"At your service."

"You set this up?"

292

"I'm not sure what you're referring to. I assume Don Julio attempted to subdue you with his mental gift . . . am I right?"

"No," said Mingolla. "I came in and he was on the phone, so I hit him."

"I think you're fibbing, David. How is Don Julio? Salvageable?"

Mingolla looked down at the plantation owner: he was in bad shape, pasty, sweating, and breathing shallowly. A little toy rightist with a silver snake in his head.

"No matter," said Izaguirre. "I'll send someone to check."

"You're not too fucking clever," Mingolla said. "Don't you think I know Ruy led us here? I see what's going on."

"There's no need to be clever. Whether or not you're aware of your situation has no bearing on the dangers you may face."

"And I'm sure you've set plenty of traps."

"The world is a trap. You just happened to stumble into one of mine. Perhaps you'll avoid the rest." Izaguirre chuckled. "I have better things to do than worry about you. You're very strong, David, but you're really not very important. There are only a few of your kind and many of us. We can control you."

He hung up, and Mingolla knelt beside Don Julio, who arched his eyebrows, strained to speak. Groaned. Mingolla set about trying to wake him, but as he made contact, Don Julio's mind winked out . . . like the hummingbird on the beach at Roatán. He felt for a pulse. Don Julio's skin was remarkably cool, as if he'd been dead a long time.

"What's goin' on?" said Ruy behind him; he was flanked by Tully and Debora.

"Heart attack or something," said Mingolla.

He added an imaginary gray goatee and wrinkles to Ruy's face. No doubt about it. The resemblance to Dr. Izaguirre was unmistakable.

"Is he dead?" Debora asked.

"Yeah." Mingolla picked up Don Julio's gun and stood. "Guess they don't make right-wingers like they used to," he said, searching Ruy's face for a reaction.

Ruy nudged the dead man's arm with his foot. "Cono!" he said, and spat. He smiled at Mingolla. "What you do, man? Scare him to death?"

293

CHAPTER THIRTEEN

In the gray light, the hills of Olanchito showed a ghostly leached green. Dirt trails wound through them, petering out into thickets and ledges, as if what they had once led to had been magicked away. Those nearest the sea were mounded sugarloaf hills, their crests bristling with stubby palms that from the coast road looked like growths of electrified hair; those farther inland were sharper, faced with granite, their peaks shrouded in rainclouds. For two days they followed the roads, and then they drove beyond the end of the roads into a wilderness whose jungles had overgrown the worst ravages of the war, but still displayed its passage in ways both subtle and distinct. For the most part—although occasionally they came across a ruin or a crater filled with ferns—everything looked normal. Trees were green, birds and insects clamored, streams plunged into waterfalls. Yet there was an air of evil enchantment to the place. It seemed the jut and tumble of the hills had been built up over a series of immense skeletons whose decaying bones pervaded every growth with wrongness. That wrongness was in the air, pressuring them, adding a leaden tone to the sunniest of days, heavying their limbs and making breathing a toil.

The Honduran hills gave way without visible demarcation

to the hills of Nicaragua, and traveling through them took a further toll on their spirits; even Ruy grew silent and morose. It was slow going. They inched down steep defiles, got stuck in streambeds, spent hours getting unstuck, were blinded by squalls that transformed the windows into smeared opacities. Each time they chanced across a bombed village, it seemed a relief to have this hard evidence of war in that it dispelled the supernatural aura. Some of the villages were inhabited, and in these they would buy red gas that was stored in oil drums and was full of impurities. The people of the villages were timorous, living like monkeys in the ruins, peeking from behind shattered walls until their visitors had left, and nowhere did they receive a sincere welcome.

There was little privacy to be had, what with Ruy's obsessiveness toward Debora and Tully's ongoing need to discuss his troubles with Corazon; but sometimes at night Mingolla and Debora were able to slip away, to walk out from the campsite, to talk and make love. Mingolla continued to be confused by their relationship. The fact that love constituted for them an actual power obscured the more commonplace fact that love required a sequence of resolutions in order to prosper; and given the tenuousness of the circumstance, none of the usual resolutions merited real consideration. But he couldn't help thinking about them, and when he did, when he looked at her and tried to imagine a future, it seemed inconceivable that they should have one. They were, he realized, scarcely more than children with guns, faced with a problem whose fantastic nature beggared logic; despite the proofs, he experienced moments when he was sure that everything they had learned was somehow in error. Trying to hold all this in focus, he would feel at sea, and forgetting the war, the unreliability of their companions, he would cling to Debora, as she did to him.

Nine days after leaving the coconut plantation, they came across a road. Not a track or an old contra trail, but an honest-to-God road of yellow dirt, wide and wonderful to drive, beginning in the middle of nowhere and winding off through the hills. Mingolla assumed it was a military road intended to connect bases that had never been constructed, because though it was plain from the wildness of the bordering jungle that it had been long since abandoned, no weeds or any other growth marred its smooth surface, and this testified to the use of chemicals available to army engineers for just that purpose. They came to the road at sunset, and while they might have traveled on into the night with such a road, Mingolla decided it would be good psychology to make camp; that way, if the road ended after a few miles, they would at least have a bit of momentum with which to ease the rest of the next day's travel. He pulled the Bronco up onto a hillside several hundred feet above the road, and they pitched their tents by a stream that had carved a ferny trench in the rock.

That night Mingolla and Debora walked down the hill and sat in the fringe of the jungle; from this vantage they could look down the road to where it curved up into a notch between the two adjoining hills. An egg-shaped moon lay on its side in the notch, and in its light the yellow dirt appeared richly mineral and moist, not like gold, but like manure of some sort, or the track of a giant snail that had gone south ahead of them. No insects, only the hissing vowels of the wind. The presence of the road made the emptiness bearable, and the quiet was so pervasive and deep, Mingolla imagined he could hear the great humming vibration of the earth. It felt wrong to talk amid this stillness, and they sat with their arms around each other, admiring the road as if it were something miraculous. Debora tucked her head onto his chest, and smelling her hair, feeling the steady hits of her heart, almost audible in the silence, it seemed that everything he had in life had acquired a comprehensible value. He believed he understood love. Not so as to be able to write a definition. But he thought that from this moment on he would be able to call it to mind as a conglomerate of imagery and sensory detail. Whatever love was, it was here, right now, conjured in identifiable form by the silence and the road and Debora's heartbeat, by a thousand other variables.

She sat up, shaking back her hair. "I heard something."

"Probably the wind."

She came to her knees, smoothing her skirt, brushing off dew. She pointed toward the opposite slope, where mist was accumulating in thick bands. "We won't be able to see soon."

"Nothing to see, anyway."

"I've been thinking," she said after a moment. "About how I've changed. We haven't been together that long, but if you measure the time in changes, it seems like years."

"How've you changed?"

"I'm not as sure of things as I used to be. When I first thought about going to Panama, I just wanted to find out what was happening. And after we started learning what was happening, then I wanted to be part of it . . . even if it wasn't my revolution, it was the revolution there was, and I knew there had to be one. I still believe that. But now sometimes I wonder if it's worth the effort. I keep imagining us running away. Hiding, letting everybody else figure out the problems of the world."

He laughed. "It's the opposite with me."

"Really?"

"Yeah . . . I used to want to get away from everything. But the closer we come to Panama, the more I realize I can't escape being involved. And the more angry I get at Izaguirre." He laughed again. "Maybe this is what they call growing together."

"Maybe," she said despondently. "At least you're changing in the right direction."

"What do I know? I've taken the same dope as the fuck-ups who're supposed to be making the movie."

"You still believe they're fuck-ups?"

"There's no doubt about it. The way they're handling us, all the games. If peace is their plan, they'll probably fuck that up. Think about it. Here's these two families who've been doing the drug for centuries. All that power, and they're just now trying to pull it together. Doesn't augur well for the peace process."

"I guess not."

He studied her face, its exoticism as pronounced as the rose in Corazon's eye. Just the sort of little treasure that would appeal to Ruy, to the man with everything . . . especially if it was beyond his reach, if his power couldn't touch them. And Mingolla was certain they had grown that strong. They would have to be careful not to reveal too much to Ruy, because

Izaguirre would be in contact with him, and he might panic if
he thought they were too strong. Try to eliminate them. It might
be time to confront Ruy. Mingolla had been hoping Ruy would
give something away, some bit of information, but maybe the
best tactic would be to bully him.

"You act like you're miles away, David."

"I'm back . . . just thinking."

"Well . . ." She settled against him. "If they are fuck-ups,
maybe we can do something."

"Given that they're into playing God, the worst we can do
is to inject some realism into the situation." He stared down the
road, trying to identify a black object that had appeared in the
notch. "Something's coming." He helped her up, and they
retreated farther into the fringe.

"It's stopped," she said.

"Naw, look. It's coming again."

After a couple of minutes they realized that the object was
in fact two objects, one light, one dark, and that they were
advancing at a leisurely clip, moving forward fifty or sixty feet,
stopping, then moving forward again; and after a couple of
more minutes they saw that the objects were a horse and a
wagon. The wagon was a little house on wheels with a peaked
roof, the walls painted dark blue and illuminated with five-
pointed gold stars and a crescent moon; the horse was white,
dappled with gray. No one was driving. The reins were lashed
to a peg on the driver's seat, and the window and door were
black with shadow. There was something horrible about the
wagon's approach, the way it lurched emptily like a body
without bones, and this, allied with its archaic appearance, lent
it an omenical potency.

The wagon drew abreast of them and stopped. The horse
shifted in its traces, eyes rolling, ablaze with moonlight; it was
an old horse, its breath wheezy. When Mingolla stepped out
onto the road, the horse tossed its head but stayed put: it was as
if it wanted to run, but was obeying a set pattern of stopping
and starting, and Mingolla had caught it just right. He grabbed
the bridle, held its head. The horse's eye swiveled, regarding
him with fear, and Mingolla—taken by its sculptural beauty, its

298

madness—knew the horse had been trifled with by someone like him, some drugged genius of the new order, and had been coerced to move haltingly along this desolate road for no reason other than that of the most pitiful folly. He was more affected than he had been by the terrible human results of similar folly. Human beings were liable to such, but horses, as beautiful and stupid as they were, should not have to put up with that kind of crap.

Debora came up beside him, and he handed her the bridle. "See if you can gentle him," he said. Then he hauled himself onto the driver's seat and ducked inside the wagon.

Before he determined the wagon's contents, he knew by intuition that it held nothing good, that it held nothing much at all, and that whatever he found would be testimony to a knowledge not worth having. An instant later he felt dread. But that was just fancy. He realized that his first intuition had embodied the true essence of terror, the comprehension that everything we dread is simply a reminder of insignificance, one we assign a supernatural valence in order to boost our morale. An angle of moonlight cut across a pallet on the floor. There was a faint cloying smell as of something once alive and unhealthy. Mingolla hesitated, not sure he wanted to poke around more. He spotted a gleam in a rear corner and reached for it. His fingers touched a slick paper surface, and he picked up a sheaf of glossy photographs, each showing a black woman intimately involved with a fat white man. His toe struck something that rattled against the wall. He groped and came up with a handful of bones. Human bones, neither fractured nor exhibiting any other sign of injury. Finger bones and sections of spinal joint. They took the light and made it seem a decaying tissue stretched between floor and window. And that was all. Except for dust and the idea of dissolution. Whether the wagon and its contents were a contrivance, a message sent from one playful maniac to another, whether one recognized it as such, Mingolla was certain that its effect upon anyone would be to make him aware of his triviality, his unlovely organic essence. He climbed back onto the driver's seat, feeling mild giddiness and nausea. The light was so vivid in contrast to the wagon's darkness, he thought he might breathe it in and exhale shadow.

"What'd you find?" Debora asked.

"It's empty." He jumped down.

"He's better now," said Debora, stroking the horse's nose.

"I'm gonna unhitch him," Mingolla said. "Let him graze."

They led the horse uphill through the accumulating mist to a clearing bounded by twisted spreading trees with black bark as wrinkled as the faces of old, old men, and they watched him graze, moving a step, munching, moving another step. Here he looked at home, serene and natural. His dappled coat blended with the mist, making it appear that he was either materializing from or disintegrating into the ghostly white ribbons clinging to his shoulders and haunches, his head sometimes vanishing when he bent to pull at a clump of grass. Moonlight slanted through the mist, haloing every object, creating zones of weird depth, coils of smoky glow, as if some magical force were dominating the clearing and illuminating its shapes of power. It was partly this perception of the magical that roused Mingolla's desire, the hope that he could evoke a magic of his own and forget the foulness of the wagon. He pressed Debora against one of the trees, opened her blouse, and helped her skin down her panties. "It's too damp," she said, pointing to the dewy grass. He lifted her a little to demonstrate an alternative. Her breasts were cool, gleaming with condensation, and felt buoyant in his hands; her eyes were aswim with lights. He drew up her skirt, lifted her again, and as he entered her, she threw her arms back around the trunk, her legs scissoring his waist. The stillness of the night was banished. The horse whuffling, munching, and the muffled noises from the jungle were gathered close, sharpened and orchestrated by the wet sounds of their lovemaking, their ragged breathing. It was a white act, seeming to kindle the moonlight to new brilliance. Mist curled from Debora's mouth, tendriled her hair, and seeing her transformation, Mingolla felt that he, too, was being transformed, changing into a beast with golden eyes and talons, gaining in strength with every thrust, every cry she made. Afterward he supported her against the tree for a long time, too weak to talk or move, and when at last he withdrew, when he turned to the clearing, he expected to find that the horse had disappeared, that it had been dissolved by their good magic. But there it was, shoulder-deep in a white sea, staring at them without curiosity, merely watchful, knowing exactly what it had witnessed, its eyes steady and dark and empty of questions.

———————

Several nights later Ruy invited Mingolla and Debora for coffee in his tent, while Tully and Corazon were gathering kindling. Ruy had apparently given up all rights to Corazon, preferring to concentrate on Debora, and though he had stopped making overt attempts at seduction, his eyes were always on her, and much of his conversation was suggestive. Mist curled through the tent flap, glowing in the radiance of a battery lamp, and Ruy lay on his sleeping bag, a coffee cup balanced on his stomach, talking about Panama, telling them more of what his long-ago passenger had purportedly told him. As he spoke, his language and his inflections grew more and more refined, and at last realizing that he was revealing himself to them, that there was no further use in circumspection, Mingolla asked, "What are you, man? Madradona or Sotomayor?"

Ruy set down his cup and sat up; shadows filled in the lines of his face. "Sotomayor," he said. "Of course most of us have grown accustomed to using other names."

"Why . . ." Debora began.

"Why haven't I told you before? Why am I telling you now? Because I . . ."

"Because it's a game he's playing," Mingolla said. "Everything's a game to them." He wanted to ask Ruy about the horse, but was afraid he might lose his temper. "And we're supposed to believe you playful fuckers are capable of making peace with one another."

"We have no choice," said Ruy haughtily. "You know a good bit of it. Would you like to hear the rest?"

"Sure," said Mingolla. "Entertain us."

"Very well." Ruy sipped his coffee. "Toward the beginning of the last century, the wiser heads among us concluded that the world was headed for disaster. Nothing imminent, you understand. At least in terms of that generation's happiness. But they could see the development of conflicts and forces that would menace everyone. They realized that the feud had to end, that we had to turn our energies toward dealing with these questions. And so we met in Cartagena and made a peace between the families."

Mingolla spat out a laugh. "Altruists!"

"That's right," said Ruy. "You have no idea how great an altruism was required to overcome centuries of hatred. It wasn't only that we had to end the feud; we had to become colleagues with our bitter enemies, because the logistics of creating a worldwide revolution were . . ." He couldn't find an appropriate term and shook his head. "We had to initiate breeding programs to begin with. The families were not large in those days, and we needed more manpower to infiltrate the political arena, the military, the intelligence communities. That's been the purpose of programs like Psicorps and Sombra . . . to swell our ranks. It's taken us more than a hundred years, but finally we're ready for a takeover. There's not an agency of any importance in Russia or the United States whose strings we can't pull."

"Then why haven't you pulled them?" Debora asked.

"We've made a number of mistakes over the years. Despite the accords of Cartagena, many of us were unable to put aside our bitterness, and from time to time the feud would flare up. We overlooked most of these flare-ups. After all, things were going well overall. But then"—Ruy let out a long, unsteady breath—"then we made a terrible mistake. About twenty of us were engaged in trying to neutralize the threat of the Palestinian terrorists, when the feud flared up again. Those twenty people became so involved in settling personal scores, they neglected their assignments. And as a result a terrorist plot to plant a nuclear device in Tel Aviv was carried out."

"Jesus!" Mingolla started to say more, but sarcasm and insult seemed unequal to the enormity of the folly.

Ruy appeared not to notice his outburst. "We renewed the accords after Tel Aviv, but even so there continued to be flare-ups of trouble, especially among the younger generation. At last it was determined that all those who were keeping the feud alive—along with those of you from Sombra and Psicorps who were strong enough to help us shape a new world—would take up residence in Barrio Clarín and negotiate a separate peace. Once the peace was successfully negotiated, then and only then would we begin the takeover."

"What if you fail?" Debora asked.

"Then we'll die, and the takeover will go on without us. I'm not sure how the sentence will be carried out. Carlito's in charge of that. An air strike, I presume. But we *won't* fail. We're making progress every day."

"Who's Carlito?" asked Mingolla.

"Dr. Izaguirre," said Ruy. "My uncle."

"Right," said Mingolla. "We're going to Panama so that crazy son of a bitch can blow us up. Sure we are."

Ruy shrugged. "If you run, you'll be tracked down. And besides"—he looked at Debora—"you want a voice in making a new world, don't you?"

"I'll pass," said Mingolla. "What you've made so far doesn't seem much of an improvement."

"You know nothing of what we've done."

"I know this goddamn war!"

"We didn't start the war! You did! What we've done over the past few years is to reduce it to a fraction of its previous scope. We've had to maintain it to an extent to cover our operations, and we don't have enough people to influence specific battles, only the command structure. But once the peace is achieved, we *will* end it. And then we'll pull the strings and end all wars." Ruy had another sip of coffee, made a sour face. "We've done shameful things, we've permitted shameful things to continue. But that's the responsibility that comes with power. You do what you have to and live with the consequences. And if the result is good, all else is justified."

"Y'know," said Mingolla, "I believe you're sincere, man. I really do. That's what scares me. You're so goddamn sincere, you think sincerity excuses everything. Every whim and atrocity."

"Your problem's not with us, man." Ruy drew up his knees, rested his arms on them. "It's with me. Debora here, she understands that the world has to change. She understands that no matter how bloody the path, things can't go on as they have. But you"—he jabbed a finger at Mingolla—"you can't see that. You haven't lived down here. You haven't seen your country violated by development bankers, by corporations and their little Hitlers. Sooner or later that lack of understanding will split the two of you."

"And that's when you move in, huh?"

Ruy smiled.

"I wouldn't count on anything," said Debora stiffly.

"I'm counting on your commitment, *guapa*," said Ruy. "I know how deep it runs. And you can count on honesty from me."

Mingolla snorted at that.

"You think we're dishonest because we've been cautious with you?" said Ruy. "Don't you know how hard it was for us to place trust in people too strong for us to control? But for the sake of the revolution, we did it." He lit a cigarette, blew a bluish plume of smoke that gave his comments visible pause. "The kind of power we've enjoyed . . . being able to take whatever you want. After a while it instills an inviolable morality. The things of this world lose their desirability, and work becomes the only passion. That's why our revolution will be pure."

"What happens to that morality," said Debora, "when it encounters something it can't have?"

"You're talking about you and me?" Ruy asked.

"Just about you . . . about the lack of seriousness implicit in a person who contrives a passion over something he can't have. It's childlike."

Ruy stubbed out his cigarette on the sole of his shoe. "You figure that's how it is with me?"

"I know it."

"What's it matter the way a passion begins?" he said. "Believe me, Debora. I'm serious."

"We can't deal with these people," said Mingolla.

"No, he's right about that much," she said. "We have to."

"What the hell for?"

"I think," she said, "it makes more sense to be a part of

this revolution than to deny it's happening. I've always thought so . . . you know that."

"They're lunatics, they're . . ."

"And your president isn't? No, we have to deal with the families. But we may not have to deal with Ruy." She said this last coldly and then reached into Ruy's pack and removed his handgun.

"It would go hard with you if you killed me," said Ruy, undismayed.

Mingolla took the gun from Debora and let the barrel droop toward Ruy's groin. "It's likely to go hard with us anyway."

Ruy couldn't take his eyes off the gun.

"Tell me some more about Panama," said Mingolla.

"You're being a fool," said Ruy. "Kill me, and they'll never stop giving you pain."

Mingolla essayed a deranged laugh. "Call me irresponsible." He cocked the gun. "Talk to me, Ruy, or I'm gonna blow away your spare parts."

"What do you want to know?"

"Back on the boat you mentioned something 'bout armies in Barrio Clarín. Armies that did the fighting whenever the families had a squabble. Let's hear 'bout them."

Ruy's words came in flurries, his eyes fixed on the gun. "The armies, yes . . . there are about a thousand, maybe more. We had no choice, you see. We couldn't keep killing one another, and passions were running so high. We had to do something."

"Calm down," said Debora. "Take your time."

"Is he going to shoot?"

"You can never tell what he's going to do," she said. "Now what about these armies?"

"They're the damaged, the hopelessly damaged. The ones whose minds are almost gone."

"Damaged how?" Mingolla asked.

"Damaged by people like you . . . like me. Their minds disrupted by too many interactions. You know. Like the people at your hotel in Roatán. Except these are even more deteriorated. They can barely feed themselves." Their stares unnerved

Ruy further. "We had no choice, don't you see? If we didn't use them, we'd be killing one another and there'd be no chance for a peace among us. We're not proud of it, believe me! But it's working. I swear it! There hasn't been a battle in over a month."

"God," said Debora.

"We don't give them guns," said Ruy weakly. "No guns are permitted in Barrio Clarín."

"Gee, that's swell of ya." Mingolla sighted along the barrel at Ruy's chest.

Ruy's voice broke. "Don't do this."

The gun seemed to be getting heavy in Mingolla's hand, and he was tempted to lighten it by a bullet. But Ruy had value alive. If they could hide their power from him, he would make a good witness when they reached Panama, would testify to Izaguirre and the rest that Mingolla and Debora were strong, but nothing that couldn't be handled. Mingolla was surprised that he hadn't argued more with Debora against continuing their journey, and he realized that what was motivating him was anger at the Sotomayors and Madradonas. It puzzled him that he should give so much weight to anger, but the strength of the emotion was enough to satisfy him, to stifle the need for self-analysis.

"I'm gonna let ya live, Ruy," he said. "Happy?"

Ruy maintained a hostile silence.

"But we're gonna pull your fangs." He picked up Ruy's rifle, cradled it under one arm. "No point in letting you run around armed and everything like you were an adult."

"You've . . ." Ruy stopped himself.

"What say, man?"

"Nothing."

"You thinking mean thoughts, Ruy. I can tell." Mingolla nudged Ruy's knee with the rifle barrel. "C'mon, man. Spit it out."

Ruy glared at him.

"Well . . ." Mingolla came up into a crouch, letting the barrel drift back and forth across Ruy's chest. "Anytime you feel the need to talk, don't be bashful." He put an arm around

Debora. "Try to make it during the day, though, will ya? We keep pretty busy at night."

Following this conversation, the character of Ruy's attentions toward Debora underwent a transformation. He took to favoring her with ardent stares and despondent looks, to scribbling poems in a notebook, to gazing listlessly at the scenery: the very image of lovesickness. It was as if in revealing his true nature, he was also revealing the sappy core of his passion. Nothing except Debora commanded his interest, and though Mingolla was grateful for Ruy's lassitude, preferring it to his previous aggressiveness, he found that he could no longer count on him for assistance in negotiating the wilderness. Ruy responded to Mingolla in monosyllables or not at all, and even when they encountered serious obstacles—obstacles as the town of Tecolutla—he exhibited no concern, but merely shrugged off Mingolla's questions and said he didn't care what they did.

Mingolla did not want to enter Tecolutla. Even from the pine ridge above it, he could sense an ominous air to the place, one that the view through his binoculars did nothing to dispel. It was big for a high-country town, sprawling across the saddle between two hills, lorded over by a cathedral of crumbling gray stone with tilted vine-draped bell towers that had the look of vegetable chessmen whose board was in the process of being overthrown. The other buildings, the houses and shops, were not so imposing, but were equally ruinous, charred and broken and fettered with creepers, and under the thin mist that covered the valley, the town appeared insubstantial, to be either fading in or out of existence.

"Ain't no way 'round it," said Tully. "Anyhow, we might find us some gas down dere."

"I don't see any movement." Debora lowered her binoculars. "It's probably deserted."

"Y'ever here before?" Mingolla asked the question of all of them.

"It's an Indian market town." Corazon nodded at Debora. "She's probably right. I doubt anyone's livin' there. When the Indians abandon a place, they rarely come back."

307

"Okay," said Mingolla. "Let's try it."

They made two passes through the town before risking a stop; they roared down the empty streets, guns poked from the windows, the engine of the Bronco sounding incredibly loud in the stillness. Finally they pulled up to the cathedral, which fronted a shattered fountain in the main square. The doors of the cathedral were massive, cracked open a foot, the wood dark and studded with iron like the door of an ancient prison, as if the Catholic God were something to be kept under restraint. The square was cobbled, weeds protruding from breaks in the stone, and facing the church was a pink stucco cake of a hotel on whose facade was written in circus-style letters HOTEL CANCION DE LAS MONTANAS. Some rusted tables and shredded umbrellas sat out front, the remains of a sidewalk café.

"Sometimes dese hotels got generators," Tully said. "Might be some gas lyin' 'round in dere."

Judging by the sumptuous rags of the draperies, the size of the reception desk, the silvercloth stripe visible in the moss-furred wallpaper, the hotel must have catered to the wealthy, but now it was tenanted only by lizards and insects. Thousands of slitherings stilled when they entered the lobby; their footsteps shook down falls of plaster dust. As they walked along a hallway past an elevator shaft choked with epiphytes, Mingolla turned to say something to Tully and saw that Corazon was missing. He asked where she was, but Tully hadn't noticed her absence and had no idea.

"I'll fetch her," he said.

"No, I'll do it." Mingolla started toward the entrance, but Tully caught hold of him.

"What's de matter, mon? She likely just wanderin'."

"Maybe," said Mingolla.

"You can trust her," Tully said.

"Who says I don't?"

"Your face sayin' it, mon."

Mingolla pulled away from Tully. "I'll check it out. You keep looking for gas."

"She ain't up to not'in'!" Tully said, but Mingolla just waved and sprinted back out into the square. Corazon was standing by the cathedral doors, peeking inside. He called to her, and she jumped.

"You scare me," she said as he came up.

"What're you doing sneaking off like that?"

"I wanna look in the church."

The rose in her eye seemed to him—as it had in the past—a Sotomayor signature, a clever advertisement of power and folly. "Who are you?" he asked.

"Nobody."

"I'm not interested in your goddamn philosophy. I wanna know what you're doing . . . who you're working for."

She stared at him deadpan.

"I don't trust you," he said. "So you better talk to me."

"You wanna know somethin'," she said, "why don't you just look inside me? You strong enough to do what you want."

"I've already done that."

She looked startled.

"Back on the boat," he said. "I checked you out a coupla times. You seem okay. But there could be things hidden inside you I can't get at. Traps. Commands. Things *you* don't even know about."

"Well, if I don't know 'bout 'em, I can't help you." She pushed the door wider. "I'm goin' in."

He followed her into the nave, and they stood facing each other beside a stone baptismal font. In the half-light the rose appeared to be hovering deep within her skull, and the tip of her braid, hanging off the side of one shoulder, looked to have vanished in inky shadow. "So tell me 'bout yourself," he said.

"Don't worry," she said. "I ain't doin' nothin' to Tully."

"What *are* you doing?"

"Just livin'."

Mingolla considered her minimalist nature, compared her to Nate and Don Julio and Amalia. It was quite possible that she was like them, a broken toy, and the fact that she professed minimalism as a policy would be just the sort of twist Izaguirre liked to employ in his creations. But he couldn't be sure, and he was still hampered by morality in his judgments; he couldn't act upon mere suspicion, especially where Tully's woman was concerned.

Corazon pushed through the inner doors, and Mingolla hurried after her, gagging on a thick fecal odor. Sounds of grunting, clucking. He started to ask Corazon another question, but then noticed that the altar was illuminated by four candelabras: an island of light floating in a black void, centered by a filigreed silver cross big enough upon which to crucify an infant. Wings whirred above their heads, and from behind them came an echoing boom, the sound of the outer doors closing and being bolted. The scrape of a shoe on rough stone somewhere near, and someone tried to snatch Mingolla's rifle. He wrenched it free, heard footsteps pattering off, and ducked behind a pew. Probing the dark, he contacted a number of minds. Maybe a dozen. He could have stunned them, but was unwilling to show his hand in front of Corazon. He fired a round into the air.

"Don't!" Corazon pulled at the rifle. "There's nothin' bad in here. I can feel it."

He shook her off, fired another round high. "I want lights in here!" he shouted. "Or I'll blow your butts away!"

"Please!" said Corazon. "Don't *you* feel it! Nothin' dangerous here."

"Don't shoot!" A man's voice speaking in English from somewhere near the altar.

"Then put on the damn lights!"

"All right, all right . . . just a minute!"

. . . David . . .

Debora's voice in his mind.

. . . I'm okay . . . stay back . . .

. . . what's going on . . .

. . . I don't know yet . . .

. . . David! . . .

. . . just hang on . . .

"Hurry up with those lights!" Mingolla called.

"Wait a second, will ya!"

The man's voice, Mingolla realized, was American . . . and not just American. It had a distinct New York City accent.

Dim yellow light flooded the church from fixtures along the walls, leaving the vaulted ceiling in shadow, and though

Mingolla had expected to see something unusual, he wasn't prepared for the extraordinary dilapidation of the church. Straw matting the floors, piles of animal waste, bird droppings speckling the pews. Swallows made looping flights overhead, swooping between the massive buttresses, flaring in the lights and vanishing. Two pigs were curled up in the center aisle, a black rooster was pecking at a dirt-filled seam between stones, and a goat was wandering along the altar rail. No one was in sight, but Mingolla could sense them hiding among the pews.

"Jesus!" said Corazon.

A priest in a black cassock came out of the entrance to a side altar some twenty yards away in the east wall, and approached them hesitantly. Skinny, with gray shoulder-length hair. He was one of the oddest-looking men Mingolla had ever seen. His features were firmly fleshed, youthful, yet his skin had the wrinkles and folds of someone in his sixties: like an actor made up to play an old man. He wore a necklace of white stones on which symbols had been scratched, and he fingered this as he might have a rosary.

"Please," he said. "You can't stay here."

Mingolla gestured toward the pews with his rifle. "Tell the others to stand up."

"They're frightened," said the priest. "They're only girls."

"They can't be too frightened," Mingolla said. "One tried to take my rifle."

"They were just trying to protect me."

Again Mingolla motioned with the rifle. "Tell 'em."

The priest called out in Spanish, and one by one the girls stood. They were all young, in their teens, and several were pregnant. Wearing white cotton shifts. With their dark skins and black hair and stoic faces, they might have been sisters.

"What's the story here?" said Mingolla.

"Huh! I tell you what's the story!" Corazon jabbed a finger at the priest's face. "This motherfucker been feedin' lies to these women to get 'em on their backs."

"No, that's not . . ."

"Don't tell me no lies!" said Corazon. "I was raised by bastards like you. Fuckin' Catholic Church been screwin' people here since they first come!"

"I can't deny . . ." the priest began.

"Goddamn right you can't!" Corazon paced away.

Mingolla was less interested in the priest's explanation than in Corazon's uncharacteristic passion, but he said, "Let him talk."

"I can't deny the Church's excesses," said the priest. "Though since before the war we have fought on the side of the people."

Corazon sniffed.

"But I assure you, I'm not taking advantage of the girls." He made a gesture of helplessness. "Something's goin' on here . . . it's extraordinary. Hard to explain."

"I bet," said Corazon.

"Who's the father?" Mingolla pointed to one of the pregnant girls.

"I am," said the priest. "But . . ."

"What I tell you?" Corazon went chest to chest with the priest. "These *holy* men . . . I know some that fuck anything that moves. Women, boys." She stuck her nose in the priest's face. "Animals!"

Something about Corazon's vehemence rang false to Mingolla. It was as if she was performing for him, putting on a show to convince him of her humanity, her untampered soul. And maybe that was what his bad feeling about the place had been trying to tell him. Not that there was danger of bodily harm, but a danger that he might buy what Izaguirre was selling.

"You're from New York, aren'tcha?" said Mingolla.

The priest looked blank for a moment, then nodded. "Brooklyn."

"I'm from Long Island."

"I hardly remember the place," said the priest absently. "So much has happened."

"Yeah? Like what? What's happening now?"

. . . *David* . . .

. . . *it's okay . . . be out soon* . . .

The priest heaved a sigh. "Maybe she's right about me." He nodded at Corazon. "Maybe I'm only erecting a justification

312

for violating the rule of celibacy. I wouldn't be the first priest to suffer delusions."

"Delusions . . . bullshit!" said Corazon. "The man ain't got no delusion, he just wanna little pussy."

"But even if they're delusions," the priest continued, "they still have substance. This place"—he looked up to the ceiling, following the flight of a swallow—"the foundations are carved from an enormous boulder that the Indians claim has magical properties. Maybe it's true. Even when I first came here I could sense life in these stones. It seems to attract life. Like the swallows. Generations that have never flown beyond these walls."

"Lotta churches like that," said Corazon.

"True, but the swallows here . . ." The priest gave a wave of his hand. "You wouldn't believe me."

"Bet your ass," said Corazon.

"Shut up!" Mingolla told her.

"The fuck I will! You don't know these bastards!"

She was about to say more, but Mingolla cut her off and told the priest to go on.

"Have you ever seen the murals they paint down here?" asked the priest. "In bars and hotel lobbies? They'll have ocean liners and volcanoes and racing cars and Jesus all in the same painting. It seems nonsensical, random. But I've come to believe that that tendency is at the heart of a syncretic process permeating the region. You see it—the process—at work in every area of life, and I believe it's all reflective of something more important going through that same process."

"And what's that?"

"God . . . or at least the idea of God." The priest held up a hand as if to ward off ridicule. "I know, I know! Ludicrous, demented. But we—the girls and I—live every day in that process, in the syncretic blending of Christ and some Indian spirit." He rushed his words to override Corazon's interruption. "You'd have to stay here to understand, to feel the truth of what I'm saying. But you must believe me! I haven't coerced the girls . . . at least not knowingly. They were drawn here, just as I was drawn to violate my vow of celibacy. Drawn by dreams, voices.

Intimations. The scheme of the new god is working itself out in us. Pagan and benign." He touched his necklace and muttered something in a language unfamiliar to Mingolla; he pointed to the girls. "Ask them if you want. They'll tell you."

"Sure they will," said Corazon. "They fuckin' brainwashed."

"What's your new god alla 'bout?" Mingolla asked.

"It's not yet clear," said the priest. "We keep adding to the image, and someday it'll be complete. But . . ."

"What image?"

"Here, I'll show you." The priest started off along the east aisle, beckoning, and they followed him toward the side altar. Standing at the back of the altar, mounted on a head-high pedestal and fronted by banks of flickering candles, was a twice-life-size statue of the Virgin clad in a stiff gilt gown whose folds looked like flows of golden lava. Gems encrusted the bodice, and a golden cross hung from her neck. Spiderwebs moored the statue to the walls, frail intricate supports billowing slightly in the wash of heat from the candles, and a beetle was crawling on the chipped forehead. Much of the pink plaster of her face had been eroded; painted symbols figured her cheeks and neck. A knife was taped to her left hand, and in her right she held a clump of flowering weeds. The dim lighting made her appear monstrous and decaying, yet there was a kind of organic magnificence about her; it seemed to Mingolla that the movement of the spiderwebs and the inconstant shadows cast by the candles were the result of imperceptible breathing.

"You've seen all there is to see," said the priest. "Will you leave now . . . please?"

"Why you want us to leave so bad?" Corazon asked. "What you hidin'?"

"Nothing, nothing at all. But you're interfering with the process. We need solitude, we need to focus on the Conception."

"I s'pose we might as well," said Mingolla.

"Ain't you gonna do nothin' 'bout these women?" Corazon was outraged.

"What should I do?"

"Take 'em outta here, man! Get 'em 'way from this fucker!"

Mingolla turned to the body of the church, saw that the

314

girls had gathered at the entrance to the side altar. "You ladies like it here?" he asked. "Or you feel like leaving?"

They edged away, silent, their eyes looking as hard as obsidian.

"Guess they're happy," said Mingolla.

"Thank you," said the priest.

"You don't know what you doin'!" Corazon shook her finger at Mingolla. "These fuckin' priests, they crazy! They get so desperate for God, they start thinkin' they God themselves. That they know everything 'bout God. And then they mess with you. I know!"

"How do you know?" Mingolla asked.

Corazon drew a long breath. "When I was little, thirteen, this priest, man, he used to take me into the rectory . . . givin' me special instruction, he tell my mama. Say he see somethin' spiritual in me. At first he just tellin' me 'bout the Mysteries, y'know. But then he start showin' me. The Mysteries! Huh! After a year I know more 'bout the Mysteries than most married ladies."

She was, Mingolla thought, quite convincing, and if what she was saying was true, it might explain much about her. But he couldn't swallow it. Her opening up to him was too sudden, too coincidental with his growing lack of trust in her, and it might be best to act on impulse and get rid of her now. But then, he realized, he'd have to deal with Tully, and he didn't want that. He could be wrong, after all, and even if he wasn't, she would be no threat as long as he kept an eye on her.

Ignoring her railing, her emoting, he shoved her ahead of him toward the front door.

"Go with God," said the priest, and then laughed. "Or whatever."

Mingolla paused in the doorway, looking back at him, feeling a momentary sympathy for a fellow New Yorker. "This ain't for real, man," he said. "Y'know that?"

"Sometimes I feel that way," said the priest. "But"—he shrugged, grinned—"I gotta be me."

"Well . . . good luck."

"Hey," said the priest. "How the Mets doing?"

"I don't follow 'em, I'm a Yankee fan."

The priest adopted a stern expression. "Blasphemer," he said, and then, with a friendly wave, he closed the door.

———————————

Soon they began to see the war in the sky, eerie sunset glows visible at every hour of the day as swirls of pink and golden light bathing the clouds. The people in the villages where they bought gas told them that the battle zone stretched for miles and that no trails existed to circumvent it. That war should have such a lovely reflection made the prospect of encountering it all the more menacing, but there was nothing to do except to go forward. The jungle became less dense, the evidence of conflict increasingly apparent. Once they came to a grassy slope upon which lay dozens of yellowish brown shapes that at a distance resembled giant footprints, but on closer inspection were revealed to be dessicated corpses that had been pressed flat, perhaps by the passage of tanks; their faces were eyeless masks, their fingers splayed like those of the clay men Mingolla had fashioned as a child. Less than a day's travel farther on, they discovered a mass grave that had been left uncovered, and that same evening they reached the base of a volcano that rose from the midst of an extensive stand of mahogany trees: Mingolla spotted large wooden platforms high in the trees, and as the Bronco threaded its way among the trunks, he saw men descending on ropes from the heights of the trees ahead of them. Though the men did not appear to be bearing arms, he threw off the safety of his rifle and told Debora to pull up. He and Tully and Debora climbed out, training their rifles on the two men who approached them.

"Hello!" one of the men called. He was a balding, stocky American in his fifties, wearing shorts and a tattered khaki shirt with a general's star on the collar; he had the sort of healthy openness to his face that Mingolla associated with scoutmasters and camp directors. His companion was an Indian, older, wrinkled, dressed in jeans and a Mickey Mouse T-shirt. "God, it's good to see new faces," said the stocky man. "Where you bound?"

"Panama," said Debora.

"Well, then you'll have to stay the night, won't you?" said the American. "My name's Blackford. Frank Blackford, U.S. Army, retired. And this"—he gestured at the Indian—"is Gregorio, my brother-in-law. You might say we're co-mayors of our little community. Come on up. We'll feed you and . . ."

"Thanks," said Mingolla. "But we want to make a few more miles before dark."

Blackford's good cheer evaporated. "You can't do that. You'll be in great danger."

"From what?" said Tully.

Gregorio muttered something in his own language. Blackford nodded and said, "There's a rather large animal that inhabits this area. Nocturnal, and very fierce. Weapons don't have much effect on it . . . which is why we've taken to the heights."

"What kind of animal?" Debora asked.

"Malo," said Gregorio. *"Muy malo."*

"That's a long story," said Blackford. "Look, you can't get much farther tonight. You'll be right in the heart of the most dangerous area. Why not stay with us, and I'll tell you about it."

He seemed genuinely concerned for them, but, taking no chances, Mingolla reinforced his concern and that of Gregorio. "All right," he said. "What about the car?"

"Be perfectly safe here." Blackford chuckled. "The Beast has no use for it."

"The Beast?" Debora glanced at Mingolla, alarmed.

"Crazy motherfuckers," said Tully under his breath.

Blackford heard him. "Crazy, perhaps. But alive! Alive! And in these times, that's the only form of sanity worth recognizing."

From the edge of a wooden platform encircling the trunk of a mahogany tree, Mingolla could see other platforms through the interstices of the branches. Charcoal fires in iron braziers glowed like faceted orange jewels among sprays of dark green

317

leaves; women were hunkered beside them, and children sat beneath lean-tos set closer to the trunks. The smells of cooking came on the breeze, mixed with the clean scent of the trees. Men slid from platform to platform on systems of ropes, passing one another in mid-air. Just below, water jumped like a silvery fish from the jagged end of a pipe, spilled into a trough that ran from tree to tree; a pump thudded somewhere nearby. Wind frayed the sounds of conversational voices and babies crying. The platform where Mingolla was standing was roofed with interlaced branches and furnished with pallets and cushions. Propped in one corner was a pale green combat suit and helmet, and after they had eaten a meal of beans and rice served in banana leaves, Mingolla asked Blackford about the suit.

"It's mine," said Blackford.

"I didn't know generals took part in combat," Mingolla said.

"They don't," said Blackford; he flicked his starred collar. "This is what they give you for twenty-five years' service with the quartermaster corps. The suit"—he seemed to be searching for the right words—"it was part of a fantasy I once had. It comes in handy these days."

"How come you people livin' wit' de fuckin' birds?" Tully asked. He was sitting against the trunk, his arm around Corazon. Ruy was lying on a pallet, staring at Debora, who sat cross-legged beside Mingolla. Darkness was settling over the treetop village, and a few stars could be seen between the separations of the leaves; to the west, visible beneath a branch, the last of sunset was a neon scar on the horizon.

Blackford stretched out his legs, took a pull from a bottle of rum. "I guess I have time for a story before I get to work."

"You work at night?" Debora asked.

He nodded, picked at the label of the bottle. "For most of my time down here," he said, "I was stationed in Salvador. I was a damn good organizer, but nothing of a military man, and that had always bothered me. I figured that if they'd give me the chance, I'd be as good as any of the glory boys. What was war, I asked myself, if not organized violence? If I could organize shipping schedules and deliveries, wouldn't I be just as efficient at running a battle? I applied for front-line assignments, but they kept turning me down. Said I was more valuable where I was. But I heard their jokes. The thought of Frank T. Blackford in combat made them dizzy with laughter. So I decided that I'd show 'em.''

Blackford's sigh accompanied a sudden dimming in the west. "Looking back, I can see what a foolish idea it was. I suppose I *was* a fool, then. At the least I was ignorant about war. Even though I should have known better, I saw war as opportunity, a field upon which a man could make his mark. And so to prove my mettle, I pulled some strings and wangled myself temporary command of a combat unit in Nicaragua, one of the long range recon patrols. This was done under an assumed name, you understand. I had some R & R coming, and my plan was to take the patrol and do great things. Impossible things. Then return to Salvador and shake my combat record under the noses of my superiors. Well, after three days in the field, I'd lost . . . I was about to say I'd lost control of my men, but the truth is I'd never had control. They'd just started using Sammy in those days, and the safe dosage was still a matter of conjecture. My men were lunatics, and once I began doing the drug with them, trying to be one of the boys, I became as crazy as they were. I remember coming into the villages, peaceful little places with fountains in the plazas. I moved through them spinning, a kind of mad dance, spraying bursts of fire that seemed to be writing weird names on the walls. I laughed at the men I shot. Shouted at them. Like a kid playing soldier.''

He lifted the bottle to his lips, but didn't drink, just stared off into the leaves. "I couldn't take it. No, that's too easy to say. I *could* take it. I relished the chemical bravery, and no moral wakening brought me to my senses. I simply outstripped my men in madness, and they deserted me. Left me without drugs, without a radio, to wander the hill country. I walked back through some of the villages we'd destroyed, and then, only then, did it begin to come home to me where I was and what I'd been doing. I saw ghosts in the ruins. They chatted with me, followed me, and I would run and run, trying to escape them.''

Blackford had a drink, shivered as if the rum had hit a raw place inside him. "The nights were awful. I figured out why dogs howl at the moon. Because they're answering it, because it's a howl frozen up there, the end of a long yellow throat opened by terror and despair. I hid in the ruins, in holes in the ground. I hid from things that were there, things that weren't. Once I lay in a ditch all night, and when the light started to gray I saw that what I'd thought was a log was actually a stiffened corpse. It had been staring at me the whole night, and I could feel the bad news its eyes had beamed into my head. I was inside madness. I'd reached the place where madness has its own continuum of correct actions and policies. The heights upon which you can sit and hold rational discourse with a sane man and be so madly fluent that you can win every point. And I would have traveled farther into madness, but I was fortunate."

Blackford started to have another drink, but remembered his manners and passed the bottle to Tully. "It was the volcano that restored me to sanity. It was such an elementary sight, it seemed to offer the promise of simple truths. There it was, a perfect cone rearing into a blue sky, like something a child with crayons might have drawn if you'd told him about Nicaragua and how it used to be. Empty except for Indians and fire in the earth. I was so taken with it, I walked around it three times, admiring it, studying it. Buddhists do the same thing, you know. Circumambulation, they call it. Maybe I remembered that, or maybe it's just something your cells instruct you to do once you reach your magic mountain. Whatever . . . I loved the volcano, loved being under it, in its shadow. And all the time I was walking around, I never noticed anyone living nearby. Not until Gregorio decided to save me from the Beast. I thought Gregorio was madder than I. He'd never spotted the Beast, never seen its track. Yet he would have sworn to its existence. In a way the story he told charmed me; if it hadn't I might have risked staying on the ground just for the sake of obstinacy, and I might have died. But I wanted to hear more, to learn about these curious people that lived in the trees."

Blackford waved his bottle at the platforms below, ragged rafts of planking illuminated by the dimming fires; human shadows knelt by the fires, and each scene was enclosed by filigrees of leaves, giving them the otherworldly vitality of images materialized in magic mirrors. "Of course scarcely any of this existed at the time," Blackford said. "The place didn't shape up until I got to work on it. Yet even then there seemed something eminently reasonable about the style of life, and after listening to Gregorio, after considering the principles embedded in his tale, I knew I'd found the field upon which I could make my mark." Blackford took back the bottle from Tully, drank, and wiped his mouth with his hand. He was intent now upon his story, his eyes fixing them not to see if they were listening, but rather—it seemed—to reinforce his words with the intensity of his stare. "What Gregorio told me was this. Years ago, a German man by the name of Ludens lived near the headwaters of the river that runs behind the volcano. No one understood why he had picked this particular spot to settle, but in those days solitary and eccentric Germans were the rule rather than the exception in Central America, and so not much attention was paid him. He ventured downstream only to resupply, and whenever he did, he would warn the Indians against penetrating to the headwaters, saying that a horrible creature dwelled there. A monster. Most heeded the warning, but naturally some wanted to test themselves and went in search of the Beast. Their mutilated bodies were found floating in the river, and soon nobody would dare journey as far upriver as Ludens's house. This state of affairs continued until Ludens's death, at which time it was learned that he had discovered a silver mine and had, according to his diaries, fostered the legend of the Beast in order to keep anyone from finding out his secret. He also wrote that he had murdered Indians so as to lend verisimilitude to the legend. Though the Indians believed that Ludens had been the murderer, this didn't disabuse them of their belief in the Beast. Monsters, at least the Nicaraguan variety, are more subtle than their North American counterparts, and it seemed in complete accord with the Indians' knowledge and tradition that the Beast had used Ludens as its proxy to kill those who violated its territory. They saw Ludens's invention of the legend as a disguise masking a harder truth, the existence of a subtle and malefic demon. And so for years they avoided the forbidden territory. It took the violence of war to drive them from their homeland into the region of the headwaters, and even then they didn't dare remain on the ground, but sequestered themselves high in the trees where the monster had no claim."

Ruy laughed. "And now you think the Beast exists?"

"It's a seductive truth," said Blackford. "And like any truth, it's most complicated in its efficacy. Consider that in all the years since Ludens's death, no one has tested the legend by spending a night below. I would encourage you to test it, but what would that prove one way or another? Your survival wouldn't diminish the legend; the Beast might be otherwise occupied. And your death wouldn't more firmly establish belief. The only real test of a truth is whether or not it serves its adherents. And who could deny that the Beast serves us? Hasn't he kept us from war? Hasn't he inspired us to create this pleasant environment? His philosophical presence alone is enough to sustain belief." Blackford smiled. "You ask if I believe in his existence. I am his existence. All this you see is the geometry of his secret form, the precinct of his wish. If you're asking me, Does he howl, does he rend and tear? my answer is, Listen. Find your own answer. I've found mine."

Sleep came hard for Mingolla that night. He lay awake listening to the rustling leaves, the myriad sounds of the high canopy. Watching the dark figures of the others. Near midnight, one of those figures got stealthily to its feet and draped what looked to be a bulky shadow over its arm: the combat suit. It was Blackford. He moved to the edge of the platform, stepped into the cage of planking that was used for an elevator. The cage vanished, the ropes to which it was attached thrummed. Mingolla crept to the edge of the platform and peered over the side. Saw Blackford disembarking from the cage at the foot of the tree, clearly visible in the fall of moonlight. Blackford stripped off his shorts and shirt, and stepped into the combat suit. He put the helmet on, fastened the seals; then he walked off among the pillarlike columns of the mahogany trunks and was lost to view.

Mingolla crept back over to his pallet and lay down beside Debora, trying to make sense of what he had witnessed; after he had made a sort of sense out of it, he tried to decide whether Blackford's actions were the mark of madness or were exemplary of an elusive and remarkably clearsighted form of sanity. Maybe, he thought, there was no difference between the two states. From the depths of the wood came a guttural wail that Mingolla recognized as the distress signal of a combat suit. It sounded three times and fell silent.

"What was that?" said Debora, clutching his arm. "Did you hear?"

"Yeah." He pushed her back down gently. "Go to sleep."

"What was it?"

"I don't know."

He held her until she had fallen asleep again, but he stayed awake, listening to the signal that sounded every so often, the roar of the Beast making its rounds.

CHAPTER FOURTEEN

On the border of war stood a work of art, both a memorial to the way things had once seemed and an indictment of how they had really always been. The work of art was a sequence of murals painted on the stucco walls of a ruined village less than an hour's drive from the front lines; it occupied the lower slope of a pine forested hill, and from the checkpoint on the road below, Mingolla could make out its bright colors through the trunks. "It's that guy, y'know, what's he called . . . the War Painter," said the corporal who had just passed Mingolla and Debora through the checkpoint, believing them to be intelligence operatives. "Some museum asshole's standin' watch over the son of a bitch, but y'can scope it out if you want. We'll give ya escort to headquarters when you're ready."

"Maybe we'll do that." Mingolla climbed out of the Bronco; he glanced inquiringly at Ruy, Corazon, and Tully in the backseat.

"We hang out here," said Tully. "I don't need to see no damn paintin' 'bout war."

Ruy, who was in a foul mood, having been shot down again that morning by Debora, offered no comment.

"Take your rifles," said the corporal. "We get snipers 'round here sometimes."

The morning was fresh, cool, the sunlight shining clear and whitish gold, glinting in the dew-hung pine needles, like a late

September morning back in New York. As he and Debora made their way through the pines, he could see that the village was small, no more than fifteen or twenty houses, most roofless, and all missing at least one wall; but on coming out into the clearing where the village stood, he found that the poignancy of the painted images caused him to forget the damage. The exteriors of the walls were covered with scenes of daily life: a plump Indian woman balancing a jug on her head; three children playing in a doorway; some farmers walking to the fields, bandannas around their heads and machetes on their shoulders. The colors were pastellike acrylics, and the men and women were rendered in a representational style that deviated from the photo-real by its accentuation of the delicacy of feature, the balletic edge given to the villagers' postures. Looking at them, Mingolla felt the artist had been trying to capture the moment when their fate first made itself known, when they first became aware of the whistle of incoming, before their expressions could register alarm or astonishment, before their bodies could react other than to begin to tense, to perfect their last unfearful poses. They were bright ghosts, still alive yet dead already, with not even the knowledge of death fully lodged in them. Wall after wall, each biting to the eye, and in their cumulative effect most difficult to bear. There appeared to be other murals painted on the interiors of the walls, and Mingolla was about to investigate these, when a fruity voice behind him said, "Isn't it fantastic?"

Walking toward them was a thin, tall man in his late twenties, with olive skin and brown hair and a kind of pinched handsomeness to his features; he was dressed in jeans and a plaid shirt, and accompanying him was an older mestizo man, who was operating a video camera.

"My name's Craig Spurlow," said the tall man. "Metropolitan Museum. Hope you don't mind if we record your visit . . . we're keeping a record of the piece while it's still in its natural environment."

Mingolla introduced himself and Debora, said he didn't mind. He doubted Spurlow had caught their names: the museum official was lost in contemplation, hands on hips, chin up, his stance conveying pride of possession.

LUCIUS SHEPARD

"Just amazing," Spurlow said. "We lost two men defusing the booby traps. And I suppose we could lose more once we start breaking it down for shipment. Who knows if we've found all the traps. But God! It's almost worth it to have finally saved one. I know everyone up there"—he nodded toward the checkpoint—"thinks it's ludicrous to save it, what with everything." His sad smile and outspread hands seemed to offer apology for the condition of "everything," to define that condition as hopeless, and to deny that it was his fault. "But you have to try to hold onto human values, don't you? Simply because there's a terrible war, you can't pretend it doesn't produce works of great beauty and power." He sighed, the aesthetician confronted by some essential boorishness that he felt to the quick. "And this one, this one's special. Even the artist must have thought so . . . it's the only one he ever titled."

"What's it called?" Mingolla asked.

" 'The Mechanics Underlying Superficial Reality,' " Spurlow said, savoring each word.

"That doesn't seem very appropriate," said Debora.

"Really, I . . ." Spurlow smacked his forehead. "You haven't been inside, have you? Come on! I'll show you around. Believe me, I think you'll find the title's most apt."

He ushered them through the door of the nearest house. Tall weeds and nettles grew from the dirt floor, dragonflies with zircon wings wobbled up among the long green stems, and the sunlight cut a sharp angle across one wall, but—because of the nature of the murals, because the walls seemed to be shedding cold—the light did not have much effect. They depicted a grotesque machinery worthy of Bosch or Breughel. Complex and filling every inch of paintable surface. Spurs of yellow ivory bone for gears; pulleys of unraveled heart muscle; ropes of tendons for string; weird assemblages of gristle. And in the darkly crimson interstices between the joints and corners of the machines were gnarled gnomish faces like those formed by grooved tree bark: it was difficult to tell whether the faces were productions of the paint or inadvertent contrivances of warping

326

and shadow. Each time Mingolla turned his head, the machines appeared to shift into different alignments. He was reminded of jogging along a country road near his uncle's farm one night, with fireflies fanned out across the cornfields; he'd been noticing the patterns they formed from second to second, jars and crescents and whatever, and—exhausted from his run—he'd become irrationally annoyed that these patterns were being imposed on him; he had tried not to see them, and just when he thought he had succeeded, a firefly had winked on right in front of him, and he had inhaled it. That was how these horrid machines affected him: he thought he would choke on each new pattern that came clear.

"Do you feel it?" Spurlow asked. "The commitment in the paint, the luminous presence of the artist, his eyes watching us." His own eyes flicked to the side, to make sure of the cameraman's diligence.

They moved from room to room, house to house, Debora and Mingolla silent, the cameraman tracking them, and Spurlow carrying on an inane lecture. "Of course," he said, "every tour of the complex has a different starting point, a different finish. But we think the artist intended this house and this particular wall to be the focal point."

The wall indicated by Spurlow depicted a bed where lay a man, his face to the wall, only his black hair and tanned shoulders visible, and a young woman who greatly resembled Debora in the East Indian cast of her features. The sheet had ridden down to expose her breasts, and her brown left arm hung off the side of the mattress. There was an energyless abandon to the attitude of the bodies that communicated the fact that they were dead, that they had succumbed to the evil processes embodied by the cables and gears of the bloody human remnants that could be seen in the shadows beneath the bed.

"End of story," said Spurlow. "Painting as narrative redefined for our age. And redefined with thrilling power."

Perhaps it was the woman's resemblance to Debora that ignited Mingolla's rage, but it seemed to him then that his passage through the labyrinth of painted rooms had been like the progress of a flame along a coil of fuse, and that he was essentially carrying out the wishes of the artist, obeying the angry impulse that had created the work and designed its destruction, and that the match that had lit him was Spurlow's adenoidal voice. He lifted his rifle and opened fire, ignoring Spurlow's panic-stricken shouts. He tracked fire across the wall top to bottom, chips of painted stucco flying, the bursts echoing, and when the clip had at last been emptied, all that remained of the painting was the woman's brown arm hanging off the edge of the mattress. . . . Seeing it that way, isolated, Mingolla remembered that he had seen it before, the brief hallucination in Izaguirre's office, the glimpse of a delicately rendered arm that had preceded the more detailed hallucination of the night street; and he became unnerved on realizing what that meant, how it ratified the sense of finality, of long years wound down into the future that had been implicit in the hallucination of pornographic America. With Spurlow still shouting at him, he went out of the room, out through a door and back into the street, where he breathed deeply of the clean sunlit air. Tully and a couple of the soldiers from the checkpoint came running through the pines. "What goin' on?" Tully yelled. "You all right?"

"It's okay . . . I just shot up the fucking painting!"

"Didja, no shit?" said one of the soldiers.

"Yeah!"

The soldiers laughed. "Awright, man! Awright!" They ran back up the slope to spread the news.

Debora moved up to stand beside him, to put a hand on his arm, as if accepting complicity, and behind him Spurlow was talking to the cameraman, saying, "Did you get it all?" and then, "Well, at least that's *something.*"

He walked over to Mingolla and confronted him. "Mind explaining why you did that?" There was bitterness in his tone, along with a tired sarcasm. "Did you feel that was something you just *had* to do, did it satisfy some barbarous impulse? God!"

Mingolla could hear the camera whirring. "It felt right . . . what can I tell ya?"

"Do you know," said Spurlow, his voice tightening, "do you know what we've gone through to preserve it? Do you . . ." He waved in disgust. "Of course you don't."

"It doesn't matter," Mingolla said. "I mean you've got the statement down." He gestured at the camera. "This is better'n art, right?"

"The loss . . ." began Spurlow with pompous solemnity, but Mingolla—experiencing a surge of anger—cut him off by grabbing Debora's rifle and training it on him.

"You getting this?" Mingolla asked the cameraman, and then said to Spurlow, "This is your big moment, guy. Any pronouncements on death as art, any last words on the creative process?"

Debora pulled at him, but he shook her off.

"Don't be actin' dis way," Tully said. "De mon ain't worth it."

"There's no reason to get upset," said Spurlow. "We . . ."

"There's plenty of reason," said Mingolla. "All the reason in the world." He hadn't been this angry for a long time, not since the Barrio, and although he didn't quite understand the anger—something to do with the painting, with its validation of the sorry future—he liked the feeling, liked its sharpness, its unrepentant exuberance. He switched off the safety, and Spurlow blanched, backed away.

"Please," he said. "Please."

"Wish I could help ya," said Mingolla. "But just now I'm so caught up in the coils of creativity, I'm afraid mercy's not in the cards. Don't you see the inevitability of this moment? I mean we're talking serious process here, man. The perfect critic stepping forth from the demimonde of the war and blowing the heart of the painting to rubble, and then turning his weapon on the man whose actions have been the pure contrary of the work's formal imperative."

"I'm outta film," said the mestizo cameraman. He seemed to be enjoying himself, and Mingolla told him to go ahead, load up. Both Debora and Tully began pleading with him to stop, and he told them to shut up.

"For God's sake!" Spurlow looked left and right for help, found none. "You're going to kill me . . . you can't!"

"Me?" Mingolla tapped his chest. "That's not the way you should see it, man. I'm merely the shaped inspiration of the work, the . . ."

"Ready," said the cameraman.

"Great!" Mingolla's thoughts were singing, whining with the pitch of the sunlight, the droning of insects, and he said to himself, *I'm really going to waste this chump, why, just because he irritates me, because he's so goddamn stupid he believes . . .*

"Stop it, David." Debora pushed the barrel aside, pressed close to him. "Stop it," she said softly. Calm seemed to flow from her, and though Mingolla wanted to reject it, he couldn't. He lowered the gun, looked over her head at Spurlow, who was frozen, stiff-legged. "Fuck," he said, realizing how close he had come to losing it, to reverting to his old insanity.

Spurlow scuttled behind the cameraman and, using him for a shield, made for a doorway. Once inside, he poked out his head and said, "You're out of your mind, you know that? You better get him some help, lady! You better get him some help!" It looked as if his head had been added to the frieze of figures on the wall beside him: a young couple arm in arm, and two old men who were apparently whispering about them. Mingolla had the urge to make his own movie. Hound Spurlow through the ruins day after day, filming his fearful decline, taping his increasingly incoherent rants on the state of art, rants that made more and more sense in relation to both the project of the film and the artifact of its setting. Call it *The Curator*. But he supposed there must be better things to do . . . though at the moment he couldn't think of any.

"Let's go," said Debora, taking his hand.

They started off up the slope toward the Bronco, where a group of soldiers had gathered.

"That's right!" Spurlow screamed. "Walk away! You've desecrated a work of art, and now you just walk away." He came a few steps out of the doorway, encouraged by their distance. "Don't come back! You do, and I'll be ready! I'll get a gun! It doesn't take intelligence to fire a gun!" He came farther toward them, shaking his fist, the last defender of his little painted fortress. He said something to the cameraman, then continued his shouting, his voice growing faint, almost lost in the crush of their footsteps on the carpet of pine needles. "You laugh!" he called out to them. "You laugh at me, you think I'm a fool to care about beauty, about the power of these walls! You think I'm crazy!"

Spurlow waited until the cameraman had moved around to get an angle on him that would incorporate the murals.

"But I'm not!" he shrieked, scuttling toward them a few steps, then darting away.

From the crest of a high hill, they could see the body of the war. A green serpentine valley stretched from the base of the hill, cut by trails so intricately interwoven that they looked to be the strands of an ocher web, and scattered among them, like the husks of the spider's victims, were charred tanks and fragments of jeeps and the shells of downed helicopters. Dark smoke veiled the crests of the distant hills, leaked up in black threads from fresh craters, and directly below, an armored personnel carrier had been blown onto its side and was gushing smoke and flame from a ragged hole in its roof. Several dead men in combat suits lay around the carrier, and a group of men in olive-drab T-shirts and fatigue pants were loading body bags, while two others were spraying foam from white plastic backpacks onto the flames. All the smoke threw a haze over the sun, reducing it to an ugly yellow-white glare, the color of spoiled buttermilk. Choppers were swarming everywhere—close by, in the middle distance, and thick as flies at the extreme curve of the valley. Hundreds of them. Their whispering beats seemed to convey an agitated rhythm to the movements of the firefighters and body baggers. Now and then a far-off explosion, a *crump*, a new billow of smoke, and the choppers would flurry around it, fire lancing from their rocket pods. Despite all the activity, despite the urgency of the men below, the sounds of battle, Mingolla sensed a lassitude to the scene, a kind of unhurried precision that accrued to the responses of both choppers and men, and he was not surprised to learn that the battle for the valley had been many months in progress.

"Can't nobody figure why, neither," said the sergeant who escorted the four of them on an elevator down through the middle of the hill. "Seem like we coulda overrun the beaners anytime, but we keep holdin' back. Guess ya gotta have faith somebody knows what the fuck they doin'."

The sergeant was a short, balding army lifer in his late forties, pale, thick-armed, and potbellied, and was obviously a man to whom faith was not a casual affair. He wore two silver crosses around his neck, he pretended to be knocking on wood whenever he said something optimistic, and on his right biceps were tattooed the words ALLEGED FAST LUCK, surrounded by representations of cornucopias, dollar signs, arrow-pierced hearts, and the number 13 surrounded by wavy radiating lines to indicate its sparkling magical qualities. He was a bit slow on the uptake, scratching his head at their every question, and when not talking, he vagued out, staring dully at the elevator door. Mingolla recognized the signs.

The corridor into which they emerged from the elevator was covered with white foam like the tunnels of the Ant Farm, and was thronged with harried-looking junior-grade officers. The sergeant conducted them through a door at the end of the corridor, and told the corporal at the desk that the I-Ops were here to see Major Cabell. The corporal punched a buzzer, an inner door swung open to a round white room with a desk and chairs, charts on the walls, and a cot in one corner.

Major Cabell was in her thirties, a tanned reedy woman whose lusterless brown hair and strained expression had hardened her good looks into a spinsterly primness redolent—Mingolla thought—of a frontier schoolmarm who had been forsaken by her lover and left to age in the prairie winds. She threw on a dressing gown over her T-shirt and fatigue pants, and invited them in. She agreed to send them across the valley with a recon patrol the next morning; but when he suggested a chopper she told him that they'd be safer with a patrol: they lost a lot of choppers on missions to the far side of the valley. She checked her watch, offered them the use of bunks and shower facilities, but asked Mingolla if he would mind staying behind and talking. Official business, she said. Once the others had gone off with her aide, she unwound, seeming to drop four or five years along with her brittle air; she broke out a bottle of gin and pulled up a chair beside Mingolla, who was becoming unsettled by her attitude toward him.

"I hope you don't mind talking," she said, filling Mingolla's glass. "It's been so long since I've been able to talk with a man."

"Why's that?"

"This place . . . the intrigues are unbelievable. It's medieval! Lieutenants scheming against captains, captains against each other, against me. It's because there's no resolution to the battle. People get bored, and for lack of anything else to do they start planning career moves."

"You serious?"

"Oh, yes! If they'd let me win the battle—and I could, in a matter of days—everything would be all right. But command insists upon a holding action. God knows why!" She began to rub the ball of her right thumb across the knuckles of her left hand. "It's really unbelievable. People trying to make fools of one another . . . that gets a lot of them killed. They write reports on each other's eccentricities, and sometimes things get back to the injured party. I've caught some of the reports they've written about me. If I did half what they say . . ." She gave a dramatic shudder. "And so I'm cut off from any possible . . . relationships. Stuck in this room. I have this recurring nightmare about it. I'm on a beach. . . . White sand, heat. I live in a house in the dunes. I'm always exhausted from walking on the beach, because it's so boring. There's nothing to look at . . . even the colors are all bleached and ugly. I'm not helping anyone by being there. It's not an escape or a retreat. I'm just supposed to be there. It's like my profession. No one needs me, no one speaks to me. In fact, I don't even know how to speak. I've always been there." She gave a nervy little laugh.

LUCIUS SHEPARD

"It's not far from the truth. So"—she affected casualness—"you're from New York. God, it's been years since I've been in New York."

"Been a while for me, too," he said, glancing around the room. There was a stack of confession magazines on a night table beside the cot, and set beneath it was a small TV, a VCR, and a number of videotapes, the word *Love* prominent in many of the titles. There was a dominant pattern in the major's thoughts, one that had obviously been trifled with, and from the contents of the room it was clear what particular delusion the pattern reflected.

To fend her off—she had begun trailing her fingers across his arm and knee—he asked about her background. He didn't want to reject her outright, to hurt her. Despite her delusion, there was something impressive about the major, a core dignity and strength that forced you to disregard her flaws, to relate to her without pity. It had been a long time since he had met anyone whom he didn't pity.

"I enlisted because my mother died," she said. "People do the damnedest things under pressure. God knows what I was thinking. It seems now that I wanted structure. Structure!" She laughed. "The army's got all the structure in the world, but it's all topsy-turvy."

She described her mother's illness, how she'd coped. "I did labor," she said. "I built a masonry wall around the house. I worked in the garden. Cutting away rotten roots . . . tough as clenched knuckles." She swirled the gin in her glass, stared into it as if hoping the liquid would reveal some oracle. "People are so simple, really. When I came home to take care of her, she put my clothes away in a drawer she'd cleared. No big deal. Just this simple inclusion in her life. Sometimes she'd ball all her pain up into a simple order, get rid of it that way. I remember once she said, 'See the seeds of that lily . . . balanced on the leaves. Get the big ones. Don't let them dry out too much. Plant them on the far side of the garden.' And after I'd done it, she felt better." The major freshened Mingolla's drink. "My sister came to help out. I hadn't seen her for years.

334

She'd acquired a southern accent and had taken to wearing a gold map of Texas on a necklace. She said she loved me, and I hardly recognized her. She'd married this Texas boy who wrote horror novels. I read some of them. They were okay, but I didn't care for it. At best it was this sort of sensual pessimism. Maybe I just couldn't identify with the self-loathing of vampires."

She got up, walked to the door, and stood looking back at him over her shoulder; when he met her eyes, she paced away. "I can't understand how I wound up in charge here," she said. "I can see the events that led to it, the colonel dying and all. But it doesn't make sense." She laughed. "Of course I'm *not* in charge. Nobody is . . . or if they are, they don't have much of a plan. You know I lose over a hundred men a day even when it's slow. A hundred men!" She walked back to the door, fiddled with the knob. "I shouldn't be talking this way to an I-Op. You might report me."

"I'm not going to report you."

"I'm sorry," she said, coming toward him. "I didn't mean that. I'm just having trouble being around you."

"Maybe I should go."

"Maybe you should." She dropped into a chair. "Why does this keep happening?"

"What keeps happening?"

She turned away, embarrassed. "I keep being attracted to . . . to men, to strangers. It's . . . it's not even a real attraction. I mean I can feel it beginning, y'know. Feel my body reacting. And I try to control it. My mind's not involved, y'see. Not at first, anyway. But I can't stop it, I can't slow it down at all. And then my mind *is* involved . . . though even then I know it's not real, it's just . . . I don't know what it is. But it's *not* real." She seemed to be asking for reassurance.

"I might be able to help," he said.

"How could you possibly? You don't know what's wrong, and even if you did . . ." Her eyes narrowed. "What are you up to?"

"Nothing," he said, and began to make her drowsy.

"Who're you working for?" she said, then yawned.

335

Among the patterns of her mind was one that showed evidence of tampering, its structure more resilient and less easy to influence than the rest, and as she nodded in her chair, he worked at modifying the pattern, reducing its dominance. The work was painstaking. He realized he could easily go too far and destroy the pattern. Destroy her mind, turn her into a clever reconstruction of human wreckage like Don Julio and Amalia and Nate. A feeling of serenity stole over him as he worked, and accompanying this serenity was a new comprehension of the mind's nature. He sensed that the patterns of thought were obeying some master template, that over the span of a life they weaved an intricate preordained shape that was linked to those of a myriad other minds; and he wondered if his old belief in magic and supernatural coincidences had not been a murky perception of the processes of thought, and if the mystical character he had assigned reality had actually had some validity. There was so much to think about, to try to understand. The woman's arm in the mural, the Christian girl he'd treated in some possible future; the idea that he had somehow dealt with Izaguirre. Even the serenity he felt was something that needed to be understood; it seemed a symptom of a deeper and more complete understanding that lay yet beyond him. And these things taken together implied a universe whose complexity defied categorization, whose true character could not be fitted inside the definitions of magic or science. He doubted he would ever understand it all, but he thought he might someday understand more than he had once believed plausible.

When he awakened the major, she sat up, looking confused. "You must have been dead tired," he said.

She laughed dispiritedly. "I'm always tired." She pressed her palms against her temples.

"How do you feel?" he asked.

"I'm not sure," she said. "Clearer, maybe." She probed him with a stare. "You *did* do something to me."

"No, I swear . . . Sleep must have been what you needed."

"But I don't understand," she said. "A minute ago I was desperate to . . ."

"Probably stress," he suggested. "That's all. Stress can do funny things."

"God, that's what this place does to you," she said. "It even makes you suspicious of feeling good."

"Do you still want me to leave?"

She appeared to be checking inside herself, sounding for an answer. "No," she said, brightening. "Why don't you have another drink and tell me about New York. About yourself. You've hardly told me anything. Of course that's always how it is with I-Ops . . . they're secretive even about trivialities." She reached for the gin bottle, paused. "But you're no I-Op, are you?"

"What gives you that idea?"

"Every I-Op I've ever met has been cold and given to drinking bourbon and gazing moodily toward the Red Menace as if he was yearning to have a Commie in his sights. You're not like that."

"I guess I'm a new breed."

She studied him for a long time before pouring. "I just bet you are," she said.

―――――――――

The patrol that escorted them across the valley consisted of ten men, bulky and alien-looking in their combat gear, their faceplates aglow with green letters and numerals from the computer displays inside the helmets, their minds awhirl with Sammy. There was no moon at first, but as they moved through the thickets, hugging the side of a hill, flares burst above them, explosions sent blooms of orange flame boiling up toward the clouds, and iridescent rains of tracers poured down from circling gunships: a constant incidence of roaring light that silhouetted twigs and leaves, and shimmered in blazes on the faceplates of the soldiers. When the moon sailed clear of the clouds, its radiance was almost unnoticeable. Mingolla and the rest had been outfitted with throat mikes and miniature speakers affixed to their ears so they could communicate with the soldiers, and he listened to their tinny voices with amazement, wondering at their delight in this environment, which seemed to him infernal.

"Son of a bitch!" said one, a kid named Bobby Boy. "See that muthafucka go, man! Musta hit a fuel cell."

And the sergeant of the patrol, a wiry light-skinned black named Eddie, said, "That ain't shit, man! Wait'll you see one of them little tanks get it. Man, one of them goes, it's the fuckin' Fourth of July. All them missiles touchin' off . . . red and green streaks of fire. That's somethin', that's really somethin'."

"I seen that," said Bobby Boy querulously. "You tryin' to say I ain't seen that? I been here 'bout as long as you, man."

Eddie grunted. "You be so fuckin' high, you liable to see anything."

"Hey," said another voice. "You fuckers watch yo' mouth! We got us a lady present."

"Shut the fuck up, Sebo," came back Bobby Boy. "That ol' girl's I-Op. They probably bugged her yummy 'fore they sent her out here. They . . . Wow! Awright! See that bitch blow, man? See that gold color in the heart? That's fuckin' weird! Wonder what the Fritos got burns gold."

"Probably all the grease they eat," said somebody new.

Mingolla, made uneasy by all this, walked closer to Debora. In the flashes of the explosions, her eyes burned red, her shadow hands looked to be seven-fingered. "You okay," he said, just to say something, forgetting the throat mike.

"I do believe," said Bobby Boy, "those two I-Ops got a little somethin' goin'."

"Bet she knows how to throw it," said Sebo. "Bet I-Op teaches 'em all kinda slick tricks."

"Shut ya hole!" said Eddie.

"Bet she gotta educated love muscle . . . make ya shoot silver bullets."

"I tol' ya, shut up!"

"Can't stop me from dreamin'," said Sebo. "I dreamin' 'bout both of 'em, slim there and the one with the rose eye."

"You can dream," said Tully. "But you be watchful, or dere gonna be one big nigger in your dream . . . unnerstan'?"

338

"Wouldn't mess with him, Sebo," said Eddie. "The man sound serious."

"Serious? Shit!" Sebo giggled. "This the wrong goddamn war for serious."

"I think," said Ruy nervously, "it would be best for everyone to keep their minds on the crossing."

"That's that skinny beaner talkin', ain't it?" said Billy Boy. "Hey, Frito! I don't like you, man! You gimme the excuse, you ain't gonna have to worry 'bout no crossin'."

An explosion nearby shook the ground, orange light illuminated the figures of the soldiers, freezing them in a tableau, transforming the outlines of trees and shrubs into a bizarre menagerie of shapes. Mingolla and Debora crouched behind a bush, but the soldiers turned their faces to the light like pilgrims brought hard upon their central mystery. The explosion seemed to calm them, and once the glare had faded, they continued on in silence.

They crossed the valley without incident, but as they crested a rise overlooking the ruined village where they would await transport to Panama, a soldier about twenty yards ahead of Mingolla was flipped into the air by a burst of flame beneath his feet, and rifle fire began striking around them. Mingolla pulled Debora down, going flat. Screams and agitated voices came over the transmitter. His mouth was full of dirt, and he was very afraid. He aimed his rifle at the shadowy brush and opened up; the sound of his fire was drowned out by the *crump* of high explosive ammunition. The voices and the gunfire seemed to be speaking as one, blending into a weird percussive language. So much noise and fury, Mingolla felt a hot wind was blowing at hurricane force, driving red splinters of fear through him. Debora wrangled her rifle out from beneath her and began to fire; he could feel its heat and vibration on his face. Then it was over. The guns fell quiet, and the moonlight appeared to reassemble, to fit around every shape, making them sharp and recognizable again. Cooling the air. Normal voices filtered in. A groan.

"Got a live beaner here!"

"Bring him, man!"

"Sebo! You in there, man? You awright?"

"It's his leg . . . suit's gone tight to his leg."

"Gimme his numbers, goddammit! What's his numbers say?"

"He's alive! Leg looks fucked, but he's alive."

"Get the I-Ops down the hill!"

"His medipac's doin' for the leg. . . . He's cool. Hell, he ain't feelin' nothin'."

"You okay, Sebo. You hit a mine but you okay."

"His leg's fucked! Check the readout . . . just little bits of bone floatin' 'round in there."

"Dumbass shit! Shut up!"

"You talkin' 'bout my leg, man?"

Two of the soldiers hauled Mingolla and Debora up, hustled them down the hill toward the village. Behind them, Sebo shouted, "Whaddaya mean . . . what's wrong with my leg?"

The village—a few acres of huts and dirt streets—looked to have been trampled by a giant: roofs staved in, walls crumpled, poles splintered. Ruy and Mingolla and Debora sat beneath the overhang of a canted roof. Tully and Corazon sat apart from them, and farther off stood a group of soldiers. Under the strong moonlight, the snapped poles and crushed thatch took on a dirty grayish black color, and the street glowed lavender gray. All the shadows were sharp and crooked like they might be in Hell. Rocket bursts flickered above the distant hills.

"Almost home," said Ruy.

"You stupid fuck!" Mingolla had to make an effort to keep from hitting him. "This bullshit tour 'bout gets us killed, and you sit there mouthin' off 'bout home."

Ruy, a cross-legged shadow, gave no reply.

"When will the plane come?" Debora asked.

"First light," said Ruy. "It'll fly us to an airstrip near the city, and we'll enter the barrio after dark."

Three more soldiers came down the street, two of them supporting Sebo, whose leg dragged in the dirt. His combat suit was scorched to the knees. They sat him down between Ruy and Mingolla and removed his helmet. He had close-cropped black hair and a weasly dark face dirtied by a growth of stubble. Mingolla recognized him as the vet who had accosted him in his hallucination, who had recognized *him*. Sebo was sweating freely, lines of strain bracketing his mouth. The other two soldiers—Bobby Boy and Eddie—removed their helmets and went to their knees beside him.

"Your suit juice ya up 'nough?" Bobby Boy asked. He was a hulking kid, crewcut and moon-faced, his features small and regularly spaced, giving him a bland moronic look.

"Yeah, I'm makin' it." Sebo slurred the words.

Mingolla stared at him, trying to put his presence together with the arm in the mural, with everything else.

"Chopper can't get here for a while, man," said Eddie, settling back on his haunches. "But you be fine."

Sebo gazed off into the sky, wetted his lips.

Eddie took out a packet of C-ration cookies. He split one of the cookies in half, licked the filling of white icing. Offered one to Mingolla, then to Debora and Ruy. They all refused. "Don't know what you're missin'," said Eddie. "These ol' sugar things make ya tranquil. Ain't that so, Bobby Boy?"

"Uh-huh."

"Yeah," said Eddie. "Cool ya right down, these fuckers. Just the thing after a firefight." He grinned, winked, his face cinching into lines of wily good humor. "Maybe they lemme do a commercial once I get home, man. I say, 'Suckin' the middles out these doobies got me through the great war.' How 'bout that?"

"Probably sell a million," said Mingolla. He looked around at the village, the sad gray wreckage, still holding a faint smell of animals and men. The ghost of a smell. Wind feathered the thatch, making the shadows tremble.

"Razors," said Bobby Boy dreamily. "Man, they cut so smooth you cain't even feel 'em. Cain't even feel when you hangin' open. Don't know you bad off till blood's comin' in your eye. Man, you can make somebody think twice 'bout hookin' wit'cha if you gotta razor, man. 'Cause he don't want

341

nothin' to touch him he cain't feel how bad it is. Razors," said Bobby Boy. "Smooth."

His lazy tone of voice gave Mingolla a shiver.

"Don't be talkin' that shit!" said Eddie. "Fuck! Boy never had no dealin's with razors. He just stoned and like hearin' hisself talk mighty. You bullshit to the bone, Bobby Boy." He licked the icing from another cookie. "To the bone!"

"Maybe," said Bobby Boy. "But I know 'bout razors now, see. From thinkin' 'bout 'em, I know 'em. Gonna get me one when I get home."

"Fuckin' retard," said Eddie, and winked at Mingolla again. "Hey, Bobby Boy! 'Member when we first come to this ol' village?"

Bobby Boy turned to him, the movement slow and distracted. He ejected an ampule from a dispenser in his hand, popped it under his nose, and breathed deep. His face seemed to lengthen, grow leaner.

"Hear what I say, Bobby Boy?" Eddie asked.

"Yeah, I 'member."

"That was ol' Bobby Boy's baptism of fire," said Eddie. "He didn't know what to make of this shit. He be poppin' Sammy every coupla minutes, screamin' and blowin' holes in the smoke. Then when he calm down a little, he wanders into one of them huts. He's gone for like minutes, y'know, and finally he comes back, he says, 'Somethin' fuckin' weird's in there, man,' he says. 'What's that?' I ax him, and he say, 'There's this beaner, man, he's sittin' there. Gotta hole in his forehead, and his brain, it's sittin' there in his fuckin' lap.' He gawks at me. 'Like he's holdin' it, y'know. Like he's wantin' to put it back in. Y'oughta come see, man.' And I say to him, 'Bullshit, man! Ain't nothin' make a wound like that.' 'Course I know the caseless ammo these rifles fire, man, they blow a shallow hole. I seen this kinda shit plenty of times. I just woofin' with ol' Bobby Boy. And he gets real upset. 'Man,' he say. 'Man, I'm tellin' the goddamn truth. Dude's sittin' there with his fuckin' brain in his fuckin' lap.' And I tell him, 'Naw, Sammy's got you all confused.' Well, lemme tell ya, ol' Bobby Boy, he's screamin', tellin' me how weird it is, how it's true, and meantime, I give the signal to my man Rat to torch the goddamn hut. And when the hut goes up, I thought Bobby Boy was gonna bust out in tears. 'I seen it,' he says, 'I swear I did.' We had the boy believin' he was crazy for 'most a week. That was really fresh, that was. 'Member all that, man?''

Bobby Boy nodded and said gravely, "I was a fool."

Eddie chuckled. "Sometime the boy come close to makin' sense, don't he? Yeah, well. We all fools to be sittin' 'round in the middle of this mess."

"Hey," said Sebo. "Hey, lady."

Debora looked over at him. "Yes?"

"C'mere, lady." Sebo's face was shiny with sweat, his grin was without mirth. "Hurt so bad, I need me some sweet talkin'. C'mere and talk at me, huh?"

"Wouldn't be doin' that, woman," said Eddie. "Old Sebo, he just wanna grab holda your jaloobies. That's all he be wantin'. Sebo, he get horny when he hurt."

"Me, too," said Bobby Boy; he reached out a hand toward Debora, moved the hand around, like an artist gauging the balance of different sections of his work.

"Cut that shit out," said Mingolla.

Bobby Boy turned his stunned moonboy gaze on him. "What say?"

"Hey!" Eddie gave him a shove. "Lowrate, will ya, cool? You got that dingy Spec Four redhead bitch for postholin', man. Leave these folks be."

"She lookin' nice," said Bobby Boy in the same tone he had used to talk about razors.

"C'mere, lady," said Sebo. "Little talk ain't gonna hurt nobody."

"Got somethin' better to do with my tongue than talk to her," said Bobby Boy.

Ruy got to his feet, menacing Bobby Boy. "This is insupportable," he said, and then, to Eddie: "Can't you control him?"

Eddie shrugged.

A smile melted up from Bobby Boy's face. "Thank ya,

Jesus," he said. "This here's Bobby Boy Macklin praisin' your name for givin' me this scrawny bastard to mess over."

"I tol' you to lowrate, man," said Eddie anxiously, and Mingolla, realizing that Bobby Boy was very much on the edge, set himself for a fight. No way was he going to try to influence Bobby Boy: Ruy must know how hard it was to influence someone behind Sammy.

"Sebo!" Eddie maneuvered himself between Ruy and Bobby Boy. "Know what I's just thinkin' 'bout? 'Member that ol' girlfriend of yours, one who wrote you the letter 'cusin' you of bein' a killer?" He gave Mingolla a friendly elbow. "We wrote her back, faked the colonel's signature, and tol' her Sebo was a fuckin' hero, went 'round feedin' the starvin' kids and all. Shit! Woman wrote back, sounded like she 'bout ready to air mail her snatch to ol' Sebo."

"Get outta my way, Eddie," said Bobby Boy. "I'm gonna crumble this Frito."

"Fuck you are!" Eddie glanced around wildly as if hoping to light on a solution. "Know what, man? Know what we can do? We can run a game!" He shouted to some soldiers gathered by the wreckage of the next hut. "Where that prisoner at? Bring his ass!"

One of the soldiers grabbed a shadowed figure lying on the ground, hauled him up, and hustled him over. Flung him down. A kid of about eighteen, skinny, long black hair flopping in his eyes. Crop of pimples straggling across his chin. He was shirtless, his ribs showing. On his right shoulder was a blood-stained bandage.

"How 'bout it, Bobby Boy?" said Eddie. "Sebo? How 'bout a game?"

"Yeah, I s'pose," said Bobby Boy sulkily.

"Awright!" said Sebo, sitting up straighter.

Bobby Boy punched the kid in his injured shoulder, and the kid cried out, rolled away.

"Bastard!" said Debora. "Leave him alone!"

Bobby Boy stared at her and made a throaty sound that might have been a laugh.

344

"Listen up, lady," said Eddie. "Bobby Boy *will* fuck with you, so you better let him have his fun."

She looked to Mingolla, and he shook his head.

Some of the soldiers moved off along the street, planting what appeared to be large seeds, covering them with dirt, patting it smooth. Planting lots of seeds.

Bobby yanked the kid up to a sitting position. "What's your name, Frito?"

The kid spread his hands in helplessness. *"No entiendo."*

"Somebody ask him in Spanish," said Bobby Boy.

Mingolla did the duty.

"Manolo Caax." The kid looked around hopelessly at the others, then lowered his eyes.

"Cash . . . huh! The beaner's named for fuckin' money," said Bobby Boy as if this were the height of insanity.

Sebo giggled, his eyes glassy from painkillers. "I'm bettin' on ol' Frito," he said. "I do believe Frito's got what it takes."

The others began making bets.

"Ask him if he got any information," said Bobby Boy.

When Mingolla asked, the kid said, "I know nothing. What are you going to do? Are you going to kill me?"

Mingolla didn't answer; he found it easy to reject the kid and realized this was because he had already given up on him.

"What's going on?" he asked Eddie.

"Got frags buried all over," said Eddie. "Coupla guys get behind the beaner, fire at his heels to keep him movin', and we see if he can run the street without triggerin' a frag. He don't move fast 'nough, the boys'll wax him." He grinned, but sounded more tense than enthusiastic.

Debora leaned close, whispered, "I'm going to stop it."

"No, don't." He caught her arm.

"We can't let them do this!" she said. "I don't care if . . ."

"You better care," he said. "You better just leave it alone. We can't save everybody. All right?"

Ruy was looking at them with interest.

"All right?" Mingolla repeated, and Debora gave a resentful nod, looked away.

Tully sidled over, Corazon at his side, and said, "I can't touch 'em, Davy. Can you do somethin'?"

"Uh-uh."

"What you talkin' 'bout?" said Bobby Boy.

"Just talkin'," said Tully. "Ain't you got not'in' better to do dan fuck wit' dis kid?"

"Naw," said Bobby Boy mildly. "Not a goddamn thing." He was almost as tall as Tully, with broader shoulders, and Mingolla thought Tully was a little afraid.

"Buncha damn chickenshits, mon," said Tully. "Fuckin' wit' a kid."

"You could be next, nigger." Bobby Boy went eye to eye with him. "How 'bout that?"

"Watch your mouth, man!" Eddie stood and shoved Bobby Boy back from Tully.

Ruy tapped Debora's arm. "Can't you do anything?"

She turned a bitter glance on Mingolla, then said, "No."

"Hey," said Bobby Boy. "One of y'all 'splain to Frito how it's gonna be."

Again Mingolla did the interpreting.

The kid glared at him with stony hatred. Bobby Boy, his eyes aglitter in the moonlight, gave the kid an affectionate pat. "I know y'can do it, Frito. Don't lemme down."

Two soldiers led the kid toward the start of the course at the base of the hill about a hundred yards away, and he kept staring back over his shoulder at Mingolla as if he alone were responsible.

"Hee-hee," said Bobby Boy. "This gonna be good!"

"Does he have a chance?" Debora asked.

"Slim," said Eddie. "Frags all over, and they be drivin' him toward 'em with fire. He be runnin' too quick to be lookin'."

Tully looked dubiously at Mingolla, and Corazon added the eerie weight of her stare. Mingolla fixed his eyes on the three figures at the base of the hill, the two soldiers in their moonstruck helmets, the kid a darker and less distinct figure between them.

"Let's do 'er!" Sebo shouted. "Get outta my way, Bobby Boy! I can't see shit!"

With a mean glance at Sebo, Bobby Boy shuffled to the left.

The two soldiers at the end of the road shoved the kid forward and fired bursts behind him; the kid sprinted left toward a gap in the wreckage, but more fire cut off his escape, set one of the crumpled huts to burning. He came zig-zagging down the street, eyes to the ground, bullets throwing up dirt at his heels. Bobby Boy whooped, and Sebo was babbling. Debora buried her face in Mingolla's shoulder, but Mingolla, full of self-loathing at his lack of moral strength, his pragmatic convictions, forced himself to watch. The kid tripped, went rolling, and Mingolla hoped one of the grenades would explode and end this cruelty. Gunfire pinned the kid down. He crawled, scrambled to his feet, was knocked sideways as a bullet detonated a grenade at his rear; he teetered beside a little mound of dirt, nearly stepped on it, but leaped aside. The soldiers followed him, their fire coming closer and closer. Eddie shifted up and down on his heels, cheering in secret, and Bobby Boy was giving out with breathy *yeahs* and shaking a balled fist, and Sebo was leaning forward, intent, his wound forgotten, and the stuttering fire was instilling a fierce tension in the air around them, and the kid sprawled, scrabbled, jittered, appearing to be moved by an invisible finger that pushed him in a dozen lucky directions, keeping him inches away from the little mounds of dirt with their gleaming seeds. It was as if he were doing a magical arm-waving dance, as if he were a crazy spirit from the heyday of the village, from the time when the sapling walls of the huts were freshly skinned and yellow, the thatch green and full of juice, and pigs were stealing mangos from the children's plates, and even in the worst of times the men would gather around the well and smoke cigarettes that they bought for a penny apiece at the store on the hilltop and boast about the milk cows they planned to buy once the crops were in, and it really seemed the kid was going to make it, not only make it—Mingolla thought—but that his mad spinning run was carving a secret design that would resurrect the old gone days, the days before the war, bring the gray wreckage into order, and restore it to color and motion and life, and everything would

begin again, and the soldiers would vanish, and Mingolla would
be a child dreaming of some unimaginable sweetness. . . . But
then the kid stopped running. Stopped dead less than fifty feet
from the end of the course. The firing broke off, and Mingolla
knew that the soldiers harrowing him must be thunderstruck by
this sudden turn. The kid was breathing hard, his chest heaving,
but his face was calm. Dark chips of eyes, mouth firmed and
stoic. Looking at him, Mingolla believed he could see his
thoughts. He realized that somewhere along the way the kid
had understood that it didn't matter whether he made it, that
the course he was negotiating was one that had been negotiated
for centuries by his countrymen, a device of excess and oppression, a bloody game for amused profit takers, and he just didn't
see any reason to continue. Maybe the kid didn't know all this
in words, maybe in his own mind he had simply reached a
point of exhaustion and malaise, a point that Mingolla himself
had reached from time to time. But that knowledge was in him,
enervating, heavy as stone. He wasn't going to run another
foot, he was going to stand there, and by standing gain the only
victory he could.

"Run, dammit!" Bobby Boy shouted.

The kid shifted his weight, let his arms dangle, waiting. To
Mingolla's eyes, he appeared to be growing more solid and
substantial against the background of wasted gray shapes.

"Kill his ass!" Bobby Boy shrilled.

Nobody fired, nobody moved.

"Kill him!" Bobby went a couple of paces toward the kid
and waved angrily at the soldiers. "Y'hear me? Kill him!"

Reluctantly, it seemed, the soldiers lifted their rifles and
opened fire. The bullets blew the kid forward in a staggering
run, and he collapsed between two of the mounds. Black blood
webbed his back, puddled beneath his mouth. His left leg beat
a tattoo against the dirt, and his entire body humped up once,
then was still.

Ruy sighed, and Mingolla let out the breath he'd been
holding; it felt hot in his throat. Debora's hand was tremulous
on his arm, as if she were poised for flight. "Shit," said Eddie.
"Shit." Corazon's mystic eye looked to be glowing, and Tully

was stone-faced. Sebo, spent and sweaty, leaned against the hut, his mouth open, eyes slitted . . . Chinese eyes.

Bobby Boy walked over and kicked the kid in the side. He turned back, his features warped by a scowl, giving his round face the appearance of a nasty man-in-the-moon. "I ain't payin'," he said to the other soldiers. "Muthafucka didn't play fair."

"You better fuckin' pay," said somebody. "You'd make us pay."

"Yeah, man," said somebody else. "You be squawkin' at us, sayin' that the bastard didn't make it, and that was what counted."

"Pay up, Bobby Boy! Y'ain't got no reason not to!"

"Hell you say!" Bobby Boy stalked back to the group beside the hut. "Hey, Eddie," he said. "You with me on this, ain'tcha? Tell 'em the rules, man. Tell 'em what's right. The son of a bitch didn't even try."

SECTOR JADE

The world is not a solid body, but rather is a point in time and space upon which a myriad of beams of light are shining, beams of every color and intensity, some waxing in brilliance, some waning, and the character of this particular point is therefore always in flux, always becoming something new. Thus it may be said that the world has ended many times, but few men have ever noticed.

—Attributed to the San Blas Indians

CHAPTER FIFTEEN

The armies of the Madradonas and the Sotomayors—more than a thousand strong—lived in the streets of Barrio Clarín, in doorways and gutters, under benches in public squares, in pitiful shelters made of cardboard or beneath no shelter at all; and every morning Mingolla would walk out among them and minister to their needs, plying them with his strength, inducing temporary frameworks of happiness and well-being. He derived little satisfaction from the work; the armies were unsalvageable, and the best he could do was briefly to restore their humanity; their minds retained scarcely any structure, and the process of their thoughts was slow and turgid like porridge slopping in a bowl. Though he gained a measure of redemption from these kindnesses, he was less trying to assuage guilt than to evade it. It seemed to him that he was suffering a peculiarly American form of guilt in that he did not want to be perceived as who he was, and thought that by disguising himself as a do-gooder, he might be able to confound whatever all-seeing moral eye governed the region.

Most of the streets in the barrio were narrow, one lane of potholed asphalt, and forked at odd angles between dilapidated four- and five-story buildings of whitewashed stone . . . old colonial-style dwellings with vented French doors opening onto ironwork balconies, and bands of faded blue and green painted along their bases like stratifications. It was the rainy season, and every day began with drizzles and ended in downpours. Swollen gray clouds passed so low overhead that their bellies appeared to be sagging between the roofs; and this, along with the extreme overhangs of the roofs, produced a claustrophobic effect, making it look that the buildings were leaning together, being pressed down by the heavy skies. Faint traffic noises could be heard from beyond the barricades, and occasionally a jeep would pass, bearing a clutch of Madradonas or Sotomayors. But there were no babies crying, no radios playing, no matrons leaning on the balcony railings to gossip with their neighbors. The apartments were empty, as were the little stores with murals on their pastel facades depicting disembodied shirts and hats, sparkling kitchen appliances, floating loaves of bread, and sewing machines the size of mastiffs.

One afternoon Mingolla ate his lunch on a stoop facing a store in whose windows and along whose aisles were arranged dozens of mirrors; ornate lettering on the facade proclaimed that within one could buy items of religious significance. He'd seen similar stores in Guatemala. Hotly lit windows thronged with golden crosses, gilt-framed Madonnas, Sacred Heart lockets . . . the gold flashing in the mirrors, brilliant images duplicated over and over, creating a dazzling maze of faith and nowhere for the eye to rest. But the only image held by these mirrors was that of his face: an infinity of gloomy young men, their expressions resigned, empty of conviction. The barrio had done this to him, he thought. Had planed away the extremes of his emotions, making him slow and dim like the members of the Sotomayor army who ranged the street, some moving hesitantly about, but most lying motionless in the drizzle that pocked the leaden puddles. Not far away, an old woman in a widow's shawl squatted by the curb and peed. Just beyond her, a haggard gray-skinned man walked with the gait of a somnambulist, stopping to touch a wall, to stare, then stumbling on. Their clothes were ripped and stiff with grime, their eyes dark and shapeless-looking like holes worn in rotted fabric. They were armed with clubs and knives and garden tools, and many bore wounds that had gone untreated. Little black receivers like drops of ebony were affixed to their ears, and it was through these that they received orders to fight or disengage. Gauzy shadows appeared to be collecting around them as if they were decomposing, adding their substance to the air. Mingolla wished he could puke, have some overwhelming reaction, but he only felt numb.

The woman sitting at his feet began to hum. A slovenly thirtyish plug of a woman, with heavy thighs and pendulous breasts and jaundiced skin. Clad in a dress that might once have been blue. After he'd finished working on her, she had told him her name was Irma and that she missed her babies.

"How ya doing, Irma?" he asked.

"I'm singing," she said, gazing off down the street. "Singing to my babies, putting them to sleep."

"That's good." He held out half his sandwich. "Hungry?"

She rocked an imaginary child in her arms, smiled and hummed.

It might not be so bad, Mingolla thought, to keep growing slower and slower like the people in the armies of the barrio, to wind up inhabiting shreds of memory. Lots of normal people were no different, and they seemed content.

"Pacito, Pacito," Irma crooned, and chucked the invisible baby under its chin. Faint Madonna smile lighting her doughy face.

Mingolla turned away, hollow with the sight, yet at the same time pleased that a human smoke still fumed inside Irma, that she had love to rely on . . . something he could no longer do wholeheartedly. He remembered one of his father's salesmen, an old earnest huckster with gray hair and a face like a rumpled dishrag. He'd played uncle to Mingolla, delighted in imparting to him anecdotes of his days on the road, the lore of insurance and selling. "First thing," he'd said once, "you give 'em the bad news. The premiums, the payment schedules. Then you work around to the benefits, just the ordinary stuff. They're not impressed. Fact is, they're disappointed. They were hoping for something better. So you let 'em stew a minute, and then you tell 'em. 'Now here's the beauty part.' " The salesman had been referring to some hidden investment potential, but to Mingolla his words had had the musty resonance of a universal constant, and he had taken from them a different meaning, a belief that the world—going on and on with its routine turn-ings, its unremarkable miseries and joys—could suddenly un-fold to reveal at its heart a luminous principle as full of serene significance as a Christmas star. Making love with Debora had always seemed to disclose this kind of beauty, but since arriv-ing in the barrio, though their lovemaking was as good as ever, too much else had changed for Mingolla to derive anything from it other than release. Debora had changed most of all. She was caught up in the process of the peace, passionate about it, and even her ordinary conversation smacked of an ingenuous idealism that dismayed Mingolla and caused him to look at her in a new light, to wonder how she could be such a fool. Like the night before, during a pause in lovemaking, lying on their sides, still joined.

. . . *it's funny* . . . she'd said.

. . . *what's that* . . .

. . . *I was thinking how I'd like to live with you, and what I decided I wanted was green places, green solitudes . . . green* . . .

The word *green* became a chord sounding in him, binding him to her, and for a split second he had a kinesthetic sense of her body and his, how she felt having him inside, the nerveless warmth and comfort of being filled.

. . . *edens,* she said. *Places without strangers, without rules, make our own rules, our own reasons* . . .

Her intensity made him aware of his own growing ambiva-lence, but he tried not to let it show.

. . . *why's that funny* . . .

. . . *I've always hated them, jungles, mountains . . . my father was always dragging us off into the wilderness . . . he loved it, loved the emptiness . . . and then after I got out of prison, I was in the jungles and mountains so much . . . I hated them . . . but with you, I want a clean place, a place no one else has ruined or touched* . . .

Troubled, wanting to shut her up, because everything she said was causing him to lose faith in her good sense, because how could she be so glad and hopeful in this terrible place, he moved inside her.

. . . David, oh God, David . . .

He clutched her ass with both hands, grinding against her, squeezing out feelings.

. . . I want you to come in me, David . . . now . . . but in my mouth, I want you in my mouth . . .

The words honed his arousal, and he thrust at her for a few seconds, then stopped, feeling distracted. Seams of light through the vents of the shutters, her skin gleaming palely in blurred stripes . . .

. . . what's wrong, David . . .

. . . tired, that's all . . .

. . . we can stop, it's all right . . .

. . . maybe . . .

. . . we'll make love in the morning . . . I want that, I want to walk out and feel you still warm inside me . . .

He held her as she drifted off, brushing the edges of her thought, their minds engaging like gears in a slow mesh, and he suddenly saw an expanse of smooth-grained golden wood, and had a sense of her personality, her anxiety and the calmness that underlay all her moods, and he heard a chirpy woman's voice gabbling about a customer she'd had to deal with, knew the woman to be his . . . or rather Debora's Aunt Juana, going a little senile now, and Debora was studying the grain of the wood, noticing how the flow crested into dark slivers like stylized waves, and looking up at the glassed-in shelves with their lumps of pre-Columbian pottery, and she wished Aunt Juana would be quiet, those same stories over and over, and if Juana kept it up, Papa would lose his temper, and then she'd have to spend all night soothing him, and she glanced at him, a heavy bulbous man, his impassive face not unlike the faces on the lumps of pottery . . . and then Mingolla was himself again, marveling at the contact, wondering at all his attempts to fathom her, because there she was, locked in her memory of another time, that mixture of poise and concern and naïveté that was the base compound of her soul, and beneath that, the frail inquiry tinged with hope that we, every one of us, are even before innocence begins. Then another memory, one so brief that he could retain only a sensation of agony and harsh radiance, and he was spinning in the stream of her memory, in a ruddy glow that was like the light of her blood coursing into the past, and memories were slipping by so quickly he could scarcely differentiate between them, and then the stream slowed, entering a region of dusky light, murky darks, dusty, ancient memories, creaky old things, and he had an image of yellowed lace veils, webs of memory lifting from brassbound chests and shaking loose dust that sang as it fell, the singing translating into a whining like the circuit of the blood, then into voices and visions and thoughts, and he was walking in a garden with a young man, the sun making an embroidery of shadow on the stones, and the duenna close behind, coy whispers and signals, and later the pain of a child being ripped loose, and later yet the heartsick perception of the sick old man a lover had become, and then a clangor of steel, shouts, the silver armor masking the horse's head gone pink from a rinse of blood bubbling from the slash on its neck, and the passage of memory speeding up again, voices and images blending into webs of golden light that wove an endless pattern, binding blood and time and history into a knot, a sexual twining. . . . Mingolla surfaced from this immersion feeling as if he had fallen a hundred floors and landed in feathers. He was sweating, his heart racing, and he was amazed to find that Debora was still asleep. He tried to put together the experience with the intimations of magical connectivity he'd had while working on Major Cabell; but he was reduced to supposition, to vague theorizing, and the only thing that seemed apparent was that the contact had spoken to the character of his relationship with Debora, that they were all flash and dazzle, and no real substance. . . .

Irma sighed, and Mingolla glanced up at her. She was leaning against the glass of the door; a Marlboro decal with the picture of a cowboy lighting up was stuck to the glass beside her mouth like a visual word balloon. Her arms cradling her dreamed-of child. She held up it for him to approve, and still thinking of Debora, seeing not the emptiness of Irma's arms but the memory they embraced, he said, "Yeah . . . nice-looking boy."

It rained every morning and every afternoon, and often during the night, and whenever it stopped raining, the heat would settle in; it seemed to have a presence, to be a huge transparent animal crouching in the streets and exhaling a foul warmth. Posters plastered to the walls of the buildings wilted at the corners and hung in scrolls; heat haze rippled above roofs and sidewalks, making it look as if the entire barrio were about to dematerialize. The surface of the asphalt melted into sludge; you could peel off rubbery hunks with your fingers. The armies floundered in humid air, the buzzing of their minds weak and intermittent like that of winter flies trapped between panes of glass. Sweat popped out in drops the size of pearl onions, and smiles were sharp and strained. Then the rain would begin again, diminishing the heat a fraction, spattering on the asphalt, drumming on the roofs, ticking the windows, and lying in bed at night, Mingolla could sense in its incessant rhythms the tension of an event taking shape. Something final and powerful. Whether good or evil, he didn't know and didn't care. He was under the spell of heavy life, heavy weather, and he had no interest in the eventual outcome, no interest in anything other than making it through each day.

They were quartered in a pension called the Casa Gamboa, a one-story building of pink stucco with an interior courtyard centered by a swimming pool whose water was so dirty that it looked like "a sector of jade amid the bright tiles." Macaws sat on perches under the overhang of the roof, cocking their eyes knowingly at passers-by and chuckling, and thick jungly vegetation grew in plots around the pool. Through a breezeway at the rear of the courtyard could be seen an old Oriental man in a wheelchair, who would sit most of the day beside a small garden and tie strips of paper to the stakes between the rows. The maid was a pretty dark woman named Serenita. All these things elements in the story *The Fictive Boarding House*. Mingolla was not surprised to learn he was living in Pastorín's (or Izaguirre's) story. He realized he had been living in it ever since Roatán, and that even the fact of his existence was to some extent a Sotomayor conceit. Indeed, he found it a comfort to be part of a fiction in that perceiving life this way tended to insulate him from the real, and when he was not working, he would spend his time in the room he shared with Debora. A large white room, much too large for its sparse furnishings of chair, table, bed, and dresser. The room was cooled by a creaky ceiling fan, and mounted on the wall beside the door was a cheap tin crucifix; a cord ran up behind the cross to the light fixture on the ceiling, giving the impression that Christ had some role to play in the transmission of the current. The figure was poorly rendered, its hands and feet disproportionately long, and its expression dyspeptic instead of soulful. Mingolla sympathized with the distorted spiritual values it embodied, and he held out hope that it would effect a miracle of a quality in keeping with its grotesque appearance.

On one occasion Debora dragged him out of the room to attend a negotiating session. She wanted him to see for himself that they were going well, and though he refused to accept this, there was no use in arguing the point. It was in her nature to cling to belief, to commitment, and he knew she would have to experience total disillusionment before giving up the idea of revolution, even one as horrific as this.

The sessions were held in a working-class restaurant with pale green walls and long tables and a glass case atop the counter containing crumbs and dead flies and crumpled wax paper. The negotiating teams consisted of five members of each family and a handful of psychics who had undergone the drug therapy. The psychics—there were thirty-one in the barrio all told—were hostile, suspicious, and neither Mingolla nor Debora succeeded in establishing a relationship with any of them; they were interested only in maintaining their relationships with various members of the families. The Sotomayors, however, were—with the exception of Ruy—gracious to a fault. They were all lanky, long-nosed, and homely . . . though their chief negotiator, a tall woman in her early thirties named Marina

Estil, had a severe hawkish beauty. She was quite tall, almost six feet, with sharp cheekbones and large eyes and black hair cut short to resemble a cowl. Her fingers were extremely thin and seemed paler than her hands. In her frankness about Sotomayor frailties, she impressed Mingolla as being someone whose concern for peacemaking outweighed the imperatives of the feud, and he came to put a modicum of trust in her.

"You have so much power, and so little interest in using it," she told him once. "But of course many of us have a problem with the way you *do* use it.

"Yeah?" he said. "How come?"

"Your devotion to the armies."

"It's not devotion. I just don't have anything better to do."

"Surely there's more to it than that."

"Maybe . . . it's not important."

"It is to us. What you're doing exacerbates our guilt. We have trouble enough bearing the weight of our sins without you reminding us of our greatest sin. Some of us take your work as an insult."

"That's tough."

She laughed. "I wonder if you understand the challenge you present to us."

"I think so."

"Oh, I doubt you can understand the extent of it. For instance, lately I've felt attracted to you. And I can trace the roots of the attraction not to propinquity or anything physical, but to your power."

He liked hearing that. Her honesty supported his impression that she was trying to control her twitches. And although he wasn't attracted to her, the thought of sex with her intrigued him in the way he'd once had the urge to reach into a cage at the Bronx Zoo and find out if the jaguar's paw was really as soft and furry as it appeared.

"Don't worry," she said. "I'm harmless."

"I'm not worried about *you*," he said. "Even if I were, you'd be low on my list."

Led by Marina, the Sotomayors arrived first at the restaurant and took seats along one side of the front table. The

Madradonas arrived five minutes later and sat across from them. They were as much a physical type as the Sotomayors: short and squat, with stolid chubby faces and luxuriant growths of black hair. Mingolla got the idea he was watching a debate between alien races. Stubby brown demons with blunt bone-crushing teeth, and pale snake-people with rubies in their skulls. The Madradonas possessed a brisk energy, their manner in sharp contrast to the diffidence of their rivals, and despite his reservations, he had the hope that their efficient shopkeeper mentality might offset the whimsy of the Sotomayors, and thus the peace would be achieved. But after an hour of talks an incident occurred that dashed his hopes.

The Sotomayors had proposed that the families remain in the background of world affairs and practice extremes of birth control in order to limit the possibility of genocidal tendencies; the Madradonas' position was not far removed from this, but the subject seemed to set them on edge and their replies grew terse and insulting. Finally a portly Madradona man with a crescental scar at the corner of his right eye stood and knocked over his chair.

"Paris, twenty years ago," he said. "You remember that, don't you?"

"There's no need of dragging that up, Onofrio," said Marina.

"Tell me how to forget it!" Onofrio balled his fists, rested them on the table, and leaned over Marina. "I remember it too damn well. I was looking out the window, listening to the baby in the next room. And Sara called to me. 'There's a package for you,' she said. 'A present, I think. Come see.' I'd just gone out in the hall when 'the present' exploded." He looked as if he were going to spit. "I won't have you bastards telling me when I can or can't have children. You've taken too many of our children as it is."

"And you haven't?" said Ruy. "What about Marina? Is her pain less than yours? Your uncle has a lot to answer for."

"My uncle had help," said Onofrio. "Remember, Ruy?"

"Stop it," Marina said. "This isn't . . ."

A Madradona woman jumped up and screeched at Ruy,

362

and the next second they were all on their feet, yelling, filling the air with accusations, listings of murders and rapes and betrayals. Mingolla started for the door.

"Don't leave," said Debora, catching up to him at the door. "They'll calm down. They always do."

Anxiety tightened her mouth, and he wanted to stay to please her; but the sound of the feud, the babbling and cursing, brought home to him the folly at work in the barrio, and he just shook his head.

She called after him. "David!"

He turned to her. "Look," he said. "You take care of this end, and I'll do what I have to. All right."

Doubt and disappointment contended in her face, and then without another word she wheeled around and went back inside.

Most of the armies kept to the center of the barrio, wandering aimlessly like herds of stupefied cattle, falling out when fatigue overwhelmed their restlessness. Strays, however, could be found in every quarter, and one afternoon Mingolla came across two of them on the steps of the palace that Juan Pastorín had built for the children of the poor. It was a futuristic dome of blue plastic alloy with the look of a gigantic cheap toy. Gold-colored doors. Clusters of needle towers spearing 150 feet above the parking lot that formed a black moat around it. The sunlight channeled shimmers along its surface, and as Mingolla approached it, the whole thing seemed to have the instability of a mirage. Curious to see the inside, he slipped through the doors into a dimly lit room half the size of a football field. The floor was fake gray flagstones, and the walls were unadorned. The dimples formed in the roof by the extrusion of the towers reminded Mingolla of the interior of a doll's body, the hollows of plastic arms and legs. He gave a shout, testing the echoes, and was about to leave, when a woman came out of a door in the far wall. Not a woman, he realized as she glided toward him. A robot painted and clothed to resemble a plump Victorian matron. Wearing a gown of stiff yellow fabric worked with a lacy design of black silk; hair netted in a bun; a prissy, daffy face with rouge spots dappling the cheeks. It was twice as wide and a head taller than Mingolla, and he retreated a few steps.

"The labyrinth is closed for repairs," it said in a fluting voice. Behind the waxy crystals of its eyes, camera lenses were swiveling. "Would you like to hear a story?"

"Not really," said Mingolla.

"I have stories for all ages. Mysteries, adventures, romances." The robot's whacky-looking eyes tracked back and forth. "I know . . . what about a love story?"

Mingolla's suspicions were roused; he wondered if someone who knew him was controlling the robot. "No thanks," he said.

"I wish you'd let me tell you one, anyway," said the robot. "I'm sure you'd enjoy it." It glided to the door, blocking the way out. "The only trouble is, love stories are so sad." It tipped its head to the side, looking at Mingolla, who became alarmed by the fixity of the stare.

"Lemme out," he said. "I don't wanna hear your damn stories."

"Oh, but you've never heard one like this. It's so sad, it'll make you happy. Did you know it's an established psychological fact that sad stories have exactly the opposite effect on a listener? It's true. You'll feel much better after you . . ."

"Goddammit!" said Mingolla. "Lemme out."

"I'm sorry . . . you can't leave without the rest of your group. Just you wait with me and listen, and soon your teacher will come to fetch you." The robot folded its arms and gazed at him benignly like a doting aunt. "Now, this particular story . . ."

A shout interrupted the robot, and an old man in a brown uniform and cap came hobbling across the hall. "What are you doing in here? We're closed."

"The labyrinth is closed for repairs," said the robot.

The old man snorted, touched a control on the robot's side that caused it to stiffen and fall silent. "They never finished the labyrinth. Never finished any of it. Just more of their foolishness." He was lean, pale, with long arms and legs, and sprigs of white hair poking from beneath his cap. It was the Sotomayor look, and though it made no sense that a Sotomayor would be serving as a caretaker, Mingolla asked if he was related.

"Used to be," said the old man.

"I don't understand."

The old man took off his cap, patted down his hair. "They stripped me. Said I'd betrayed them. And I suppose I did, though they've let greater betrayals pass. I hated them for it at first. But I came to see I was better off. What's power ever done but make them miserable." He peered at Mingolla, shook his head sadly. "Make you miserable, too."

"What do you mean they stripped you?"

"They gathered a threesome and skewered my brains. Stripped away my power. They said they were sorry afterward, but by then I was glad they'd done it. You've heard the saying 'power corrupts'?"

"Uh-huh."

"Well, it does worse than that, believe me. At least to them. It ennobles, makes them believe everything they do is right." The old man blew air through his lips like a horse. "They're loaded with noble intentions, but they're wrong all the time. They're monsters. You should know that, you're just like them."

Mingolla decided to change the subject. "Did Izaguirre build this place?"

"Izaguirre, Pastorín . . . whatever name Carlito's using." The old man made a noise of disgust. "Even as a child he was a madman. Took whatever he wanted and pretended it was the act of a saint no matter who was hurt."

"Tell me 'bout him."

"Just look around you. Look at this place, look at the barrio. Hah! Look at the others. They think they're in control, but they're only Carlito's pawns. Made in his image." The old man jammed his cap down over his eyes. "Best thing would be for you all to throw yourselves in the sea. Now go on, get out. We're closed."

"I just wanted to—"

"Get out, I say!" The old man gave him a push. "It depresses me to be around you." He shooed Mingolla off with a flapping of his bony hands and slammed the door behind him.

Mingolla blinked at the intense sunlight. The two men on the steps stirred like leaves in a soft wind. He felt less inclined to help them now, but it would at least pass some time. One of them—bearded, blond, wearing clothes that appeared to have been rolled in soot—was leaning against the doorframe. His face was abraded, the cuts crusted with grime; his hair was long and stringy, and though he was sitting in the shade, the pupils of his blue eyes had shrunk to pinpricks, as if he were living in some internal brilliance. Resting across his knees was a machete, its blade fretted with brown stains. The other man lay beside him, his face turned to the golden doors. Mingolla dropped to his knees, preparing to work; but as he met those blue eyes, as he noticed the petulant set of the man's mouth, the slight bulge of his brow, he was flooded by a feeling of despair.

"Gilbey?" he said, and then knowing it *was* Gilbey, he shook him. "It's Mingolla, man! Hey, Gilbey!"

Gilbey stared at his scabbed, broken knuckles.

Mingolla focused his power, trying to restore Gilbey's patterns, talking all the while, desperate to make that sullen punkish spirit burn high again. "C'mon, man," he said. "Remember the Farm . . . 'Frisco? You gotta remember 'Frisco." He was in a panic, like a kid fitting together the pieces of a valuable vase he'd broken.

After a few minutes, Gilbey responded. "Mingolla," he said wonderingly. "I . . ." He nudged the other man. "This here's Jack."

Jack grunted, knocked Gilbey's arm away.

Gilbey seemed to fade, then perked up again. "Know who this is?" he asked, tapping Jack's shoulder. "He's . . . he's famous. Hey, Jack! Wake up!"

Jack rolled over, eyes slitted against the sun. His face was partially obscured by a heavy black beard, but his features—cleverly made, foxy—looked familiar.

"He's famous," Gilbey repeated. "Tell him, Jack. Tell him who you are."

Jack rubbed his forehead with the heel of his hand. "Name's Jack," he said foggily.

"Naw, man!" said Gilbey. "The guy's . . . Shit! Tell him, Jack!"

"It doesn't matter," Mingolla said.

"I'm . . ." Jack squeezed the sides of his head as if trying to still his thoughts. "I'm a singer."

"Yeah, yeah!" said Gilbey. "That's it. You 'member, Mingolla. Prowler."

Mingolla stared in disbelief, saw Jack Lescaux's face melt up from the beard and dirt. "How'd you wind up here?"

Jack rolled back over to face the door.

"He ain't feelin' so hot," said Gilbey. "But it's him, ain't it?"

"Yeah, it's him." Mingolla stood, suddenly exhausted. "You come on back with me. I'll find ya a bunk at my place." He plucked the receiver from Gilbey's ear.

"I dunno," said Gilbey. "We gotta . . ."

"It's okay . . . I'll be responsible."

Gilbey plucked at Jack's shirt. "Let's go, man."

"Just leave him."

"I ain't leavin' him, man," said Gilbey, displaying a flash of his old contentiousness. "Me'n him are tight."

"All right." Mingolla set to work on Jack and soon had him standing. He was shorter than Mingolla had assumed from watching him on TV; his clothes were as filthy as Gilbey's, and he had a crowbar in his left hand. In their rags, leaning together, they looked like zombies at the end of their term. Dead men with blue eyes.

They shambled at Mingolla's heels across the parking lot and down an empty street lined with groceries and butcher shops and bakeries. Murals of cakes with halos of painted flavor, ice cream bars surrounded by exploding stars, bananas wreathed in music notes. Little coiled nests of human shit everywhere testified to the passage of the armies.

Gilbey picked up his pace, stumbled alongside Mingolla, searching his face. "What happened to you, man?" he asked.

"You mean back in 'Frisco?"

"Un-uh." Gilbey tripped, regained his balance. "What happened to you here." He tapped his forehead, very gently, as if afraid he might punch a hole.

"Bad drugs," said Mingolla. "War. Shit like that."

Gilbey nodded, his brow furrowed. "Same here," he said.

CHAPTER SIXTEEN

On a night not long after he had found Gilbey and Jack Lescaux, Mingolla was about to enter his room at the Casa Gamboa, when he heard Ruy's voice issuing from an open shutter. He flattened against the wall and peeked through the window. Ruy was standing at the foot of the bed, dressed in jeans and a black windbreaker; his hair was combed straight back, and the collar of the windbreaker was turned up, framing his face in such a way as to give it the austere nobility of a vampire.

"Leave me alone!" said Debora.

Mingolla couldn't see her, but the distaste in her voice was clear.

"I've been trying to," Ruy said. "But I can't."

"You have to," she said. "I don't love you . . . in fact, you're beginning to disgust me. Don't you have any self-respect?"

"Not where you're concerned." Ruy moved out of Mingolla's line of sight. "Don't you understand how he's stifling you, stunting you? God, you should be—"

"I'm not listening to this! Get out!"

"Debora, please."

"Get out!"

"For God's sake, Debora. Don't do this!" There was a catch in Ruy's voice. "If I could just touch you once . . . like a lover."

369

"I want you to leave right now."

"Sometimes," said Ruy, "sometimes I think if I could touch you just once, that would be all I needed . . . it would sustain me the rest of my life."

A pause, shuffling of footsteps.

"Are you saying that if I let you touch me, you'd leave me alone afterward?"

"I . . . I don't know. I . . ."

"Suppose I were to let you touch me," said Debora coldly. "Would you swear not to bother me again?"

"You shouldn't treat me like this," said Ruy. "I love you."

"Answer me."

"You'll let me touch you?"

"Only if you promise to leave me alone."

His anger growing, Mingolla went to the door.

"Please don't do this," said Ruy.

Another pause, and then Debora said, "I'll tell you what. You can touch me, touch my breast, if you swear you won't even talk to me for at least a week."

Mingolla put his hand on the doorknob.

Ruy was silent, and Debora said impatiently. "Well? Do you want to or not?"

"I . . . yes." Shame in the quaver of the words.

"All right," said Debora, and then: "No, I can't. The idea of you touching me . . . it's repulsive. Get out of here."

Mingolla opened the door, and Ruy spun around to face him.

Debora was standing in the bathroom door. "He was just going," she said calmly.

"That right, Ruy?" said Mingolla.

Ruy shot Debora a resentful glance, then stalked from the room.

"I was . . ." Debora began.

"I heard," said Mingolla.

"I was trying to degrade him," she said. "I thought if he could see what a fool he was acting, he'd leave me alone. I think it worked."

"It won't last," said Mingolla, throwing himself onto the bed. "The son of a bitch isn't going to quit."

"Maybe not . . . but I want to handle him myself. Please don't do anything foolish."

"How foolish am I allowed to be?"

She lay down beside him, flung an arm across his chest. "Please don't do anything. Promise me."

"Sooner or later he'll do something even if I don't."

"He might not, he might get over it."

"Depends how far you're willing to go. A quickie in some dark corner might diminish your air of unattainability."

She frowned and edged away. "You don't understand how hard it is having to fend him off. I know you don't think—"

"The thing is," he cut in, "I know you're capable of screwing him if you thought it'd save the goddamn revolution. Maybe that's the right attitude to take. Maybe we should all hop in the sack together and get rid of our frustrations."

She tensed, and he felt her anger thickening the air. Laughter from the courtyard. Relaxed, confident Sotomayor laughter.

"I'm sorry," he said. "It's not you, it's everything."

"Just be quiet," she said, turning to face the wall. "Let me alone."

"Okay," he said. "But only if you let me touch you."

Shortly after that he fell asleep with his clothes on, without making up. It had been a long time since he'd had a dream that he remembered, but that night he dreamed he was lying in a featureless void and straining to dream. At length he saw a dream approaching, a thin slice of vivid color and motion against the blackness. He awaited its arrival eagerly, but as it drew near he realized that the dream had come in the form of an enormous blade, and he awakened just in time to avoid being cut in half by it. He sat up in bed, frightened, wanting to be comforted, consoled. Debora was inches away, but half-believing that the dream had spoken to their irresolute condition, he doubted she could provide what he needed.

Two days after this, Mingolla broke into Ruy's room and stole his notebook filled with poems and meditations about Debora. The notebook, he had decided, would give him the tool with which he could defuse Ruy as a threat; and yet he was not altogether sure why he wanted to defuse him, because he did not perceive Ruy as a serious threat. It seemed to him a whimsical act, one predicated on a desire to recalibrate his emotions, a motive similar—he suspected—to that underlying Ruy's decision to pursue Debora. Seeing this resemblance to Sotomayor behavior in himself was alarming, but he was unable to deny the impulse.

The contents of the notebook made Mingolla envious. Ruy's observations on Debora's character were more detailed than his own, and though he chalked this up to the fact that Ruy had the advantage of distance, the rationalization failed to diminish his envy. A few of the passages were quite well written, and one in particular struck Mingolla with its intensity and sincerity.

. . . It's the thought of your beauty that makes me wake, sometimes, from the middle of dreams I can't remember, it's not the image of your face, the softness of your skin, but just the sudden awareness of beauty, that first strike before any of the details come clear, that jolts me hard into the world and leaves me broken on the shoals of my bed. For a moment I'm angry that you're not there, but then anger planes into longing, and I stand up, pace, and haunt the darkness of my bathroom, thinking of remedies. I see there's no reason for anger, no reason we should make the right choices, no reason we shouldn't ruin our lives . . . after all, our lives are ruined already, and what sense is there in denying the world that waits to transform us into lumps of pain and wizened hairless dolls, and why should we assign value to love or any emotion that menaces our conception of the expectable? And having agonized for an hour over all this, having explored hope and hopelessness, in the end it's the thought of your beauty that makes me lie back on the bed, heavy in the head, weighting me down so that I plummet through the edges of sleep and drown in the middle of dreams I won't remember.

This passage and others firmed Mingolla's resolve in that they caused him for the first time to see Ruy as a man; he was not inclined to see him that way, and so in order to reduce Ruy once again to the status of a characterless enemy, he took an irrevocable action against him.

Twice a week Marina Estil held what she called "group therapy" in her hotel. She had tried to persuade Mingolla to join in, but he had refused, not wanting to involve himself more than necessary in Sotomayor business. However, on the night after he stole the notebook, he went to the hotel for the purpose of attending one of these sessions. Marina's hotel was located three blocks from the Casa Gamboa and served as lodging for the leaders of the negotiating teams, both Sotomayor and Madradona. Mingolla arrived a half-hour early, and rather than standing around the lobby, he went into the lounge and sat down in front of a TV set that was hooked to a satellite dish on the roof. He asked the lounge's sole occupant—a young Madradona man—if he minded the TV being on, and then flipped through the channels until he came to one showing a line of plodding soldiers moving up a hillside under an overcast sky, and superimposed on this, shot in fiery letters, the legend: *William Corson's War Stories.* Corson had visited the Ant Farm during Mingolla's tour, and though Mingolla hadn't met him, by all reports he was a good guy. Baylor had done an interview with him, and when Mingolla had asked what sort of man the journalist was, Baylor had only said, "The guy gets high." Which had been Baylor's standard for acceptance. The credits rolled, and Corson strolled into view of the camera, the line of soldiers continuing uphill at his rear. He was bearded, tall, dressed in fatigues, with a hooked nose and fleshy lips; he looked, Mingolla thought, a little bit like a thinner, younger Fidel Castro.

"Behind me," Corson said, "you see members of the First Infantry heading toward the fighting north of Lake Izabal. Once they cross that hill they'll be in a hot zone, a zone that's been hot for nearly three years, a battle without resolution. That fact speaks to the character of the war. Battles flourish like hothouse plants in the midst of pacified territory with no apparent justification other than a command strategy that can be best described as cryptic. All wars have their character. World War

One was called the War to End War. World War Two was a righteous crusade against a legitimate madman. Vietnam has been countenanced as both an exercise in the demonic and as a gross political misjudgment. And this war . . . well, the poet Kieran Davies has pronounced it 'the vast sputtering signal of the Age of Impotence, the evil counterpart of topless tennis matches and fast food solutions to the nutritional problem.' Davies's imagery has a basis in . . .''

"Very sad," said a voice beside Mingolla.

The Madradona man had taken the adjoining chair. He was in his twenties, pudgy, smiling, wearing a red Coca-Cola T-shirt and chinos. "But soon," he went on, gesturing at the screen, "it will be all over, yes?"

Mingolla shrugged. "I guess."

"Oh, yes." The man patted his chest. "We will end it soon."

"Terrific."

"You are Meengolla, no?"

"Yeah."

"I am Chapo. Pleased to meet you." Chapo held out a hand, and reluctantly Mingolla shook it. "Where are you from in the United States?"

"New York."

"New York City? But this is wonderful! I am living a year in New York, in Green-witch Village."

"How 'bout that." Mingolla tried to get back into Corson's monologue, but Chapo was relentless.

"I love New York," he said. "I love especially the Mets. Such a wonderful team! Do you like the Mets?"

"No."

"The Yankees, then?"

Mingolla nodded.

"They are good, too," said Chapo with some condescension. "But I think the Mets are a little better."

Mingolla stared grimly at the TV.

"You are interested in this show?"

"Right."

"I'm so sorry. I will watch with you."

Corson had begun an interview with a crewcut kid younger than Mingolla, who was wearing an Air Cav patch on a nylon flight jacket. "Would you like to say anything to your parents . . . or your friends?" Corson asked him.

The kid wetted his lips, looked at the ground. "Naw, not really."

"Why not?"

"What's there to say?" The kid gestured at the soldiers, the jungle terrain. "Picture's worth a thousand words, right?" He turned back to Corson. "If they don't know what's goin' on, me tellin' 'em ain't gonna help."

"And what do you think is going on?"

"With the war? Fuckin' war's bullshit, man. This place'd be all right, wasn't for the war."

"You like Guatemala, then?"

"I dunno if I like it . . . it's weird, y'know. Kinda neat."

"What's neat about it?"

"Well . . ." The kid studied on it. "This one time, I hitched a ride to Réunion with these minitank guys . . . they were convoying oil trucks along the Petén Highway. So one of the trucks turns over in the middle of the jungle, oil spills all over the fuckin' place. Nothin' can move till the spill's cleared up. And alla sudden out of the weeds comes all these Fritos, man. They got little stoves and shit. They start cookin' food. Fritters and chicken and stuff. Selling pop and beer. Like they been knowin' this is gonna happen and they was just waitin' for us to show. And there was girls, too. They'd take ya into the weeds and do ya. They wasn't hard like the city girls. Sweet, y'know. It was 'bout the best time I had down here, and it was weird the way they was waitin'."

"You served in Guatemala, no?" Chapo asked.

This time Mingolla was glad for the interruption; the interview had made him feel that he was watching a depressing home movie.

"Yeah," he said. "Artillery."

"It must have been horrible," said Chapo, and made a doleful face.

"Wasn't great."

Chapo nodded, apparently at a loss for words. "Perhaps we can be friends," he said. "Perhaps you will come to visit me in my room. I live on the third floor."

Startled, Mingolla said, "Maybe . . . I don't know. I'm pretty busy."

"I would like it very much."

"We'll see."

On the screen, the kid was talking about his duty. "These choppers, man, they are fuckin' *fast*. You come in off the sea, you're so far out you can't see land, and then the land pops up, green mountains, cities, whatever, like one of those pop-up birthday cards. And then you're into the clouds. I'm talkin' 'bout hittin' at the guerrillas, now. Up in the mountains. So you're in the clouds, and when you unbutton your rockets, all you see is this pretty glow way down under the clouds. Like glowing marble, that's what it looks like. And the only way you can tell you done anything is that when you make a second pass, all those little hot targets on the thermal imager ain't there anymore. You don't feel nothin'. I mean . . . you do feel somethin', but it's different."

That was enough for Mingolla, who still felt the deaths he'd caused. He got up, and Chapo, too, stood.

"I hope I will see you again," Chapo said. "We can talk more about New York City."

Stupid blocky brown face. Earnest smile. Common clay of the Master Race. Chapo's ingenuousness—similar to that Mingolla had encountered in dozens of young Latin men—had sucked in him. Maybe it was for real, but Chapo was no less his enemy for all that.

"Not a fucking chance," said Mingolla, and walked out into the lobby.

Marina's bedroom was a touch more luxurious than those of the Casa Gamboa. Carpeted with a patchy shag rug. Wallpaper of a waterstained oriental design that might have been plum blossoms, but had worn away into a calligraphy of indefinite lines, with pale rectangles where pictures had once been hung. The bed was draped in a peach-colored satin spread that rippled in the light from a lamp on the night table. Seven Sotomayors, including Ruy, were seated on the bed and floor, and Marina, enthroned in an easy chair, led the discussion . . . less a discussion than a bout of fabulous confessions. Mingolla stood by the door, watching, listening. He had been disconcerted by Ruy's presence, but he was now considering changing his tactics and confronting Ruy with the notebook rather than sandbagging him.

"It was in April of the year," said one of the Sotomayors, a man named Aurelio, slightly older than yet strikingly similar to Ruy in appearance. "All that month I'd been feeling at loose ends. Even though I was involved in settling the Peruvian problem, my involvement wasn't enough to prevent idle thoughts, and my thoughts came to settle on Daria Ruiz de Madradona, the daughter of my father's murderer. She was also involved in the Peruvian operation, but that was not a factor in my decision."

As Aurelio described the process of plotting that had led to his abduction of Daria, he maintained a downcast expression as if he were revealing a matter of great shame; yet his tone grew exuberant, his description eloquent, and the others, though they sat quietly and attentive, seemed titillated, leaning forward, breathing rapidly. Especially Marina. She had on gray slacks and a silver-and-gray blouse imprinted with a design of black birds flying between stylized slants of rain. Crimson lipstick gave her mouth a predatory sexuality, and her cheekbones looked as if they were about to pierce her skin. With each of Aurelio's revelations, she appeared to sharpen, to become more intent and alive.

"I don't think," said Aurelio, "I've ever known myself as I did in that moment. My location in the world, in the moment. Certainly my senses had never been so clear. I took in every detail of the walls. The grain, the knotholes and wormtrails. All in an instant. I could hear the separate actions of the wind in the trees outside, and how it was flapping a piece of tarpaper on the roof. Daria was not a beautiful woman, yet she seemed unbelievably sensual. Fear drained from her face as she met my eyes, and I couldn't hate her any longer, because I knew that this moment was more than mere vengeance. It was drama. Ritual and destiny coming together. And knowing this, knowing

377

that she knew, there arose a kind of love between us . . . love such as arises between a victim and the one who is both torturer and bringer of mercy."

After Aurelio had finished, the group analyzed his story, dissected it in terms of its bearing upon Sotomayor psychology, all with an eye toward repressing their baser instincts; yet their dissection had the prim fraudulence of sinners who were justifying their wickedness and pretending to be sad. Other stories were told, and Mingolla—seeing in their gleeful descriptions, their delight over their violent traditions, and their penitent pose a perfect setting for his presentation—bided his time.

After an hour of this, Marina asked if he had any questions, and stepping to the center of the room, he said, "Sure do. They might annoy you, but I hope you'll answer them."

"We'll do our best," she said.

"From what I've heard tonight," he said, "and what I've heard before, it seems that a good many of your operations have been undermined by someone suddenly reestablishing the feud. And this usually happens at the last minute, right when success is at hand. Is that fair to say?"

One of the men started to object, but Marina interrupted, saying, "It's not unfair."

"What makes you think that won't happen here?"

"That's what we're trying to prevent," said Ruy haughtily.

"Right." Mingolla beamed at him, surprised to feel some fondness for him now that he had him in his grasp. "Anyway, there's a casualness to your operations that makes me nervous."

"What are you leading up to?" Marina asked.

He ignored the question. "Everybody except you has admitted to some sin. Don't you have anything to confess?"

"Marina is our exemplar," said Ruy with a measure of bitterness. "She's blameless in all this."

A smile carved a little red wound in the gaunt planes of her face. "Thank you, Ruy."

"You must have been affected by the feud in some way," said Mingolla. "At one of the negotiating sessions, Ruy mentioned something about your pain . . . something somebody's uncle had done to you."

"Yes? What about it?"

"I'd like to hear what happened."

"I don't see the point," she said coolly.

"There's something I want to say, but I want to be sure of everyone before I commit myself."

"Very well . . . but I trust it isn't just curiosity." She smoothed wrinkles from her slacks. "Some years ago I was married to a Madradona. . . ."

"I didn't know that ever happened," Mingolla said.

"It was an attempt at ending the feud," she said. "I balked at it, of course. I'd been living in Los Angeles, and I'd become rather a free spirit. Quite undisciplined. Perhaps it was my father's intention to check these tendencies, for the Madradonas are nothing if not disciplined." Laughter from the others. "Despite my attitudes, after the wedding I grew to respect and care for my husband . . . though I can't say I ever really loved him. But I had sufficient confidence in the marriage to become pregnant. Things were going well for us, but then one day an old lover of mine came to visit, purportedly to offer his congratulations on the baby. In the course of our conversation he drugged me and laid me out naked on the bed. It was his plan to have my husband return home and catch us in flagrante delicto. And so it happened. I was just waking from the drug when my husband entered. He and my lover got into a terrible fight, and though I was still groggy, I tried to intervene. I received a blow in the stomach, and as a result I not only lost the baby, but was unable to conceive another. Later I discovered that my lover hadn't been entirely to blame. My father-in-law had manipulated him with tales of my husband's cruelty to me. He'd never accepted the marriage, and I guess the prospect of a child was too much for him." She glanced up at Mingolla. "Will that do?"

"Sorry," he said. "It was important."

"Now what's this all about?"

He let his gaze swing around the room, lingering on Ruy, who was sitting on the bed. "I hear the negotiations are going well."

"Extremely well," said Aurelio. "So?"

"Would you say they're on the verge of success?" Mingolla asked. "Isn't this time frame the time of greatest risk, the time when someone is likely to loose it? To find some reason for blowing everything out of the water. Like with Tel Aviv."

"If you have something to tell us," said Marina, "I suggest you get on with it."

Mingolla took the notebook from his hip pocket, unfurled it, and saw Ruy stiffen. "Ruy knows what I'm talking 'bout . . . don'tcha?"

"Where did you get that?" Ruy asked.

"I thought so," said Marina, relaxing. "This has to do with Ruy's fixation on your girlfriend."

"It's more than that."

"I doubt it. I've seen this before. Ruy learned long ago that he can't indulge his fantasies."

"Give me that," said Ruy, coming to his feet and holding out a hand. "You had no right to take it."

"We're talking rights, are we?" Mingolla shoved him back down. "How 'bout the right to some privacy?"

The other Sotomayors looked to Ruy as if expecting him to retaliate, but he only sat there.

Mingolla passed the notebook to Marina. "See if you don't think this is evidence of something more than a fixation."

Two of the men read over her shoulder as she studied the notebook, turning the pages with a flick of her forefinger. "Oh, Ruy," she said after several minutes. "Not again."

"You don't understand," said Ruy. "You don't see how he . . . how he . . ." He stood, sputtering. "She can't bloom, she . . ."

"You're fucking ridiculous, y'know that, man?" said Mingolla.

Ruy sprang at him, but Mingolla sidestepped, grabbed his shirt, and flung him against the wall face-first. Ruy sagged to the floor. Blood from his mouth left a red snail track on the wallpaper. "See there?" said Mingolla. "Man's outta control."

"You aren't helping the situation by goading him," said Marina.

"I want you to see what he capable of," said Mingolla.

"It's not my fault he's the way he is, and if you don't think he's a threat . . . Hey! Let him go on with this shit. It won't be long before he does something really stupid."

Ruy groaned, rolled onto his back. Blood smeared his mouth and chin.

"What do you suggest we do?" Marina asked.

"I met an old guy at the palace the other day . . . the caretaker."

"Eusebio," she said. "We can't strip Ruy for something he *might* do."

"Then put him on notice. Seems to me the worst thing Ruy could imagine would be to lose his power."

He could see the idea working in her face, in all their faces. They liked the thought of punishment.

"Perhaps that is the best way," said Marina, and Mingolla thought he detected a deep satisfaction in her voice.

Ruy sat up, wiping his mouth with his sleeve. He gazed blearily at the others; he must have seen something in their faces, because he scrambled to his feet and made for the door. One of the men blocked his path.

"You can't listen to him!" said Ruy, flicking his hand toward Mingolla. "He's not one of us."

"Be quiet," said Marina.

"You can't do this," he said. "Not just on his word."

"We have your word, Ruy." She held up the notebook, and Ruy looked away.

"Carlito won't let you," he said weakly.

"We're not going to do anything," she said. "Not yet. But if anything happens to Debora or David, you'll be held accountable. And not even Carlito will be able to help you then."

Ruy stared hatefully at Mingolla.

"You been a bad boy, Ruy," Mingolla said, and grinned.

"I don't want you talking to either of them without my permission," said Marina. "Is that clear?"

"That's hard to avoid," said Ruy. "I live in the same building, and I'm bound to run into them."

"Move," she said. "Move tonight. You can move in here,

Ruy. You used to tell me how much you liked being near me. Now you have your wish."

Ruy looked stricken. "I'm going to talk to Carlito about this. Right now. He's not going to be happy."

Marina turned to Mingolla. "Would you mind leaving us, David. Ruy apparently needs proof of our seriousness."

"What you gonna do to him?"

"Give him a taste of what he's risking."

"No!" Ruy shouted it, wrestled with the doorknob, and was thrown back by two of the men.

"Please, David." Marina gestured toward the door, and Mingolla crossed to it, taking pains to avoid Ruy's eyes. "Oh, David!" Marina called as he went out into the hall.

"Yes?"

Her smile was the gracious smile of a hostess acknowledging the departure of a favored guest. "Thank you so much for bringing this to our attention."

CHAPTER SEVENTEEN

Gilbey's friendship with Jack Lescaux gave Mingolla hope that he might restore Gilbey completely: friendship was such a human thing and so untypical of the armies. He was strong enough to effect this; he could feel strength like a heavy stone inside his head, wanting to explode, to exert itself upon some target. But he must not have had sufficient knowledge. Even had he been stronger and more knowledgeable, he doubted he would have been able to do anything for Jack. Most of the time Jack was barely capable of movement, and on the one occasion that Mingolla succeeded in getting him to talk at length, an afternoon they spent on the steps of the palace, it made him very unhappy. Mingolla asked how he had become involved with the families, and he replied, "It was somethin' in the music they wanted . . . somethin' they made me do." Mingolla assumed Jack had been forced to inject subliminals into his recordings, perhaps ones that would appeal to psychics; but the particulars didn't interest him. If he were to try and root out every Sotomayor game, he would have time for little else.

Jack hummed, broke off, then rocked back and forth, smacking a hand against his thigh as if trying to recapture a rhythm. "Wish I had a billion dollars," he sang. "I'd buy myself . . ." He made a fist, pressed it to his head. "I got a little of it," he said. "Little bit."

"Let's hear 'er, Jack," said Gilbey.

Jack, a stressed look on his face, sang out again.

"Wish I had a billion dollars, I'd buy myself an armory.
I'd deploy my men, get high and then I'd fuck with
                                                    history.
I'd build a palace out of skulls, eat steak, screw beauty
                                                    queens,
And every other week I'd go on nationwide TV,
and make a speech entitled 'That's What America Means
                                        To Me . . .' "

He faltered, appearing worried. "There's more. I . . . I
can't get it."
"Take your time, man," said Mingolla.
After a minute, Jack sang some more.

"Wish I had my own religion, I'd be a brand new kind of
god. I'd burn down all the churches and give Las Vegas to
the poor . . ."

Again he faltered, and Mingolla boosted his good feeling,
started him singing a third time, but singing a different song,
softer, almost chanted.

> "Angel, angel, are you receiving,
> won't you try to answer me?
> Has my signal grown weaker than moonlight,
> does this transmission convey my grief?
> We are lost in wars and silence,
> dark November colors all our lives,
> strangers pass by without speaking
> of the important sadness in their eyes.
> Many of us have taken refuge
>   in religion or in lies,
> But I know we can't last much longer
> without the truth that only you supply.
>
> Angel, angel, it's getting darker,
> the wind is bringing shocks and flowers,

and black ice forms beneath my nails.
I never meant my heart to matter,
especially to a girl like you,
I swear I'll fix all that I've broken
if you'll only answer me.
Angel, angel, are you in Heaven,
or are you in prison, longing to be free,
huddled for warmth, afraid of breathing,
too weak to press the transmit key . . ."

"There's more," he said. "Lot's more."

"Y'should write it down, man," said Gilbey, pretending to write with the point of his machete. "Get some paper, and write it down."

"Yeah, okay," said Jack, scratching his head, and then burst into tears.

Mingolla put far more effort into Gilbey. Once, thinking a sexual experience might enhance his work, he dug up a woman for him, primed her with horniness, and staked her out in one of the empty buildings, a room with depressions in carpets of gray dust that testified to the long-ago presence of chairs and tables. The woman was pudgy, worn-looking, and Gilbey said, "She's a fuckin' beast, man. I dunno 'bout this."

The woman smiled and jerked her hips in invitation.

"Well," said Gilbey. "I guess she got okay tits."

Mingolla left them alone, and when he returned he found them both asleep, Gilbey's hand resting in proprietary fashion on her hip. He wasn't sure anything had happened, but afterward Gilbey did seem more his old self.

That same evening they walked out behind the palace, a spot from which they could see the barricade: a long flimsy wall of planks nailed into a gapped barrier ten feet high, with two guardhouses of equally crude construction behind it. Like kid's clubhouses. A dirt road led across a grassy meadow from the barricade toward green hills in the distance, and Mingolla imagined stealing a jeep, ramming through the wall, and heading up into those hills. It was a pleasant fantasy, but he knew Debora would never go along with it. And anyway, it was likely they'd be killed in the process.

Jack curled up in the dust, and Mingolla and Gilbey sat on the rear steps of the palace. Mingolla could make out riflemen pacing behind the barricade. Twilight had thickened to dusk, and a scatter of stars picked out the slate-colored sky. The windows of the buildings set away from the palace showed black and unreflective, rectangles of obsidian set into palely glowing stone; the breeze drifted scraps of cellophane along the asphalt, and a scrawny cat with scabs dotting its marmalade coat came prowling past and stopped to regard them with cold curiosity.

Gilbey had stumbled across a splintered baseball bat, one that had probably been used as a weapon, and he was turning it in his hands. "Be neat, y'know," he said.

"What?" Mingolla was watching the shadowy figures of the riflemen.

Gilbey was silent for such a long time that Mingolla wondered if he had lost his train of thought. "Get up a game," he said at last. "Be neat to get up a game. Think we could."

"A baseball game?"

"Yeah, we could get some guys." He stared at the bat, gave it a tentative swing.

The idea of Gilbey with his dulled reflexes playing baseball depressed Mingolla. He pictured the ratty blond hair sheared away, the grime washed from the cheeks, the expression firmed into one of sour indulgence. But it didn't work. The old Gilbey was dead, and the new Gilbey was moribund.

"We could, uh . . . we could . . ." Gilbey waggled the bat. "What's wrong with me, man? Somethin's fucked-up wrong, ain't it?"

"How ya figure?"

"With me . . . wrong with me. And you're tryin' to fix it."

"Yeah," said Mingolla. "Somethin's wrong."

"Can ya fix it?"

Mingolla didn't feel like lying. "I don't think so."

Jack stirred in a dream, muttered, and Gilbey let out a thready sigh. "I couldn't play too good, anyhow," he said, the words coming slowly, one at a time, like dollops of thick syrup. "Be okay to try, though. I could maybe play right field. Nobody ever hits one out there." He tapped the head of the bat against the asphalt. "Be okay, y'know. Right field's not so bad . . . y'can see a lot from right field."

Mingolla drew up his knees, rested his forehead on them, and closed his eyes, wishing he could shut himself down.

"I used to play second . . . Babe Ruth League. That's a tough league, man. 'Specially in Detroit. Them niggers come in all spikes and bad grins to second base, y'know." He put the bat on his shoulder, setting himself for an imaginary pitch. "Jack's worse off than me, huh?"

"He's not so hot."

"He could just watch, then . . . or sleep. He likes sleepin'."

What would really be neat, Mingolla thought, would be to take a gun and line up the Madradonas and Sotomayors in a row. Shoot them from the legs up, kill them a piece at a time. Or trigger whatever attack Izaguirre had planned in case the talks failed: Mingolla realized he had been hoping the talks would fail, that they would glance up one day at the whistle of an incoming rocket.

"I could probably still hit a little," said Gilbey.

"Let's talk about it later, okay?" said Mingolla. His heart felt lumpy, made of something disgusting and oily like lard.

"Sure, it's awright. Sure."

The stars had brightened, the sky gone cobalt. Somebody at the barricade switched on a spotlight; a shining sword of light dazzled the windows of the empty buildings, swung above their heads.

"Mingolla?"

"Whatcha need?"

" 'Member Baylor? What happened to Baylor?"

"He went Stateside."

"Stateside." Gilbey said the word several times as if by repetition he could comprehend it. " 'Member all them books he used to read? That science stuff?"

"Science fiction."

"Yeah, science fiction." He appeared to be considering the term. "They was dumb, y'know, them books."

"Uh-huh."

" 'Cept for one. I read this one was pretty good."

The spotlight swept back over them; the cat scampered for cover, and Jack rolled onto his side away from the glare.

"Yeah, there was this one," Gilbey said. "I got into it."

"Which one's that?"

"It's 'bout this alien. There's only one of 'em . . . I mean there's more'n one of 'em somewhere, maybe, but far as we know there's only this one we found. And it don't look like much. Kinda looks like this big brown rock, 'cept the surface of the rock is alla time movin', shiftin', and that's cause it's so fulla thoughts, the thoughts is pushin' against its skin, y'know, makin' it change shape a little."

Out of boredom Mingolla had read most of Baylor's books, and this one didn't sound familiar. "So what happens?"

"Nothin' much," said Gilbey. "See, the thing is they wanna find out what the alien's thinkin', 'cause they found him driftin' 'round out in space, and they figure he's been 'bout everywhere, and they wanna see what it's like where he's been. So they look for somebody who can read his thoughts, but nobody can 'cause his thoughts are sharp, man! They hurt. It makes ya scream to feel his thoughts. But, anyway . . ."

Gilbey faded, and Mingolla rekindled him.

"So did they find somebody?" Mingolla asked.

"Huh?"

"Somebody to read the alien's thoughts."

"Oh, yeah . . . yeah, they found this one guy who could stand the pain. And so he squats down beside the alien, touches him, y'know, and soon he realizes the alien's thoughts ain't nothin' but memories shiftin' 'round under his skin. Memories of every place in the universe, every place that ever was. This guy, now, he's tough, but even so, man, he can't take it for very long, and he can only stick with the alien a coupla minutes, long 'nough to get this one memory. After that he can't deal with the alien no more, 'cause his . . . his . . . his tolerance, that's it, his tolerance is all wore out. But he's got this one memory, and that's pretty good."

"What was it . . . the memory?"

"It's 'bout these people that live out on the edge of the galaxy, and when they die their bodies is stored on these big black ships that float 'round out in space, and once every while a captain comes on board each of the ships and starts flyin' 'em toward the center of the universe, to this place where the stars is so thick there's light all over. Big ol' suns, man! Burnin' every color, fuzzy-lookin' like Japanese lanterns. The light from 'em kinda overlaps, y'know. Makes prisms and all. Energy's flowin' from everywhere. And the alien ain't clear why this happens, why the bodies is shipped there. It ain't 'cause alla energy and light gets 'em reborn or nothin'. It just does somethin' to the bodies, maybe changes them into somethin' that gets used again or somethin' . . . I dunno. But whatever, it's a hard trip. Real hard. Mostly it's hard 'cause it's so bright, and the closer ya get to the center, the brighter it is. And it's slow . . . the light slows things down. It's so bright, it's almost solid, the air out there, y'know. And the captains, as the voyage goes along, the less they see. They goin' blind from the light. Their eyes get like crystals, hard and shiny and busted-looking. And if they was by themselves, they wouldn't be able to steer. But each of 'em's gotta woman 'long with 'em, and as they come closer and closer to the center of the universe, the women they're gettin' more 'n' more beautiful. And the captains, they so tight with these women, they love 'em so much, it don't matter none they blind, they can still see the women. The women they so beautiful, blind men can see 'em, and that's how they steer, by keepin' their eyes on the women, by watchin' how beautiful they get, and what way they beautiful, and from that they can always tell where they are, what part of the center they travelin' through. And in the end that's how they come safe back to home."

Mingolla had been trying to recall the book, but when the story broke off at this inconclusive point, he realized it must have been something of Gilbey's own invention. It pleased him that his work with Gilbey had unearthed the story, for it substantiated his belief that Gilbey had always been hiding his intellect; but he was also saddened, because he had the feeling that the story was a core myth, a jewel Gilbey had been hoarding, and his having yielded it up now seemed a bad sign.

"You made that up, didn'tcha, man?" he said.

LUCIUS SHEPARD

"Naw, uh-uh." Gilbey ran a hand along the cylinder of the baseball bat. "I read it somewheres."

But in his face was sly delight, and Mingolla knew he was lying. "C'mon, man! You musta made that up."

"You liked it, huh?"

"Yeah, it was good. How'd ya come up with it?"

"Wasn't me, man."

"Well, it was pretty goddamn good . . . good story."

Looking pleased, Gilbey shook Jack and said, "Wake up, man. Hey, Jack! Wake up."

Jack rolled over, blinked, his face a map of fatigue and befuddlement.

"I wanna tell ya this thing," said Gilbey eagerly. "It's like . . ." His eagerness evaporated, and he gazed off toward the barricade. "Goddammit, man! Ya missed it." Then he added in a tone of pride, "I 'membered this really cool thing."

Mingolla had never questioned the existence of the old Oriental man in the wheelchair until he disappeared. Every previous morning, he had sat beside his garden, fiddling with his strips of paper, his back to the courtyard. But on this particular morning he was nowhere to be seen, and the maid Serenita informed Mingolla that he had been taken to the hospital. Disconcerted, Mingolla went to stand by the plot and was surprised to see that the garden had long since gone to seed, implying that the old man's conscientiousness had been either a product of senility or mind control. But this wasn't the thing that troubled Mingolla. He had been interested in the old man, had always intended to speak to him, and the fact that he hadn't brought home the verity that this was how it went with other people: you had intentions toward them, imagined yourself developing relationships, fulfilling certain goals, and—as if intent were all that mattered, as if the function of other people were merely to provide a sort of inadequate moral tinder—you never realized any of them. Like with Tully, for instance. He kept thinking that they were going to grow close, but they had both been too busy to spare time for each other, he with his fraudulent acts of kindness and Tully with Corazon; the sense of

390

imminent closeness had been sufficient to make him believe that they were satisfying the requirements of the bond of experience between them. It occurred to Mingolla that his father had been right about war, that it had, indeed, made a man out of him. He could see intricacies that he had never before suspected, he understood the nature of his responsibilities and felt able to handle them. But the problem was that he had not become a very nice man. Not even average. His capacity for violence and indifference bore that out.

The garden was small, about twelve by twelve, the dirt crumbly and pale brown, interwoven by crispy tomato vines, lumped by shriveled melons and the husks of dried squash. Wanting to feel dirt under his feet, Mingolla kicked off his shoes and stepped over the retaining wires. Clods broke apart between his toes, vines snagged his ankles, pebbles bruised his soles. He stood at the center of the garden, looking up at the white globe of the sun veiled by frays of gray cloud, and felt—as if the garden were a plot of free land—that from this vantage he could see the twisted processes of history that had brought the world to this moment: the invasions, the mercenaries, the manipulations of the United Fruit Company, the blundering American do-gooder, the development bankers and their evil puppets, the vast unprincipled sprawl of business interests. All that on one hand, and on the other, the bizarre tapestry of murder and revenge fabricated by the two families, a Borgialike progression of poisonings, stabbings, explosions, and kidnappings that spread across the centuries, enacting its bloody scenarios in mansions and poverty-stricken villages and on battlefields. And these two vines of history grappling, twining, crowding out every other growth, leaching the earth, reducing it to an arid garden in which nothing would grow except an old man's fantasies.

"David! Where are you?" Debora's voice calling from the courtyard. She came running through the breezeway. Behind her, Sotomayors and Madradonas were gathered at the entrance to the pension, shaking hands and talking. "David," she said. "It's over. We've done it!"

He was unable to break himself out of his shell of gloomy speculation and stood waiting for her to continue.

"Peace," she said. "There's going to be peace."

Her face looked like peace. A beautiful, dusky, smiling Third World peace. But he couldn't relate. "Good," he said, stepping out of the garden. He sat on the tiled walk, began putting on his shoes.

"Don't you understand?" Her smile had faded. "The negotiations are over. The treaty's going to be drawn up tonight and signed tomorrow at the party."

"A party?" That, he thought, would be an appropriate absurdity.

"Yes, there's going to be a celebration at the palace."

"Swell."

She frowned. "You act like nothing's happened."

"Look . . ." he began. "Never mind."

Her face softened, and she knelt beside him. "I know you haven't had much faith in all this, but it really has worked. You haven't seen how hard these people have been trying."

"Hope so."

She drew back from him as if needing a new perspective. "Do you? Sometimes I think you hope just the opposite, though I can't understand why."

He felt distracted, disinterested. Her words seemed parental in their reflex and cautionary morality.

She slipped an arm around his shoulders. "You've been working too hard. But you'll see. Come with me. Talk to everybody. That'll make you feel better."

He was torn between the urge to convince her of a sober truth and the hope that she would remain happy. But deciding that a moment's peace was better than nothing, he let her lead him out into the congratulatory melee of the courtyard.

That night, an overcast night with a few stars showing between glowing strips of cloud, he fell into a conversation with Tully outside the pension. Gilbey and Jack were sitting by a potted fern in the entranceway, and Tully was standing with Mingolla about a dozen feet away, talking about Corazon.

"Sometime I t'ink she gonna drop de act," he said. "But den de nex' minute, she go inside herself again and I can't touch her. Damn, I'm gettin' used to it . . . used to bein' wit' a woman dat frown when she feel a smile comin' on."

"Maybe she'll still come around." Mingolla looked back into the courtyard, where, illuminated by spills of light from the windows, three Sotomayors were sitting and chatting in aluminum chairs by the pool.

"I guess it ain't 'portant whether she do or she don't," said Tully. "I be fah her even if she start t'rowin' t'ings at me." He sucked at his teeth and pointed at the Sotomayors. "What you be t'inkin' 'bout dis shit, Davy?"

"Tell ya the truth, I haven't thought much about it at all." He studied the Sotomayors, taking the measure of their languid gestures. "Debora seems convinced that everything's great."

"Dat don't tell me what you feelin'."

Mingolla let the question penetrate. "I guess I figure they'll screw things up somehow. But there's nothing I can do 'bout it."

"Yeah, dat's my feelin'." Tully scuffed the sidewalk. "You still got dat map I give you?"

"Uh-huh."

"You hang on to it, y'hear?"

"You thinking 'bout running?"

"All de time, mon. All de time." Tully stretched his arms overhead, his elbow joints popping. "Dis de kind of night it be good to have a drink or two."

"I gotta bottle."

"Dat's not my meanin'," said Tully. "I'm wantin' some riot." He clapped Mingolla on the back. "Like dem nights over in Coxxen Hole. 'Member dem?"

"Sure do," said Mingolla. "That was all right."

"Better dan all right." Tully made a disgusted noise. "Dat's how I know dis barrio ain't got no future. Dere ain't no riot, no livin' wild. De place dead already. Y'can't make peace in a graveyard and 'spect anyt'ing good to come of it." He cast a sad eye on Jack and Gilbey. "How de fuck I ever wind up here?"

"Beats me," said Mingolla. "I used to hate Roatán, but it'd sure look good to me now."

"Yeah, dat little island not so bad." Tully kicked a loose pebble on the concrete. "Ain't it fuckin' strange, Davy. How you start out wantin' to rule the worl', and in de end all you wanna do is hide from it?"

Mingolla had the impulse to open up to Tully about all his conflicting emotions, his regrets, but couldn't find the words.

"Look like you 'bout to choke on somethin', mon."

"I was just thinking about intentions."

"Intentions? What 'bout 'em?"

"Seems to me that if something gets to be an intention, that's a guarantee it's not going to get to be any more than that."

"What you talkin' 'bout?"

"Just bullshit, man. I'm all fucked up."

"Well, you ain't alone in dat."

They talked some more, but said little, and when Tully headed back to his hotel, Mingolla—followed by Jack and Gilbey—went back into the courtyard. The Sotomayors had vacated the pool area, and Mingolla sat in one of the chairs. Gilbey and Jack settled on the tiles nearby. The murky water in the pool shimmered with light from the windows along the courtyard, and watching the play of the ripples, Mingolla recalled the story in which it had been featured, described as "a sector of jade." The story had told how each afternoon the local newsboys would come running into the pension after selling their papers and dive in, vanishing beneath the surface, and the author had imagined them plunging down through moss and kelplike growths to some mysterious country. Feeling desolate, disoriented, Mingolla pretended his gaze had penetrated the depths and was carving a tunnel through the water, and after a second his pretense manufactured a reality, a future he was becoming less and less able to deny. He was standing in a dimly lit room furnished with leather chairs and glassed-in bookcases and an antique globe and a massive Spanish-colonial-style desk. The walls were of a grainy dark wood, and the rug was midnight blue emblazoned with tiny stars, making it seem you were having an audience in the vault of heaven with its chief magistrate, Dr. Izaguirre, who sat at the desk, astonished, his gray goatee waggling as he said, "We thought you were dead."

Through the picture window behind Izaguirre, Mingolla could see the desert glowing luminous white beneath a half-moon, and on the horizon a seam of infernal red brilliance that he knew were the lights of Love City, where soon—after taking an overdose of the drug that had funded this entire bit of history, taking it out of despair, out of the hope that it would bring him a vision of some tolerable future—he would wander in a delirium. And despite knowing the result of the overdose, he would go through with it, because even certain knowledge could not defuse his hope.

Izaguirre slipped one hand beneath the desk, and Mingolla said, "The alarm's been cut, Carlito. And they're all dead out there."

"Except for upstairs," said Debora bitterly, moving up next to him. "They're alive upstairs . . . at least they're breathing."

Izaguirre was wilting under their stares, his waxy skin losing its tone, his flesh appearing to sag off the bone. "What are you planning to do?"

"It's already been done," said Debora. "Almost all of it, anyway."

"What are you saying?"

"All but three of you have been eliminated," said Mingolla. "The three in the Pentagon. And we're going to let you take care of 'em for us."

"That's impossible! Only yesterday I was talking . . ."

"That was yesterday," said Mingolla.

"I'm going upstairs," said Debora. "Maybe some of them are salvageable."

"Don't injure them," said Izaguirre.

"Injure them?" Debora laughed. "I've been fixing your broken toys for five years . . . all that had enough left to fix." She turned to Mingolla. "Can you handle him?"

"Yeah . . . go on."

"What will you do with me?" Izaguirre asked as Debora closed the door behind her.

"You can figure it out, Carlito. Strip you down to nothing,

then put you back together. You'll be a time bomb like Nate and the rest. You'll be almost alive like your friends upstairs."

"You killed them all . . . all but three?" Izaguirre seemed unable to absorb it.

"It wasn't even a challenge. We've learned a lot the last five years." Five black coffin-shaped years, each filled with the ashes of violence and betrayal.

"If only three are left," said Izaguirre haltingly, "then there's no need to . . ."

"You know I'm not going to listen to this."

Izaguirre straightened, composed his features. "No, I suppose not." His Adam's apple worked. "All the work . . ." He passed a hand across his brow. "What will you do afterward?"

"There's nothing left to do."

"Oh, you'll find something. You've become like us, and you'll have to do something." There was a note of triumph in Izaguirre's voice.

"I'm going to put you to sleep now," Mingolla said.

Izaguirre opened his mouth, but didn't speak for a long moment. "God," he said finally. "How could this happen?"

"Could be you wanted it this way. Like your story about the boarding house . . . it ends with the death of the author. This ending's got your style, Carlito."

"I'm . . . uh . . ." Izaguirre swallowed again. "I'm afraid. I didn't think I'd be afraid."

Mingolla had often imagined how he would feel at this moment, and he was surprised to feel very little, mostly relief; he had the idea that despite Izaguirre's fear, the old man felt much the same.

"Isn't there anything I can do?" Izaguirre asked. "I could . . ."

"No," said Mingolla, and started to make him drowsy. Izaguirre half-stood, then dropped back into the chair. He tried to rouse himself, shaking his head and gripping the edge of the desk. A look of panic crossed his face. He sagged in the chair. His eyes widened, focused on Mingolla. "Please." The word came thickly like a final drop squeezed from him, and his head lolled back. His chest rose and fell in the rhythms of sleep, and his eyelids twitched.

Everything in the room—the whine of the air-conditioning, the gleams on the antique furniture, the false night of the rug— seemed to have grown sharper, as if Izaguirre's wakefulness had been a dulling agent. The hard clarity of the moment made Mingolla uneasy, and he spun around, certain that some trap had been sprung behind him. But there was only the closed door, the silence. He turned back to Izaguirre. The old man struck him now as a kind of monument, a sad misguided monster trapped in a tar pit, a repository of history, and he realized how little he knew about the families, that most of his knowledge was factual, fleshed out by sketchy impressions. He perched on the desk, engaged Izaguirre's sleeping mind, and went flowing down the ornate corridors of the blood past the memories of his life and into the memories of other lives, the years igniting and fading like quick candles, and he was the boy Damaso Andrade de Sotomayor on the day of his majority, standing in the gloomy main hall of the old house in Panama. All the family was there, silent in their ebony chairs, the arms carved into serpent's heads, letting their thoughts blend in the dream, and he could feel the drug in his belly, a distant ache, and he knew the dream as voices, thousands of them speaking at once, not in words but in a wordless whisper that was the soul of the passion. The pale figures of his parents and cousins and uncle and aunts began to flicker like white flames in cups of black wood, and he, too, was flickering, his flesh becoming insubstantial, and the dream firing his thoughts with the joy of vengeance and power. And when the dreaming was done, when he was strong and steeped in the passion, it was his time to travel the path of truth, and without a word he went down the stairs into the labyrinth beneath the house, into the lightless corridors that led to the seven windows, toward the one window that would show him his place in the pattern. He walked for hours, afraid that he would never find his window, that he would be lost forever in the chill, clammy depths. But the stones of the wall, mossy and rough, were friends, and touching them he felt the energies of the past guiding him into the future, which was only the pattern of the blood extending forever. They were ancestral stones, as much of his blood as his family, and their domed shapes had the familiar textures of the Sotomayor skulls in his father's library, and from them he derived a sense of direction and grew able to choose turnings that had the feel of the blood knot. And when he came at last to his window, he did not see it but apprehended it as a tingling on his skin. He thought this strange. Shouldn't a window admit light . . . and then he saw light. Two crimson ovals like pupilless eyes that burned brighter and brighter as he approached. The window, he realized, was made of smoked glass, the sections fitted together with lead mullions into the image of a coal-black man wearing a crown of thorns, the eyes left vacant so as to allow the light of the setting sun to penetrate. The image fright- ened him, but he was drawn to it, and he pressed against the glass, fitting his eyes to those empty ovals, and across the valley he saw the blocky stone house of the Madradonas, looking monstrous in the sanguine light, appearing to be crouched, preparing to spring. He had seen the house many times, but this view affected him as had none other. Rage choked him, and he came to feel at one with the black burning-eyed figure against which he stood. The network of lead mullions seemed to corre- spond to the weavings of his nerves, to channel the bloody color of the west along them, filling him with a fierce intent, sealing the image of the ebony Christ inside him, and he knew that of all the children of his generation, he had been chosen to lead the rest against the Madradonas, that he was the arrow notched to the family bow, and that his entire life would be a flight toward the heart of that dark beast hunched and brooding on the far hill.

Mingolla broke contact and got up from the desk, went to the window. Pressed his forehead against the pane. The glass was cool and transmitted the vibration of the air-conditioner. He looked off at the distant city lights, thinking about the Christian girl, the holograph of Jesus walking around on her hand. It had always seemed that beyond that moment lay a beginning, but he had never been able to know it, to make it clear. Probably, he thought, it was just another glimmer of hope. Izaguirre stirred in his chair, and Mingolla realized he was delaying the inevitable. It wasn't that he was troubled by what he had to do; he was simply weary of the procedure, of exposing himself over and over to the bad news about the human condition implicit in the fact that you could strip the mind to zero. He'd wait a few minutes more, he decided. A few minutes wouldn't hurt. He pushed Izaguirre's chair to the side and began emptying the desk drawers, wondering where the old man kept his drugs. . . .

The swimming pool, blank and gleaming, with wavelets lapping the sides. Mingolla sat bolt upright, looked around, certain someone was sneaking up on him. But nobody was in sight. Voices from one of the rooms. A radio playing violin music. Gilbey and Jack still sleeping. He leaned back, stretching his legs, arranging his three visions of the future in chronological order. First the diner, the chat with the waitress; then the confrontation with Izaguirre, and then Love City. The aftermath of a hollow victory. He couldn't understand how the picture drawn by the visions was compatible with the peace. Maybe they weren't accurate. But he couldn't bring himself to accept that. They felt real.

Gilbey shook himself, came to his knees, and, grateful for the interruption, Mingolla said, "How ya doing?"

"I was dreamin'," said Gilbey. "Dreamin' 'bout the Farm."

"What 'bout it?"

"Nothin', just dreamin'. " Gilbey sat cross-legged, stared at the rippling pool. "Y'know, it wasn't so bad there . . . the Farm, I mean."

"It was a different bad than here."

"Yeah, I guess." Gilbey mumbled something else.

"What'd you say?"

"Didn't say nothin'. I was gonna, but . . ."

"You forgot, huh?"

"Naw, I didn't forget." Gilbey's stare tracked around the courtyard, then settled on Jack. He bowed his head, rubbed the back of his neck. "I got it all right here to say . . . it's all right here. But it just don't fit into words."

The emptiness of the palace's main hall was scarcely compromised by the long tables that had been set up along the walls, bearing punchbowls and trays of sandwiches and pastries. Harsh white lights shone from the ceiling, giving the plastic the look of sweating blue flesh. Several hundred people were milling around, and the storytelling robot trundled back and forth, its Victorian drag striking an odd note among the celebrants, who were for the most part drably clothed. Speeches were given, proclaiming all present to be members of a single family dedicated to the principles invoked by the Peace of Panama . . . this a phrase much used during the evening. Piped-in music began to play, and Mingolla was persuaded to dance by a dwarfish Madradona woman, who smiled up at him with pointy-looking teeth, and whose torpedo-shaped breasts—confined by a tight red blouse—bumped against his belt buckle.

"I've been dying to meet you," she said.

"Looks like you made it just in time," he said.

She acted confused, then her smile returned. "Yes," she said. "I've been wanting to talk to you about our genetics program. Are you familiar with it?"

"Nope." He maneuvered Dwarf Woman between couples. Clutzy dancers, all. Considering the significance of the party, it was—he thought—pretty fucking déclassé. Kind of a cross between a prom and a country club mixer.

"Well . . ." Dwarf Woman frowned at a Sotomayor man who had backed into her. "We've been hoping you'll donate."

"Donate?"

"You know . . . genetic material." Dwarf Woman put a girlish emphasis on the last words and tittered. "I apologize for being blunt, but I'm so excited by the prospect of blending the lines."

"Blending the lines, huh?" The image of himself fathering generations of Mingolla-Madradonas and Mingolla-Sotomayors touched off a wave of giddy good humor in Mingolla. "Tell you what," he said, laughing. "Why don't you and me slip out back, and I'll jerk off on ya. Maybe you can bottle it 'fore it dries."

He'd expected an offended reaction, but Dwarf Woman

400

dug her stubby fingers into his waist and kept smiling. It was an eerie screw-loose smile, and for a second he thought she might accept his proposition.

"I've been warned about your iconoclastic tendencies." She said this in a dire tone as if warning him that she knew his secret. "This is no joking matter."

"I can see that," he said. "I mean just from looking 'round the room, I can tell you people are in need of new blood. Especially you Madradonas. I never seen such twinky little fuckers. You could use a few height genes, right?" He gave her a lascivious thrust of the hips. "Yeah, sure. I can put a little length in your whatsitz."

Dwarf Woman struggled to free herself, but Mingolla held her in a death grip, whirling her around. "Crudity is hardly responsive," she said.

"That's me . . . hardly responsive." He bounced Dwarf Woman into a Madradona man who was dancing with a Sotomayor woman. "Oops," he said, and grinned.

"Let me go!" said Dwarf Woman.

"Never," said Mingolla. "It's just you and me from now on, shorty." He slung her into yet another couple and apologized, saying, "Sorry, she stepped on my foot."

"I'm not going to forget this," she said venomously.

"Me neither. God, what a night we're gonna have! Somehow we'll overcome the difference in height. Ever done it with ropes and pulleys?" He hugged her even tighter. "Aw, babe! I can hardly wait till your teeny belly starts poppin' out."

Dwarf Woman writhed, wriggled, straining to get loose.

"Jesus, that feels good!" he said. "Do it again . . . a little lower."

"Let me . . . !"

He muffled her words by pulling her head into his chest. "On the first date?" he said, lifting his voice so all could hear. "Well, if you're game, I'll give 'er a try."

Suddenly weary of this, he turned her loose and performed a mock bow. "Thanks for the struggle," he said.

She stood fuming, sputtering.

"You motherfuckers oughta be in cages," he said by way of farewell.

He walked over to the nearest table, swilled down a cupful of punch. Farther along the table, Tully, Corazon, and Debora were talking with several Madradonas. The Madradonas, it appeared, were busy consolidating their role as Masters of Efficiency. Marina Estil, all dolled up in a white silk dress and jade beads, disengaged from another group and came toward him. She was flushed, excited, and in her eyes, her smile, was an intensity that seemed a product of more than natural well-being. He wondered if she had taken something.

"How are you?" she asked. "I've been so busy, I haven't been able to get back to you about our little problem."

"Everything's fine," he said.

"I knew it would be." She called a hello to a passing Sotomayor, then turned back to Mingolla. "Are you having a good time?"

"Marvelous," he said. "I'm in a transport of delight." He noticed Ruy sidling up to Debora.

Marina followed his gaze. "Don't worry, David. He told me he was planning to apologize tonight. That's all that's happening. So"—she sipped punch, looking at him over the rim of the glass—"have you been meeting people?"

"Oh, yeah! Lots." He told her about the Madradona woman.

She giggled. "They're so officious, aren't they? Sweet in their own way, of course."

"Of course."

"You're in a strange mood," she said.

"I might say the same about you."

"Oh, I'm just exhilarated. You see, everything's coming together tonight."

Her words were oddly weighted, but he chalked that up to chemicals: he was now certain that she was stoned. "Everything?" he said.

She stroked his arm, a seductive move. "Yes, and you're responsible for a great deal of it."

"Is that right?"

"I'll tell you about it sometime," she said. "But not now." She pointed at the storytelling robot; it had rolled up to the table beside them a few feet away. "It's time for the entertainment."

"Gather 'round, gather 'round!" called the robot, and the crowd formed a semicircle about the table, chattering and laughing. From their ranks came one of the Sotomayor men leading a pale thin girl dressed in a white jumpsuit. She had a withdrawn, blank look, and Mingolla felt that this blankness was a sign of retardation. She stood half-hidden behind the robot's skirts, nervous, twisting her fingers together.

"Music, maestra!" cried the robot, clapping its pink plastic hands.

The girl jumped, ducked her eyes.

"Please, *chiquita!*" The robot gave her a tickle, and she squirmed away. "Just a little music to make us all happy."

The girl smiled wanly, and a moment later bell-like tones began to resound inside Mingolla's head, tones of such purity that he was stunned by their beauty and failed to notice at first the simplicity and awkwardness of the tune they played. A nursery school tune. Played badly, the timing all wrong. Mingolla realized the girl was in essence a music box whose lid had been opened, a toy with faulty springs. The tune continued for far too long, and the crowd's applause was polite but unenthusiastic. The girl was led off, and a young man with a similar blankness of expression was presented to the crowd. His eyes were deep-set, dark; he had a pinched, bony face, and his scalp showed through his crewcut. After being prodded by the robot, he stared at a point in midair, and a color materialized before Mingolla's mind's eye, a shade of blue so deep and rich that it seemed an emotion, embodying a sense of absolute tranquility. Other emotions were projected, each of them powerful in the extreme, and the crowd applauded each one wildly.

Marina stepped forward and addressed the crowd. "I believe we should show our appreciation to Carlito for this great work, for bringing forth flowers from these stones."

The crowd applauded, and the applause evolved into a chant of "Carlito, Carlito, Carlito!" that ended only when the dance music was struck up again. Mingolla stared into one of the punchbowls, thinking that he'd seen six-legged movement among the floating bits of rind and fruit pulp.

"Hello, David," said a high-pitched female voice at his shoulder.

403

He spun about and looked up into the robot's eyes. Behind occluded crystals, the cameras swiveled.

"Don't you recognize me?" The robot clasped its hands over its ample belly.

For a moment Mingolla was at sea; but then, remembering the chopper and its divine pretense, he penetrated the disguise. "Izaguirre," he said.

"Good to see you again," said the robot. The pudgy pink face seemed to be regarding him with paternal favor.

"Are you here in person?" asked Mingolla, hoping this was the case, not knowing what he would do, but hoping all the same.

"Oh, no. I'm in Costa Rica. But I've been keeping my eye on you." He essayed a daffy wink. "I'm most impressed with the work you've been doing."

"Are you now?"

"Indeed! It's remarkable. The results you've achieved put my poor efforts to shame."

"You're just saying that." Mingolla offered the robot punch and spilled a cupful over its stiff yellow dress. "Gee . . . lucky you didn't short-circuit. By the way, what is your work? Entertaining at birthday parties?"

"Still angry, I see. That's good, David, that's good. Anger can be a useful tool." The robot dabbed at the spill. "To answer your question: No. No birthday parties. My work is much like yours, though I've been limited to producing singular effects as opposed to the overall rehabilitation you've been attempting."

"I haven't been attempting shit. Just passing the time."

"Don't belittle your efforts. No one would put in the hours you have without a strong commitment."

"Beats hanging out with your nieces and nephews."

"I won't insist you agree," said the robot. "However, I do have a proposal for you. I'd like you to come work with me after all the loose ends are tied up down here."

"Naw," said Mingolla. "I'm going home, gonna sit on the beach."

"You can do both."

"You work in the States?"

The crystal eyes tracked back and forth across the dance floor. "I see no harm in admitting it at this juncture. Yes, I have a home there. I think you'd find it an amiable atmosphere."

"Where is it?"

The robot gave out with a fey titter. "I believe I'll keep you in the dark about that for the time being."

Not as much in the dark as you think, asshole, Mingolla said to himself. Some place with dry desert heat and a lot of horny people. "Why?" he asked. "Scared of me or something?"

"Not really, David. You're quite formidable, I admit. But we've been around for a long time, and we know how to deal with strength." The robot trundled back a foot, then forward the same distance, as if gearing up for a leap. "Now about my proposal . . ."

"I'll think about it."

"A talent like yours won't lie dormant, David. What else is there for you to do?"

"Could be I'll go back into the killing business. The world can always use another assassin."

The robot's great oval head twitched. "I'm sorry you have so much resentment."

"It's not resentment," said Mingolla. "It's disgust."

"I'm aware that—"

"You aren't aware of shit!" said Mingolla. "The things you bastards . . ." He caught himself, not wanting to lose it completely. "Maybe you're right. Maybe all I can do is try to fix what you people have broken."

"Don't you understand?" said the robot. "That's exactly how I feel."

"Really?"

"Do you think I'm without feeling?" the robot asked. "Don't you know how appalling I find what we've done, what we've had to do?"

The robot embarked upon what Mingolla was coming to view as the classic Sotomayor rap, You Can't Make an Omelet without Breaking Eggs, and We Will Spend Our Lives Redressing All Wrongs. Izaguirre's version was superb, heartfelt, and eloquent, and Mingolla had no doubt that he believed every word. He promised Izaguirre that he would give serious consideration to his proposal and that he would try to put his resentments behind him; but after the robot had trundled off to visit relatives, he found that his tolerance of the proceedings had been reduced to zero. The scales had fallen from his eyes. Everywhere he looked he detected the residues of old hatreds. Whispers behind hands, scowls, poisonous stares. And there were fresh hatreds as well. Those he detected in the standoffishness with which the Madradonas and Sotomayors treated their new allies, the drug-induced psychics. The shoddiness of the party, the schmaltzy music, the whirling unlovely couples, the mutant sideshow, the high tech grotesquerie of Izaguirre's robot: the sinister aspects of all this seemed to have undergone an intensification. He might, he thought, have been standing in Berlin decades ago, watching the burghers ratify their allegiance to the lean, cold National Socialists, disguising their intrinsic meanness and paucity of spirit with shabby pomp and sprinklings of glamour. This gathering had no less potential for nastiness, for vicious perversion, and he perceived in it the shape of the world to come, one not so different from the old. The feud would resurface, with the added bloodiness of a new feud between the families and their drugged creations, and the result would be a world of back-fence wars and heavy tensions and near-apocalypses. Or perhaps a total apocalypse. The families' propensity for oversight might well allow for this significant difference. But whatever ultimacy they might contrive of the future, of one thing Mingolla was sure: he would not survive to see it. Wherever he turned, people looked away from him, not wanting to be caught staring. That consensus interest alone was enough to damn him. Sooner or later somebody would decide that he was too powerful to trust, or would make a judgment based on a more personal issue.

He spotted Debora standing with Tully and Corazon on the far side of the hall, and he crossed to them, bumping into ungainly Madradonas and graceful Sotomayors. "I'm gonna take a walk," he said to Debora as he came up. "You be all right?"

"You look pale," she said. "Are you sick?"

"Something I ate."

"You be missin' all de fun, mon," said Tully drunkenly; he gave Corazon such a fierce squeeze that Mingolla half-expected to see her rosy eye pop out.

"I'll go with you," said Debora; but she didn't seem eager to leave.

"Naw, I just wanna walk a little. I'll take Gilbey and Jack, and I'll catch ya back here or at the pension."

He turned to go, but she stepped in front of him. "Is anything wrong?"

It was a temptation to tell her all he'd been thinking, but he knew she wouldn't buy it. "Nothing serious," he said. "I'll see ya later."

As he headed for the door, various of the families acknowledged him with smiles and nods. So sincere, so unassuming. He smiled back, hating them all.

Clear night, the stars pointy and bright, so regularly spaced that the strip of blue darkness overhead looked like a banner laid across the rooftops. Mingolla felt at ease walking out among the dead. The dead could be trusted, at least. Their dim urges were not informed by greed or lust; their memories did not inspire perversity, but were merely unresolvable longings for a world they could not quite recall. He liked the silence of the street, too. Silence was a blue-dark flow through the claustrophobic canyons of the barrio, carrying his reflection smoothly along in the windows of the stores, past the logjams of shadowy figures in the gutters, and he thought it might not be so bad to enlist in those shadow armies, to breathe the poison that made them slow, to follow the orders that permitted them to indulge in the last red reason for living. He increased his pace, swinging his arms, marching, and Gilbey and Jack had to break into a stumbling run to keep up. At last he stopped in front of the store that once had sold religious items and looked at himself in the ranked mirrors. An infinity of starlit Mingollas, all of them dark, with glittering eyes. Studying the reflections calmed him. He turned his head, and the reflections followed suit. He put his hands on his hips, moved toward the window, and an army of Mingollas, bold and undaunted, approached for consultation.

Pity, he thought, that they weren't magic mirrors. He'd summon his friends and family to appear, give them the benefit of his wisdom. Not that he had a lot to give. Just one word: Panama. He'd say it differently to each of them. Softly to old girlfriends, to Long Island Woman, letting them know how lucky they were as Americans to be insulated against so much painful reality. And to his old buddies, he'd offer it as an admonition, shock them into draft-dodgery. And to his father, yeah, to his father he'd pronounce it as a cross between a whisper and a hiss. The word would cloud the mirror, translating into a gas the color of the night sky and the shadows, one that would envelop his father's head and convey to him the dark flash of being, send him reeling, choking on quintessential Panamanian truth, and a moment later actuarial reality would knock on the door, and Mom would have lovers in Florida till she was eighty. Wow! What a gal!

Panama.

Not what he'd expected, nosiree!

He hadn't reached the topless country of white beaches, the tanned coast of movie star tits and *coco locos*, the loll of brochure-portrait dewy daughters of the idle isles, and you got American money, Jim, this land is your land, for rape, rent, and shopping mall development . . . whatever's your pleasure. No, he'd reached the bloody republic of history, where Colombian pirates raided the coast and screwed their victims' corpses, where once a band of white sailors had become headhunters and cannibals, where Chinese railroad workers had drowned themselves by the hundreds when their opium ran out, where a little weed grew that gave you the power to raise armies of the dead.

Where a man named Carlito had been born.

Panama . . . little shiver of three syllables.

Then the word seemed to acquire a new meaning, to tell of green hills rising beyond a barricade, of Darién, the cloud forest, the lost tribes, the witch-men and their thoughts like streamers of mist.

That Panama, now . . . that might just be an option after all.

Jack and Gilbey edged closer as if his longing for escape had spoken to them, and something stirred in the gutter at Mingolla's feet. A thin shred of a man wrapped in tatters of brown cloth, stinking of garbage. Mingolla went to his knees beside him, looked into eyes empty and doting as a dog's. The man's lips were scabbed, and his nose had been broken; strings of bloody mucus hung from his nostrils, thick and webbed like macramé. He reached out his hand, clutched at Mingolla's arm, and Mingolla, his bitterness swept away, began to work on the man's mind. Behind him, a rustling, a shifting, but he paid it no attention.

Then Gilbey said, "Watch it!"

Mingolla glanced up, saw figures silhouetted against the stars, looming above him, and one, cowled, its face an oval of darkness, swung at him with something long and crooked. He twisted away, but the club struck the side of his head, sending white lights shooting through his skull, and he fell on his back. Gilbey hauled him up, dragged him onto the sidewalk, and he had a dizzy glimpse of hundreds of people choking the street, shuffling forward, making no sound other than the glutinous passages of their breath. Eyes like holes cut in dirty sheets, and weapons at the ready.

Glass shattered.

Gilbey jerked him around to face the store. Jack was smashing the window with his crowbar, clearing away hanging icicles of glass. Gilbey dragged him through the window, into the mirrored showroom. He kept blacking out, floating back to consciousness, seeing himself in the mirrors. Open-mouthed; a black forking of blood from his hairline. Behind them, the army converged on the broken window, pressing inside, unmindful of the spears of broken glass that pierced them. Mingolla tried to strike at them with his mind, but couldn't focus and was pulled past his floundering mirror images and down a narrow corridor toward the back door. The knob turned in Gilbey's hand, the door gave a little, but was stuck. Gilbey dropped his machete and wrangled with the knob.

Mingolla leaned against the wall, looking down at the machete. It was a long way off, spinning, receding, and he wasn't sure he could reach it. But if he could reach it . . . well, he knew about machetes. Yes, indeed! He bent at the waist, swayed, and in righting himself, managed to scoop up the machete. The hilt was greasy with Gilbey's sweat, the rust and blood on the blade gleamed in the light from the transom. Its heft stabilized Mingolla, and he turned to face the army.

The corridor was just wide enough for two abreast, and the army surged into it, grunting, bumping into each other, unable to master the tactics of two-at-a-time. Mingolla swung at the first to come within range, slashed a chest, a belly, drawing lines of blood in gray flesh. Two of them fell, then a third. He chopped at the shoulder of an old woman whose shawl had slipped down to blind her, he spitted a young man and kicked him away. With a screech, the door came open, and Mingolla backed into an alley almost as narrow as the corridor. Blocked at one end by a high brick wall, at the other by more of the army. Gilbey took a stand beside him, wielding a two-by-four, and Mingolla, retreating toward the brick wall, slashed the gut of a shirtless man whose skin hung in folds about his waist. He should be feeling something, he thought. Fear at the least, because he likely was going to die: there were too many of them, their heads bobbing, eyes slits of ebony, pale skin showing through rents in their clothing. And regret at killing his ex-patients. Surely he should feel regret. But it was as if the blow to his head had reduced him to their state, to an emptiness empowered by a command, swinging the machete, a little faster and more accurate than they, yet equally single-minded. No shudders flowed along the blade—their lives weren't stubborn enough to produce such phenomena—and when their blood spattered him, it dripped from his arms with the slowness of heavy machine oil. Flesh Dummies with Real-Life Organs. There was a sweet brainless appeal to cutting them down, a muscular pleasure in a stroke well conceived and nicely executed, and Christ, was he ever doing a good job! Piling up the bodies. They slipped and flailed as they clambered over the pile. Easy to pick off. He swung, connected, biting to the bone. Swung, connected, swung, connected. Should be a work song to sing while he chopped. *Well, I'm gon' take dis machete . . .*

Jesus fuck! The alley snapped into horrid focus for Mingolla. He saw his last victim writhing as slow as an earthworm at his feet, shoving guts back into his belly. Once again he tried a mental assault, and as he did, this time succeeding, he realized that in hiding his power from the families, he had hidden its true extent from himself as well.

He felt a sun was inside his head, a heavy black sun shedding lines of force, and he sensed the minds of the armies, those in the alley, those in the store and on the street, sensed them in the way a constellation might know the fires that comprised its shape. Sensed their fragility and vacancy. Some of those near him fell, others staggered and leaned against the walls for support. He had no pity for them. They were unimportant, incidental, and he had wasted too much time with them as it was. A feeling of grim righteousness stole over him, so profound an emotion that it seemed a physical condition, a cellular affirmation of the need to strike back at whoever had tried to kill him. He exulted in the feeling and imagined himself confronting his enemy.

Ruy.

Oh, yeah! Had to be Ruy!

The army rustled, stirred by the wind of Mingolla's anger.

He pushed through the men and women in the alley, shouldering them aside, unconcerned by their proximity . . . although he didn't like touching them, subject to an irrational fear that bits of their substance would flake off and cling to him. He weaved through the motionless dark figures thronging the store, catching sight of himself among them in the silvered mirrors, a man hiding among mannequins. He'd forgotten about Gilbey, but as he moved into the street, he noticed him missing. He turned to the store. Gilbey was kneeling next to a body that lay half-in, half-out of the shattered window. A crowbar beside the body's outflung hand.

"C'mon, Gilbey," he said.

Gilbey's hand fluttered over the body; he might have been searching for a switch with which to reactivate it.

"There's nothing you can do for him," said Mingolla, laying a hand on Gilbey's shoulder.

"Leave me alone!" Gilbey knocked away his hand.

His eyes were glistening, and Mingolla wondered at this, at tears from Gilbey.

"I . . ." Gilbey looked at Mingolla and said his name a couple of times in a quizzical tone as if it meant something rare and unfathomable.

"What is it?"

Gilbey shook his head, smoothed Jack's rumpled shirt.

It was useless to continue their charade of friendship, Mingolla realized; it had been a sentimental mistake to distinguish Gilbey from the others, to pretend he was alive and well. There was no room for sentiment here. He walked away from Gilbey, resisting the impulse to say goodbye, and, using his reflection in a store window, he set about cleaning the blood from his face and arms. Around him, the dead stood stockstill like statues in a street scene by De Chirico. He could almost hear the vibration of their emptiness, their longing for purpose, and he knew how to ease that longing, he knew the purpose for which they had been made.

Anger had always been big in him, but what he felt now was anger come to fruition, anger that seemed a separate shape walking in his body, a glittering man of furious principle. His anger spread to infect the army, and as he hurried toward the palace, shadows pushed themselves up from the curbs and doorways and fell into step behind him. The moon was up, and the walls of the buildings glowed with such brilliance that he could make out the gray patches where the whitewash had flaked away. More than ever, the narrow streets reminded him of canyons, and with their ragged hair and primitive weapons, the army might have been cavedwellers on their way to engage a neighboring tribe. Their skin looked as pale and crumbly as cheese, and their eyes had the reflective blackness of the window glass.

When he reached the street that opened onto the parking lot in front of the palace, he divided the army into two forces, sending one on a circuitous route in back of the palace toward the barricade and instructing the others to wait in the shadows until summoned. Walking across the parking lot, he felt calm in the midst of anger, as if the core of his personality had separated from the rest and was observing the goings-on. Parked by the steps were a number of jeeps, and he was pleased to see that most had keys dangling from their ignitions. Inside, the party was in full swing, the atmosphere more drunken than when he had left. Madradonas and Sotomayors tripping the light fantastic to the strains of a jazzy dance tune; the storytelling robot stood unmoving in a corner, switched off. Probably past Izaguirre's bedtime. As he worked his way through the dancers, Mingolla smiled and nodded to whoever caught his eye. "Lovely evening," he said. "Wonderful party." And then, pitching his voice so low that they couldn't be sure what they had heard, he would add, "You're gonna die," and smile more broadly. Debora was hemmed in against a table by a group that included both Ruy and Marina, and Mingolla insinuated himself into the group, stood next to her. "Where's Tully?" he whispered.

"I don't know," she said. "I think they went back to their hotel." She looked at him askance. "You're bleeding! What happened?"

He touched his brow, his fingers came away red. "Got a little bump," he said, smiling at Ruy. It was too bad about Tully and Corazon, he thought. But he wasn't going to postpone things. They would just have to fend for themselves.

"That looks serious," said Marina. "You should have it tended to."

She was acting nervous, fidgeting with her skirt, unwilling to meet his eyes.

"It's nothing," he said, feeling a heady mixture of rage and glee. The blue plastic shell of the palace suddenly seemed the inside of a vast skull, Carlito's skull. In the beams of light slanting from the ceiling he saw the haywire geometries of Carlito's thought; the air had the stink of his stale brainwaves, and the dancers, the group by the table, the inanimate robot, all of them were the sorry creatures of Carlito's imagination, whirling and talking and pretending to be real, each of them moved by some strand of plot or whimsy. But that was coming

413

to an end. He pictured the blue walls cracking, unable to contain the power that Carlito had inadvertently kindled.

"I've had an interesting time tonight," said Mingolla. "What you might call a real eye-opener. Isn't that right, Ruy?"

"I don't know what you mean," Ruy said.

"No, I bet you don't."

"You should have that cut seen to," Marina said with some agitation. "I'd be . . ."

"Don't trouble yourself." Mingolla glanced around at the others; they were staring at him with puzzlement as if they sensed something imminent, but weren't sure what, and though he had planned to wait until he and Debora got clear, he realized that now was the time, that he couldn't leave without at least witnessing the beginning of the end. That he, like Carlito, delighted in dramatic presentation.

He took Debora's arm, steered her away into a clear space at the edge of the dance floor. He turned back to the group by the table. They looked nervous.

"Somebody tried to kill me tonight," he said.

Somebody turned off the music, and everyone was whispering.

"It's not that important for the culprit to be singled out" —he raised his voice—"because every damn one of you is guilty. But I think it's appropriate that some punishment be meted out."

Marina pushed through to the front of the group. "How did it happen, David?"

"Somebody sicced the army on me while I was walking," he said.

"Ruy!" She spun about to face him.

"It wasn't me!" he said. "I've been here all night."

"Doesn't matter." Mingolla called out to the dancers, "How 'bout some more entertainment, folks?"

"I wouldn't risk myself just to get back at you," Ruy said to Mingolla.

"Who was it, then?"

Ruy was caught without an answer for a moment. He searched the crowd for a likely candidate. "Marina?" he said.

She looked injured, disappointed, like a teacher let down by her prize pupil.

"It was her . . . don't you see?" Ruy said to Mingolla. "She's trying to get back at me, trying to set me up."

"My God, Ruy," Marina said, and gave a pitying laugh.

"It had to be her," said Ruy. "All these years she's pretended that she's forgiven me, but I knew she hadn't."

"Forgiven you for what?" Debora asked.

"Years ago," said Ruy. "I did something to her. I didn't mean to, I was crazy about her. But . . ."

"You're the one who made her lose her child!" said Mingolla, putting together Marina's flighty behavior that evening with her pleasure in punishing Ruy, with other hints and clues.

"This is ridiculous!" said Marina.

"Yes, yes!" Ruy moved closer to Mingolla, eager now. "And she's been crazy ever since. But she's managed to make everyone think her craziness is something else. Dedication, efficiency. She's just been waiting her chance. She knew I'd be accused if anything happened to you."

Guilt was plain in Marina's face, but Mingolla was unable to redirect his anger; the fact of her treachery was not at all surprising, considering what Ruy had done, and he had hated Ruy for too long to give up his vengeance. In any case, he wasn't concerned with specific guilt, but rather with example, and Ruy, with his pleading manner, his sweaty fear, made a perfect example.

" 'Bye, Ruy," he said, and struck with stunning force.

Ruy sagged, his knees buckling, and went down on all fours. His saturnine face emptied, and he collapsed onto his side. Mingolla stood over him, plucking at his mental knots, undoing them one by one. "What we call this, folks," he said in a lectoral tone, "is field-stripping the human mind. Easy as pie once you get the hang of it." Ruy tried to speak, but succeeded only in making ugly dream noises. His hands scrabbled on the floor, his legs twitched, and he gazed up at Mingolla, his mouth working, his brow creased, as if trying to recall something important, something that would save him. "Doesn't take long at all, as you can see," Mingolla said. "Be glad to give lessons."

The Madradonas and Sotomayors were silent, their expressions ranging from the horrified to the bemused.

"Know where you are, Ruy?" Mingolla asked with vast solicitude.

Ruy looked worried. "I . . . unh . . . I . . ."

"Real good, Ruy." Mingolla gave his shoulder a pat. "You'll make a terrific soldier. Defending the Sotomayor honor. Shitting in the street, clubbing the other zombies. You'll do just fine."

Ruy ventured a weak smile.

"But it's gonna be tough. Know how tough it's gonna be?"

Ruy had no idea, but was all ears.

"Lemme show ya." Mingolla seized Ruy by the shirtfront and began to slap him. Each slap seemed to win a little battle in his heart, to wipe out the last vestiges of compassion.

Somebody grabbed Mingolla from behind, but he shook them off and sent a wave of hatred across the dance floor, a signal powerful enough to summon the army. The families retreated, leaving him and Debora and Ruy in a cleared circle. He studied them, and they returned measuring stares, looks of appraisal. He saw that they weren't upset by what he'd done; they were merely gauging his relative worth, the risks involved in dealing with him. They appeared to have no conception of defeat.

"We understand your reaction, David," said one of the Sotomayor men. "But we can't let you take matters into your own hands."

"Show's not over, folks," said Mingolla. "Time for the big finish."

A noise behind him. He turned, saw Marina kicking Ruy, who was curled up, trying to protect his head. Mingolla caught her arm, ripping a seam of her silk dress, and backhanded her to the floor. She rolled onto her stomach, sat up, demented-looking, all her elegance dissipated. She went crawling back toward Ruy. Mingolla shoved her away with his foot.

Hubbub at the entrance, a scream, people milling.

Ragged figures were crowding through the door. Mingolla pulled Debora against the wall.

"What did you do?" she said, pushing him away.

"They tried to kill me, dammit!"

"You shouldn't . . ." She broke off, looking broken, defeated. Her shoulders slumped, and she stared out at the dance floor.

It was strange, those first moments of confrontation between the families and their former victims. Haggard men and women, stumbling, blinking at the lights, looking—despite the urgency of Mingolla's powerful command—bewildered, uncertain, like beggars allowed into the throne room. Some stood fingering their rags, hands to their mouths, in attitudes of humility and shame. But only for a second. Then they shuffled forward, intent on their chore. The Madradonas and Sotomayors were aghast, less terrified than affronted . . . or so it seemed to Mingolla. And as the attack began they fixed their eyes on the army, confident, trying to influence them. It was only when they discovered that Mingolla's influence was too ironclad for them to affect that they displayed fear, and by then the army was upon them. A grizzled heavyset man struck first, impaling a pale skinny woman with a pitchfork, walking her backward into the center of the room; she plucked at the tines, openmouthed, too shocked to scream. An old woman stabbed at a fallen man, her head thrown back like that of a triumphant animal. Marina Estil turned to run and was struck in the neck with a hoe wielded by a young boy; he hacked at her, miring her white silk dress with blood. There was an awful clumsiness to these assaults, a dreamlike momentum, and had the odds been less, the families might have survived; as it was, quite a few were managing to escape out the door. But the odds were too great. All around the room, huddled groups of the families were trying to beat off dozens of attackers; their shouts and screams, bright splinters of sound, were too energetic to suit the slow murders taking place. The blood of the families shimmered like a rich yield seeping up from between the seams of the fake gray stones, and everywhere were instances of courage: Madradonas saving Sotomayors and vice versa, as if in

417

death they were at last uniting in a common cause. He felt no pity for them, yet he saw in their dying a sad inevitability, a summation of centuries of death, a pattern resolving into a knot of blood and fear, cinching tight about the neck of a monster whose neck stretched back into colonial days. And he saw, too, the indulgence of his own act of vengeance, how it had been a reaction worthy of the families, equally as unthinking and with a typically horrid result. But he wasn't tempted to interfere.

He guided Debora along the wall, shielding her against anyone who headed their way, warding them off with doses of fear, and they moved through the massacre unscathed, like saints immune to fire. But as they drew near the door, Mingolla began to feel an intense sadness and to hear a pure simple music inside his head, tones of crystalline purity. Faint at first, but stronger and more pervasive with every second. His step faltered, and he spotted the girl and the young crewcut man who had "entertained" the gathering standing beside the door, their faces empty, their eyes squeezed shut in concentration. Bells and sadness, sadness and bells. Mixing into a fluid heavy as mercury, slowing and dimming him. He tried to throw off the sadness, to muffle the bells, but his panic didn't catch, just flared briefly and went out, and it didn't seem worth the effort to fight anymore. The sad blue music was killing him, chilling him, tolling and tolling, a mournful angelus that made him long to grow slower and slower, to fade with the vibration of the ringing notes, receding forever into a place he could almost imagine, gray and secret deep, the bottomland of the spirit, a little hollow large enough for the soul to curl up in and sleep, and even the screams and shouts were knitting into music, a choral counterpoint. He wondered why Debora wasn't doing anything, why she was just standing there, wasn't she going to help . . . it didn't matter, it was better to fade, to lean against the wall and let the sadness and the music vibrate inside him, breaking down the structures of his thought, and it wasn't really so bad, this emptying, this winnowing, like the way you disappear into sleep, cell after cell shutting down, vision narrowing . . . and then there was something hot inside him, something charged and driven, and he felt Debora joining her strength to his, that twisting fevered energy building into a red noise of thought, of anger and loathing for what was happening, and the little girl shrieked, staggered away, and the crewcut man began to shake, he was biting his lower lip, blood filming over his chin, and the music and sadness splintering into fragments of terror and cool sound.

Mingolla stepped close to the crewcut man, grabbed the front of his jumpsuit, kneed him, let him fall. He turned to Debora, pulled her through the door. "What the hell were you doing . . . waiting like that?"

"You weren't doing anything! Why should I?" She reached out to him, but withdrew her hand. "For a second, I just didn't care anymore . . . about anything."

"Dammit!" he said. "You . . ."

"Don't tell me you didn't feel like that!" she said, halfway between anger and tears. "You feel like that all the time, and it's all I can do to keep going in spite of it. I . . ."

She twisted away from him, and he stood a second, looking at her back. His chest ached with some feeling he couldn't identify, and his face was hot. Debora was taking deep shivery breaths. "Fuck it," he said. "Let's get outta here."

As they climbed into one of the jeeps, a Madradona man, blubbering, came running up and struck Mingolla on the cheek, a feeble blow, but one that sobered him, alerted him to the fact that other men and women were converging on them from the corners of the parking lot. The man went to his knees, swayed, clutched at Mingolla's leg. Mingolla kicked him away, gunned the engine, and sped off, weaving among the survivors, who cried out in frustration, reached for him with bloody hands. He turned down the street leading to the barricade, bouncing over the potholes. The crests of the distant hills were outlined in stars, the glowing walls jogged in his vision. Dark figures were scaling the barricade, some falling when gunfire flashed between gaps in the boards; but many more were making it over, and more still were massed at the foot of the wall. Mingolla laid on the horn, and some of the ragged men and women scattered; others stood and gawked, but he didn't slow down. "Hold on!" he said to Debora as the wall loomed high, and then, amid splintering boards and gunfire and the thud of bodies impacting the hood, they crashed through the barricade, slewed sideways in the dirt. He fought for control of the jeep, managed to straighten it out. Saw that they were in the middle of a battle much like the one they had fled. Groups of soldiers firing at larger groups of attackers on a field of yellow dirt tufted with grass that showed black in the moonlight. And beyond, a meadow of taller grasses stretched toward the hills.

Debora beat on his shoulder, pointed to a shack with a tarpaper roof, isolated from the battle. "They'll have extra guns in there!"

A bullet pinged off the fender.

He pulled up behind the shack, kept the engine running while Debora darted inside. A second later, she returned with two rifles, shoving a wiry mahogany-skinned man in fatigues ahead of her. She forced him into the back of the jeep.

"Who the hell's he?" Mingolla asked.

"Hostage," she said. "He was hiding."

He was astounded by her transformation from hopelessness to martial efficiency. She seemed at home in this chaos, desperate, yet her desperation contained, channeled.

"Come on!" she shouted. "Let's go!"

He swerved out from behind the shack and across the meadow. Bullets zipped past, one striking sparks from the frame of the windshield, and for the first time Mingolla was afraid. His asshole clenched, and a cold spot formed between his shoulder blades.

Debora knelt in the seat, facing behind them, and began to fire. In the rearview mirror he saw three sets of headlights in pursuit. He floored the jeep, and they went sailing over depressions in the meadow, skipping like a stone. The windshield was blown out by a round, and Mingolla threw the jeep into a zigzag course, sending Debora into his lap. She righted herself and kept firing.

"Head north!" shouted the man in the backseat.

"Why?" said Mingolla, hunching his shoulders, turtling his neck, expecting a bullet at any second.

"There's a road! Trails! You can lose them there!" The man's head poked between the seats. "Make for that big hill!"

An explosion at their rear, and in the mirror Mingolla saw a fire burning in the meadow, two sets of headlights giving it a wide berth.

"Damn!" Debora's rifle had jammed. She flung it down, picked up the second rifle.

With every jolt and bounce, the jeep felt as if it were going to take flight, and Mingolla urged it to stay earthbound with body English and wishes. He made promises to God, get me out of this, Jesus, and I'll sin no more, and his heart was hammering to the rhythm of Debora's fire, and the hill was swelling huge and black above them, and the man in the backseat was shouting directions, and then they were swerving up into thick jungle along a narrow dirt track.

"Pull over . . . here!" Debora elbowed him, pointed to a shadowed avenue leading off between two large trees. He did as she instructed, shut down the engine. She propped her rifle on the top of the windshield, covering the road, and as another jeep, its headlights piercing the darkness, swung around the curve, she opened fire. Screams, silhouetted figures against a flash of flame, and the jeep flipped over, the husk of a dead olive-drab beetle crackling in its own juices. "There's one more," she said. "They must have seen."

Mingolla reached with his mind. Found three frail minds less than a hundred yards away. He made them afraid . . . so afraid that they whirled, flared bright, and winked out one by one.

"We're okay now," he said.

Everything was still, a stream chuckling somewhere near, insects and frogs bubbling, and even the crackling of the flames was compatible with the stillness. All the dark confusion of the escape might never have happened. The shapes of branches and leaves overhead were sharp in the moonlight, and Mingolla felt the aches and tremors of adrenaline as if the moon were illuminating his weaknesses, pointing up their isolation. It seemed that none of what he remembered of the past hour had happened, that they had been disgorged from a nightmare and left on this hillside to sort out reality.

"Are you going to kill me?" said a voice from the backseat.

Mingolla had forgotten their hostage. The man was sitting up, looking alert but not afraid; he had a feline cleverness of feature and crispy black hair. Mingolla saw in him an opportunity for some good, a last chance to practice mercy.

"You can go," he said.

"We can't . . ." Debora began.

"Let him go." Mingolla laid a hand on her rifle. "Just let him go."

The man climbed out of the jeep. "I won't tell anybody," he said as he backed away.

Mingolla shrugged.

The man backed, stumbled, and broke into a run, his figure standing out for a second against the flames of the jeep, then vanishing around the curve.

"You shouldn't have done that," said Debora; but her voice lacked conviction.

Mingolla fired up the engine. He didn't want to look at her, he didn't want her to see his face for fear of what might be written there. As he pulled out onto the road, her hip pressed against his; she left it there, and the contact made him feel close to her. Yet he also felt that the closeness wasn't important, or if it was, it was of memorial importance, because things were changing between them. That, too, he could feel. Old postures were being redefined, connections tearing loose and reforming, shadowy corners of their souls coming to light. He put it from mind, put everything from mind, and concentrated on the road, driving north toward Darién.

CHAPTER EIGHTEEN

By five o'clock the next afternoon, after two car changes to throw off pursuit, they were high in the Darién Mountains, their pace slowed to a crawl by a dense mist. Visibility was no more than a few feet, and Mingolla had to clear condensation from the windshield to see even that far. Finally he gave up and pulled off the road. Debora went to sleep in the backseat, and he sat staring out into the mist, at vague green loops of vines and foliage that resembled fragments of a florid script, the signatures—he imagined—on a constitution not yet manifest in the land. Now and then he heard cries from the mist, cries that seemed as complex and strange as the shapes of the foliage. Birds, he figured. But recalling Tully's stories of the region, the brujos and ghosts, he pictured little brown men sitting in huts, sending out winged spirits; and once the moon had risen, setting the mist aglow, he thought he could feel them fluttering around the car, dispersing into eddies and streamers whenever he turned his eye their way. He was only a little afraid of spirits; he was much more afraid of his memories and potentials.

After a half-hour he nodded off and was awakened sometime later by a tremendous feeling of anxiety. Something had happened, something bad. He tried to dismiss the feeling as the hangover from a dream, but that wouldn't wash. His heart was pounding, he was sweating, and when Debora spoke from the backseat, he jumped at the sound.

"I just had a terrible feeling," she said. "A dream or something."

"Yeah . . . me too."

She sat up. "Do you . . ."

"What?"

"I wonder if something happened back in the city."

It rang true, but he didn't want to think about the city, about anything that lay behind them. "Maybe," he said.

"Come and sit with me . . . all right?"

He crawled over the seat, and once he had gotten settled, she lay down, resting her head in his lap.

. . . David . . .

"I'm here," he said, rejecting the easy solace offered by that kind of intimacy.

. . . I love you . . .

Her sending had a wistful flavor, as if she were trying to resurrect the emotion.

"I love you." His voice sounded flat, tinny, like a recorded message.

She shifted to a more comfortable position, and out of reflex his hand slipped down to cup her breast. He thought he could go for years without touching her that way, and his palms would remember the weight of her breasts, their exact conformation. The contact relaxed him.

. . . my father used to love places like this . . .

. . . you told me . . .

. . . high, misty . . .

. . . you like them . . .

. . . I can't help liking them, I've spent so much time in them with my father . . . we used to visit a village in the Cuchamatanes Mountains called Cahuatla, it was so strange, the men wore shirts with big floppy embroidered collars and monkey-skin hats, and some of them looked a little like monkeys, they were all tiny and wizened-looking, even the young ones . . . and when they'd come out of the mist at you, you imagined they were monkey spirits . . . we'd go there every May for this festival, my father was amused by it, he couldn't see it too many times . . .

424

. . . what sort of festival . . .

. . . it was really nothing special, all the men would ride horses from one end of the village to the other, and at each end they'd drink some aguardiente, and then they'd ride back and drink some more, and they'd keep getting drunker and drunker . . . the whole thing was to see who could stay on their horse the longest . . .

She continued telling him about the festival, and he could see it, the scrawny little monkey men, their striped shirts with red and purple collars shiny as velvet, swaying drunkenly on their bony mounts, and for a while it was enough to listen to her, hear her, watch her memories unfold; but not for long. He sensed her fraying attention in the patchiness of the memories, and he felt her arousal, knew that she wanted to make love, that she was open, wet, and her readiness seemed to him obscene, because something bad had happened, something no amount of lovemaking would erase. But there was no use in dwelling on it, he decided, and there was nothing they could do except make love. She skinned out of her jeans, her panties, sat on his cock, lifting and lowering herself, using the front seat for leverage, and he got into it on the level of prurience, watching her ass come down and sheathe him. At the end her cry sounded as eerie and distant as those of the birds lost in the mist.

They talked for a bit afterward, but their hearts weren't in it, and soon she was asleep again. Mingolla tried to stay awake, to keep watch. He was troubled by the lack of pursuit, and he suspected they were being spied on from above by choppers with thermal imagers. But realizing that if this was the case, no amount of watchfulness would save them, he gave in to sleep and fell into a dream.

In the dream he climbed out of the car, leaving Debora asleep, and walked farther up the hillside into the mist, picking his way through vines and ferns, his trousers growing heavy with dampness accumulated from the leaves. Before long, he saw a crumbling glow in the mist that resolved into an oblong of yellow light defined by the doorway of a hut. He was not afraid to approach the hut; in fact, it seemed he had been searching for just this hut for a very long time. He ducked inside and sat down facing a gnarled root of a man with black hair and wizened features and coppery skin: an old man, yet with the vitality of youth about him. He was wearing a loose-fitting shirt striped with red and purple and black and yellow, and trousers of the same fabric. The light came from three lanterns hung on pegs and made the freshly skinned poles of the walls gleam like rods of gold.

The brujo—for such Mingolla knew him to be—nodded on seeing him enter and went back to staring at a complicated pattern traced in the dirt floor of the hut. Mingolla, too, stared at the pattern. It took his eye ever inward like the chart of the labyrinth, and he realized that this pattern was the core pattern of the world and time, the one that all the patterns of thought and movement of all living creatures were destined to create. As he followed its course, he found the particular point at which he and Debora made their contribution to the weave, and understood that his visions of the future—of which this was one—were nothing inexplicable or magical, but were a result of being attuned to the pattern, of intersecting its flow and seeing along it to other points that were pertinent to his course. He was on the verge of looking along it into the future, past the time of their meeting with Izaguirre, when the brujo, with a sweeping gesture, rubbed out the pattern and grinned at him.

"Why'd you do that?" Mingolla asked.

The brujo reached out and touched his forehead, and when the brujo spoke in a harsh language that had the sound of a language of crows, full of hard *h*s and aspirates, he understood every word.

"I had no choice," said the brujo. "It was given me to do."

Though this answer seemed an evasion, Mingolla was satisfied by it and could think of no other question he wanted to ask.

"Tell me what you've learned," the brujo said.

This at first struck Mingolla as an impossibility, because he had learned so much; but he found himself giving quite a concise answer, as if the brujo's demand had sought out the

level of answers and dredged up the exa
edge required.

"I've learned that everything men prize
"An illusion. That what men see as their esse
stripped away by the power of a whim, th
value, that peace and war are the same, that
are the convictions of fools, and that fools rul
the name of a wisdom that exists like music, li
moment and is gone."

"You know all this," said the brujo, marvel
you are sad?" He burst into peals of laughter, and
choreographed the pale streamers of mist furling in
into the likenessess of dancing women.

"Why shouldn't I be sad?" said Mingolla. "I t
pretty goddamn sad."

"It's only sad because you don't really believe it,"
brujo. "You don't want it to be true. But once you acc
true, then other truths will become applicable, and yo
things aren't so bad."

"I doubt that."

"Doubt is fine for now," said the brujo, and then, doi
perfect imitation of Mingolla's voice: "Whatever works for
right?"

Irritated, Mingolla asked, "What am I doing here?"

"I'm just checking on your progress," said the brujo.

"And who the hell are you?"

"Your cousin," said the brujo with a mad cackle. From
beside him, he picked up a weed that had tiny violet florets
with magenta centers; he waved it in Mingolla's face. "Those
idiots back in Panama City aren't the only ones who know
about this, and they certainly weren't the first to discover it . . .
just the first to abuse it. Now they've paid for their abuse."

"Did something happen back in the city?" asked Mingolla.

"You'll know soon what happened," said the brujo. "There's
no use in dwelling on it now. But when you find out, remember
that you weren't the agency, only the spark."

Mingolla couldn't frame a response.

You've got a lot to learn," said the brujo. "Remember
too."

There was something hopeful in the brujo's words, his
, and Mingolla looked up at him, ready for some good
s, but none was forthcoming.

"It gets a lot worse before it gets better," said the brujo,
o—along with the hut—was fading, growing as insubstantial
the mist. "And when it does finally get better, you won't care
e way or the other. At least not the way you'd like to care
w."

Despite its air of unreality, the dream was so vivid that
hen Mingolla awakened back in the car he expected to find
ome talisman, some proof that his meeting with the brujo had
actually occurred. A piece of fern stuck to his trousers, or a
portion of the weed. There was nothing like that, but there was
a proof of sorts. The knowledge of the disaster in Panama City.
As real and palpable as a gold coin in his hand.

Debora was still asleep, scrunched into a corner of the
backseat. He ran a hand along her flank, loving her, wanting
love to mean more than the meaning it had acquired in Panama. She stirred, blinked. "What is it?"

He leaned down, brushed hair from her cheek, and kissed
her. "Go back to sleep."

She struggled up to a sitting position, looked around at the
misted windows as if awakening somewhere unfamiliar. "Did
something else happen?" she asked.

In the morning they followed the road through the hills into
gray light, to a ridge overlooking a valley. Tres Santos was
situated at the far end of the valley between two jungled cliffs
that nearly formed a natural arch overhead; from their vantage,
the cliffs had the look of two cowled figures gazing down at an
unlucky throw of the dice: little white houses with shadow-
blackened windows and doors. Green mountains surrounded
the valley, appearing to extend forever in every direction; roads
wound through them, visible as red threads. Dark cloud bellies
swirled and changed shape above the cliffs, lowering, intensifying the atmosphere of gloom.

They drove down from the ridge and into the village along a dirt street broken by gray mica-flecked boulders and parked outside a cantina with the faded mural of an armored man on horseback upon its facade: Cantina Cortez. The door was open, and several men were standing at the bar, watching a portable TV. Short bandy-legged men with impassive pre-Columbian faces, wearing blankets and white cotton trousers and straw hats. When Debora and Mingolla entered, carrying rifles under their arms, the men acknowledged them with nods and turned back to the TV; an agitated voice was issuing from the speaker, and on the screen was a flickering image of ruins.

"A bomb?" said Debora. "In Panama City . . . a bomb?"

"Yes," said the bartender, a man older than the rest, with gray streaks in his hair. "An atomic bomb. Terrible."

"It must have been very small," said another man. "Only one barrio was destroyed."

"But many are dying in the other barrios," said a third man. "Who could have done this?"

Mingolla was sick with the news, heavy with it. "I'm looking for someone," he said finally. "A big black man named . . ."

"Señor Tully," said the bartender. "He arrived this morning. Take a left at the next corner, and you'll find him in the third house on the right."

Mingolla listened a minute longer to the voice detailing casualty figures, recounting the horror of Carlito's punishment, the punishment of Tel Aviv, a little irony he'd probably never expected to employ. When he went back outside, he found Debora sitting on the hood of the car. "Tully's here," he said. "Maybe he'll know what happened."

"I know what happened," she said. "Izaguirre blew them up. Shit!" She jumped down from the car and kicked at the red dirt. "I've been acting like a stupid girl. I never should have believed them!" She walked off a few paces, whirled on Mingolla. "We have to kill the rest! Or else they'll kill us. Your dreams, your hallucinations about the future . . . they must be accurate. I didn't understand before, but it's clear now."

He was more stunned by her reaction than by the news of

429

the bomb. She looked as if she were about to explode, swinging her rifle back and forth, unable to locate a suitable target.

"Let's get Tully," she said.

As they walked he watched her out of the corner of his eye, noticing how anger . . . no, not anger, but the restoration of commitment, how that had carved weakness and worry from her face, left her more beautiful than ever. And in her face, in its clean rigor, he saw the insanity of their relationship. How first one pushed, then the other pulled. How her desire for commitment would drag them so far, how his anger would carry them on until she had another chance for commitment. How they fed off this exchange and called it love. And maybe it was love, maybe the insanity incorporated love. Even realizing all this, he loved her, loved love. Loved it to the point that rejection became unthinkable. To reject it he would have to stop loving himself, and while that was something he would have had no qualms about under other circumstances, he couldn't afford that kind of honesty now.

Tully was sitting in a chair outside one of the houses, a rifle across his knees, and as they came up, he waved: a languid, boneless wave. "Glad you made it, Davy," he said in a weak-sounding voice. His eyes were bloodshot, and he seemed energyless, depleted.

"Where's Corazon?" Mingolla asked.

"Inside," said Tully. " 'Pears she cotch a dose from de bomb. 'Pears I cotched one, too."

"Radiation?" said Mingolla, guilt-stricken.

Tully nodded. "Look like you two got away clean."

"What went on back there?" Debora asked.

"Hell, I don't know. Somethin' happen at de palace, but I never sure of what. All de day dere's not'in' but riot. People 'cusin' each ot'er of dis and dat. Fightin' in de streets. Took me and Corazon most of de day to get clear. And we not get clear 'nough. Must be dat bomb were battlefield ordnance, or else we be shadows on de stone." He coughed, wiped his mouth, and checked his hand to see what had come up. "We took de coast road and make it dis far. Bet you got lost in de mist."

"Yeah," said Mingolla.

430

Tully let out a sigh that Mingolla thought might go on forever. "Mon," he said. "Here I been t'inkin' better must come, and now dis." He cocked an eye at Mingolla. "Seem like you 'bout to choke on somethin', Davy."

"Tully, I . . ."

"Get on outta here, Davy. I don't wanna hear no bullshit 'bout sadness and de back-time. Dis de way it have come, and dere's not'in' to do more. Be worse places dan dis to have a funeral." He laughed, and the laughter started him coughing. When he had recovered, he said, "De fools 'round here, dey wash a body wit' lime juice and wrap it in white cloth and sing over you. Lime juice! Dey t'ink lime juice be fah everyt'ing. Cure de dysentery, cure de fever, and make you sweet fah Jesus." He gestured with his rifle. "Go on, now. Dat stream what's marked on de map, you find it at de end of dis street. You can spy de trail from de bank. Just cross dem two big hills east, and you be square on one of dem villages I told you 'bout."

Mingolla fought the urge to do something stupid like insist upon staying. This was the way Tully wanted it, fast and low-key, and the least he could do was to go along. He allowed himself to say, "I'll miss ya, Tully," and then wheeled about, leaving Debora in his wake, not wanting to hear Tully's response, not wanting any more knowledge or guilt. But as he passed by the window of the house, he heard the click of a safety being disengaged. He went into a shoulder roll, heard the popping of a rifle, felt bullets pass close, and as he brought his rifle to bear on the window, in the instant before he fired he saw Corazon, her face empty of emotion, her rosy eye looking full of blood. His bullets knocked her back from the window, pumped a hoarse grunt from her chest.

He got to his feet, unsteady. Debora was covering Tully with her rifle, and he was trying to stand, having a hard time of it. Mingolla went to the window, peered into the darkened room. Corazon had been blown back onto the bed and was spreadeagled on a white coverlet made into a severe abstract by angles of shadow and the scatter of her blood. Her rifle lay on the floor. Tully stumbled into the room, stopped dead.

"What you do, mon?" he cried. "What you do?"

"She tried to shoot me," said Mingolla. "I didn't have a choice, I didn't even have time to think."

"She wasn't tryin' to shoot nobody!" Tully dropped to his knees beside the bed, his hands hovering over the body; blood was still leaking from Corazon's mouth and breast, and it looked as if Tully was unsure where to put his hands, what hole to plug.

Voices behind Mingolla. He turned, saw Debora explaining things to a group of men who had come to investigate. When he turned back to the window, he found that Tully had picked up Corazon's rifle and was training it at his chest.

"Goddamn you, Davy!" he said. "You ever was low on de spirit."

"Listen," said Mingolla. "She tried to shoot me. What else could I do?"

"Why she shoot you, mon?" Tully was trembling, his finger poised on the trigger. "She got no cause to shoot you."

"I don't know, man. Maybe somebody put something in her head that made her want to do it . . . or maybe she was just crazy, too sick to think straight. I don't know."

"You tellin' me she like dem ot'ers, dem empty shells dat de Sotomayors pump fulla dere shit? Don't be tellin' me dat! I know her, mon. Dere were more dan dat in her!"

Suddenly Mingolla wanted Tully to pull the trigger, to end the suspense. "What was I s'posed to do?" he yelled. "*Let her kill me?* Let you get all fucking soulful 'bout me dead? This is crap, man! You wanna kill me, go ahead! Go on! Pull the fucking trigger! Maybe somebody put something in your goddamn head, told you to do it. Maybe this whole fucking shuck 'bout Tres Santos is just more Sotomayor bullshit!" He pushed his chest to the window, puffed it out, daring Tully. "C'mon, man!"

"You t'ink I won't?" said Tully. "Ain't but one t'ing holdin' me back, and dat's de knowin' how I helped make you dis way."

Instead of Tully, Mingolla saw a big black shadow, a creature of blackness, empty, hateful, a nothing with muscles and a sweaty forehead and bloodshot eyes. "Fuck you, Tully," he said, and focused his anger in a stream of poisonous energy that sent Tully reeling. Tully's gun discharged. Wild misses aimed at the ceiling, the walls, the floor. He tried to bring the gun to bear on the window, dropped it, clutched his head, letting out a hiss that turned into a scream. Then he fell across the bed, twisted onto his side, his fingers shaking at his temples as if trying to push thoughts back inside, thoughts crowded out by the anger roiling in his skull. And then he was gone. Winked out, truly empty, his blind eyes staring at a cross of black wood on the wall, like an incision into a region of darkness.

Mingolla was crying. He knew it by the wetness on his face and by no other sign, because he felt almost nothing. The tears might have merely been an excess, as if he had been filled to overflowing and was experiencing a necessary spillage. He turned from the window, and the bandy-legged little men moved back from him, staring incuriously, betraying neither fear nor any sort of strong emotion. They had, he realized, seen nothing out of the ordinary. Tears and violent death were part of their millieu, and though they might not comprehend the specifics of the situation, they understood that it was none of their business; they already had a sufficiency of tears and death, and had no interest in sharing the grief of strangers or involving themselves in moral judgments. All this he saw in their faces, all this he perceived as admirable and right.

From the bank of a narrow stream at the base of the hill, Mingolla could look back and see the edge of the village less than a hundred yards away. He could see all its sweetness, the bougainvillea in window planters, smoke curling from a jointed tin chimney, an old man picking his way among the ruts. The view was unobstructed, but Mingolla knew this was an illusion. Doors had been closed, and there was no going back. He looked up at the hill, its green slope as imposing as the hill of the Ant Farm. But this hill was even more menacing. Its blank, silent enormity presaged the grimness of a five-year-plan with no joyful goal at the end, and Mingolla was reluctant to set foot upon it.

"Are you thinking about Tully?" Debora asked.

"No," he said.

She looked surprised.

"I don't know why," he said. "The thoughts just aren't coming."

"I know how it is . . . sometimes you can't think about important things right away. You have to let them diminish."

"Maybe," he said. "Or maybe it wasn't important."

"That's not true."

"You don't know what I'm feeling."

"Yes, I do." Her eyes were wide, her mouth tight, as if she was trying to hide some emotion. "I know exactly how you feel."

They sat awhile on a boulder by the stream, gathering themselves for the climb. The stream was the only thing of energy in the entire landscape. Its tea-colored water raced over a stony bottom, foaming at the breaks into lacy white threads; orange iron-bearing rocks thrust up from the surface, and midges danced above them. Clumps of small flowers fringed the bank, the blossoms a pale creamy yellow with a magenta splash at the center, the stems furred with dark filaments. Wherever Mingolla turned, his eye met with an infinity of detail, with complicated mosaics of life, with patterns too intricate to unravel, and this complexity afflicted his sense of competence, made him aware of the ineptitude of his judgments, the fallibility of his hates and loves. It might be best just to sit there, he thought, and wait for the ones who soon would be hunting them. The sun's light came grayish white and watery through a rift in the clouds, and seemed to search out all the fine stems and tendrils and cottony fibers, to course along them and fill the air with a single disturbance, a constant fluctuation of pressure and heat that unsettled Mingolla as might have a background of slow shadows or shouts in many languages. Nothing was clear, not even the urge to sit and wait. But at last he was moved by some vague impulse to stand and begin the climb.

The hill was slow going. They tripped and stumbled as if their many uncertainties were posing an impediment. But on reaching the top and gazing out over the mountains of Darién, jungle-shrouded and rumpled to the horizon, it seemed they had come to one of the strange green places of God where the structural immensity of life was made plain, all paths delineated. The low sun had broken clear in the west, and its heavy golden light, reflecting off ridges of slate-gray cloud, mined a mineral brilliance from every color. The slopes were a luminous green, the air held a shine in every quarter, and the view was so intricate yet at the same time so comprehensible, it offered a promise of hope and magical possibility. Above one hill a rainbow arched into oblivion; a hawk circled another, and dark slants of rain stroked the summit of a third. Like signals, portents. As if each green dome were a separate identity with its own character and values. The sight boosted Mingolla's spirits, and as they started downhill, his confidence returned. They walked swiftly, stealthily, twitching branches aside with their rifle barrels, moving with an efficiency that comes only with a surety of purpose, and it seemed to Mingolla that he was growing lighter, the past falling away with every step . . . and it was, he realized. The past was becoming weightless, frail, and they were leaving behind everything familiar, leaving friends and enemies. . . .

. . . David . . .

. . . yes . . .

. . . you're going too fast . . .

. . . it's easy downhill . . . make time . . .

. . . it only feels easy, downhill's harder on your legs than uphill . . . you'll start to feel it soon . . .

. . . okay . . .

. . . leaving behind memories and attachments, honesty and duplicity . . .

. . . look, David . . . that bird . . .

. . . yeah, weird . . .

. . . did you see the tail, the ruby feathers on the breast . . . it was a quetzal . . .

. . . so . . .

. . . they're very rare . . . it's good luck to see one . . .

. . . luck . . . yeah, sure . . .

. . . don't make fun of luck . . . we've been lucky . . .

. . . Tully . . . luck? . . . Panama . . . luck? . . .

. . . luckier than most . . .

. . . leaving behind the fear of death and the desire for life, leaving hope and hopelessness . . .

. . . when I first joined the movement . . .

. . . I don't wanna hear this crap, Debora . . .

. . . no, you listen . . . when I was first in the movement, about thirty of us spent the rainy season in the Petén . . . it was awful, we lived like amphibious animals, our shelters rotting, our clothes mildewing . . . we caught fevers, dysentery . . . some of us had leishmaniasis . . .

. . . leaving behind the usual, the expected . . .

. . . what . . .

. . . it's a parasite, it eats the cartilage in your ears, your nose . . . anyway, we were there for months . . . it seemed endless, and I lost sight of why we were there . . . we were just there, we were just part of the decay, the rain, and nothing I'd thought of achieving seemed worthwhile any longer . . . sometimes I was so depressed I could hardly lift my head, and then this kid came to the camp, this young boy from a village near Cobán, and he'd sing, he'd tell stories . . . lovely stories . . . I hated him at first, because it seemed immoral for him to be so happy, for him to make me forget my misery . . . misery was important to me, I saw it as integral to the revolutionary ethic . . .

. . . leaving behind dreams and the conception of dreaming, for dreams and reality were being fused into the idea of purpose . . .

. . . and once he told this story, I can't remember what it was about, but I remember some of the words . . . they spoke to me . . . he was talking about someone who was very sad and they were thinking that there had to be another country after this, but the only one they could imagine was this secure dull place where life was as cozy as a Christmas kiss, and that wasn't enough for some people, for this particular person, and the secret of living through the sadness . . .

. . . leaving sadness and joy behind . . .

. . . was to find a story, an emotion, a fable so alluring that

it was like another country, a continent rising from the sea, with flamingos and golden melons and animals more beautiful than sin, one that gave you strength to be the person who you always pretended to be, even to yourself, and if you could do that, if you could search inside yourself and find that country, no matter if it was a lie, no matter if it was foolish and childlike, then you could survive all the terrible realities that denied it . . . at least for a little while . . . that's what we've found . . .

. . . did the kid make it . . .

. . . no, but we survived the rains because of him, and after we left the jungle, we had the strength to keep fighting . . .

. . . leaving behind the thought of peace, and entering the precincts of a violent dutiful morality with its own continuum of behaviors and possibilities . . .

. . . do you understand, David . . .

. . . just more bullshit . . .

. . . of course it is . . .

. . . then why . . .

. . . I remember more of what the kid said . . . some of it had to do with a story a man was telling a woman in order to frighten her, to make her come close so he could seduce her . . . it was a story about the devil's green cat, glowing in the darkness of the throne, how it prowls the earth and inspires sin . . . not just sin . . . extremes of life, of action . . . because although it belonged to the devil, like all cats it was independent, it had its own biases, its own idea of what was appropriate . . . and after the story ended, after the man had seduced the woman, they were lying together, happy, and the woman realized that the story had merely been a tactic, that she had been taken in, but she didn't care, and when she asked the man if that was the case, if the story had just been a clever lie, he laughed and said, 'No, there's no such thing as the devil's green cat that glows in the darkness of the throne, striking sparks with its claws from the stones of Hell, scenting the burning from the Pit, hissing a wind full of words, saying, Live or be lifeless, Love or be damned . . .'

. . . and leaving even love behind, at least for a while

because love was changing into its martial equivalent, denying of sentiment and admitting only to the virtues of its strength . . .

. . . *don't you see, David . . . it's the same story with us, it's always the same story . . . I love you, and it doesn't matter why . . .*

. . . leaving behind logic, leaving behind all ordinary truths . . .

. . . *I love you . . .*

. . . yet in the single-mindedness of their intent, the purity of their anger, and their lack of choice, they were taking with them everything that mattered.